LIBRARY SPIRITS

ALSO BY ALICE DUNCAN

The Mercy Allcutt Mystery Series

Lost Among the Angels

Angels Flight

Fallen Angels

Angels of Mercy

Thanksgiving Angels

Angels Adrift

Christmas Angels

Hollywood Angels

Celluloid Angels

Dancing Angels

LIBRARY SPIRITS

A DAISY GUMM MAJESTY MYSTERY
BOOK 19

ALICE DUNCAN

Paperback ISBN: 978-1-64457-623-6
Hardcover ISBN: 978-1-64457-623-6

ePublishing Works!
644 Shrewsbury Commons Ave
Ste 249
Shrewsbury PA 17361
United States of America

www.epublishingworks.com
Phone: 866-846-5123

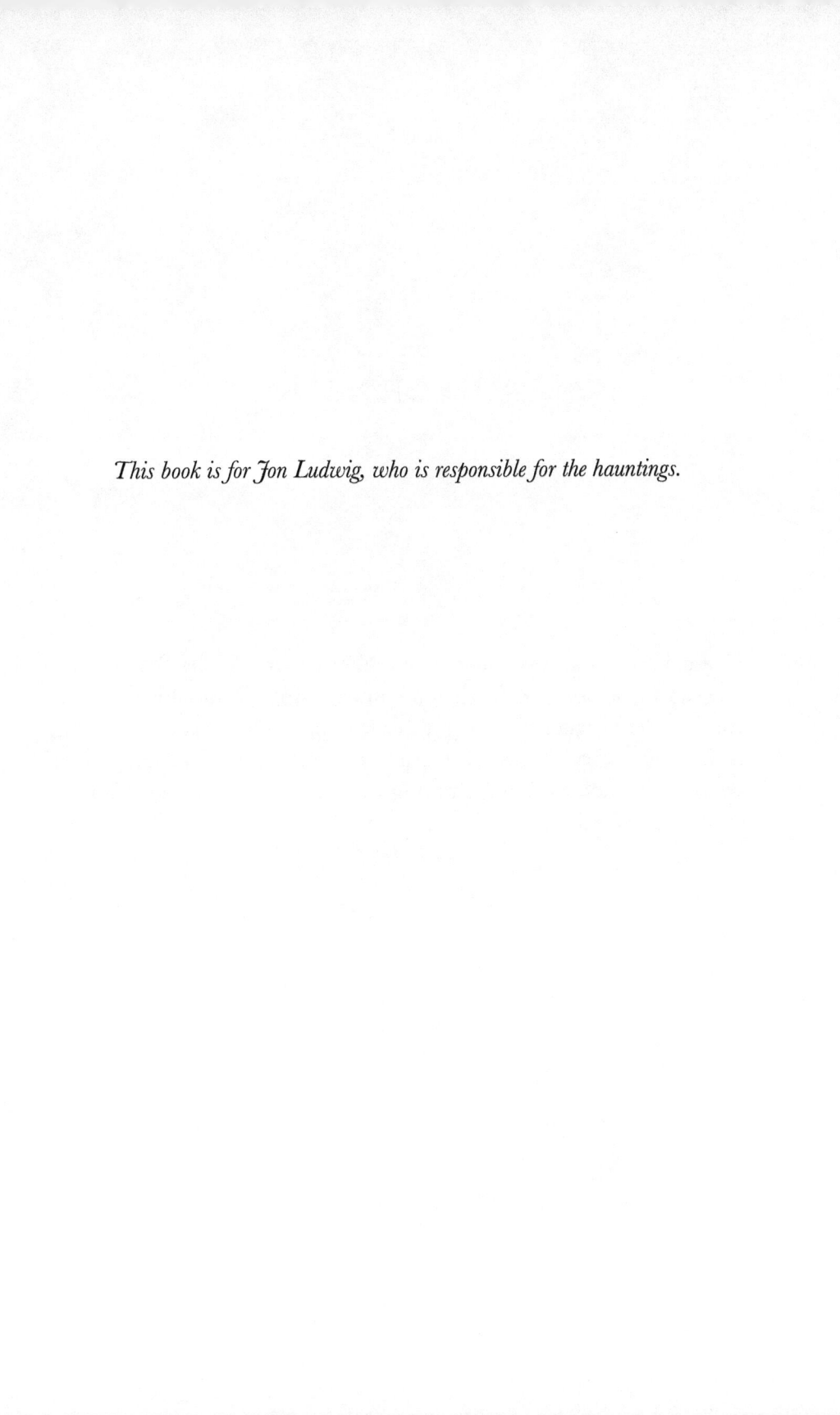

This book is for Jon Ludwig, who is responsible for the hauntings.

AUTHOR NOTE:

Please know that I've been a member of the United Methodist Church for as long as I can remember. I sing in the choir (in case you wondered where Daisy got her leanings). Please know, too, that within this story, Daisy and I are not maligning *any* religion or system of belief. We're attempting to point out the perils of fanaticism of any kind, in any place.

ONE

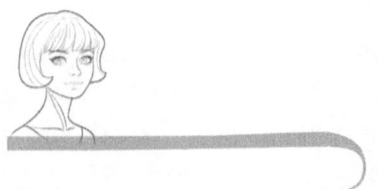

As I sat at my dressing table preparing for the day, I stared at the array of small objects before me. Then I glanced at the dainty gold chain Sam had given me a couple of years ago and thought I might just need to get a heavier chain one of these days.

"Why are you staring at the table?" asked Sam, who stood behind me, looking into the dressing table mirror and tying his tie. As a detective in the Pasadena Police Department, he had to get dressed and go to work. The only activities I aimed to undertake that day were taking a walk and going to the library, and I'd already dressed for those two tasks.

"Not sure precisely," I told him. "But when I put all these things on the gold chain you gave me, my chest is lumpy."

"You don't want a third lump?" asked Sam, who occasionally thought he was funny.

"I've already got three lumps if you count the baby," I said.

"True, but not on your chest."

"Yes, but look here." I picked up each item individually. "Billy's ring. The juju Mrs. Jackson gave me. The woven basket the Tongva ghost gave me at the séance. And then there's the little carved baby Mr. DeLoera presented to me a month or so ago."

"Hmm, yes. I see," said Sam, at last taking in the enormity of my problem.

Very well, so enormity isn't the correct word, but I didn't like having a lumpy chest. However, I also didn't want to leave any of these charms home when I went out. I cherished them all and...this will sound stupid...I thought they were lucky. Or as lucky as any inanimate object can be.

Speaking of which..."You still wear your juju, don't you?" I asked him, turning on the vanity seat and staring up at him.

"Of course I do. You'd kill me if I didn't."

"There you go. See? It's a lucky charm. It keeps you from being murdered on a daily basis."

"Do all of those things keep you from being murdered?" he asked.

"I don't know." I heaved a big sigh.

"If it's any comfort, I wouldn't kill you if you didn't wear them all," said Sam in a voice he was forcing to sound solemn.

"But I love them. I know it's silly to be attached to objects, but I'm attached to every one of these and I don't want to leave the house without them."

"Understood. Can't think of a solution offhand though. I can buy you a heavier chain, but it'll still hang around your neck and make you lumpy."

"Exactly."

"How about a charm bracelet?"

"Already thought about that," I said. "I'd bump them against stuff, and bumping might damage them."

"Right. Well, I don't know what to suggest, but let me think on the matter. There must be a way to carry your trinkets that doesn't make you lumpy. Although I do like your lumps, you know."

"The natural ones, I know," I said, grinning in the mirror at the man I loved.

He grinned back, stooped, and kissed the top of my head. "Until we come up with a better solution, just wear a loose-fitting top. Maybe the trinket lumps won't show. You and Lou are going to the library this morning, aren't you?"

"Yup. As soon as I take Spike for his walk with Pa and Rosebud." Spike was my practically perfect black-and-tan dachshund.

"Is Rosebud settling down any better?" asked Sam.

Rosebud was a not-so-perfect female black-and-tan dachshund.
Mrs. Bissel, a very nice woman who lives in Altadena and who
breeds dachshunds, gave her to me in payment for conducting a
séance at her house a couple of months back. That's the séance
during which the Tongva ghost delivered the tiny woven basket
to me.

Huh. That sounds insane, doesn't it? Perhaps I should explain.

It's like this: Until I, a widow, married Sam Rotondo, a widower,
a few months prior to this conversation, I earned my living and that
of most of my family via my talents as a spiritualist medium. In
those days, not long after the so-called Great War and the so-called
Spanish Influenza pandemic, I don't think there was a family
anywhere on earth that hadn't suffered a bereavement or two. Or
three or four. I mean, life was rough.

Grieving folks claimed I offered them comfort, which was nice to
hear, even though I knew I was a fake. I began my accidental career
on Christmas Eve, 1910, when my beloved aunt, Viola Gumm,
brought home an old and tattered Ouija board given to her by the
woman for whom she worked, Mrs. Pinkerton (who was in those
days, Mrs. Kincaid).

When I was seventeen, right after I graduated from high school,
I married my childhood sweetheart, Billy Majesty. He'd gone off to
war in order to make the world safe for democracy and come home
about a year later, a crippled, lung-damaged, wheelchair-bound
unhappy man. My darling father, Joe Gumm, had suffered a heart
attack and could no longer serve in his former capacity as chauffeur
to wealthy residents of Pasadena, California, our fair city. My Aunt
Vi had not merely lost her husband to the influenza, but her only
child, Paul, had perished in the war.

My brother and sister had both married and were living elsewhere, and Vi had come to live with my mother, father, and me in
our bungalow on South Marengo Avenue. So you see, the women in
the household had to earn the bread.

Because there was plenty of grief to go around, people hired me to get in touch with deceased relatives or read tarot cards or the crystal ball for them. Yes, I was a fraud, but at least I was an honest one.

That doesn't sound right, does it? However, I never pretended to foresee the future. Both the spirit guide, a Scottish gent named Rolly, and my spiritualist name, Desdemona, had followed me from my tenth year until 1926. I swear, I wish I'd had to read *Othello* sooner. I'd have chosen a better name for my spiritualist self. Ah well. Too late now. Anyhow, Rolly and I generally dispensed what I considered to be sensible advice to the people who hired me.

Sometimes—often, in fact—the absurdities of one's childhood follow one into adulthood.

Oh, and the reason I still wore my first wedding ring (Billy's) every day on a chain around my neck is because I'd loved him with all my heart. He finally managed to do away with himself after suffering years of constant pain, leaving me devastated. Sam's first wife, Margaret, whom he'd loved with all his heart, had died of tuberculosis approximately two years prior to Billy's demise, leaving him devastated.

And now I loved Sam with all my heart, and he claimed to love me with all his heart. See how much love a couple of hearts can hold? So why are human beings unable to get along with each other? Is what I want to know. There's probably no rational answer to my question, perhaps because human beings are an irrational species.

Ahem.

Back to walking with Spike, my wonderful black-and-tan dachshund, and Rosebud, my father's rather not-quite-so-wonderful black-and-tan dachshund.

"Pa has been attempting to teach her to obey his commands, but I think we'll have to take her to the Pasanita Dog Obedience Club for their next session," I said.

"Do you know when that will be?" asked Sam as he headed for the bedroom door, preparing to descend the staircase.

"Not sure," I said. "I aim to call Mrs. Hanratty and ask." Mrs.

Pansy Hanratty had taught the Pasanita Obedience Club's class to which I'd taken Spike two years earlier. Spike was now the best-behaved dog in Pasadena, according to me.

Spike was also at present waiting for Sam and me in the kitchen. Sam had built a ramp up our staircase so that Spike didn't have to climb up and down lots of stairs. Sam was probably the most wonderful husband in Pasadena, also according to me.

Anyway, I hurried to fasten my chain around my neck, prepared to be lumpy again that day. I was already clad in the nice skirt, sweater, and jacket I aimed to wear on my walk and then to the library. I had created the skirt and jacket on my mother's side-pedal White sewing machine out of a lovely brown-checked fabric I'd bought to go with the sweater Aunt Vi had knitted for me for Christmas. Fortunately for my expanding middle, both the skirt and the sweater were loose. When I stood and squinted into the mirror, I decided my chest didn't appear too lumpy.

As mentioned earlier, the women in my family had earned the bread, not to mention the bacon, for the Gumms and the one remaining Majesty (me) for years. It had long been my opinion we were lucky to have Vi cook them for us because both my mother and I were disasters in the kitchen. Since my marriage to Sam, I'd been making a concerted effort to learn to cook. What's more, I was having some slight success in the endeavor. Sam never complained, although that might be due more to Sam's good heart than my kitchen skills.

Fortunately for me, Sam had hired a kindhearted woman named Mrs. Elvira Rattle to come in and clean for us every day. She also prepared meals when I was too busy (or slothful and lazy) to do so.

I was on firm culinary ground this morning, though, because I'd mastered the art of making eggs-in-a-nest. And, as we had a small orange grove in our backyard, we could round out our breakfast of eggs and toast with fresh orange slices. Because we had both navel and Valencia oranges in our grove of trees, we could have fresh oranges pretty much all year long. Come March and April, a person could by-golly swoon from the spectacular aroma blessing us from all the citrus blossoms.

"Thanks for cutting the bread," I said to Sam as I walked into the kitchen. Bless his heart—and his common sense, because he knew I couldn't cut a straight slice of bread—he already had several slices of bread resting on the cutting board.

"Not a problem, sweetheart," he said. I heard the grin in his voice, but I didn't resent it.

I grabbed a bowl from a cupboard, walked to the Frigidaire, and transferred several eggs from it to the bowl. "How many eggs would you like this morning?" I asked sweetly.

"Two will be fine, thanks," said Sam.

"Would you like me to make a sandwich for you to take for your lunch?" I asked, still sweetly.

"No, that's all right. Some of the guys and I will probably walk to the Crown Chop Suey Palace if we're at the station at lunchtime."

"We still have chicken left over from dinner last night," I said as an inducement.

"You have that for lunch. Dinner was delicious, by the way."

Good old Sam always attempted to boost my ego when it came to cooking. In reality, last night's dinner had been pretty good. I'd roasted a chicken! All by myself! And made mashed potatoes and gravy! The gravy had been a teensy bit lumpy because I didn't stir the flour into the chicken grease quite well enough. Still, everything had been tasty, and I'd cooked green beans to go with the chicken and potatoes. Perhaps I'd overcooked them a weeny little bit, but still…I was learning.

Spike had followed me to the Frigidaire, so while I was there, I lifted the waxed paper cover on the leftover chicken and snabbled a piece of chicken for him. Under orders from both Mrs. Bissel, who had bred him, and Mrs. Hanratty, who had taught him, Spike was *never* supposed to gain weight. That's because dachshunds' backs are long, and those long backs can't support too much weight.

Still and all, Spike, being the best-behaved dog in all of Pasadena, deserved a little treat now and then, so I tossed him his chicken; he snapped it out of the air, gulped it down, and thanked me. Okay, so he wagged his tail at me. Thanks are thanks.

Breakfast was a smashing success, and Sam left for work a happy and well-fed man. Spike and I walked him to the front door and watched as he backed his Hudson out of the driveway, turned north on Marengo Avenue, and headed for the Pasadena Police Department, which sat behind the Pasadena City Hall and Courthouse on the corner of Fair Oaks and Walnut.

By the time Sam left for work, it was approximately eight a.m. Spike and I washed the dishes—Spike cleaned the plates before I rinsed them and dumped them in hot, soapy water. After I finished drying the dishes and putting them away, I wandered through the house, looking for any stray books. Sam and I loved to read. We were supposed to put our already-read books on the table beside the front door, but every now and then we missed one. Not that day.

"We did it, Spike!" I said to my hound.

He wagged at me again.

"Want to go for a walk?" I then asked him. Stupid question. Spike *always* wanted to go for a walk.

Unfortunately, I'd asked it a little too soon because Mrs. Rattle hadn't arrived yet. She knocked a minute or so later, though, so all was again well in the Rotondo household.

Mrs. Rattle, Spike, and I greeted each other, and then I got Spike's leash, Mrs. Rattle headed for the utility porch for the mop and bucket, and Spike and I headed across the street to my parents' house. There we were greeted by an ecstatic Rosebud (called Rosie by pretty much everyone) and my darling father.

Rosebud didn't tug on the leash too much, and she responded pretty well when Pa called her to task for nearly yanking his arm out of its socket when she saw a cat and decided to give chase. Guess she forgot she was on a leash, because she almost choked herself. Except for two or three minor incidents of a like nature, our walk was peaceful and happy.

When we got back to my parents' house, Pa picked up the already-read books from their house and carried them to the Chevrolet sitting in his driveway. I was the only one who drove the Chevrolet, but we kept it at my parents' house for the heck of it. I kept a shopping basket in the backseat of the Chevrolet to hold books.

"Is it all right if Spike stays here with you and Rosebud while Mr. Prophet and I go to the library?" I asked my father as we walked back to the house.

"Sure! He and Rosie like to romp together."

"I'm glad they romp and don't fight," I muttered.

"Every now and then, if one of them gets too rambunctious, the other one will growl. Generally, when that happens, the growler calms down. If he or she doesn't, I intervene."

"Don't get bit!" I warned him.

"I won't. Don't fret, sweetheart. The dogs adore each other."

"I'm glad," I said, happy to hear it.

"Have a good time at the library," said Pa as I headed across the street to Sam's and my house.

"Will do. And I'll bring back any new Edgar Rice Burroughs or Zane Grey books if there are any."

"Thanks!" Pa laughed, but he knew I'd do precisely as I'd said. I was the family book hunter and gatherer. It was a job I liked, so it worked out just fine.

TWO

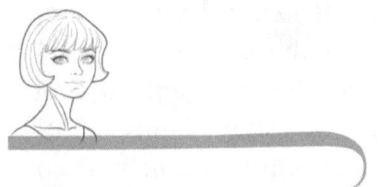

When I walked into my house, I heard the gentle rumble of conversation coming from the kitchen, and I knew Mr. Lou Prophet had come over with his own to-be-returned books. Sure enough, when I entered the kitchen, I saw him sitting at the kitchen table gabbing and watching Mrs. Rattle chop carrots. Guess she aimed to cook for us that evening. Fine with me.

"Good morning, you two," I said cheerily when I joined them.

"Good morning again, Daisy. I decided to fix a chicken dish from a recipe I got out of an old issue of *Good Housekeeping*. Hope you don't mind if I use your left-over chicken."

"Why would I mind?" I asked, honestly curious.

"Well, I know you've been cooking a lot yourself lately," said Mrs. Rattle. "But Mr. Prophet said you have a busy morning planned, and I thought that if I prepared this dish and put it in the Frigidaire, you can just retrieve it and heat it up at suppertime."

"Thank you."

I eyed Mr. Prophet, who sat at the kitchen table, trying to appear innocent. He wasn't, and we both knew it.

Perhaps a word about Mr. Lou Prophet wouldn't come amiss here. Sam and I had met the old curmudgeon almost two years ago when he'd thwarted Sam's idiot nephew, Frank Pagano, in an attempt to murder me. This startling event occurred at the church my family attended, the First Methodist-Episcopal Church on the corner of Marengo and Colorado.

What had drawn Mr. Lou Prophet to Southern California wasn't in any way related to my safety. In fact, when we'd first met and for a long time afterward, he'd had little use for me. I'd used him as a dictionary into the esoteric world of Wild Western slang.

In his youth and adulthood until a short few years ago, Mr. Prophet had been a by-golly bounty hunter in the Wild West. Modern life didn't suit him well, but he'd come to Los Angeles to consult on the sets of some of the millions of western flickers then being filmed. He disapproved of the home of his young adulthood as depicted in the flickers because it didn't display the West he knew. From what I'd been able to gather about his personal old west, it had been a filthy, violent, drunken, wild place in which I'd feel extremely uncomfortable. So if you reversed our attitudes and the reasons for them, perhaps you can understand his yearning for the bad old days.

Of course, the reasons he'd got along so well there might have had something to do with his relative tallness (six-foot-four before the rheumatics shrank him) and his ability with firearms and different languages, primarily Spanish and Apache (Mescalero, in particular). Because we were now in the throes of Prohibition, his boozy days were relatively over, although he still managed to secure a bottle of something every now and then. Because Sam was what Mr. Prophet would term a lawman, he confined his drinking to his own home.

His career as a consultant for the flickers had lasted until he, two ladies of the night, and a crate of bootleg liquor drove off a cliff in Malibu. Not sure who was driving at the time. Mr. Prophet was the only survivor of the accident, but he lost a leg. After he recovered, more or less, he'd gone to live at the Odd Fellows Home of Christian Charity in Pasadena. And if ever a place was misnamed, it was that one.

Sam and I had sprung him from the joint, and he now lived in the small cottage at the rear of our property on south Marengo and acted as our caretaker. These days, he was a wrinkled, gray-haired, crabby old man with a leg and a peg and a generally snarly attitude toward life, although he had a few good points if you looked hard enough.

He'd also recently adopted a striped orange kitten that was just about as beat-up as he was. I don't know what had happened to the poor cat, but Mr. Prophet had discovered it whilst Sam and I were on our honeymoon on the East Coast. He'd taken it to the veterinarian, nursed it back to health, named it Yuyutsu (Yuyu for short), and crooned lovingly at it when there was no one around to hear him. I'd caught him at it one evening and had held my knowledge over his old gray head ever since.

Yuyutsu means "Loves to fight," in case you wanted to know. Mr. Prophet had decided the name suited the mangled cat.

Oddly enough, while I was petrified when Spike and Yuyu first met, fearing flying fur, blood, etc., nothing of the sort happened. They actually *liked* each other! In fact, they even played with each other from time to time. I'd never seen a dog and a cat become pals before. I thought it was kind of sweet. Unlike Mr. Prophet. I doubt he'd ever been sweet in his entire misspent life.

After staring at each other for several seconds, Mr. Prophet finally said, "There's a lot o' that chicken left. Figgered Elvira here could fix a good meal out of it."

"So I wouldn't poison Sam?" I asked, sounding deadly enough that Mrs. Rattle turned at gave me a horrified look.

"He never said any such thing!" she exclaimed.

"I never said any such thing," Mr. Prophet repeated. He'd stopped even attempting to appear innocent, however, and grinned at me sort of like a Halloween jack-o'-lantern might have if it were October instead of March.

"Huh," I said. "Well, if you're ready, let's go to the library." Turning to Mrs. Rattle, I said, "Thank you very much for fixing us dinner, Elvira. I appreciate it, even though it isn't necessary."

"I hope you enjoy it. I'll leave the recipe for you, and then you can make it again if you want to. It's sort of like a shepherd's pie, only with leftover cooked chicken. I'll just sauté some onions with these carrots and dump in the rest of those beans. The leftover mashed potatoes will go on top. Thus its resemblance to shepherd's pie."

"What a brilliant idea!" I said, forgetting to be annoyed at Mr. Prophet. At least he'd ceased openly criticizing me for my paltry kitchen skills, even if he used insidious means to show me he still thought I was a rank amateur as a cook. The fact that he was correct didn't make me appreciate him any better.

"I'm ready," said Mr. Prophet, pushing himself up from the table. I probably should be kinder to the old reprobate. After all, he was an elderly cripple. And he'd murder me if I called him that.

"I left Spike with Pa," I told Mrs. Rattle. "So he won't be underfoot."

"Dear Spike is never a problem," she said, sweet woman that she was.

So, with each of us holding a heavy stack of books, Mr. Prophet and I left the house, walked across the street, and deposited the books in the Chevrolet's backseat shopping basket. Then Mr. Prophet maneuvered himself into the front seat of the car as I got behind the wheel. I'd purchased this Chevrolet after I'd exorcised a ghost—or it might have been a spirit—from Mrs. Bissel's basement about three years before this trek.

Um…It wasn't a ghost or a spirit. It was a runaway girl who had out of desperation taken refuge in Mrs. Bissel's basement. The girl's mother had been so grateful I'd saved her, she'd handed me enough mazuma for me to replace our old rattletrap Model-T Ford with this nice self-starting Chevrolet. I don't know if you've ever had to crank a car into life, fiddle with the clutch wire and the high-speed pedal and the low-speed pedal, but it's no darned fun. I loved our newish Chevrolet.

I also loved the Pasadena Public Library, located on the southeast corner of Walnut and Raymond. It sat in a park complete with a pond, a gazebo, and paved walking paths. Unfortunately for me, the city had outgrown the library, and a new one was scheduled to open early the following year, which would be 1927. Sam, Mr.

Prophet, and I had all seen the proposed plans for the new library. According to me, it wasn't a patch on the old one, although it would be huge enough to house twice or thrice the number of books our current library held—and I'm including the children's wing, which was across the street from the main library.

One of my dearest friends worked in the Pasadena Public Library, too. Mrs. Robert "Regina" Browning (no relation to the poet) hadn't given up her job when she married, being a modern woman and all. Besides, she loved being a librarian, so why should she stop being one?

"Oh, good, there's a parking space right in front of the building," I said when I drove the automobile west on Walnut after I turned left from Marengo.

"Good. Won't have to walk too dern far," said my companion, sounding grumpy.

Because I saw no reason for him to be grumpy, I decided to tease him a bit. "I'm glad you're no longer afraid of Mrs. Rattle," I said sweetly.

"Weren't never afraid of Elvira," he declared.

"Fiddlesticks. I remember when you couldn't even stand to be in the same room with her because you feared for your virtue. Not that you have any."

"Hellkatoot," he growled. "Thought she had designs on me."

"At least you admit it," I said, laughing.

"Well, she acted like it."

"She was just being nice to an old one-legged coot."

"Huh. Didn't know she was married, did I? Gotta watch out for them old widder women."

"Who'd want you?" I asked, perhaps unkindly.

"Miss Li don't mind me much," he said, with a wealth of satisfaction in his voice.

"Some women have no taste at all," I said, although he was right to be satisfied. Miss Li Ahn was a gorgeous Chinese woman whom he'd met in Tucson many moons ago. She lived down the street from us in a huge mansion owned by a wealthy woman named Mrs. Mainwaring. Mrs. Mainwaring had become rich via a number of

ALICE DUNCAN

unspecified—and more likely than not disreputable—ways, but the only one most Pasadenans knew about was her orange empire.

I parked close to the curb because I knew it was difficult for my passenger to get in and out of automobiles. As he grunted his way out of the car, I picked up the book-laden shopping basket. It was heavy as sin, but I didn't even huff when I picked it up from the backseat. Although I hate to admit it, this might be in part because I'd been attending weekly exercise classes at my church. I also had residual muscles leftover from when I'd had to maneuver my Billy in and out of his wheelchair and help him walk. For a while there, I had shoulders like a linebacker.

"Lemme carry that thing for you," said Mr. Prophet gruffly. "You shouldn't be carryin' it in your condition."

"Fiddlesticks. I'm strong as an ox. There are too many steps for you to climb and carry the basket too."

"Yer gonna have a baby, fer chrissakes!" snarled Mr. Prophet. "If you drop that kid before it's time, Sam will kill me."

"Nonsense. I'm not going to hurt myself. Besides, your buddy, Mr. DeLoera, said I was going to have a healthy baby boy, remember?"

"Yeah, I remember," the old sinner growled. "I still don't like it."

Sam, Mr. Prophet, and I had met Mr. Emilio DeLoera a few months back when we'd visited the Mission San Gabriel Arcángel in order to learn about the Tongva people who used to live in the Pasadena and Los Angeles area. Mr. DeLoera was something of a shaman, and we still visited him every now and then. Nice old fellow, unlike the snarly, snappy Mr. Lou Prophet.

Oh, very well, that's not fair. Mr. Prophet wasn't always snarly and snappy. Only most of the time and generally only around me. He didn't appreciate my charms as much as Sam did, I reckon.

Back to the library steps. I held the basket of books in front of me and was about to start climbing when I heard an exclamation behind me.

"Daisy! Here, let me take that!"

I was in no condition or position to whirl around, but I looked over my shoulder and smiled to see Mr. Robert Browning hurrying along the sidewalk toward Mr. Prophet and me. "Robert!" I said. "Good to see you. Are you visiting Regina?"

He caught up with us, greeted Mr. Prophet, who grunted back at him, and then said, "Actually, I'm here to do some honest-to-God research for work."

"Good grief, you do research here? I thought you used the Millikan Library at Caltech." Robert was a scientist who worked at the Underhill Chemical Company on South Fair Oaks Avenue in Pasadena.

"Every now and then I need to find more mundane information. Today I'm in pursuit of a recipe for lemon curd."

"Lemon curd? What in the world for?"

"For my secretary, Miss Partridge. She even gave me the name of the cookbook it's in. She said she copied it down and now can't find it and asked me to visit the library since I had to go out anyway. So I said I would. Besides," he added as he took my heavy book basket, "I want to take Reggie to lunch."

"Smart man," muttered Mr. Prophet.

"Darned right," I said. "He's a scientist."

"Not all scientists are smart. Trust me on this," said Robert wryly.

"If you say so. I couldn't even get past algebra," I told him.

The three of us continued on our way to the library, up the several short staircases, and made it to the big library door. Robert opened it for us, and we entered. Robert carried our basket of books to the returns table, emptied it, and handed the empty basket back to me.

"Thanks, Browning," grumbled Mr. Prophet.

"You're more than welcome, Mr. Prophet. It's good to see you again."

"Yeah. You too," said Mr. Prophet. Not sure about Robert, but I didn't believe him.

The last time the two men had met had been over the corpse of a murdered man after Robert and Regina's wedding, but that's another story.

"Try not to fill the basket so full this time," Robert suggested.

"I'll try not to," I said, "but your wife keeps finding books for my family and Mr. Prophet to read."

"You should get Sam to make you a dolly with wheels and a handle so you can set your book basket on it," said Robert.

"That's a good idea," said Mr. Prophet, smiling at Robert for the first time. "Hellkatoot, I kin make one o' those my own self."

"It is a good idea," I said, wondering why I hadn't thought of something so useful, and deciding the reason I hadn't was probably one of the reasons I wasn't a scientist but a fake spiritualist-medium. All I needed to be as a fake medium was an imagination. You actually had to *know* things in order to be a scientist.

The three of us walked together to Regina's desk across the library. I glanced around as we walked, knowing as I took in all the old wood and windows and book shelves and so forth that I was *really* going to miss this place. I was sure the new library would be nice and big and so forth, but I'd pretty much grown up in this library, and I'd be sad to see it go. Not to mention the park and gazebo and pond. The new library would be part of what the newspapers were calling the "Pasadena Civic Center" and would include a new courthouse and a new city hall. I'm sure it would look okay, but it wouldn't be *this*.

Ah well. One lone woman couldn't stop progress. Darn it.

THREE

M r. Prophet and I spent quite a while in the library. Regina and Robert made plans to meet for lunch after he'd found his secretary's recipe for lemon curd.

Regina, who knew Sam and Mr. Prophet were both interested in history, had found several books for each of them. She'd also snagged quite a few mysteries and westerns for my mother, father, aunt, and me. In short, she managed to fill up my shopping basket with books again, bless her.

"Here, let me carry the basket out to your car, Daisy," said Robert.

"Please do, Robert. Daisy shouldn't be carrying heavy baskets in her condition," said Regina.

I felt heat creep up my neck and invade my cheeks. "It's not *that* heavy," I said.

"Nonsense," said Regina. "If Robert and I ever have children, I'm going to make him carry *me* everywhere, much less heavy baskets full of books."

We were whispering, by the way. I mean, we were in the library. However, we did chuckle at her statement. I even heard Mr. Prophet's rusty chortle.

Regina had told me something that made me feel a teensy bit better about the replacement of the old library. Evidently, the children's wing was going to be moved to Lamanda Park, which was an eastern neighborhood recently annexed to Pasadena, to serve as the library there. So the whole of my dearly beloved library wouldn't be entirely gone from the earth. Just most of it.

A huge crash sounded from a far stack. We all jumped. "What the heck was that?" I asked.

Regina, appearing suddenly nervous, said, "I don't know. Books have been falling off the shelves recently, and nobody can figure out why."

I saw a library employee rush to where the crash had sounded, and we went on our way. Maybe this lovely library was more dilapidated than I'd thought if the stacks gave way under the weight of books. Ah well…

After Robert set the basket of books in the backseat of the Chevrolet and bade us farewell, Mr. Prophet said, "Wanna go sit in the gazebo and read for a while?"

His question surprised me. While he didn't pick on me as much as he used to, I hadn't thought he enjoyed my company so much that he'd want to linger with me in the library's beautiful gazebo for any length of time.

On the other hand, it was a glorious day, and the gazebo wouldn't be around for much longer.

"Sure," I said. "The new library won't have a beautiful park and pond."

"Yeah. It'll be a big, ugly building, and all this open space will be gone and filled with more buildings. That's called progress."

"I wouldn't go that far," I told the cranky old man, even though I'd been thinking the precise same thing only moments earlier. "I think the new building is…Elegant. Dramatic. You know, impressive. It's part of a grand plan to make a civic center in Pasadena, along with the new city hall and everything."

"Huh."

"Oh, very well, I agree with you. I love this library, and I'm going to miss it like fire."

"Figgered as much."

As we approached the gazebo, which had been built near the library pond, my heart held a whole gob of conflicting emotions. I was madly in love with my husband, thrilled beyond measure that we were expecting our first child, and loved my hometown of Pasadena. What's more, I was learning how to cook better and more easily than I'd ever expected. In short, I was happy.

I was also kind of annoyed because Sam was too over-protective of me in my current condition. I was also darned sad that my beloved library was going to be demolished, even if it did seem to have some issues regarding shelving.

Then there was a niggling anxiety about Stacy Kincaid, daughter of my most lucrative client, who had escaped a week or so earlier from the jail ward at the Castleton Hospital. What vexed me was the notion that Stacy might not leave Pasadena, as she would if she had the sense God gave a goose. I worried she might stick around and do more mischief.

In particular, because she blamed me for the death of her late felonious gentleman friend, I worried she might wish to do me harm. It would be just like her. She'd hated me almost as long as we'd known each other. The sentiment was returned by me in full measure. Still, *I* never tried to harm other people. Stacy had tried to kill me two or three times.

"Pretty day," said Mr. Prophet, startling me out of my confused thoughts.

"Yes," I said, "it is. Sometimes March can be chilly, but today is perfect."

"Never gets chilly here, if you ask me," grumbled Mr. Prophet.

"If you wanted cold weather, you should have moved to Maine or Minnesota or some other northeastern state. You didn't get chilly weather in Arizona or Mexico, did you? Or Georgia, your old home state?"

"Naw, but at least Arizona, Mexico, and Georgia were kinda normal. This place is…not normal."

"Bother. You're just grumpy because you're old and have a cat instead of a horse." It still astonished me that Mr. Prophet had adopted Yuyu and seemed to be totally in love with the animal. In his younger bounty-hunter days, he'd had a horse he'd named Mean and Ugly. Whatta guy.

"Huh," said the old sinner again.

I began squinting as we approached the gazebo. "I think somebody's already in there. Darn."

"Well, it's a purty place. Besides, I'm sure we can fit. It's got benches all around it."

"Yeah, you're right. I guess we don't *have* to be alone together." My tone was sarcastic because the occasion seemed to call for it.

"Huh."

"Oh, fiddlesticks, I think whoever's in there is asleep," I said, frustrated. Why couldn't people sleep in their own homes? Why'd they have to sleep in the library gazebo and make everybody else who wanted to sit in the gazebo feel bad for waking them up?

Not awfully charitable, was I?

Naturally, Mr. Prophet said, "Huh," once more.

Whoever occupied the gazebo was deeply asleep because she/he didn't move, even though we didn't lower our voices. I'd taken a step into the lovely hexagonal structure when suddenly Mr. Prophet stopped me by means of gripping my arm with one of his gnarled hands. I gave a start of alarm and turned to glower at him but didn't when I saw his face.

"Don't go in there. That ain't no sleeping beauty. It's a dead woman."

"What?" I squealed. Then I whirled around and saw what Mr. Prophet had seen: a pool of blood on the floor of the gazebo. The blood no longer dripped from the dead, cold body of…

"Oh, my God!" I shrieked. "That's Stacy Kincaid!"

"Shit," said Mr. Prophet, for once not attempting to modify his crude language. "You can move faster'n me, so you go to the library and call Sam. I'll stay here and make sure nobody else goes into the gazebo."

"Good idea," I said as I shoved the book I carried into his hands, turned, and started running toward the library.

"Don't run!" Mr. Prophet hollered after me. "Remember the baby!"

I didn't even bother with a retort. My heart was thundering, and my feet and the rest of me just kind of had to thunder along with it. Good heavens, Stacy Kincaid had been murdered. Stacy! Who'd wanted to murder me! I could hardly believe it, but I'd seen her dead body with my own eyes.

I think. Maybe I'd been mistaken. Maybe that dead woman with all the blood on the floor wasn't Stacy after all. Maybe it was...

No. It was Stacy. I'd recognize her anywhere, even dead and bloody.

Oh, Lord; oh, Lord; oh, Lord.

Mrs. Pinkerton was going to have hysterics. And I *knew* I'd be given the task of calming her down in my role as spiritualist-medium. I'd been attempting to cut back on my spiritualist-mediuming since my marriage to Sam, but she'd pester me about this disaster for sure. Well, it was a disaster for her. For the rest of the world, it would almost certainly come as a relief. Stacy had never been good for much besides driving her mother nuts and consorting with undesirable people.

I was puffing like a grampus—which is some kind of sea crea-ture about which I knew nothing, but I'd heard the expression—when I finally flung the library door open and raced inside. My precipitate entry caused several people to turn and gawp at me, but I didn't slow down.

Rather, I raced to the main counter and panted to the clerk behind the desk: "Please, may I use your telephone? It's an emergency."

"But...But our telephone isn't for public use," said the startled clerk.

"It's an *emergency*," I repeated more loudly.

"Shhh," said the clerk.

"Daisy! Whatever is the matter?" Regina had hurried up to me and put a hand on my shoulder.

I whirled around, grateful for her arrival, and said, "I need to use the telephone. It's an emergency. A *major* emergency!"

"Please, Miss Chalmers, let Mrs. Rotondo use the telephone."

"Very well," said the clerk. Miss Chalmers, I presume.

She pushed the candlestick telephone at me. It didn't have a dialing plate, so I had to depress the switch hook several times. When the operator answered, I tried not to holler when I said, "Pasadena Police Department. It's an emergency."

Thank heaven, the operator was on her toes, because she almost instantly put my call through to the reception desk at the Pasadena Police Department.

"Sam Rotondo, please. It's an emergency," I told the officer who answered the phone.

"What's the matter, ma'am?" he asked, not being nearly as cooperative as the telephone operator.

Still panting like a grampus, I was now swelling like a balloon with pent-up fright and fury. Trying not to shout, I said distinctly, "Sam Rotondo, please. It's an emergency."

"What is the emergency, ma'am?" asked the thick-headed officer.

Wanting to utter several of the new words I'd learned since Lou Prophet came into my life, I restrained myself and said in a low, lethal voice, "A woman has been murdered in the library gazebo. Now *let me speak to Sam Rotondo!*"

Regina and Miss Chalmers both gasped, and I heard clicking sounds as the officer *finally* transferred my call to Sam.

"Rotondo," came his voice, which always sounded gruff when he was at work.

I told him, whispering, what Mr. Prophet and I had found, and he said, "I swear to God, Daisy. Only you could find a body in a gazebo."

"Mr. Prophet found it!" I snapped, still attempting to whisper. "Well, he's the one who recognized it for what it was. I'm the one who recognized the body as Stacy's. He's guarding the gazebo so I could come in here and call you."

"Be right there," he said. And he hung up on me.

I let out a sigh of mingled exasperation and relief. When I looked up from the telephone, I found both Regina and Miss

Chalmers staring at me in horror. When I glanced around, hoping nobody else in the library had heard my message to the police, I saw that most of the patrons had gone back to their library business, although a few still glanced my way.

What sounded like several books fell from a shelf in a far stack, making a huge noise. Another problem with another stack? I didn't know, but everyone in the library jumped and stared in that direction. Glad they weren't staring at me any longer.

"Daisy, is it true?" asked Regina, recovering from the shock of the falling books. She didn't speak as if she didn't believe me, but as if she couldn't believe somebody could be dead in the library's gazebo.

"I'm afraid so," I whispered. "But I can't talk about it now. I have to get back out there with Mr. Prophet and keep people away from the gazebo."

"Tell me later, okay?" said Regina.

"Will do," I said.

Shaking her head, Regina then said, "So many strange things are happening here lately."

I wanted to ask her what things besides falling books, but that explanation, too, would have to wait until later. I hurried out the library's front door, ran down the steps and to the path leading to the gazebo—where I saw Mr. Lou Prophet being harassed by two uniformed policemen, one of whom was holding a pair of handcuffs in a menacing manner. A couple of women stood nearby, clutching each other and gawking at Mr. Prophet with horror.

Good God, what now?

I sped up, running faster than I had since I was a kid in school. "Stop! *Stop!*" I hollered.

"Slow down, Miss Daisy!" Mr. Prophet hollered back. "These idiots think I done her in."

I didn't slow down. I raced, yelling like a demented banshee, up to the police contingent. "What the devil are you doing? This man didn't do it!"

"We *saw* him!" said one of the women in the clutch.

"You did not!" I snapped, panting. "He and I found Stacy dead in the gazebo. Mr. Prophet stayed here to guard the gazebo while I went into the library to call the police! He didn't do a single thing to that woman in there except find her body." Then I slapped a hand over my thundering heart and bent over to try to catch my breath. Perhaps I had overdone the running thing a bit, but for heaven's sake!

"Who are you?" asked a policeman.

"And who's he?" asked the other one.

"But we saw him come out of there!" said the other woman from the clutch.

Still attempting without much luck to catch my breath, I said, "I'm Mrs. Sam Rotondo. He's...he's...Oh dear." I grabbed onto one of the posts supporting the gazebo's roof and sort of sagged, breathless for a second.

"Rotondo?" said the first policeman.

"Yeah," said Mr. Prophet, who had a reason to be grumpy for once. "This here's Sam Rotondo's wife, and I'm a friend of theirs. Miss Daisy and I came to the library today, and we found that dead woman when we came out here to sit a spell."

"But..." said one of the clutching women.

"But nothing!" I barked, getting some of my breath and equilibrium back. "You assumed because Mr. Prophet is elderly and...a little rough-looking, that he must have killed the woman in there. But he didn't! We found her together. I mean, we both found her when we wanted to sit in the gazebo. Just like he said!"

"Oh dear," said one of the women.

"*What the devil is going on here?*" came a roar I recognized. It came from near the street. When I turned to look, I saw Sam stamping up to the gazebo between the palm trees, not bothering to use a path.

"These idiots think Mr. Prophet killed Stacy Kincaid," I told Sam.

"Now just a minute here," said one of the policemen. "We didn't—"

"But we *saw* him!" cried one of the women.

"Oh, hush!" I snapped at her.

"Everybody, be quiet!" bellowed Sam. He squinted at me. "Have you been running?"

"Well, yes. I had to run to the library to use the phone. And then, when I came out here to join Mr. Prophet, I saw these policemen trying to arrest him and these two idiotic women screeching about him killing Stacy! So I ran up here to stop their asinine doings."

"Well, *really*," said one of the clutchers.

"Hush up," I told her brusquely.

"Dammit, you shouldn't be running anywhere in your condition," said Sam, frowning severely at me.

"Applesauce! These idiots were blaming Mr. Prophet! I had to stop them from hauling him away in handcuffs," I growled back at my husband. "Look! Look, he's holding handcuffs. What a quartet of dunces!"

"How dare you call me names!" said a woman.

"Be quiet, you nitwit," I told her.

She huffed angrily, but didn't speak again. Good thing too, or I might have been forced to…do something. Not sure what.

"Now let's just get this figured out here," said one of the policemen.

Two other uniformed policemen, a fellow named Doan, who was Mrs. Rattle's son; and a fellow named Oliphant, who generally photographed crime scenes, joined us. Sam turned to them. "Doan, take statements from these two women. They didn't see what they thought they saw, but take 'em anyway."

"But, we *saw* him!" sniveled one of the women.

"Be *quiet*!" I snarled. "You only thought you did!"

"And you two," said Sam, directing his attention to the two uniforms who still had their hands on Mr. Prophet's arm, "turn loose of that man and go away. We'll take care of everything from now on."

"B-but——"

"*Now!*" said Sam.

The two strange-to-me uniforms saluted, let go of Mr. Prophet's arms, and backed off.

Mr. Prophet shook out his arms as if trying to get life back into them. "Hellkatoot," he said.

"As for you," Sam said to the two women, "after Doan takes your statements, leave the premises. You're only in the way here."

"Well, *really!*" cried a woman.

"Go away," I snarled at her.

Both women backed away from me. Doan took each one gently by an arm and led them a few yards from the gazebo.

FOUR

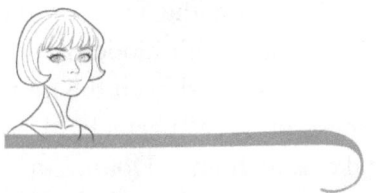

After the extraneous people left the scene, Sam turned to me, frowning.

"Whatever the provocation, you shouldn't have been running in your condition. Don't you care about the baby?"

"What?" I squealed, hardly able to believe my ears. "Of *course* I care about the baby, darn you! I also care about those blinking fools thinking Mr. Prophet murdered Stacy Kincaid!"

"Still—"

"Still nothing," I snarled, interrupting my mostly wonderful husband. "Mr. Prophet and I found Stacy dead in the gazebo, so stop scolding me and start solving the crime, will you?"

"God," mumbled Sam, but he stopped pestering me and returned to his sworn duty.

After what seemed like a confusing hour and a half, but could only have been five or six minutes, Sam, Mr. Prophet, Doan, Oliphant, and I were left alone at the gazebo. We stared in at the spectacle of Stacy Kincaid.

She wasn't a pretty sight. She'd managed to shed her hospital garb and somehow found clothing more to her taste, which had always been appallingly flashy. She'd grabbed onto the "flapper" look and gone wild with it. I think she wanted to be a heroine in an F. Scott Fitzgerald story.

The dress she wore now was a flimsy red gauze thing that might have looked almost good on a dance floor but was absurd for outdoor wear. She'd also got someone to paint flowers on her knees. One red, high-heeled patent-leather shoe dangled from a foot. The other one lay in the congealing blood on the floor of the gazebo. A broken bottle, its pointy edges crusted with blood, had rolled away from the blood puddle, but I expected it had been the murder weapon. Ugh.

After taking in the grotesque spectacle for several seconds, Sam said, "Daisy, you take Lou home. Doan, stay out here and keep people away. Oliphant, take as many photos as you can take."

"To heck with that," I said. "We found her. I want to know what you learn about how this happened."

Scowling at me over his shoulder, Sam said, "Nonsense. A bloody murder scene won't do you or the baby any good!"

"Nertz. How's the baby going to know? Osmosis? Anyhow, I need to know what happened here, because you know as well as I do that Stacy's mother will fall into a flying frenzy and call upon me to settle her spirits—so to speak—as soon as she hears about this."

"Cripes," muttered Sam. "Looking at this horror won't help you deal with Mrs. Pinkerton."

"Are you going to call the doctor? An ambulance? The coroner?" I asked, ignoring his silly statement.

"Already done," he said. With his lips pinched together, he continued to glower at me for another several seconds. Then he let out a sigh, his shoulders slumped, and he said, "Aw, hell, I guess I can't force you to leave." He turned to Mr. Prophet. "Will you take her to a bench or something where she can rest up from all the dam — all the running she's done?"

"I kin do that," said Mr. Prophet. "I gotta sit, too. My stump is hurtin'."

"Thank you," said a clearly unhappy Sam. "Keep her calm until Doan, Oliphant, and I can more or less figure out what happened here. She needs to rest, curse it, not run around all over the place."

"I'm right here, you know," I said, irked that Sam was talking about me instead of to me. "I didn't run around all over the place. Out of necessity, I ran to the library and back out again. And it's a good thing I did, or Mr. Prophet here would probably be in the back of a police car in handcuffs."

"She's kinda got a point, Sam," said Mr. Prophet reluctantly.

"All right, all right," said Sam. "Go sit on a bench. And *rest*, curse it, Daisy."

"Yes, sir," I said, snapping him a salute.

He didn't appreciate it, but he said no more. So Mr. Prophet and I moseyed over to a bench several yards away, beside the pond. The pond would go away too, once the new library opened. I heaved a sigh.

"That didn't turn out the way we planned, did it?" said Mr. Prophet.

"No, it did not. Lordy, I wonder who did Stacy in. And why. Well, she was a horrid human being. If I could have got away with it, I might have killed her myself, actually, although I'd never be so messy about it."

"Naw, you wouldn't," said Mr. Prophet. "You don't have it in you."

"I battered a woman over the head with a chair once," I told him a trifle huffily. "Mind you, she'd just shot Sam, but still...."

"Okay, maybe you do have it in you, but not like that." He jerked his gray old head toward the gazebo.

"You're right. I think the best way to have done Stacy in would have been to drive a wooden stake through her heart. Like Dracula."

"Who's Dracula?" he asked.

Peering at him in surprise, I said, "You've never read *Dracula?* Oh, dear, we should get that out of the library for you. It's a great story, although it's pretty scary. Dracula's a vampire."

"Ah. I've heard of vampires."

We sat in silence for a few minutes, and I glanced around the pretty library park, wishing we could still have it *and* the new library, but I knew it wouldn't happen. Something caught my eye, and I squinted at it.

"Hey," I said, "look over there. Are those footprints in the dirt there?"

Mr. Prophet's gaze followed my pointing finger, and he squinted too. "By God, I think you're right. They're headin' to the gazebo, ain't they?"

"Looks like it to me," I said. I turned to him. "You're a world-famous scout and bounty hunter. Why don't you go check them out? Maybe they're prints of Stacy and her killer from when they walked to the gazebo from…I don't know. Somewhere."

"Ain't a world-famous nothin'," he grumbled. But he rose from the bench and hobbled over to the prints. Bending over, he peered narrowly at them.

"Are there two sets of prints?" I asked.

"Yeah."

Rising from the bench, I said, "Are they a man's and a woman's?"

Mr. Prophet straightened, pointed at me, and said, "Sit down there and don't move. I'll take care of this. Sam will kill me if I let you move from that bench."

"Oh, bother the both of you!" I said, irked, although I sat. I didn't want Sam to get mad at Mr. Prophet because I'd disobeyed him. Honestly, though, you'd think I was the only woman in the world ever to become "with child," as polite people put it. "Are they a man's and a woman's prints?"

Bending over and squinting again, Mr. Prophet took his time responding. When he did, he shook his grizzled head and said, "Nah. Two women. These are prints of two people wearing them stupid high-heeled shoes."

"You wore high-heeled boots, didn't you?" I said, a trifle irked.

"Them boots served a purpose. Gripped the stirrups. Ladies' shoes with them high heels are stupid."

Thinking about several times when my feet had ached horribly after wearing high-heeled shoes for a long time, I decided he had a point. "You're right, but that's interesting. Do you think a *woman* killed Stacy? That seems strange."

"I've known killer wimmin in my time," said the old, banged-up voice of experience. "Stay there. I'll tell Sam about these. Mebbe that feller with the camera can take pictures or something."

"Good idea," I said, still irked that I had to sit still while other people were solving a crime. The crime of Stacy Kincaid's murder.

I couldn't help myself. I grinned. No more Stacy. Amazing. I wished like heck I could call Harold, Stacy's brother, and tell him. Harold had as much use for her as I did. Maybe he and I could go out and celebrate somewhere.

How unkind, huh? That's only because you didn't know Stacy.

Oh dear. I should also tell Flossie and Johnny Buckingham. Johnny was the captain of the Pasadena Salvation Army, and he'd done his level best—and then some—to save Stacy from herself. He hadn't succeeded. Flossie, his lovely wife, had also done her best for Stacy.

Stacy hadn't deserved their best. At least that's what I thought as I sat on the bench in the library's lovely park. Heck, Stacy had even ruined the gazebo.

If we Methodist-Episcopals practiced confession, as do the Roman Catholics, I should have gone to confession and told the priest my evil thoughts. Try as I might, though, I couldn't be sorry that Stacy no longer polluted the earth with her presence.

Crumb. I should go light some candles even though I'm not a Catholic.

So lost in thought had I become that I started when Oliphant's shadow suddenly appeared on the spot of grass at which I'd been staring. I looked up and saw he had his camera with him.

"Going to take pictures of the footprints?" I asked. Stupid question.

"Yes, ma'am. Mr. Prophet will show me where they are, and maybe we can follow them to their origin."

"Good. Might give you an idea of how Stacy got to the gazebo."

"No, really?" said Mr. Prophet sarcastically.

All right, so maybe my statement had been superfluous. Darn it,

I felt left out! Nevertheless, I sat on the bench like a good girl for the most part.

Daring rebuff once more, I said, "Can you, like, take plaster casts of the prints or anything so you can match shoes to them?"

"Not sure," said Oliphant, clicking away with his Kodak. "Might not be deep or distinct enough. We also don't have the plaster preparation with us. Might have to wait until tomorrow."

"Hope it doesn't rain overnight," I said.

"Me too," agreed Oliphant.

"Can you tell if they came from different shoes? I mean, different sizes or shapes or something?"

"Yeah," said Mr. Prophet, answering for Oliphant. "Both had high heels, but the fronts were shaped different. So were the heels, for that matter."

"If you can't take casts, can you draw pictures of them? A drawing might give more detail than a photograph in this light. A drawing might help if you can find the other pair. If one of those sets of prints is from Stacy's shoes, I mean. The other one might belong to her murderer."

"Not a bad idea, Miss Daisy," said Mr. Prophet, surprising me. He didn't generally give me credit for anything at all, much less having a good idea.

"It is a good idea," said Oliphant. "I'm not much of an artist."

"Sam is," I told him. "I mean, he does sketches of all sorts of things. I'm sure he could sketch those footprints."

"Really?" Oliphant sounded surprised.

"It's true," said Mr. Prophet. "I'll go fetch him."

And he did.

A few minutes later, Sam walked up to the bench upon which I sat, scowling to let me know I shouldn't move therefrom. "Good idea about the sketches," he said, softening his expression.

"Thank you. I haven't moved, so there's no need to frown at me," I told him.

"Good. Stay there."

I did. And as I did, an ambulance showed up on the street. So did Dr. Benjamin, our family doctor, and all-around good man. He helped the police occasionally when called upon to do so. I guess Sam had called him this time.

As he strode to the gazebo, he waved at me. I waved back.

Ambulance attendants carried a stretcher to the gazebo, but Doc made them stand outside while he inspected the interior and Stacy. Didn't envy him that job.

By the time Dr. Benjamin was through with the contents of the gazebo, Sam was finished sketching the footprints, and Mr. Prophet and Oliphant had traced the prints back to where they'd started; I was quite bored and was glad I'd brought a book with me. Having a book turned out to be of less use than it otherwise might have been, because I was distracted by the goings-on of the police and couldn't concentrate.

"Very well," said Sam in a booming voice behind me, making me jump, "we can leave now. I think we've managed to gather all the information there is to gather here for now."

"Thank heaven," I said. "I was bored out of my mind, just sitting there. I couldn't keep my mind on the book I brought with me."

With a grin, Sam came over to me, leaned down, and kissed my cheek. "I'm sorry, sweetheart, but you already did too much running around this morning, and I didn't want you to exhaust yourself."

"Huh. You didn't want me getting in your way, is what you mean," I said.

"Well," he admitted. "That too."

"Bother you, Sam Rotondo."

"But there's more excitement in store for you, because you and Lou have to come to the police station with me and give formal statements."

"Oh. Okay," I said, pleased. Very well, so giving formal statements wasn't precisely exciting; it was better than sitting on a bench while people were doing interesting things all around you and you couldn't participate.

"And then you, Lou, and I can go to the Crown Chop Suey Palace for lunch."

"Oh, that sounds like a great idea," I said, getting happier by the second.

However, as Sam and his uniformed helpers walked to his police Hudson, Dr. Benjamin walked to his car, and the ambulance attendants carried the covered body of Stacy Kincaid to the ambulance, I couldn't help shuddering. As little as I cared for Stacy—and I cared so little, it wouldn't fill a bottle cap—what happened to her had been really ugly.

The good Lord alone knew how Mrs. Pinkerton would react to this news.

FIVE

"Darn it, Sam Rotondo, that's not fair!" I said to my beloved after I'd given my statement to a uniform at the police station. He, Mr. Prophet, and I were walking up Fair Oaks to the Crown Chop Suey Palace. "You wouldn't let me move from that stupid bench when you did all your investigating, but you want me to go with you when you break the news to Mrs. Pinkerton? She'll shriek and make a gigantic fuss. That'll do me more harm than running or finding Stacy's body!"

"Relax, Daisy. I've already called Harold so he can be there with you to break the news."

"What do you mean, 'break the news'? *You'll* break the news because that's a policeman's lot. Which, as W.S. Gilbert pointed out, is not a happy one. But you chose it. I guess Harold and I can help pick up the pieces, but I'll be darned if I tell that woman her miserable daughter is dead. Murdered. Ewww."

"I'll tell her. I just want you and Harold to be there because she'll need you. You know she will," said Sam.

I heaved a huge sigh as Sam opened the door to the restaurant, and I preceded him and Mr. Prophet into it. It smelled *really* good in there, and my hackles unfluffed slightly.

They smoothed down even more when the food came. I love Chinese ribs, and I munched three or four of them along with my rice and chop suey and so forth.

"So, who do you think killed that gal?" asked Mr. Prophet during a break in the chomping.

"I don't have any idea," said Sam. "What about you, Daisy? You know anybody who'd like to do Stacy Kincaid in?"

"Me," I said. "Harold. Pretty much everyone else who knew her."

"Johnny Buckingham sounded cut up when I told him," said Sam.

Surprised, I lifted my gaze from the fried shrimp I'd just speared to Sam's face. "You already called Johnny? I'm so glad. Thank you, Sam. I'm sure he felt bad about Stacy. Johnny and Flossie were always good to her. Never gave up on her, which is some kind of miracle, actually."

"You, he, and Flossie were about the only people on the face of the earth I could think of who might be of some comfort to Mrs. Pinkerton. Along with Harold Kincaid. He's going to meet us here."

"Wow," I said, amazed and proud of my husband. "You've thought of everything, haven't you?"

"Probably not, but Kincaid can let me know whom else I should telephone. Isn't there an Episcopal priest on Mrs. Pinkerton's list of friends?"

"Yes," I said. "Father Frederick. I can't remember which church he's attached to, but Harold will know."

"Good. That should provide the woman with plenty of support."

"There you are!" came Harold's rather high-pitched voice from the dim interior of the restaurant. "It's so dark in here compared to the brightness outside, I couldn't find you for a few minutes."

"Harold, I'm so glad Sam found you at home!" I said, rising to greet him, even though I'm a woman and according to etiquette, men were supposed to rise and greet women and not vice-versa. Phooey on etiquette, I say. My morning had been made hideous by

Harold's sister—and not for the first time—so I not only rose to greet him, but gave him a hug when he joined us.

"Daisy," muttered Sam. "We're in public."

"Who cares?" I said. "I'm so happy you're here, Harold. I thought I'd have to call you, so I'm glad Sam got you first."

"Me too," said Harold. "Good day to you, Sam, Mr. Prophet," said Harold, who was a polite fellow.

"Kincaid," said Mr. Prophet, nodding at him.

"Glad you were home," said Sam to Harold. He had risen too. My Sam was also a polite fellow.

"Not sure I'm pleased about it," said Harold frankly. "I was almost to the automobile when Roy ran outside and hollered at me that you were on the telephone." Roy Castillo was Harold's houseboy. Nice young man and a very good cook. He'd been taught his culinary skills by none other than my own Aunt Vi, the best cook in Pasadena.

As long as we're on the subject of Harold Kincaid, I might as well explain him. There had been a time when Sam had disliked Harold for what I considered no good reason. Harold, you see, wasn't what you'd call a manly man. In actual fact, Harold lived—in a fabulous mansion in San Marino—with another man named Delray Farrington. If they were a man and a woman, they'd be married, but they weren't allowed to marry each other because they were both men, if you see what I mean.

Harold had, for many years, been my very best friend, followed closely by Flossie Buckingham and Regina Browning. He was a truly kind, generous, and all-around marvelous person. However, his mere existence was against the law, which leads me to believe the laws don't know what the heck they're talking about. Harold had absolutely no say in the matter of his being-ness and, therefore, shouldn't be punished for it, according to me.

Golly, I have a lot of opinions, don't I? Well, I'm correct about that one. I know I am, because Harold has told me so. He'd even asked me more than once, "Why would I choose this? To be vilified, persecuted, thrown in prison, laughed at, humiliated, and otherwise discriminated against? I didn't choose to be this way. If I could be other than what I am, believe me, I'd be it."

According to Harold and my own observations, there are lots of people like Harold in the world, both male and female, and none of them had a say in the matter. They are what they are.

There. That's over with. So now you know about Harold.

"I'm *so* happy to see you, Harold!" I told him as he sat in a chair at our table. "I couldn't bear the notion of facing your mother without you there to help soften the blow."

"You think either of us will be able to soften the blow?" asked Harold. "You know damned well she'll have hysterics and make everyone's life a pure misery for days, if not months. I'm not sorry somebody finally put an end to my vile sister, but it would be easier on Mother if she'd fallen off a cliff or something. She won't take kindly to Stacy having been murdered."

"Can't say as I blame her fer that," observed Mr. Prophet.

"True," said Sam.

"I guess," I said. "Have you ever met her, Mr. Prophet?"

"Which one? The mother or the daughter?" he asked.

"The mother. I'm pretty sure you never met Stacy."

"Lucky you," muttered Harold.

"Once or twice," he said. "Ain't seen her in a snit, but I've heard plenty about her. Not an easy woman, I take it."

"You couldn't be more right," I said with a sigh. "Hey, Harold, want a rib or a shrimp or something?"

"I already asked the waiter to bring me another plate," he said.

Sure enough, the words had barely left his lips when a waiter showed up with not merely a plate, but another two bowls full of food, which he managed somehow to fit onto the already-crowded table.

"I've got this, by the way," said Harold.

"There's no need for that," said Sam, sounding not precisely offended, but a little off.

"Nertz," said Harold. "You had to deal with my sister this morning, and pretty soon you're going to have to deal with my lame-brained mother. The least you deserve is lunch."

"Thanks," said Mr. Prophet.

"Yes. Thanks, Harold. I'm so glad you're here," I said, repeating myself. Bad habit.

"Thanks, Kincaid. Have to admit I'm not looking forward to breaking the news to your mother."

Harold rolled his eyes heavenward as he bit some delicious pork off the rib he'd picked up. "I'll be glad when the day's over." He evidently had another thought because he turned to Sam. "Have you called Dr. Benjamin? He probably should be at Mother's side too. She'll need a pill or a posset or an injection or a gallon of Scotch or something."

"He's aiming to be at your mother's house in"—Sam shook his coat sleeve down, pushed up his shirt cuff with his right hand, and said—"thirty minutes."

"Better eat fast then," said Harold, proceeding to do so.

"What about me?" asked Mr. Prophet. "Do I have to be there too?"

"Would you mind taking a red car?" I asked him.

"It would probably be best if you drove him home, Daisy. After thinking about it, I believe it would be better if you weren't there when I break the news."

"What?" I asked, incredulous. "Why? That's crazy, Sam."

He appeared a trifle taken aback. "I just don't think it would be good for you in your condition to endure a huge scene, and you know she'll enact a huge scene."

"Fiddlesticks on my condition," I told him roundly. "Women have been giving birth since Adam and Eve. They can't *all* have lived scene-free lives during their pregnancies!"

People at nearby tables turned to glare at me. Whoops. I grinned at them, and they all swiveled back to mind their own business once more.

"Sorry. Didn't mean to yell," I said more softly. "But that's a really stupid thing to say, Sam Rotondo. You know Mrs. Pinkerton, and you know how she'll act."

"She's right, Sam," said Mr. Prophet.

"Gawd, yes," said Harold. "I won't go if Daisy isn't allowed. My mother is a pain in the ass at the best of times, and this definitely won't be one of those."

"Oh, very well," Sam chuffed out, as if he were a train letting off steam. "But if Mrs. Pinkerton gets out of hand, I'm taking you home."

"Precisely how 'out of hand' do you expect her to get?" I asked. "My guess is that she'll faint, Dr. Benjamin will shove ammonia salts under her nose, then she'll wake up again and start shrieking and crying. Then Doc will give her a sedative, and she'll cry some more and beg me to perform a séance or something."

"Sounds about right to me," said Harold after swallowing another bite of yummy food. "There will be a lot of noise, and then the good doctor will step in and stick her with a needle, and she'll go to sleep." He peered at me across the table. "She's going to drive you crazy for the next few weeks, though. Wish you didn't have to go through it."

With a shrug, I said, "I'm used to it. I don't like it, but I'm used to it. Since she started seeing the Swami Vivekananda, she hasn't been bothering me quite so much, but I expect this news will change that."

"I don't want Mrs. Pinkerton pestering you," said Sam.

"Good luck with that," said Harold.

"How you gonna stop her?" asked Mr. Prophet. Then he shrugged and added, "Guess you can have Elvira answer the telephone for a week or so."

"That's a good idea," said Harold.

"It's all right," I said, not happily but with resignation. "Mrs. Pinkerton has been my primary source of income for more than half my life. The least I can do is assist her through this ordeal."

"Cripes," said Sam. "You're in a delicate condition. You don't need her problems piled on you."

"Too late," I said. "You might almost say I volunteered for the position as hankie-in-chief. She's become accustomed to calling on me in times of trouble. Even when there's no trouble, she's just accustomed to calling on me. Can't imagine she'll quit now. Especially now."

"I don't like it," said Sam.

"Daisy won't like it, either," Harold told him. "But I've never been able to convince her to let my mother stew in her own juices. She's too nice for her own good."

"Miss Daisy? *She's* too nice fer her own good? That who you're talkin' about?" Mr. Prophet squinted at me. "Ya never been too nice to me."

"You've never paid me to listen to your woes," I said. "Besides, you've never been nice to me either."

He tilted his head in something akin to agreement. "Ya got me there."

"All right, you two," said Sam. "Have we about finished here?"

There was still enough food on the table to feed a family of six, but we all claimed to be too full to eat any more of the delicacies remaining. Not sure about the others, but I was telling the truth.

"I'll have them pack it up, and you and Daisy can take it home, Detective. You'll have meals for days," said Harold.

"Mrs. Rattle already fixed our dinner for tonight," I said. "Mr. Prophet? You want to take these leftovers home with you?"

"On a red car? No thanks."

"This place packs food in great boxes to take home," said Harold, rising from his chair. "I'll just go tell Wally to pack this up, and you can eat it tomorrow. And the next day too no doubt."

Before anyone could ask Harold who Wally was, he'd left the table and was almost to the main counter where the cash register sat. The man behind the register gave Harold a big smile. I got the impression they knew each other of old.

"Harold seems to know everybody, doesn't he?" I asked no one in particular.

"Handy feller to be friends with," said Mr. Prophet.

Sam chuckled.

Sure enough, in a very few moments, two waiters came and whisked all the dishes from our table and carted them off. A few minutes after that, a cardboard box appeared on the counter next to the cash register, and Harold returned to tell us, "Everything's all packed and ready. Just stick it in your Frigidaire when you get home, and you'll have meals for days."

"Thanks, Kincaid," said Sam. He sobered. "Are you ready for this?"

"No, but Daisy and I can take my car to my mother's place. We'll wait for you there."

"And I'll go home in a red car, thank gawd," said Mr. Prophet.

"Lucky," I muttered at him.

Sam carried the cardboard box full of food from the restaurant. Harold's red Hispano-Suiza sat at the curb, looking gorgeous and slightly out of place in front of a Chinese restaurant. Sam looked at the Hispano-Suiza and at the cardboard box and said, "Say, Kincaid, would you mind carrying this box? We have to walk to the police department to pick up my Hudson. I'd probably better get another officer to go with us, too."

"I'll take the food and Daisy and meet you at Mother's place," said Harold, taking the box from Sam. "Hope the doctor's there. I'll telephone Father Frederick from Mother's house. Crumb. I hope Algie's there, too."

Mr. Algernon "Algie" Pinkerton is the extremely nice, plump, pink man who married Harold's mother after her first husband, Mr. Eustace Kincaid, turned out to be a stinker and almost ruined the bank he ran. So she divorced him and married Algie.

"I hope so too," said Sam. "Didn't have his number, or I'd have called him."

"He's probably home," said Harold. "Algie doesn't get out much these days. He's happy to be home with Mother, which is a darned good thing."

"Yes, it is," I agreed.

"Yeah," said Sam.

"Don't know how he can stand it," said Mr. Prophet.

"And you don't even *know* Mrs. Pinkerton!" I said.

"Don't have to. I wouldn't want to be at any woman's beck and call all day, every day."

And there you have another aspect of Mr. Lou Prophet in a nutshell, I guess.

"Oh, it's not all *that* bad," said Sam.

I whacked him on the arm for his effort. He laughed as he opened the passenger side door of Harold's magnificent automobile for me to climb in.

SIX

Harold and I arrived at Mrs. Pinkerton's palatial palace several minutes before Sam and his Hudson did. When Harold pulled the Hispano-Suiza up to the closed gate, Mr. Jackson, Mrs. Pinkerton's gatekeeper, gave him a huge smile.

"How-do, Mr. Harold. And is that Miss Daisy with you?" Mr. Jackson said, his smile broadening.

"It is, Jackson. How are you today?"

"Doin' all right, thanks, Mr. Harold. Good to see you."

"How's your mother, Mr. Jackson?" I asked, leaning forward so I could see him better. "Please let her know I'm still wearing the juju she gave me."

"Will do, Miss Daisy. She'll be glad of it. Swears by them things, she does."

Mr. Jackson's mother, Mrs. Jackson, was a real live Voodoo mambo from New Orleans, Louisiana. She fashioned the juju for me after we'd all had a rather severe altercation with the Ku Klux Klan, which invaded Pasadena in 1923. Stupid people. The Klan, I mean, not the Jacksons, who were all lovely. What's more, Mrs. Jackson not only made jujus, but she baked the tastiest beignets I've ever eaten. Truth to tell, I'd never even heard of a beignet until Mrs. Jackson brought my family a plate of them as a thank-you.

"But Jackson, you might want to prepare for some ructions," said Harold. "I'm afraid Mother is going to get bad news about Stacy in a very few minutes."

With a sardonic expression, Mr. Jackson said, "She ought to be used to bad news about that child by now."

"This time is even worse," Harold told him. "Somebody killed Stacy. Daisy's husband will be here in a few minutes to break the news to Mother."

"Sweet Lord have mercy!" said Jackson. "I never much cared for your sister, Mr. Harold—and I apologize for that—"

"No need to apologize," Harold said, interrupting him. "I couldn't stand her myself."

"I suppose the girl was trouble," said Jackson, "but this news will break your poor mother's heart."

"Yes," said Harold, expelling the word along with a huge sigh. "That's why Daisy's here. And Dr. Benjamin will be here soon too. I'll telephone Father Frederick and hope he'll be able to come as well."

"The more folks she has to help her in this time of sorrow, the better," said Jackson.

"True," grumbled Harold.

"How's Jimmy doing?" I asked Mr. Jackson before Harold could drive the car through the gate Mr. Jackson just opened for us.

"He's doing just swell, Miss Daisy. I'll tell him you asked about him."

"Glad to hear it," I said honestly. Jimmy Jackson, Jackson's son, was a good kid. "He still playing at the Cocoanut Grove?"

"He is indeed, Miss Daisy."

"Good for him!"

Jimmy Jackson played the horn. The first time I'd seen him play had been shocking to me because it had been in a speakeasy. As Prohibition had been in effect for several years by then, neither one of us should have been there, but we both were—and both in pursuit of making a living, too, by Jiminy. Huh. I just realized Stacy

Kincaid had provoked my involvement in *that* debacle, too. You know, I'd never attempted to ascertain if Stacy had any good qualities because her bad ones have always predominated, but if I did, I doubt I could find one. The world—according to me, as usual—would be better off without her.

But I still felt sorry for Mrs. Pinkerton. And really, if Stacy hadn't been such a worthless blob of humanity, I wouldn't have earned nearly so much money for my family during the many years of my spiritualist-mediuming.

"You know, Harold," I said as he drove through the open wrought-iron gates and up the winding, deodar-lined path to his mother's mansion, "I've finally decided that your sister had one good quality."

He whipped his head around to gape at me. "No! How'd you do that?"

"I just realized that if it hadn't been for Stacy, I wouldn't have made nearly as much money over the years as I did. My good income was due directly to Stacy being a deplorable person."

"Well, there you go. Maybe cockroaches have some good qualities, too. Never much thought about her that way."

In spite of everything, I laughed. Then I said, "But drive up to the kitchen entrance, please. I'd better warn Vi of impending storms so she can prepare tea and possets or whatever your mother will require."

"Good idea. I'll call Father Frederick from the kitchen telephone."

"Thanks, Harold."

So Harold drove past the curving road that would have taken him to the circular drive in front of Mrs. Pinkerton's massive home on Orange Grove, and took us straight to the kitchen entrance of the establishment. Mrs. Pinkerton's Rolls-Royce sat in the drive, dripping. That's because Quincy Applewood, who generally worked for Mr. Pinkerton taking care of his sons' polo ponies, had the hose running and was washing the expensive automobile. He turned when he heard Harold's Hispano-Suiza and grinned at Harold and me. After quickly rinsing the soapy slush off the Rolls, he shut off the hose and walked over to open my door.

"Hey, Daisy and Mr. Harold. You don't generally use the back entrance."

"There's a good reason for it today, Quincy. How's Edie?" Edie Applewood, Quincy's wife, was an old high school chum of mine. She now worked as Mrs. Pinkerton's lady's maid.

"She's fine, thanks. She's inside if you want to chat or something."

"Listen, Quincy," said Harold. "We came to this entrance because something pretty bad happened, and Daisy thought we'd better warn as many staff members as we can before we see my mother."

"Yeah?" Quincy's smile vanished and he appeared confused.

"Somebody murdered Stacy," I told him bluntly. "Mrs. P is going to be in a state and a half."

"Holy Moses! You're kidding!" said Quincy. Then he shook his head hard. "No, I know you're not kidding. Good God, though, this stinks. I mean, I didn't like the girl, but this is going to be a huge blow to Mrs. Pinkerton."

"I know. That's why we wanted to warn you and Vi and Featherstone and anybody else. To be prepared, you know?"

"Yeah. Okay. Thanks, Daisy and Harold. Your aunt's in the kitchen, I'm pretty sure."

"Thanks, Quincy."

"Shoot, I'd better finish with the Rolls before it dries and streaks," said Quincy, who looked as if he'd like to enter the house with us and find and warn Edie.

"Leave the car be," said Harold. "Mother won't notice if it's streaked. I doubt she'll be going anywhere for a while. Anyhow, you can fix it later, can't you?"

"Yeah. Yeah, I can. Thanks, Harold."

"Not a problem." Harold looked at me.

I looked at him.

"You ready for this?" he asked.

"No."

"Neither am I, but we'll have to do it anyway."

Harold opened the door to the kitchen entrance of the house, which led onto a utility porch. Quincy came with us and we walked through the utility room to the kitchen and found Vi stirring a pot over the kitchen range. When she heard us coming in, she glanced our way and began to smile. Her smile didn't quite achieve its full radiance as she took in our bleak demeanors.

"What's wrong?" she asked.

"Better come over here and sit down, Vi," I said, patting a chair at the kitchen table.

She let go of the wooden spoon with which she'd been stirring, reached to turn off the burner, and turned to stare at me, aghast. "Is it your father? Has something happened to Joe?" She slapped her hands to her cheeks. "It's not *Peggy*! Oh, Daisy, not your mother!"

Peggy, in case you didn't guess, is my mother. I held up both hands. "No. Vi, calm down. It's not our family. It's Stacy."

Vi visibly sagged, reached for her spoon, and relit the burner. "Oh, for goodness' sake, it's always Stacy. Why do you want to scare a body like that?"

"Somebody murdered her!" I said, perhaps a trifle loudly.

There went the spoon and burner again. Vi turned and gaped at Harold and me.

"Murdered? Stacy?"

"I'm afraid so," said Harold. "We wanted to warn the staff before Sam gets here to tell my mother."

"Oh, my Lord God Almighty. This might kill your mother, Harold."

I heard Harold mutter, "If only," but I'm sure Vi didn't.

"We're here to see that doesn't happen," I told Vi, giving Harold a hard elbow in the ribs. "In fact, Harold wanted to use the kitchen telephone to see if he can get in touch with Father Frederick. The more people she has to assist her through the shock, the better."

"Good idea," said Vi. "Quincy, see if you can find Edie. Harold, I think Featherstone is in the butler's pantry. Will you see if he's there and tell him?"

Featherstone was Mrs. P's elegant, unflappable butler, so the butler's pantry was a good place for him. I've always admired Featherstone. He even had an English accent. How butlerine can one person get, you know?

Anyhow, Harold and I went to do Vi's bidding. Pretty soon, the Pinkerton kitchen was full of Vi, Harold, Featherstone, Quincy, Edie, and me. Edie looked stunned, which made sense. While it is true no one who knew Stacy liked her, learning of her murder came as a shock to everyone. I'd been shocked as all heck when Mr. Prophet and I had found her, for instance.

Harold managed to get hold of Father Frederick and relayed the news. After only a few seconds, he hung up the receiver, turned, and told us, "Father Frederick will be here shortly."

"I'll make tea," said Vi, moving from the human cluster to the kitchen sink.

"And I'll go upstairs and get her smelling salts," said Edie, also breaking away from the crowd.

"Sam should be here pretty soon," said Harold a trifle fretfully.

"Perhaps we should walk down the hall so as to be close to the front door and the drawing room," suggested Featherstone.

With a shrug, Quincy said, "Heck, guess I'll finish washing and waxing the Rolls. There doesn't seem to be anything I can do in here."

"Good idea," I told him.

As Vi prepared tea and whatever other magical panaceas she could create to soothe Mrs. Pinkerton's soon-to-be savaged spirits, Harold, Featherstone, and I crept from the kitchen and down the hall. For some reason, we reminded me of Natty Bumppo leading a rescue party through the woods of New England. Featherstone was Natty. Harold and I were Uncas and Chingachgook, although I'm not sure who was which. When Featherstone silently held out a hand, we stopped like good little scouts and waited.

I heard a car drive up and stop in front of the huge front porch. Another car followed it. I thought I recognized Sam's Hudson's engine. I hoped the other car contained Dr. Benjamin and that he had a good supply of whatever Mrs. Pinkerton was soon going to need.

Sure enough, after several seconds, the brass knocker whacked the knocking plate. I saw Featherstone suck in a deep breath—I didn't hear him, because he was too elegant for that—straighten his already-straight shoulders and walk to the front door. He opened it, and sure enough, there was Sam, Officer Stephen Doan, and Dr. Benjamin standing on the porch.

Softly, Featherstone said, "Mrs. Rotondo has informed us of the unfortunate event. She and Mr. Harold are here to be of service. As, of course, am I."

"Thanks, Featherstone," said Sam.

I waved at him but he didn't wave back. He just gave me a curt nod and followed Featherstone to the drawing room. Poor Featherstone. He'd have to be right there when Sam broke the news. But Harold and I were handy, and so was Doc Benjamin, so he wouldn't have to be alone with Mrs. P for long.

Featherstone left the door to the drawing room open, so Harold and I crept up to it and listened.

Sam broke the news as gently as he could.

Didn't matter, of course. Letting out a shriek that could probably have been heard in the New England forest through which Featherstone, Harold, and I had just tiptoed, Mrs. Pinkerton then fainted. At the first screech, we rushed into the drawing room. We both noticed that Mrs. P had conveniently fainted onto a sofa so she didn't hurt herself.

Harold and I exchanged a cynical glance, which did neither of us credit. The poor woman might be accustomed to staging dramatic collapses, but that didn't mean this one wasn't genuine, or that her grief was feigned.

As Sam, Featherstone, Doan, Harold, and I watched, Doc Benjamin hurried to her side, adjusted a sofa cushion, and said, "Daisy, will you please open my bag? I want to give Mrs. Pinkerton a sedative."

"Sure," I said, hurrying to do his bidding.

"What in the world is going on?" came a querulous voice from the door of the drawing room.

We all swiveled to see Mr. Algernon Pinkerton, clad in a

smoking jacket and with a fez on his head, standing at the open doorway, staring at everyone, a bemused frown on his face.

Crumb! We'd totally forgotten to tell Mrs. Pinkerton's husband the news! Of all people to forget. Unforgivable.

Thank the good Lord, Harold was quick on his feet.

"Algie," he said, hastening to take his stepfather's arm. "I'm so sorry we didn't get to you in time for you to be with Mother."

What a diplomat! And what a fibber, but it was his diplomacy I admired then.

When he told Mr. P what Sam had just imparted to Mrs. P, Mr. P hurried over to his fallen wife. Sitting on the coffee table before the sofa, he picked up one of Mrs. P's hands and chafed it.

"Madeline! Oh, Madeline, what horrible news," he crooned, his voice oozing sympathy. I'm sure he hadn't cared for Stacy any more than did the rest of us, but he loved his wife. "What a terrible blow for you, my darling."

Opening her eyes after giving them a flutter or two, Mrs. Pinkerton sat up and threw her arms around her husband.

"Oh, Algie! Whatever will I *do*? *Stacy*! She's *dead*! Somebody *murdered* her!"

"I'm so sorry, my dear," said Mr. P gallantly as his wife all but smothered him. She was a large woman.

"Who did it?" asked Algie.

Interesting. To my knowledge, this was the first time anyone had bothered to ask the question. Mr. Pinkerton lifted his chin far enough to gaze at Harold.

Slapping a hand to his chest, a startled Harold said, "It wasn't me!"

With a nod, Mr. P went back to endeavoring to soothe his wife. To put it mildly, his chore wasn't an easy one.

SEVEN

I'm not sure how long we, as a group, stayed in the drawing room of the Pinkerton estate, but it was far too long for my peace and comfort. When she wasn't sobbing onto her husband's smoking jacket, Mrs. Pinkerton was calling on me to summon Rolly and get the Ouija board and the tarot cards, etc. I could see my husband's anger build with every demand of hers on me and my time. I prayed for rescue.

Rescue came eventually, thank God, in the form of my beloved aunt. Almost staggering, she appeared in the doorway carrying a heavily laden silver tray. From his stoic position just inside the room, Featherstone gave a start—the first time I'd ever seen him the tiniest bit rattled—and rushed up to take it from Vi and carry it to the gang of people surrounding the sofa.

"Ahem," he said loudly. "Mrs. Gumm has kindly brought tea for Mrs. Pinkerton, if you will allow me to set the tray on the table.

With a leap of which I wouldn't have believed him capable if I hadn't seen it for myself, Mr. Pinkerton rose from the table, clearing the way for Featherstone's tray. When I glanced at my aunt, she was taking in the scene at the sofa and shaking out her aching arms. I sidled up to her.

"Thanks, Vi. You should have called Quincy or Edie to bring the tray. Or me, for Pete's sake."

"Don't be ridiculous. I wanted to see for myself what was going on," said my honest aunt. "Hysterics seem to be the order of the day."

"I'm afraid so," I agreed.

"Besides, you shouldn't be carrying heavy things in your condition," she said, frowning at me.

"I'm fine. The only thing wrong with me is that I want to get out of here. I've suffered years and years of Mrs. Pinkerton's fits and starts, and I'm not enjoying this one at all."

With a sigh, Vi said, "Well, I can't blame the woman. She may have more money than is good for her, but I know what it's like to lose a child, and it's hard."

"Oh, Vi." I hugged my aunt hard. "I know you do. And Paul was a *good* person, too, unlike…" I deemed it better not to finish my sentence.

Vi understood. She only said, "Yes. But listen, Daisy. I'm going back to the kitchen. Please let me know if Mrs. Pinkerton or anyone needs anything else. I'll finish dinner preparations, although I doubt anyone will want to dine this evening."

"Thanks, Vi. You're a brick."

"Very well," said Dr. Benjamin from his position near the sofa. "I'm going to give you a sedative now, Madeline. You need to lie down. You've had a shock, but Daisy's in no condition to help you at the moment."

"Oooooh!" sobbed Mrs. Pinkerton. "I forgot! Oh, Daisy!" She glanced to where I'd been before I'd gone to my aunt, blinked, and said, "Oh, dear. Did she run away? I'm *sorry*! Oh, Daisy, I'm so sorry!"

After one quick prayer—and why I hadn't thought to pray before, I have no idea—I left my aunt's side and went to Mrs. Pinkerton's. "It's all right, Mrs. Pinkerton. This was a terrible thing to have happened. But I fear Dr. Benjamin is correct. I'm expecting a child now and am unable to be of help to you. Um…" I tried to think fast but didn't have much luck.

Fortunately for me, Harold stepped into the fray. "Have you been seeing the Swami Vivekananda? Perhaps he can assist you."

"Or Johnny Buckingham," said Sam, who could often be absolutely brilliant.

"Yes!" I cried. "Johnny is the very person you need right now. He never once gave up on Stacy, even when…" I decided not to finish that sentence too.

Dr. Benjamin pushed up Mrs. Pinkerton's sleeve and jabbed a needle in her arm. She squeaked, although I think it was from surprise and not pain. Then she kind of slumped back onto the sofa. Mr. Pinkerton had taken up residence behind the sofa, and he gently massaged his wife's neck and shoulders. He was a kind man.

The door knocker sounded once more, and Featherstone went to the door to admit Father Frederick. The good father walked to the sofa, too, and knelt to speak to Mrs. Pinkerton. He softly asked her to bow her head in prayer with him, and she complied. Have I mentioned she was leaking tears through all of the above actions? Well, she was.

Sam took the opportunity to walk over to me. Harold joined him.

"Why don't you get out of this hellhole?" Sam asked me. "I telephoned Buckingham from the station, but he was out with the band. I told Flossie, and she said she'd shoo him over here as soon as he got back home."

"Poor Johnny," I said. "And poor Flossie. He's always out blowing his horn on the streets while she's left home with the kids."

"They both love it," said Sam. He was right. "But I really want you out of here. You've already been through too much today."

"Fiddlesticks," I said. "I feel fine."

"That's good, but you need to be careful. The Chevrolet's at the library, right?"

"Right," I said, having forgotten this pertinent fact.

"I'll drive her," Harold volunteered instantly. "I need to get out of here, too, and I'm not even pregnant."

"Harold!" I managed not to laugh, which wouldn't have been appropriate under the circumstances.

"Good. I'll make your excuses to the Pinkertons," said Sam. "I need to question both of them, but I doubt I'll get anything out of the missus. Maybe Mr. Pinkerton can tell me if Stacy got in touch with her mother after she escaped from the prison ward. I need to know if she had any friends and get their names too."

"I doubt Stacy got in touch with Mrs. P. She knew her mother is about as good as a wilted lily when it comes to doing anything useful for anyone."

"Unkind, Daisy," said Sam gruffly.

"But true," said Mrs. Pinkerton's loyal son, Harold.

Sam grinned. "Anyhow, get out of here now before she sees you and calls you back. I'll be home as soon as I can. Might be a long night."

"Okay. See you. Try not to be late. Mrs. Rattle has prepared a special dish with the leftover chicken for our dinner tonight." I got on my tiptoes and kissed his cheek.

Then Harold and I scrammed out of there.

"I'll follow you home," said Harold as he drove library-wards. "All the Chinese leftovers are in my machine, and I know you have six tons of books in yours."

"Thanks, Harold. You're a true friend."

"I know I am, and you'd better appreciate me. Speaking of which, what did your lady do with leftover chicken?"

Have I mentioned Harold was a trifle plump? Well, he was. He loved his food, and he always took note when a new recipe or dinner idea appeared in his orbit.

"I roasted a chicken last night, and there was a lot of it left over. There were also leftover mashed potatoes and green beans, so Mrs. Rattle made a...I don't know what you'd call it. Kind of a stew with the leftovers and the gravy, and she said she'd use the leftover mashed potatoes as a topping."

"Oh, kind of a chicken a la king, only with potatoes instead of a crust."

"Right. Or a shepherd's pie with chicken instead of lamb."

"Sounds tasty. I might just have to stick a spoon in it and test it for you before you put it in the oven."

"Fine with me," I told him. "I'm just glad I don't have to cook tonight. I am kind of weary. Wouldn't mind a little nap, actually."

"You probably should nap," said Harold. "In your condition and all."

"Oh, boy, everybody talks about my 'condition' as if I had some deadly disease instead of being pregnant."

"Sam seems quite protective," Harold said musingly. "He evidently thinks you're delicate, even though he knows you."

It felt good to laugh. "I *am* delicate," I said when I stopped chortling. "At least I'm in what they call a delicate condition."

"Boloney. You're healthy as a horse." He glanced at me. "You really do look good, Daisy. Pregnancy becomes you."

"Thanks, Harold."

We'd made it to the library, so Harold maneuvered so that he could park behind the Chevrolet. "You can open your own door, can't you?" he asked.

"Yes, thank you," I said. "But thanks for the offer. You're *such* a gentleman."

"Damned right I am," said Harold. "I'll meet you at your place."

"Pull up in front of our house," I told him. "I left Spike with Pa, so I have to fetch him and leave the Chevrolet in their driveway."

"Have him come over to your place, so we can tell him the grisly news together. But wait to empty the books out of the car. I know you're healthy as a horse, but you still probably shouldn't cart a thousand pounds of books around, and neither should your father, with his dicky heart and all."

"Thanks again, Harold." He was a true pal.

As luck would have it, when Harold and I drove down Marengo Avenue, we saw Pa sitting with Mr. Prophet and Spike and Rosebud on Sam's and my front porch! The front porch had a little gate to prevent the dogs from escaping and running into the street. As soon as the two men saw us, they both rose. I drove the Chevrolet into our drive instead of the one across the street. Mr. Prophet walked over to unlatch the gate to the porch while Pa more or less controlled the two hounds.

Mrs. Rattle worked at our house until twelve-thirty most days, so she was long gone, in case you wondered.

"Wow, Daisy, Lou's been telling me about your adventures this morning. So somebody finally did Stacy Kincaid in, eh? Her mother must be devastated."

"She is," I told him.

"You need help getting the books out of the car?" he asked me.

"No, thanks. That's why I brought Harold with me," I said.

"Did he bring that Chinese chow too?" asked Mr. Prophet, who didn't dwell on little things like murder, but preferred to think about good food.

"I did," Harold hollered from his car, which he'd parked on the street in front of the house.

"I love that car," said my father wistfully. He adored automobiles and still liked to tinker with them. He wasn't able to do much in the line of tinkering except when he was helping one of his six thousand friends with their cars. My father is one of those people of whom it is sometimes said, "He never met a stranger." Great guy, my father.

"Feel free to check it out all you want," said Harold, hefting the cardboard carton full of little white boxes stuffed with Chinese food up to the porch. "I like it a lot, although it's a trifle larger than I'd prefer. I swear, nothing can beat my old Stutz."

"It damn near beat me to death when you drove me to that lion farm," growled Mr. Prophet.

"That was my fault," I told him. "I thought it might be funny for you to be so low to the ground after being on horses all your life. Guess not, huh?"

"No," he said grimly.

I suppose it had been mean of me to make him travel with Harold in his little Stutz Bearcat when we went to Gay's Lion Farm in Westlake Park in Los Angeles. Sometimes I don't think. And I'd never say that out loud to Sam, Harold, or Mr. Prophet, because they'd agree with me.

"Well, it worked out okay in the end," I said, trying to sound perky. "When that awful man dumped me into the lion's den, you saved the day."

"Yeah. I seem to save your days a lot, don't I?" the old curmudgeon said.

"Yes, and that's why Sam and I love you."

"Hellkatoot! Don't say things like that! Cripes."

"You're embarrassing Lou, Daisy," said Pa with a chuckle. "Come here and greet your hound and my hound, and I'll start carrying books in from the car." He stepped aside so Harold could cart the cardboard box onto the porch and to the front door. Mr. Prophet opened the door for him. The old misery wasn't completely useless.

So I obeyed my father and greeted my ecstatic hound Spike, and Pa's ecstatic hound Rosebud. They were so adorable together I could hardly stand it. I don't know where Mr. Prophet's cat Yuyu was, but he was nowhere on the front porch. He might have ventured there if Rosebud wasn't, but she was, so he wasn't. Did that even make sense?

Eventually, we got dogs, food, books, and people inside the house, and Harold carried the carton of food to the kitchen. He and I emptied all the cunning little white cartons from the box and stuck them in the Frigidaire. Mrs. Rattle had left her chicken dish covered in waxed paper on the middle shelf. I took it out to show Harold.

"Hmmm," he said. "Looks good."

I opened a drawer, got out a spoon, and handed it to Harold. "Try it."

So he did. "Excellent," he said after thinking about it like the connoisseur he was. "Heated up, this will make a delightful, if simple, meal."

"If you're me, it's not so simple," I told him.

"Yes, dear, I know, but your aunt says your cooking skills are coming right along."

"She tells me the same thing. And really, the chicken dinner I fixed last night was pretty good."

"Excellent. Well, I'll be going now. I think I'll give my mother's place a miss. If she needs me terribly, she knows my telephone number. Unfortunate that, but she *is* my mother. And if she telephones here, don't answer the call."

"How will I know if it's from her if I don't answer the telephone?"

"Drat," said Harold. He slid Mr. Prophet a look.

Lifting his arms as if he were being arrested, Mr. Prophet said, "Don't look at me! I ain't in the telephone-answering business."

"I can stay for a while," said my father doubtfully.

"No, you can't," I told him. "You need to get Rosebud home so you can both take a nap. Spike and I are going to nap, too, so I won't even hear the telephone if it rings."

"Doc Benjamin shot Mother full of sedatives, so she'll probably be too groggy to call you anyway," said Harold.

"Cheery thought," I told him.

Pa and Mr. Prophet laughed.

Then all the men in the house, except Spike, left. So Spike and I went upstairs. I took off my going-to-the-library outfit, donned a loose-fitting house dress, and Spike and I napped.

EIGHT

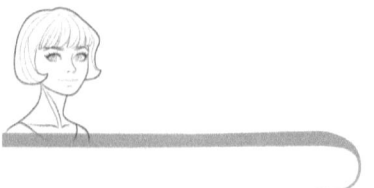

Oh, boy, what a great nap! When Spike and I rose, I looked at the bedside clock and discovered we'd been down and out for more than an hour.

You want the truth about pregnancy as I knew it then? The truth is that I was almost always tired and *always* needed to use the restroom. Other than that, I felt fine.

Anyhow, I decided to keep my loose house dress on for the rest of the day. Sam was used to me in all states of dress (and undress, but don't tell anyone) and Spike didn't care. If Mr. Prophet came over for supper, he wouldn't care either.

It was then approximately four-thirty, and I went to the telephone table in the hallway and dialed Flossie Buckingham. I should have telephoned her earlier, but I didn't think of it. However, she and Johnny had done their very best for Stacy Kincaid under all circumstances.

When Stacy had joined the Salvation Army, her mother had been horrified but Johnny and Flossie had been kind to her. When Stacy had bolted from the Salvation Army, her mother had again been horrified, but Johnny and Flossie had still been kind to her. They were, in short, the two kindest people I'd ever met, and I felt guilty for not having telephoned Flossie earlier to report on Stacy's demise.

"Salvation Army, Mrs. Buckingham speaking," came Flossie's gentle voice after a couple of rings. I heard a baby wailing in the background.

"Is that Daisy I hear crying?" I asked her.

Yes, it's true. Johnny and Flossie had named their children William, after my late husband Billy, and Daisy, after me. I guess it was sweet of them, but I'd never much cared for my name, so I wasn't as overjoyed as I probably should have been. Anyhow, their Daisy had been a fusspot from birth, approximately three and a half months earlier, and little Billy called her a "bwat". There's brotherly love for you.

"Daisy! Of course, it's Daisy. The other Daisy, I mean. She's not as colicky as she used to be, but she still fussier than little Billy ever was. Oh, but Daisy! What happened? When Sam telephoned earlier today, he said somebody had killed Stacy Kincaid and that you and Mr. Prophet found the body!"

"Yes, that's precisely what happened. I should have telephoned you earlier, and I apologize for not doing so. By the time I got home, I was tuckered so Spike and I took a nap."

"No need to apologize," said the lovely Flossie. "When I was pregnant, I was tired all the time. And I always needed to piddle."

"Me too!" I exclaimed, glad to know I wasn't the only one. "Exactly! But I figured you deserved to know what was going on, and I really am sorry I didn't call sooner. Did Johnny make it over to the Pinkerton place?"

"He did. And he ought to be back pretty soon. He's been there for more than an hour, and I can't imagine why. I mean, Sam said Doc Benjamin was about to shoot Stacy's mother with something to make her sleep."

"He did. And I hope she's still sleeping. But you know Johnny. He's probably talking to Mr. Pinkerton and Father Frederick and seeing if he can help with whatever arrangements need to be made. I don't know what the police or the coroner or whoever takes in murdered bodies does with them. I mean, do they perform autopsies on everyone who's been killed?"

"I believe they do," said Flossie. "I think they have to. And I don't know how long they'll keep the body before it's released to the family."

"If they have any sense, they'll release it as soon as the autopsy's performed and all clues collected. Otherwise, they'll have Mrs. Pinkerton calling them all day every day until they do."

"I just hope she doesn't torment you with her demands," said Flossie, who was a peach of a person.

"Both Harold and Sam have told her not to, so I hope she doesn't. For pity's sake, *I* can't do anything for her. I'm a fake spiritualist! She should be talking to Johnny and Father Frederick, not me."

"True, but you've always been there for her. You're like her rock, and she's accustomed to leaning on you," said Flossie. She was serious; I could tell.

"I don't feel very rocklike at the moment." I considered my Frigidaire full of food. "Say, Flossie, would you and Johnny like to come over for supper tonight? Along with Billy and the bwat? We have tons of leftover Chinese food, Mrs. Rattle prepared a nice chicken dish, and there's only Sam and me. Maybe Mr. Prophet. But after dealing with Mrs. Pinkerton all afternoon, I'm sure Johnny can use a break. And after dealing with everything else connected with the Salvation Army and two little children, you *definitely* need a break."

"How kind!" Flossie exclaimed.

"You think I'm kind to be offering you leftovers? If you say so, Flossie. But really, I'm hoping Sam will be here for dinner too. If you and Johnny come over, we can gossip to our hearts' content and pretend we're only discussing current events." I thought of something else almost pertinent. "And if I can get Mr. Prophet to have dinner with us, too, he can keep little Billy entertained."

Flossie's peal of laughter made my heart glad. When I first met her, she was a gangster's moll. What's more, her gangster had taken great joy in beating her to a pulp every time he got mad about anything. I'd kind of thrown her in Johnny's way on purpose, but they'd fallen madly in love with each other, so my connivance had turned out to be a good thing in the end.

"What time should we be there?" asked Flossie.

"We usually dine—if you can call it that—at about six or six-thirty, so time your arrival for whenever you can get here if our mealtime is agreeable with you."

"That's about when we eat, too," said Flossie. "Great. I'm *so* glad I won't have to cook tonight."

"I'm always glad when I don't have to cook," I admitted. "Although, according to Sam and my aunt, I'm getting better in the kitchen as the days pass. Not sure I believe them, but so far neither Sam nor I have died of ptomaine, so I guess maybe it's true."

"Let me bring something," said Flossie, her kind heart speaking again.

"Nuts! You have to cook all the time *and* deal with a husband, two kids, and a church!"

"It's not all that hard really, Daisy. The ladies of our congregation are always bringing me casseroles, cakes, cookies, and so forth. So I'll just see what I have, and I'll bring some of our leftovers to go with your leftovers."

"If you're sure you won't be put to any bother, then sure. Thanks, Flossie."

"Golly, I wonder who killed Stacy. I know several people who would have liked to, but I wonder who actually did the deed."

"Don't know. Mr. Prophet and I discovered some footprints near the gazebo where we found her. But let's not talk about that now. We can chat all we want when you get here. Oh, I'm so glad you can come over!"

"You might not be so glad once we get there. Daisy truly can be a bwat sometimes, you know."

"Well, Sam has already built a crib and a bassinet, so she can test one of them for us," I told Flossie.

With a laugh, Flossie said, "Good for Sam!"

We said our goodbyes, and I decided to walk out to the cottage behind our house where Mr. Prophet lived. When I asked Spike if he'd like to go with me, he was overjoyed. I believe I've already mentioned that Spike and Mr. Prophet's cat, Yuyu, were pals. Their relationship is one of those mysteries of life.

When Spike and I walked up the gravel path to Mr. Prophet's porch, we found him perched on his rocking chair, Yuyu draped over his shoulder, reading one of the books he'd checked out of the library that morning. When he heard us, he looked up and frowned. Yuyu hissed at me, but when he spotted Spike, he jumped from Mr. Prophet's shoulder and shot down the porch steps to leap at Spike. Spike leaped back, and off they tumbled in a black-and-orange ball.

"Ow!" said Mr. Prophet. "Damn cat always manages to stick a claw in me when he jumps off my shoulder."

"I'm sorry," I said.

"Sure you are," he said.

"Bother you! I came to ask if you'd like to come to dinner tonight. Johnny and Flossie will be coming, too, and they'll bring little Billy and little Daisy. For some reason known only to him, little Billy adores you, so I thought I'd invite you too. But if you're going to be mean—"

"I ain't mean," said the mean old man. "Sure. Thanks. I'd like to see my pal Billy again."

Listening to him talk about his pal Billy made me think of something totally unrelated to Pasadena. "Say, did you ever meet Billy the Kid?" I asked him.

"Billy the Kid? Why would I have met that little punk?"

With a shrug, I said, "I don't know. Just thought I'd ask."

"He shot most of his victims in Lincoln County, New Mexico. I made it through there a couple of times, but not when he was killin' folks."

"Okay. Well, we'll probably have supper at six or six-thirty as usual. Not sure when the Buckinghams will show up, but I imagine they'll arrive a little before six."

He creaked up from his rocking chair and grabbed the crutch he used when he took off his peg leg. "Think I'll go see if I can find some treasures for little Billy. I like that kid."

"He likes you too," I told him. "There's no accounting for taste, is there?"

"There ain't," he said. "Fer instance, Sam married you."

"Oh go chase yourself," I said.

He chuckled.

When I got back to the house *sans* Spike, who was still playing with Yuyu, the telephone was ringing. I ran to answer it.

"Rotondo residence," I said into the mouthpiece.

"Daisy, were you running again?" Sam sounded irked.

"The 'phone was ringing when I came inside, so I trotted a bit to pick up the receiver," I said, irked by Sam's totally uncalled-for protectiveness. "I just took a long nap, so a little running is probably good for me."

"I could have called back," he grumbled.

"Well, now you don't have to," I grumbled back.

I heard him heave a huge sigh. "Just wanted you to know I'll be home in time for dinner tonight."

"Oh, good!" I said, grumpiness forgotten. "I asked Flossie to bring Johnny and the kids over, too. Mr. Prophet will join us, so be prepared to tell us everything you can about the Stacy case."

"Oh, boy," said Sam. "You don't let any grass grow, do you?"

"Heck no! This is the most exciting thing to happen in our lives since…Well, since a couple of months ago, anyway."

"Nothing ever remains calm around you for long," muttered Sam. "I've never known *anyone* who could find dead bodies the way you can."

"That's not fair. Mr. Prophet found this one. And the two before that were dug up by Yuyu and Spike."

"If you say so. Do we have enough food for everybody?"

"Sure. Mrs. Rattle made a nice chicken dish for us, and we have all that leftover Chinese food."

"Oh, yeah, I forgot about the Chinese grub. Well, good. It will be nice to see Flossie and the kids again. I talked to Johnny for quite a while today at the Pinkerton place. He's attempting to remember any enemies Stacy might have accumulated during the months he was in touch with her."

"There must be dozens of those," I said. Unkind, Daisy Gumm Majesty Rotondo. But true.

"I suppose. Anyway, I have to get back to work. I also asked him if he knew the names of any of her friends."

"Did he?"

"No. See you in a while."

"Thanks for calling, Sam. I'm glad you'll be here for dinner."

"Me too," he said.

We hung up our mutual receivers. I walked to the kitchen and noticed a piece of paper sitting under the sugar bowl on the kitchen table. When I picked it up, I saw Mrs. Rattle had left me a note about the proper heating of the meal she'd made for us. What a nice woman!

I read it aloud. "Preheat oven to medium. When oven is hot, place baking dish on the middle rack. Heat for thirty or forty minutes until dish is heated through."

"That's not too tough," I told myself. Glancing at the kitchen clock, I saw it was already a little after five o'clock. I figured it might be a good time to start pre-heating the oven. I'd learned all about pre-heating ovens from Vi, bless her.

As soon as I'd lit the oven and turned it to the correct—that is to say, medium—heat, I heard a woofing at the back door. So I went back there and let Spike in. Then I mused about supper and what might go with a chicken casserole and leftover Chinese food. Because we had lots of citrus trees—and I had become an expert at making fruit salads with oranges and grapefruit—I decided to go back outside and pick some oranges and grapefruit. So I did. Spike accompanied me.

When I returned to the kitchen, I put on an apron. Then I peeled two oranges and a grapefruit, sliced the fruit, and decided to get creative.

Ha! Creative. Me. Daisy Gumm Majesty Rotondo, who was renowned in the family for being the only member thereof who could actually burn water. Well, I'd show them! I dumped the sliced fruit into a bowl and mixed the slices together. Then I bethought me of the cellar and hied myself down there to fetch some walnuts and some of the dried cocoanut Vi had given us. Dried cocoanut was quite the luxury item, but she'd told me she'd found some at Jorgensen's Grocery Store, where the rich folks send their servants to shop for foodstuffs, and she'd picked up some for the whole family.

Therefore, I grabbed the jar containing the dried cocoanut, stuck several walnuts in the pocket of my apron, and trotted back upstairs. There I proceeded to crack five walnuts, made sure they were clean, chopped them into large chunks, and dumped them in with the orange and grapefruit slices. Then, greatly daring, I sprinkled some of the dried cocoanut over the whole mess.

"What do you think, Spike?" I asked my dog, to whom I'd given a piece of walnut because he liked nuts. "Should I add anything? Sugar maybe? Honey?"

Spike advised me to taste the concoction first, which sounded like a good idea to me, so I did. It wasn't half bad! Shocked, I decided a drizzle of honey couldn't hurt it, so I added that, put some waxed paper over the top of the bowl, and stuck it in the Frigidaire.

I was darned near proud of myself. Shortly thereafter—it was then almost six o'clock—I heard Sam's big Hudson pull into the driveway and remembered I'd left the Chevrolet there. Whoops. I guess it's a good thing I'd forgotten to move the Chevrolet; otherwise, I might have become swell-headed about my marvelous citrus salad.

That's a joke.

NINE

"Sam!" I called, racing out the front door. "I'm sorry I forgot to move the Chevrolet! Do you want to back out so I can drive it across the street to my parents' place?"

"Stop running!" He hollered at me. "I'll move it. You just stay there."

"I wasn't running," I muttered, knowing I'd just fibbed.

But what was the big deal about running? Yes, I was expecting a child. But I'd hardly begun to show yet. I could understand Sam complaining if I was, say, eight-and-a-half months along. I probably wouldn't be running then anyway. Mind you, I'm glad Sam cared, but he was becoming as much of a fusspot as Flossie and Johnny's Daisy!

Ah, well. As long as Sam was home, I figured I might as well stick Mrs. Rattle's chicken dish in the oven, which was pre-heated enough. I hoped. So I did. I slid the dish into the oven on the middle rack, just as Mrs. Rattle's instructions had told me to.

As soon as the oven door shut, I heard Mr. Prophet coming in the back door. Poor Spike didn't know what to do, but I guess he figured he might as well greet Mr. Prophet, as Sam was taking his own sweet time about entering the house. Only, of course, because I'd neglected to return the Chevrolet to my parents.

"Evening," Mr. Prophet said as he walked into the kitchen, Spike frolicking at his feet. He frowned when he saw I was the sole inhabitant of the room. "Where'd Sam go? Thought I heard the Hudson."

"You did. He'll be here in a minute. He's moving automobiles."

"Ah. Yeah, ya didn't take the car back to your folks' place."

"Precisely." I waited for a snipe or three, but he forbore. Maybe that's because we both heard voices coming from the front porch. "Ah, I think Flossie and Johnny are here!" I began to trot to the front door, but slowed to a fast walk before Sam could open the front door and accuse me of running.

"Look who's here!" Sam said happily as he ushered into the house Flossie with a baby in her arms and then Johnny holding a basket in one hand and little Billy's hand in the other.

"So happy to see you!" I told them all.

Little Daisy hadn't begun shrieking yet, and I was almost afraid to approach Flossie. Flossie knew what she was about, however, and hurried right up to me. She even gave me a little hug with the arm not holding the baby. I hugged her back. Flossie was *such* a great person.

"Baby's not being a bwat," little Billy announced as he strode into the house. He was a darling little kid. Almost three years old now, he no longer staggered when he walked. Well, not much anyway.

"Unlike her namesake," muttered Mr. Prophet at my back.

I turned and stuck my tongue out at him. I know, not terribly adult and dignified, huh? He cackled, so he clearly didn't mind.

"Do you want to come into the kitchen or plop yourselves down in the living room?" I asked our guests.

"I'll go to the kitchen with you," said Flossie. She turned and reached a hand out to her husband, who gave her the basket. Then she unloaded the sleeping baby into her father's arms. The baby's father's arms, I mean. "The church ladies have given us so much

79

food recently, I figured we might as well bring some of our own leftovers to go with yours."

"Brilliant idea," I said.

Sam, who carried a briefcase with him, said, "I'll stick this thing and my tie upstairs. Be down in a minute. Make yourselves comfortable wherever you want."

"Mr. Pwophet!" cried little Billy, observing his hero leaning against a far wall. "Mr. Pwophet!"

"How-do, little Billy?" the old reprobate asked. He lurched away from the wall and met the kid, who had started running over to him. Little kids have adorable runs, kind of stiff-legged and side-to-side. "I got somethin' special fer you today."

I heard little Billy's laughter all the way into the kitchen.

As soon as Flossie and I entered the room, we both stopped and sniffed.

"Smells like something's burning," observed Flossie.

"I only put the dish into the oven about three minutes ago, when Sam got home," I said. Nevertheless, smoke was definitely rising from the oven, so I hurried over to it, opened the oven door and was appalled to be met with a huge puff of black smoke. I batted it away while Flossie opened a window over the kitchen sink.

Arming myself with a couple of oven-proof gloves—made from fabric scraps by my own two hands and the sewing machine—I flapped at the smoke, attempting to aim it at the open window.

"I'd better open the other one, too," said Flossie.

"And maybe the back door," I said.

"Good idea." Flossie hurried to the back door and opened it. I heard a hiss. Guess Yuyu had been sitting on the porch waiting for Mr. Prophet to return to his proper place in the universe. "I don't think Mr. Prophet's cat likes me," she said, laughing as she returned to the kitchen.

"That cat doesn't like anyone except Mr. Prophet and Spike," I told her.

The air in the kitchen was becoming less hazy as Flossie and I created more open spaces for the smoke to escape. We each got dish towels and flapped them at the dark cloud, directing it to the windows and the back door.

When the air was bearable to breathe once more, I reached into the oven (with my oven mitts on) and withdrew the dish I'd put in it approximately seven to ten minutes earlier. It was a black heap of inedible coal.

"How in the world did this happen?" I asked no one in particular, dismayed. "I stuck it in a medium oven when Sam came home. That wasn't long ago at all." I set the dish on top of the range in despair. "It's burned to a crisp."

Flossie patted my shoulder. "It's all right, Daisy. We still have plenty of food."

"But I don't understand!" I darned near wailed. "I haven't burned anything in the kitchen for ages and ages, and I swear I turned that stove to medium and only stuck the dish in five minutes ago.

"Well, the temperature is hot now," said Flossie. "Maybe you bumped the dial?"

"I didn't!" Despair almost made me cry. "Honest to goodness, Flossie. I've been trying *so hard* lately! And I swear I looked at the dial and double-checked it because I don't trust myself in the kitchen. I don't know what could have happened. Poor Mrs. Rattle's special chicken concoction is ruined. I hope I can save the dish it burned up in."

"Very strange," said Flossie, who sounded as if she believed me and wasn't merely being polite. "Even if the dial got turned to high by accident, the dish couldn't have been in the oven long enough to burn it like that."

"Exactly," I said, wondering if providence could turn against a person for pretending to talk to dead people.

"What the heck's going on in here?" came Mr. Prophet's crotchety voice from the hallway.

"A catastrophe," I told him. "And don't you *dare* blame me for it! I followed Mrs. Rattle's instructions to the letter. But her lovely chicken casserole burned up anyway."

"Huh. Back to your old tricks, eh?" he said.

"No, darn you! I don't know how this happened!"

"What's going on?" came Sam's voice from behind Mr. Prophet.

"Daisy burned your dinner," said Mr. Prophet.

"If you weren't an old cripple, I'd stamp on your foot!" I barked.

"Daisy," said Sam in a placating voice. "I'm sorry something went wrong, but there's no need for violence."

"Yes there is," I said, feeling like a bwat myself. "I swear, I did everything right, Sam. But that chicken thing Mrs. Rattle made nearly burned the house down. And I only put it in the oven when you drove home!"

"Huh," said Sam, sounding as though he were taking my words seriously. "Maybe there's something wrong with the range. I'll take a look at it after it cools down." He came over to where I was sagging over our charred chicken dinner and put his arms around me. "Don't worry about it. We have lots of food to eat."

"But Mrs. Rattle made that specially," I said, sounding pitiful.

"Well, there's no need to worry about it now," said Sam, all efficiency.

"What's going on in here?" asked Johnny, following Sam into the kitchen with little Billy. Good thing our kitchen was large.

"Just an overdone dish," said Flossie, who now stood at a kitchen counter opening the lid of the basket she'd swapped the baby for. "Where's Daisy? Little Daisy, I mean."

"Sam brought down the bassinet he made for your little one, and she's in the living room sawing logs like a lumberjack," said Johnny, laughing.

"Baby's sawing logs?" said little Billy, looking up at his father in awe. "Lemme see!"

"Not really, Billy," said Johnny. "It's just an expression. I just meant she's sleeping soundly."

He barely got "soundly" out of his mouth when an unearthly shriek came from the living room.

"Good Lord!" exclaimed Sam. "Sounds like the saw got to the baby!"

Everyone except me raced out of the kitchen to see what had disturbed little Daisy. After looking glumly at what had been intended for our dinner and was now nothing but ashes and soot, I took the dish to the utility room, set it on a table there and shut the door on it. By the time the evening was over, the dish would be cool enough to evaluate. The chicken casserole was gone for good, but I might be able to salvage the baking dish.

Then I hurried to the living room to see why the baby had begun shrieking.

"How did this happen?" asked Sam, sounding befuddled.

As well he might. When I joined the others in the living room, Flossie had picked up the screaming baby, and Sam held my letter opener, whose proper home was in the drawer of the telephone table in the hall.

"How did that get in here?" I asked, confused.

"I have no idea," said Sam.

Johnny turned to his son, who had his fingers stuffed into his ears. "Billy, did you find this and bring it into the living room?"

Billy shook his head, fingers still in his ears, but evidently not tightly enough to prevent him from hearing his father. "No, Papa."

"Did it hurt her?" I asked, rushing over to Flossie and the baby, who was snuffling and calming down some.

"I don't think so. I think maybe it fell on her and startled her."

"But how did it fall on her? I keep the letter opener in the drawer of the telephone table. Unless somebody brought it in here, but who would…? I don't understand."

The five adults in the living room stared at each other, shaking our heads in puzzlement.

"Holy cow, catch that lamp!" Sam cried, not waiting for anyone to figure out what he meant but running to the piano to stop the perfectly gorgeous peacock lamp Harold Kincaid had given us from finishing its slide to the edge of our baby grand piano and falling on the floor. He stopped it just before it took the plunge. "What the heck's going on?"

"I don't know," I told him. "Are we having an earthquake? What else could make the lamp move?"

At the word "earthquake", we all stood still in order to judge for ourselves if the earth was moving.

It wasn't.

"Maybe it was a little earthquake?" said Flossie, patting little Daisy's back. Daisy had a fist stuffed in her mouth and had stopped sniffling.

"I didn't do it," declared little Billy.

Laughing, Johnny swept him up in his arms. "We know you didn't, Billy. But we don't know how the lamp moved, either."

"Maybe Spike got under the piano and caught the cord?" I suggested, bending to peer under the piano. Spike took that moment to bound into the living room from the hallway. He met me under the piano and licked my nose. The lamp's cord remained firmly plugged into its usual electrical socket. I unplugged it, just to be on the safe side.

I rose from my bent-over position, wiping my nose. "Wasn't Spike," I announced. "But I unplugged the lamp."

"Yuyu ain't in here, either," said Mr. Prophet. He sounded defiant, as if daring anyone to accuse his cat of bad behavior.

"No, he was on the back porch. He hissed at me when I opened the door," said Flossie. "I think he ran off in another direction entirely."

"I don't think he's ever once entered this house," I said after contemplating Yuyu for a second.

"Yeah, he don't like civilization much," observed Mr. Prophet. "Kinda like his owner."

"Well, for the sake of caution, we'd probably better put the lamp in a closet somewhere," said Sam, carefully wrapping the cord, which he'd fished out from behind the piano, around the lamp's base. He started to hand me the vase, and then stopped himself. "I'll carry it upstairs."

"Oh, for goodness' sake, I can carry the lamp upstairs. I'm pregnant, not crippled," I snapped. My feelings had become a trifle frayed with each new unsettling occurrence in the house I loved so much.

"That's all right," said Sam. "I'll just stick it in here." He opened a closet near the front door and carefully set the lamp on the floor.

Suddenly Spike yipped in pain. I whirled around to see him jumping and snapping at…nothing.

"Spike?" I said, confused.

Spike ran to me and huddled at my feet. I leaned over, scooped him up and settled him on my lap on a nearby sofa.

"What's the matter, boy?" asked Sam, coming over to see where —and how—Spike had been wounded.

"I can't find any puncture marks or blood," I said, smoothing my hands over his sleek black-and-tan body.

"I can't either," Sam concurred.

"Doggy hurt?" asked little Billy. When I glanced at him, I saw he had tears in his eyes. Sensitive child. I approved.

"I don't know, Billy," I said. "I can't find where he was hurting."

"Maybe something fell on him too?" Flossie said in a doubtful voice.

Across the room, a big puff of ash whooshed out of the fireplace. I gave a start of alarm. "What the heck? What's going on here?"

An eerie—and somehow familiar—sound of nasty laughter rent the air. Then the ash whooshed back into the fireplace and seemed to fly up the chimney along with the laugh.

A series of startled glances passed from person to person to person to dog, who flinched in my lap and hid his head in my armpit.

"Cripes," said Mr. Prophet. He and I exchanged a significant look. "Ya got another ghost in here?"

"Oh, no!" I wailed. "It can't be!"

TEN

Both children began crying after that, and it took a few minutes to calm them down. It took a good deal longer to calm me down. In actual fact, I couldn't be calmed, although I tried not to show little Billy how angry and terrified I was.

"She can't be haunting me," I whispered to Sam, Johnny, and Mr. Prophet. "She died in the gazebo. If she's haunting anything, it should be the gazebo."

"But she hated your guts," said Mr. Prophet, who'd heard enough about Stacy Kincaid to understand how evil she'd been.

"What precisely did you mean about 'another' ghost?" asked Johnny, sitting on a living-room chair with little Billy in his lap. Little Billy, by the way, was engrossed in playing with a large silver-and-turquoise piece of jewelry that looked as if it might be a brooch that had lost its back clasp. Johnny directed his question to Lou Prophet, who had uttered the fateful words.

"Cripes," muttered Mr. Prophet, who sent a beseeching glance at me. Guess he wanted me to explain our recent experience with the ghost of an ancient Tongva shaman that had taken up unhappy residence in our backyard.

"Might as well spill it, Daisy," said Sam.

"Phooey," I said. But I told the story.

"Good heavens," said Flossie, who had soothed little Daisy so much, she had again fallen asleep and lay once more in the bassinet. Sam had moved the bassinet over to the sofa where Flossie sat, so if anything else of an odd nature happened, she'd be right there to fix it.

"Huh," said Johnny. "Interesting. And sad, really, when you think about all the native peoples who have been shunted aside to make room for Europeans wanting their land. The land of the natives, I mean."

"Yes," I said gloomily. "Human beings are an invasive species."

"That's one way to put it," said Mr. Prophet with a crooked grin.

Johnny went on. "I have no reasons to doubt you, by the way, in case you thought a minister of God might not believe in ghosts. I've been through too much and seen too much to doubt the existence of life after death. But if you've got Stacy Kincaid's ghost haunting you, I'm afraid you're in for some rough times, and I'm not sure what to do about them. I'm not personally an exorcist, although I know a couple of priests who do exorcisms."

"Really?" Sam sounded intrigued.

"Yes, but I'm not one, and I don't know what to do about your ghost if you have one."

"Same here," I said gloomily.

"Any way you can bless the house so she can't get in it again?" asked Sam of Johnny. Then he said, almost to himself, "I can't believe I asked that question. I didn't even believe in the Tongva ghost until I saw it for myself."

"I can try," said Johnny uncertainly.

"What about that Voodoo woman you know?" asked Mr. Prophet. "Them Voodoo folks have some powerful magic."

"Mrs. Jackson!" I cried, not having thought about her since I put the Voodoo juju she made for me on my chain earlier in the day. "That might be a really good idea."

The ringing telephone startled all of us into leaps of alarm. Slamming my hand over my heart, I rose and walked into the hallway to answer it. I took the letter opener with me. "Rotondo residence, Mrs. Rotondo speaking," I said into the receiver, putting the opener in the drawer where it belonged while at the same time hoping the call wasn't from Mrs. Pinkerton. With good luck, she'd still be drugged.

"Daisy?" came a tentative voice.

"Regina?" I asked, surprised. Regina Browning didn't ordinarily telephone me at home.

"Yes, it's I," she said.

She said no more for so long, I began thinking maybe she'd hung up. "Regina?" I said. "Is there something you wanted to talk to me about?"

"Yes."

Silence.

"There is? Something you want to talk to me about?" I hope she wasn't not speaking because I'd phrased my question ungrammatically. "That is, is there something about which you wish to speak to me?" There. If she didn't like that construction, our conversation that hadn't started yet wouldn't start some more.

"Oh, Daisy, I'm sorry. I'm calling about something so ridiculous, it's…well, ridiculous."

"I doubt that," I told her, recalling what had been going on in my own home only minutes earlier. "Is something wrong at the library? You mentioned something of the sort this morning."

After heaving a huge sigh, she said, "Yes. You'll doubtless think I'm insane for even saying this, but I think there's either a bad person or a bad ghost disrupting things in the library."

"You mean, like when we heard those books fall?"

"Yes. And it's not just books falling. They're flying through the air! Or being thrown. But everyone who works there has looked *everywhere*, and we can't find an interloper or anywhere an intruder could enter or anything. I mean, there are no broken windows, and all the locks are working properly. Then I thought about you and your job and…Oh, Daisy, this sounds *so* stupid, but I wondered if a ghost might be causing the trouble. Card catalogs are falling apart when we pull them out, and books are being rearranged on the shelves, and…and…and things are just *crazy* in there! I don't know what's going on, but I figured either you or the police might be able to help us."

"Good heavens," I said. "I'm so sorry. I can certainly visit the library again tomorrow and look around. Also, Sam can send a couple of uniforms to see if someone's tampering with things."

"It's getting scarier and scarier," said Regina in a small voice. "I was the last employee to leave this evening because I had some research I wanted to finish. Well, the electricity suddenly went off, and I couldn't open the door. And then…This sounds preposterous, except it happened—someone started hurling *books* at me! I have a huge bruise on my arm. Robert is threatening not to let me go to work tomorrow."

"I'm so sorry, Regina. What time do you have to be at the library tomorrow? I can meet you there. If there are two of us there, maybe whoever it is will think twice about playing tricks."

"Would you really? Oh, Daisy, I feel so stupid, but these crazy things are happening, and they're frightening!"

"Yes, I understand. Believe me, I understand." I almost told Regina about our evening with Stacy Kincaid's ghost but restrained myself. If Regina doubted her own sanity, she'd probably think I'd slipped totally 'round the bend if I regaled her with Stacy's shenanigans. I almost didn't believe them myself, except I couldn't think of another way to explain what had happened.

"Thank you. And if you could have a police officer or two visit, that would be nice, too."

"The police will probably be in the neighborhood of the library tomorrow anyway, because of…Well, because of what happened in the gazebo this morning."

"Good grief, that's right. If these weird things in the library hadn't begun a couple of weeks ago, I'd *really* think a ghost was haunting the place," said Regina, as if she were backing away from supernatural causes of the library's problems. Couldn't fault her, really. So few honestly uncanny things occurred in the world, I wouldn't believe in them myself if I hadn't witnessed them along with other people who'd witnessed the same things.

"Okay. Please give Robert my best, and I'll see you a little before nine tomorrow morning."

"Thank you so much, Daisy," said Regina. Her thanks were heartfelt; I could tell.

I walked back into the living room to find all inhabitants—except for little Billy and the bwat—staring at me.

"What's going on?" asked Sam.

"That was Regina Browning. The librarian. Something's haunting the library." I knew as soon as the words left my lips that I should have rephrased my explanation of Regina's call. "I mean, weird things are going on in there. She wanted to know if I could meet her at the library in the morning, and we can go through the place together and try to figure out who's causing the trouble."

"What was that about haunting?" asked Sam in a thin, sharpish tone.

"Just a little joke," I said, trying to laugh. Then I stopped. "No, it's not a joke. Books are flying through the air, the card catalog drawers are falling apart, the electricity fails, and doors don't open, and when I was in there calling you this morning, a big stack of books hit the floor and sounded like a bomb. It's either somebody up to mischief, or a ghost that's irked about something. My guess would be the demolition of the library."

"Cain't say as I blame it much," muttered Mr. Prophet.

"No, I can't either," I said. "But I hope it's some living human bent on making mischief. Humans are easier to deal with than ghosts."

"I can't believe we're talking about ghosts," grumbled Sam. "I didn't even believe in ghosts until I saw that Tongva fellow myself."

"Most of the ghosts in my life haunt my dreams," said Flossie, shuddering slightly.

"It's all right, sweetheart," said Johnny, giving her a loving glance. "We all have those."

"I guess," I said, thinking my own personal dreams had been quite nice of late. "But let's go to the kitchen, Flossie. We can get some kind of dinner prepared from your basket and our Chinese leftovers."

"Sounds good to me," said Sam. "I'm hungry."

"Me too," said Mr. Prophet.

"Need any help?" asked Johnny, which was just like him.

"No thanks. You stay here and watch the little ones. Flossie and I can handle the foodstuffs," I told him.

Mr. Prophet said, "Huh," but I was so used to him picking on me, I didn't even scowl at him.

The basket Flossie and Johnny had brought contained a baking dish filled with beef stew, a dish filled with cooked carrots, and some beautiful rolls someone had baked.

"This all looks delicious," I told Flossie.

"It probably is. Mrs. Weiss bakes the best breads and rolls I've ever eaten, and I think that's her special beef stew. I fixed the carrots. Why don't I heat these things up, and you get the Chinese food out of the Frigidaire. Ours might not be a conventional every-day dinner, but it should be tasty."

"I think I'll let you heat everything. I'm afraid to go near the range," I told Flossie. "And I made a citrus salad that's pretty good."

Sam appeared at the kitchen door. "Do you think I should look at the stove before you try to use it again?" he asked.

"I guess it couldn't hurt. Do you know much about gas ranges?" I asked him.

"No, but I can make sure the connections are...connected properly."

"I think Stacy's ghost went up the chimney," I said, hardly believing my own words. "I just hope it doesn't come down it again any time soon."

Sam was on his hands and knees, checking out the connections on the lovely gas range. It was a nice O'Keefe and Merritt range, and it hadn't been used a whole lot. That's mainly because Sam had bought it new when he bought our bungalow, and I was just barely learning to cook meals in and on it.

"Everything looks okay here," said Sam, grunting slightly as he got to his feet. "I don't know what happened to the dish that burned up earlier."

"Stacy happened to it," I told him.

Sam gazed at me for a few seconds. Seemed like hours. Then he heaved a sigh and nodded. "I fear you're right. You know, Daisy, when I married you, I thought you were a fake spiritualist-medium. I didn't believe the séances or card readings or any of that rubbish were real."

"If it's any comfort," I told him, "I didn't either when I started plying my trade. But I'm now beginning to direct my clients to other mediums. Media. Whatever they are. I'm tired of the spiritualist trade."

"Good. I've discovered I don't much like having ghosts around," said Sam. He walked to Flossie and me as we stood at the counter, ladling foodstuffs into various pots and pans in order to heat them. He gave me a hug. "I hope to God we won't be troubled by any more of them. I'll send some men to the library tomorrow. Isn't it a stretch to think there are *two* ghosts within haunting distance of you and your friends and loved ones?" He tried to sound comical, but he didn't succeed awfully well.

"Sounds weird to me," said Flossie. "Although something happened to the baby and Spike, and we all heard that screech. And don't forget your burned chicken dish and the fireplace ash."

"I'll never forget any of it," said Sam, sounding nearly disconsolate. "But I hope if these things *are* hauntings, you can get rid of them, Daisy. Cripes. I thought the Tongva was bad enough. I also figured he was a one-time thing. Besides, he was only unhappy. He didn't want to hurt any of us. I sure didn't expect more—and malevolent—ghosts to show up."

"Surprise, surprise," I said, also attempting to sound cheery and failing.

"It will be all right, you two," said Flossie in an encouraging voice. "Johnny will deal with Stacy. The good Lord knows he's been dealing with her for years now."

"True," I said. "He and you are the only two people in the world who still believed she might overcome her evil tendencies and do some good in the world."

"Yes. Johnny especially," agreed Flossie. "I think I've met more people like Stacy than he has. I hate to say it, but I think some people are just born without a conscience. Or something happens to them in their youth that turns them into evil beings."

"Yeah, my career as a policeman has led me to the same conclusion," said Sam. "My career and my idiot nephew."

"Oh, dear," I said. "This is kind of a melancholy conversation. As long as you think the stove is safe, Sam, I guess you can go back to the living room. After we heat all the food and set the table in the dining room, we'll call you."

"Thanks, ladies." Sam kissed me on the top of my head and turned to join the others in the living room.

As soon as he left the kitchen, Flossie whispered, "Oh, Daisy, please tell me how you exorcised the Indian ghost from your yard!"

So I did. By the time I finished telling the tale—it hadn't been I but Emilio DeLoera who'd exorcised the Tongva ghost—everything was all heated up and in dishes, and I'd set the dining room table with my pretty Spode Wickerdale china.

For the sake of caution, Johnny carried the bassinet into the dining room with the still-sleeping baby in it when he, Billy, Sam and Mr. Prophet came in to dinner. We didn't yet have a high chair, but little Billy sat on a chair upon which Sam had placed a couple of cushions so he could reach his flatware and food.

Johnny said an elegant prayer before we began eating. He also blessed Sam's and my house and entreated the ghost of Stacy Kincaid not to re-enter its portals.

As Sam said to me as he and Spike and I walked upstairs to bed that evening, "I only hope prayers work."

So did I. I had my doubts, though. If anyone could overcome good with evil, that someone was Stacy Kincaid. I had a sinking feeling she wasn't going to leave me alone, even if she *did* stay away from our home.

ELEVEN

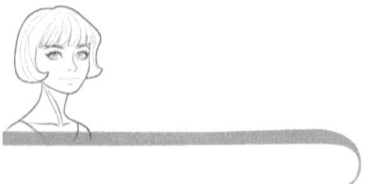

On Tuesday morning, I telephoned my father to say I'd have to take a quick walk with him and Rosebud because I had to be at the library at nine o'clock.

"Okay with me," he said, bless his heart.

So we walked our dogs and got back home before Mrs. Rattle rang the doorbell at eight-thirty. Again, I left Spike with Pa and Rosebud so he wouldn't get in Mrs. Rattle's way.

Also, I'd taken the precaution of removing the burned baking dish from the utility room and carrying it across the street to dump in my parents' outdoor trashcan. The dish couldn't be salvaged because it had sort of melded to what had once been the chicken dinner Mrs. Rattle had made for us. I didn't want there to be even a possibility of Mrs. Rattle seeing what had become of her kind-hearted effort.

Therefore, one of the first conversations I had that day, other than those I'd had with Sam and my father, began with a big fat lie.

"The chicken dish you prepared for us was absolutely delicious, Mrs. Rattle. We had guests over last night, and we all enjoyed it." I probably shouldn't have mentioned guests, which only added to my lie. But heck, I'd lied for a living for more than half my life; I'm not sure why this particular lie felt so wrong coming out of my mouth.

"So glad you enjoyed it," said Mrs. Rattle, beaming with pleasure, which made my heart pinch up and ache.

"Mornin', Elvira," came a rusty voice from behind us.

It was one of the first times in ages when I've been truly glad Mr. Lou Prophet was in my vicinity. I mean, he'd saved my life on a couple of occasions, but he hadn't done that for a year or two, so I'd found him more annoying than heroic recently. That's mainly because he took such pleasure in teasing me.

"Good morning, Lou," said Mrs. Rattle, still smiling. "Daisy said you enjoyed my chicken casserole last night."

After shooting me a sly glance, Mr. Prophet said, "It was real good."

I vowed to myself to thank him as soon as we were out of Mrs. Rattle's hearing.

As Mrs. Rattle hung her sweater on the rack and put her hat on the shelf, Mr. Prophet said, "Say, Miss Daisy, is it all right with you if I come with you today? I'm interested in what you were talkin' about last night."

"Sure," I said. "The more, the merrier."

"Where are you heading out to today?" asked Mrs. Rattle as she aimed herself at the kitchen.

"We're going back to the library," I told her. "I don't know if the news has hit the papers yet, but a young woman was murdered in that beautiful gazebo in the library's park yesterday. Mr. Prophet and I had the misfortune to find the body."

Swirling around, horror writ large on her usually happy features, Mrs. Rattle said, "Oh, my goodness! What a terrible thing to find! And what a terrible thing to happen!"

I could have set her straight on some of her thinking but figured telling her what a louse Stacy had been wouldn't show me in a very good light. Therefore, I said, "It was awful."

"It was," agreed Mr. Prophet. "Especially when Miss Daisy ran to the library to telephone the police and some ladies started screamin' that I'd killed the woman."

"Good Lord, no!" said Mrs. Rattle, even more aghast than she'd been before.

"Yes, they did," I said, reinforcing Mr. Prophet's claim. "What's worse was that they managed to find a couple of policemen who believed them. One of them was about to handcuff Mr. Prophet and haul him off to the clink. I saw them, and shouted at them that he hadn't done it. They didn't believe me at first. Honestly, Mr. Prophet and I thought we were being good citizens and should stand guard at the gazebo so nobody else would see the gory mess we'd seen. Unfortunately, those two silly women didn't wait for me to return to the scene of the crime."

"Merciful heaven," said Mrs. Rattle. "What a terrible experience for both of you."

"It was," I agreed. "Your son can tell you more about it, too. He was there, helping Sam."

"Stephen? He got home so late and left so early, I haven't even seen him. I'll have to have a chat with him this evening."

"Yes. He'll probably be at the library park again today. They're not through gathering evidence." I turned to Mr. Prophet. "Let me get my hat and handbag, and we can borrow the Chevrolet again."

"Sounds good to me," said Mr. Prophet, taking a seat at the kitchen table to wait.

He and I left for the library shortly thereafter. I wanted to give us plenty of time to reach our destination before Regina tried to enter the library. Whatever was going on in there, it sounded malevolent, and I didn't want Regina to have to face it alone.

Our trip was a short one, the library being not far from our residence on South Marengo Avenue. It started out well enough. It wasn't until I'd turned left from Marengo onto Walnut, that things took an eerie turn. Literally.

"What the heck?" I cried as the steering wheel suddenly seemed to take on a life of its own. I had turned it to the left and meant to straighten it out at once. But the cursed thing kept moving to the left. The Chevrolet didn't merely turn onto Walnut Street, but attempted to make a circle in the street regardless of any other automobiles that might be in the way. Boy, you should have heard the honks. Fortunately for the car, Mr. Prophet and me, there wasn't a lot of traffic.

"What the hell?" shouted Mr. Prophet.

"Grab the wheel!" I shouted back. "I think Stacy's got it!"

So he reached over, seized the steering wheel in both of his large, strong—if knobby—hands, and the two of us wrestled the wheel back under control. I was so rattled and upset that as soon as I could, I drew the machine up to the curb and parked it.

The two of us sat in the car, staring straight ahead. The library was only a couple of hundred yards away from where I'd parked, and it was on the same side of the street. However, I was afraid to start the car and try to get closer for fear of what might happen.

"You didn't do that on purpose, right?" asked Mr. Prophet as if he already knew the answer.

"No, I didn't do that on purpose. Maybe I can get Johnny to say a prayer to keep Stacy away from the Chevrolet."

"You really think it was her who did it?"

"I can't think of another explanation," I said. I'd begun shaking. "Stacy really must hate me."

"*I dooooo!*" came a weird howling sound from above the car.

"Cripes." Mr. Prophet opened his door and struggled to get outside and look up. "I don't see nothin'."

I bowed my head and leaned it against the steering wheel. "Oh, Lord, I don't know what to do."

"You gotta call that Voodoo woman," said Mr. Prophet, stuffing himself back into the passenger-side seat. "I think the Kincaid bitch might be too hard a nut for Johnny Buckingham to crack. He's too nice. Them Voodoo wimmin are scary as hell."

Turning to stare at him, I said, "You really think so?"

"I really think so."

"Okay. I'll have to figure out a way to get in touch with her. Now I'm afraid to drive anywhere."

"Call Harold. He's a good man. He'll help you."

Listen to him. My first husband Billy and Sam both used to dislike Harold because he wasn't a "manly" man. But Lou Prophet, who had lived what most people might consider the manliest life to which anyone could aspire, didn't give a rap about Harold's sexual preferences. His harrowing, hard life had introduced him to ghosts too. The only reference he'd made about Harold when Sam (I think it was Sam) told him about Harold's orientation had been: "Ah. He's one o' them lavender cowboys, is he?" That was it. He only cared about important stuff. I appreciated him more in that moment than I probably ever had before. Or since, if it comes to that.

"Good idea," I said. "Harold can talk to Mr. Jackson, Mrs. Pinkerton's gatekeeper. It's Mrs. Jackson, Mr. Jackson's mother, who's the Voodoo mambo."

"Let's you and me walk to the library. I'll walk next to the street so Stacy can't push you in front of a car."

"Oh, Lord," I whimpered. Rather than exit the vehicle on the driver's side of the car, I slid across the front seat and got out on the passenger's side.

As good as his word, Mr. Prophet took my left arm and marched me along the sidewalk to the library. Several police vehicles were parked at the curb, and we saw three or four uniforms and a suit or two at the gazebo. One of the suits turned and waved at us. Sam! I was so glad to see him, I nearly cried. He strode across the lawn to us.

"Thought I'd greet Mrs. Browning with you," he said when he reached us. "Why'd you park so far away?"

"Ghost," said Mr. Prophet.

"What?" Sam squinted at Mr. Prophet and then at me.

I nodded. "It was Stacy. She's definitely got it in for me. When I turned from Marengo onto Walnut, the wheel kept turning left. The car almost hit two other cars and a pedestrian. Mr. Prophet and I managed to wrestle it away from her grip, but I'm afraid even to get in the Chevrolet again."

"Good God," said Sam. He glanced at Mr. Prophet, who nodded.

"She's tellin' the truth, Sam. I told her we got to call that Voodoo woman to get rid of Stacy. If we don't do something, that ghost will do something really nasty to Miss Daisy here."

"Good God," Sam muttered again. "I can't believe this is actually happening."

"You might as well believe it," I told him. "Because it seems she's not through with me yet. Oh, Sam!" Embarrassing as it is to admit, I broke down right there on the sidewalk and began sobbing onto my husband's suit coat.

"It's all right, sweetheart. We'll figure this out." He patted me on the back. "Damn Stacy Kincaid. You don't need to deal with her any more than you need to deal with her mother. Not in your condition."

I wanted to scream that my condition had nothing to do with my aversion to Stacy Kincaid. Or her mother, for that matter. But I didn't. We were in public, and I was already making a scene.

Feeling stupid and silly, I pulled away from poor Sam, grabbed a hankie from my bag and wiped my eyes. "I'm s-sorry, Sam."

"It's all right, sweetie, but we'd better get to the library before your friend shows up. It's almost nine o'clock."

"Right," I said. "Right. Regina needs us now."

So we all continued our march to the library, I between two tall men, feeling almost protected. With Stacy, one never knew. And that was true when she was alive and earthbound. Who knew what she would do now that she was an evil emanation? But I shoved my personal fears away and fingered my Voodoo juju under my blouse. Then I fingered the tiny baby Mr. DeLoera had carved for me.

My impulse to rid the world of Stacy's ghost began building into a firm resolution. She was *not* going to hurt my dog, my husband, my friends, me, or my unborn child, curse it. Stacy Kincaid had been immoral through and through in life and in death, and somehow or other I aimed to neutralize her. Big brave words as I walked between two sturdy men, huh? Well, I aimed to try anyhow.

Regina had just arrived at the library's front door. She held the key in her hand, but hadn't stuck it in the lock yet. Rather, she stood before the door and looked this way and that. I suspect she hoped I'd show up and enter the library with her, because her last library experience had been so terrifying.

I understood her fear, even though I knew whatever evil had

invaded the library didn't involve Stacy Kincaid. At least I hoped like heck it didn't. Stacy'd had other friends and lovers, now deceased, who were as awful as she'd been. None of them, however, had ever hung out at the library so I couldn't feature the ghost of, say, Mr. Percival Petrie, haunting Regina. He'd probably never set foot in a library in his life.

"Oh, Daisy!" Regina cried when she saw us, relief ringing in her voice. "I was hoping you'd be here when I opened the library. Good morning, Detective Rotondo and Mr. …uh, Prophet?"

"Yes, ma'am," said Mr. Prophet, politely tipping his hat, as had Sam. "Mr. Lou Prophet, at your service." He sounded almost courtly.

"Thank you all so much!" said Regina.

"We'll go in with you," I told her. "And Sam and Mr. Prophet can look over the library and try to find anything out of whack."

"I do so appreciate this," said Regina, trying to turn the key in the lock. It didn't seem to want to turn. "Oh, dear. I'm sure this is the correct key." She looked at it, then took her handbag from under her arm and opened it. "Maybe…No, that's the only key I have except the key to the house. I took the red car line to the library because we only have the one automobile."

In those days, the Pacific Electric Company ran trolleys all over the Los Angeles area. They were extremely convenient, cheap, and efficient. I used to take a red car—that's what we called them—to call on clients in Altadena, which is a small township north of Pasadena, before I purchased our trusty Chevrolet. The red cars were ever so much more reliable than our old Model-T Ford. Plus, you didn't have to crank them into life.

"Hmm," said Sam. "Maybe I can give the key a try."

Regina handed him the key. He stuck it in the lock. It wouldn't turn.

"Well," said he, "This is strange. Do you have a janitor around here, or do you expect some of the rest of the staff to be here soon?"

"Most of the staff enter through the back door, the one leading to the offices," said Regina. "Perhaps if we knock, someone who's inside can let us in."

Mr. Prophet gave the big, heavy door a side-eyed look. "If anyone can *hear* you knock." He gave the door a kick with his wooden peg. He was right about the relative effectiveness of knocking on that big old door. There was a thud, but I doubt anyone inside the building could hear it.

I gave the door a couple of raps myself and only succeeded in hurting my knuckles. "Well, this is no fun. Maybe we should walk around to the back?"

"I guess that would be——" Regina stopped speaking when the door suddenly opened. A young man in a natty suit stood there and stared at us, surprised. The four of us who'd been fighting with the lock jumped back a little.

"Mrs. Browning!" said the young man, almost as startled as we. "I didn't think you'd arrived yet, so thought I'd better open the front door. It's just about nine o'clock."

"Yes," said Regina. "Thank you, Mr. Smith. My key wouldn't work in the lock for some reason."

Mr. Smith shook his head. "I don't know what's going on in here," he said darkly. "I came in the back way, and an entire file cabinet had been overturned during the night. There must be someone sabotaging things in here, but we've looked everywhere."

"Yes," said Regina. "I was the last one out of the building yesterday, and the electricity suddenly went off and the door wouldn't open. Then—this sounds insane—someone started throwing books at me!"

Mr. Smith shook his head and appeared troubled. "I'll be glad when this library closes. It's becoming downright dangerous to work here. A library, of all places."

"Please let me introduce you to my friend Mrs. Rotondo and her husband, who's a detective with the Pasadena Police Department. He and their friend, Mr. Prophet, agreed to join me today. They'll search the library."

"Thank you," said Mr. Smith, who sounded relieved when he

heard the words "Pasadena Police Department." "There must be some logical explanation for the weird things happening in here. I think it's probably children, because they're small and can hide easily and can fit through spaces adults can't." He frowned. "Although Pasadena doesn't have too many delinquent children capering about."

"The police have found a few delinquent children in Pasadena, Mr. Smith. They exist," said Sam.

"I'm sorry to hear it," said Mr. Smith. "But thank you for coming to help us."

"You're welcome," said Sam.

Regina, Sam, Mr. Prophet, and I all walked into the library. The lights were on, and the place looked peacefully normal to me. So far. Of course, I hadn't opened a card catalogue drawer or seen an overturned file cabinet yet.

TWELVE

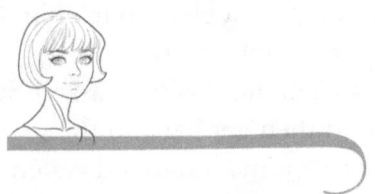

"I hope Stacy can't get me in here," I whispered to Mr. Prophet as we walked behind Regina and Sam, who were chatting with Mr. Smith.

"If a ghost is haunting this place, it probably won't welcome another ghost into its territory. Ghosts are touchy like that," said Mr. Prophet. I swear, you'd think we were chatting about neighborhood cats and dogs.

Honestly, when I began messing around with that Ouija board at the ripe old age of ten, I had *no* idea it would lead to this!

"Kin you call Harold Kincaid from here?"

"I'll ask Regina. Maybe I can telephone from an office. I'd as soon not talk about ghosts in front of a library full of patrons."

Lifting an eyebrow, Mr. Prophet said, "Don't have to worry about that problem at the moment, do you?"

Glancing around, I saw he was correct. So far, we seemed to be the only people in the place. All at once I thought of something else that might or might not be disturbing. I trotted up to Regina and tapped her on the shoulder. She turned, and I saw I'd caused her alarm.

"I'm so sorry," I said. "I didn't mean to scare you."

"Oh, no," she said, trying to laugh and failing. "I guess we're all a little jumpy these days because of the weird things going on in here."

"That's for sure," muttered Mr. Smith.

"I'm still sorry. I didn't think. It's a common enough problem with me." I shot Mr. Prophet a glare to tell him I didn't want any of his sass. He only winked at me. He would.

"Did you need something, Daisy?" asked Sam. "I've got to go through this place and then get back to the gazebo. They're taking impressions of those footprints you found yesterday."

"Oh, good!" I said. "Too bad they didn't take impressions yesterday. A hundred people have probably wandered over that ground by this time."

With a sigh, Sam said, "We put up a blockade of sorts, but you're right. However, we had to get the equipment together and the cement mixed."

"I just wanted to ask Regina if this is the only building where strange things are going on, or if the children's annex across the street is having problems as well."

"We're the only lucky ones," said Regina. "Believe me, I asked. Apparently whoever's behind the vandalism in this building is leaving the children alone. I'm glad of that, but still…."

"Don't blame you," I told her. "Thanks. Also, is it possible for me to use a telephone? I need to get in touch with a friend about another situation requiring attention."

"Can't you telephone from home?" asked Sam.

I gave him a *look*. He understood.

"Oh," he said. "That's right."

"What's the matter?" asked Regina, clearly confused.

"Nothing really," I fibbed. "But I can't drive the car right now."

"I'm so sorry. Did something happen to it? I hope you weren't in an accident or anything."

"Oh, no," I said airily. "I just can't drive it at the moment. The problem will be fixed soon." I hoped. "But if you have a telephone I can use, I'd appreciate it."

"Of course. The head librarian, Miss Drake, is at a conference in San Diego for another couple of days, so why don't you use her office? You can be private in there."

"Excellent! Thanks so much, Regina."

"Thank *you*. I never thought I'd need your…uh…specialized services, but unless we find a physical reason for the odd goings-on in here, well…." Her words trailed off. I could tell she felt stupid even implying the possibility of a supernatural reason for the library's problems. "Anyhow, let me take you to Miss Drake's room."

"Thank you."

So she did. When we got to the closed door of the head librarian's office, Regina took a deep breath for courage before turning the knob and slowly pushing the door open. "Ah, good," she said after she'd glanced around the room. "So far, Miss Drake's room seems to be untouched."

"I'm glad of that." I walked into the room and whispered, "If it *is* a ghost haunting the place, do you have any idea whose it might be? I mean, did someone hate the library or a member of the staff? Or maybe you can think of a late patron who bitterly resented this library being demolished and a new one built?"

For a few moments, I watched Regina think. Watching people think is usually a boring pastime, but after several seconds, I saw Regina's eyes open wide behind her spectacles and her mouth drop open. "Oh, my word!" she said.

Astounded, I said, "You thought of someone?"

"It sounds crazy, but I did."

"Doesn't sound crazy to me," I told her. "Whom do you suspect?"

"A cranky old man named Mr. Enoch Whitehall used to come to the library all the time. He'd sit here all day long doing what he claimed was research into his family's history. He said his grandparents were among the original settlers of the Los Angeles area. When he learned this building was scheduled to be demolished and another one erected to take its place, he became absolutely outraged. He wrote letters to the papers, the governor, the mayor, and his congressman. He was *furious*! He even berated the staff. Even I, who always tried to help him with his research."

"He sounds kind of nutty."

"He was. And you know something?"

"Probably not," I admitted.

"Things started going crazy in the library about three days after Mr. Whitehall died. He died of an apoplectic fit, which we thought was appropriate although it's not nice to say so."

"He had no business taking his wrath out on you, though," I said. "The librarians and staff have nothing to do with this library's closure."

"Well, we were consulted, and I have to admit we all agreed this building was becoming frightfully crowded."

"Oh." I glanced around Miss Drake's room. It did appear somewhat overstuffed with file cabinets and bookcases. "I suppose you're right."

With a small shrug, Regina said, "It's too small, Daisy. Our collection keeps growing, but we're confined to this relatively small building."

"I suppose so, but I wish they could maybe build an addition on this property and keep the park and grounds and so forth."

"According to the city officials, the *new* Pasadena Public Library will be part of what's planned as the Pasadena Civic Center," said Regina without much conviction.

"Yes, I've read that, too. Still, I was pretty outraged myself when I learned this building was going to be closed. I love this old place and its grounds so much."

"I think we'll all miss this lovely building," said Regina. "But honestly, Daisy, it's much too small for our growing collection. Why, we've had to open a branch library in east Pasadena and another one in north Pasadena and still another one in northeast Pasadena. Even with those other libraries, books keep being published, and news keeps happening. We're the central branch, and we *really* need to keep up. We've just outgrown this building."

"I understand, but I'll miss it a lot."

"If it's any comfort, they're planning to move the children's library to Lamanda Park, so there will be a branch library in Lamanda Park, too."

"Yes, I read about that. Actually," I said, "I'm glad to hear it." A library sounded *much* more savory than the speakeasy in Lamanda Park where one of Stacy's old beaux pulled out a Tommy gun and shot up the place while Flossie and I huddled on the floor. It took hours to get the plaster dust and wood chips out of my clothes and hair.

"Well, I'll leave you to the telephone. Thank you so much for coming today, Daisy."

"You're more than welcome. I hope we can find a living person who's causing the trouble, but if the malefactor turns out to be Mr. Whitehall's ghost or spirit or revenant or whatever, it's possible I might be able to get rid of him for you." Whoo boy. What a big fat stretcher. The only exorcism with which I'd been involved had been performed by a Mestizo gentleman. But maybe Mrs. Jackson would have an idea about getting rid of the library ghost as well as Stacy's ghost.

Good Lord, I sound like a lunatic, don't I? I heaved a sigh as Regina left me to the head librarian's telephone. I felt like a peon using an instrument belonging to a monarch. But I used it anyway.

"Mr. Kincaid's residence," came the voice of Harold Kincaid's houseboy, Roy Castillo, after the telephone in Harold's house rang twice.

"Good morning, Roy. This is Daisy Rotondo. Has Harold left for work yet? If not, I'd like to speak to him."

"Miss Daisy, Mr. Harold's not going to be at work for several days. He's at his mother's house this morning. I'm surprised he hasn't telephoned you yet. I guess what I mean is that I'm surprised his mother hasn't telephoned you yet. She's in a frenzy because of that daughter of hers."

"Oh. Of course! How silly of me not to realize Harold would have to deal with his mother after Stacy's murder. Lordy. Maybe I should call her house. I really need to talk to Harold, but if I call her home, I'm afraid I'll have to talk to *her*."

With a chuckle, Roy said, "I know what you mean, Miss Daisy, but I'm sure Mr. Harold would appreciate it if you'd call his mother's place. She's driving him crazy."

"And if I were home instead of at the library, she'd probably be driving *me* crazy."

"I expect you're right."

"Thanks, Roy." I heaved a sigh that lifted the one and only paper residing on Miss Drake's otherwise tidy desk. I whacked a palm on it before it could flutter off the desk. "Hope you have a good day."

"You too, Miss Daisy."

So I hung the earpiece on the hook provided for it and stared at the telephone for what seemed like a long, long time. Then, berating myself as a coward and a slacker, I telephoned the Pinkerton residence, hoping the line would be busy.

It wasn't.

"Pinkerton residence," came Featherstone's upper-crust British accent across the telephone wire.

"Good morning, Featherstone. This is Mrs. Rotondo. I was hoping to speak to Harold. I'm sure Mrs. Pinkerton wants to talk to me, but I need to talk to Harold first, please."

"Mrs. Rotondo? Oh! Of course, Mrs. Majesty Rotondo. I beg your pardon."

"It's all right. I was Daisy Majesty for so long, people often forget my new name," I told him.

"Of course. Mrs. Pinkerton is quite eager to speak to you, Mrs. Rotondo. Will you hold the line for a moment?"

"Don't forget Harold. I need to talk to him first!" I yelled before he could lay the receiver down.

"Of course," said Featherstone in a voice reminding me he didn't forget things like that, even if he *had* forgotten my married name.

So as I sat in Miss Drake's chair—which was really uncomfortable—I braced myself and waited. I became so tense because I expected Mrs. Pinkerton to pick up the receiver and shriek at me that when I heard Harold's calm and rational voice on the other end of the wire, I let out a whoosh of air and dislodged that single paper again.

"Harold! I'm so glad it's you!"

"Who did you think I'd be?"

"You know what I mean. I feared your mother would get on the 'phone and hystericize at me."

"Do *what* at you?" said Harold.

"Have hysterics. I'm so glad you picked up the receiver instead of her."

"I figured you didn't need her this morning. But I'm sorry to say she needs you. Where the devil are you? Mrs. Rattle said you'd gone to the library again, but I never took you for one of those grisly ghouls who *have* to visit scenes of crimes. What are you doing at the library, or did you just want to make sure my sister was really dead."

"Oh, I know she's really dead," I told him ominously. "She's begun haunting me."

Silence greeted my bald statement.

"She hurt Flossie and Johnny's baby, our dinner, and my dog last night."

More silence.

"And this morning when I drove to the library, she grabbed the steering wheel and nearly crashed the Chevrolet."

Yet more silence.

"And besides Stacy haunting *me*, we think there's *another* ghost haunting the library because he doesn't want it to be torn down. He turns off the electricity and throws books at the library staff and stuff like that."

Silence.

"But I'm mainly worried about Stacy haunting me, because she'll murder me if she can. You *know* she will, Harold, because her stupid fiancé tripped over me and killed himself falling down those cement steps."

Nothing.

I'd begun to feel desperate. "And I'm *scared*, Harold! I'm afraid even to get into the car, much less try to drive it. She'll run it into one of those big old pepper trees on Marengo and kill me!"

Zero. Silence.

"Mr. Prophet thinks we need to get Mrs. Jackson to do some Voodoo in order to get rid of her," I said, starting to panic and wonder if Harold had hung up on me.

After another short spate of silence, Harold said, "You're serious, aren't you?"

THIRTEEN

J ust in time, I recalled I was in the Pasadena Public Library. Just in time, because I was about to shriek like a bwat. Instead, I sucked in a huge breath and said, "Yes. Yes, I'm serious. Dead serious. Almost dead serious, anyhow. If your sister'd had her way, I'd be *dead*. Seriously."

"Good Lord." Harold sounded stunned, as well he might.

"So I'm afraid even to go outside. I think I'm safe in the library because whatever's haunting the library won't let Stacy in. That's what Mr. Prophet thinks, anyway. Oh, Harold, I don't know what to *do!*"

"Um…"

"But Mr. Prophet, who seems to know about these sorts of things, says we need Mrs. Jackson to create a Voodoo spell to drive Stacy away. And maybe the library ghost too. Are you able to talk to Mr. Jackson and ask if his mother is available for something of the sort?"

"You want me to ask my mother's gatekeeper to ask his mother to create some sort of Voodoo magic to keep the ghost of my evil dead sister from haunting you? And to rid the soon-to-be-demolished library of another ghost? Did I get that right?" He sounded incredulous.

I understood why he might not quite believe me, but surely my terror was plain to hear. "Yes," I said firmly. "Yes, you got it precisely right. It's urgent. I'm afraid to step foot outside the library for fear Stacy will drop a rock on me or something."

"If she's a ghost, how can she pick up rocks to drop?"

"I have no idea. But last night, she not only managed to burn our dinner to a crisp, but she dropped my letter opener on the Buckingham's baby and she did something that hurt Spike, but I don't know what. And then today, she twisted the steering wheel so that I almost turned a circle on Walnut Street and hit a couple of cars and a pedestrian."

"Um..."

"Please, Harold?" I begged.

"Wait a minute," said Harold. "Let me think about this for a sec. There's got to be a way to keep you alive even if my evil sister is haunting you."

"Take your time. I don't dare leave the library."

"Yes. You've told me so several times. But let me think for a minute, okay? That means please don't talk."

"Right. Right. I'll shut up now."

"Thank you."

This time when silence ensued, I didn't panic because I knew Harold was on the other end of the wire. I almost certainly could have figured it out the first time, because there's a slight humming noise that always travels through the 'phone wires, but I'd been too panicky to listen for it. So I waited. And waited. And I tried not to get frustrated and itchy and feel abandoned and bellow at Harold.

It's a good thing he didn't have to think for more than the seven years, forty-two days, three hours, five minutes and twenty-six seconds he took, because I was about to break the tension with a scream when he spoke at last.

"Stay there," he said.

"I don't dare *not* stay here," I told him. "I already said so."

"Yes, yes, I know. But I'll come over there and pick you up. Then you can talk to Jackson yourself. And then you can see my mother."

"I don't have my Ouija board or other spiritual accoutrements with me," I told him.

"Damn. Well then, I'll take you home and we can go in together and fetch them. After that I'll take you to talk to Jackson and then my mother. Dr. Benjamin will be here soon, so he'll probably shoot Mother with something or other."

"Will we be safe in your car?" I asked him.

"How the hell should *I* know? Did Stacy's ghost attack you when you walked with Sam? I'm only assuming you walked with Sam, of course."

"No, she didn't. I walked to the library between Sam and Mr. Prophet, and nothing happened to me. Or them."

"I doubt Stacy would dare attack Lou," said Harold. I heard the grin in his voice. I still didn't feel like grinning.

"You're probably right. But let me talk to Sam and Mr. Prophet. I know Sam has to stay here, at least in the park, because they're still going over the crime scene." Which made me think of something. "Say, Harold, you don't know any of Stacy's friends, do you? I mean, one of them most likely helped her break out of the jail wing of the hospital and maybe killed her."

"I don't know any of my sister's friends," said Harold with major emphasis. "Nor do I want to."

"Don't blame you, but we might need to find some of them."

"I don't need to find any of them," said Harold, still emphatic. "That's Sam's job."

"I suppose. All right, I'll ask Sam if he and Mr. Prophet have finished their search of the library. Probably Mr. Prophet would like a ride home when you take me there to get my spiritualist paraphernalia."

"All right by me. I really like the guy. He's one of the few so-called 'normal' men I've ever met who never even blinked an eye when he found out I *wasn't* so-called 'normal'."

"No, he doesn't care what people are as long as they leave him alone."

"My kind of guy."

"Lordy, don't say that in front of him!"

"Just joking, Daisy. My sister's ghost has clearly driven your sense of humor away."

"You're right," I told him. "I'm too scared to find anything funny at the moment."

"Be there in a bit."

"Thanks, Harold."

"You're welcome, Daisy."

I hung up the telephone in Miss Drake's office, pushed her chair away from her desk—I hope she had a cushion or something to sit on or lean against when she was working, because that stupid chair was really hard and unforgiving—and went in search of my husband. Found him in the biography section, trying to find something he might want to read.

"Did you and Mr. Prophet do a thorough search of the library?" I asked him.

"Yeah. Didn't find any place where a person might have broken in. And while Lou and I were going through the stacks, somebody pushed books out at us from the other side. Only there wasn't anyone there."

"Ghost," said Mr. Prophet, sneaking up behind me and making me nearly leap out of my skin.

Whirling around, I whispered sharply, "Don't creep up on me like that!"

He gave me a dubious squint. "I can't creep up on anybody these days. My creepin' days are long over."

"Well, you surprised me. I'm…a little nervous today."

With a shrug, he said, "Yeah, I know. I'd be nervous too if that ring-tailed polecat's ghost was hauntin' me. But it's someone else's ghost in the library."

I bowed my head, attempting not to believe his words. I couldn't not do it. "This would be unbelievable if it weren't happening."

"True. Say, Daisy, will you check this book out for me?" said Sam, handing me a book titled *Marching on Tanga*, by someone named Francis Brett Young.

I looked on the spine, and saw it wasn't a biography. "What's this about?"

"British fellow in the medical corps during the Great War in East Africa. Sounded interesting."

Sounded like a narration of hell to me, but that's because my Billy had fought and died because of the Great War. As far as I was concerned, there was nothing noble about war, any war. People tend to romanticize wars, but even thinking about my darling Billy being shot and gassed in the mud and blood of Europe made me sick.

"Will do," I said, keeping my opinion to myself for once.

"Thanks. I have to get back to the gazebo and direct operations out there. What are your plans?"

"Harold is driving to the library, and he's going to take me home to get my Ouija board and so forth. I'm going to have to visit with Mrs. Pinkerton, I fear."

He frowned. "Do you really have to see her today? The woman's a wreck."

"That's why I have to. Don't forget she virtually supported my family and me for many, many years. Her awful daughter was just murdered, and I honestly think I need to see if I can help her. *And*" —I shot a glance at Mr. Prophet—"I aim to have a chat with Jackson and see if he can talk his mother into doing some Voodoo that can keep Stacy away from me. And maybe send the library ghost away."

"I can't believe I'm hearing and believing this," said Sam, giving his head a hard shake.

"Pert' near laughable, ain't it?" said Mr. Prophet.

"It might be laughable if my wife didn't seem to be in danger."

"And don't ferget the library," said Mr. Prophet. "And the people who work here."

"True," said Sam. He shook his head less forcefully. "It's still hard to believe."

"I'd find it hard to believe if Stacy's phantom hadn't attempted to murder me this morning. And don't forget she burned up our dinner, tried to smash our peacock lamp, and hurt Spike."

"And the Buckinghams' baby," said Sam.

"That too," I agreed.

"Kin you and Harold take me home when you go?" asked Mr. Prophet. "I don't see any point to me hangin' out in the library all day."

"Yes, we'll be happy to. Harold already said so."

"Thanks, Miss Daisy. You ain't all bad, I reckon."

Sam laughed. I didn't.

So Sam went back outside to the crime scene where various uniformed policemen were doing various policemanly things. I checked out *Marching on Tanga*. Then Mr. Prophet and I stayed inside the library, attempting to be of some comfort to Regina.

"Maybe I can perform a séance in the library," I said doubtfully. "I mean, I don't really believe in my powers to do anything in the spiritual realm, but every now and then odd things happen during my séances."

"That's fer durned sure," said Mr. Prophet, being polite. If it were just I in his audience, he'd have used a word other than durned.

"Can you think of another way to get rid of the ghost?" asked Regina, who appeared both worried and disturbed. "I can't even believe I'm asking that question," she added in an agitated mutter.

"It does sound silly, doesn't it?" I said soothingly.

"Mebbe the Voodoo woman can help with the library too," suggested Mr. Prophet.

"Yes, that's an excellent idea," I told him, forgetting for a second that I didn't want him to think I appreciated him for fear he'd resume picking on me.

"I want to meet that woman," said Mr. Prophet thoughtfully. "I've met me a couple of ladies from New Orleans who knew Voodoo magic. It'd be nice to meet one more before I croak."

"It's fine with me, if it's all right with Mrs. Jackson," I told him. "Maybe she'll make a Voodoo juju for you." I fingered my own personal juju through my blouse.

Perhaps I could create a small pouch for my treasures and wear them around my waist. Which was expanding daily. Very well, so that wouldn't work. I'd think of something eventually.

"I'd like that," said Mr. Prophet, who smiled, so I believed him. "Got me some other good-luck charms other folks have give me, but I never got me a Voodoo juju." He nodded happily.

"Um…" Regina's glance bounced between Mr. Prophet and me a couple of times. "Um…What's a Voodoo…whatever you called it? I've heard of Voodoo, but not one of…those things."

"I'm sure you haven't," I said with a small sigh. I lifted my chin and fished for the chain around my neck, withdrawing it and its four small charms. "Here. This"—I held up the Voodoo juju—"is the juju Mrs. Jackson made for me. It's supposed to bring me good luck, although the results seem to vary." I showed her the other items in order. "This is Billy's wedding ring. I wear it on a chain Sam gave me because he understands how much I loved Billy, just as I understand how much he loved his Margaret. She died of tuberculosis about two years before Billy died from his war injuries."

"I'm so sorry, Daisy," said Regina. I saw tears gathering in her eyes. She'd always been empathetic, and I liked her for it.

"Me too, but Sam and I found each other, so that's a good thing—"

A loud "Huh!" came from Mr. Prophet, but I pretended to ignore it.

"Then," I went on, "this is a tiny woven Tongva basket that— well, this sounds nuts, but it happened—was dropped onto a table in front of me by the ghost of a Tongva shaman during a séance."

Regina's mouth fell open. I paused, but she snapped her teeth together and shook her head hard, so I guess she aimed to hold any questions she might have had.

"And *this* one," I said, holding up the tiny carved baby, "was given to me by Mr. Emilio DeLoera, a descendant of the Tongva natives who first settled the Los Angeles area hundreds of years ago. He's the one who helped us…" Did I really want to explain about the exorcism of the Tongva ghost from our backyard? I decided I didn't. "He helped us out a few months back. Do you recall when I was trying to find out about the Indians who used to live here?"

"Yes, and we couldn't find anything except about the Navajo and Hopi," said Regina.

"Exactly. Well, he's a descendant of the Tongva who lived here, and he carved this for me."

"How sweet," said Regina, reaching out to finger the carved baby.

"He's a very nice man. We still see him from time to time." I quickly shoved my charms back under my blouse. I trusted Regina as much as I trusted anyone, but I didn't want people fingering my treasures for fear they'd wear them out. Well, except for Billy's ring. That would always remain round and golden and dear to me. I heaved another sigh just because.

"You've both lived lives far more interesting than mine has ever been," said Regina, almost sorrowfully.

"That's the truth," said Mr. Prophet with a reminiscent, faraway look on his rugged face.

"I never thought of my life as interesting before," I said honestly. "Like the rest of the people in my family, I've only used whatever abilities I possess to earn a living. This sounds terrible because it is, but being a spiritualist after the Great War and the influenza pandemic was a more lucrative way to make money than if I were, say, an elevator operator or a clerk in a store."

"You probably make more than a librarian, too," said Regina.

"Possibly," I said. "Which is just wrong. You've been to school and worked hard to gain your position. I'm more like an actor in the flickers. Actors only have to look good in order to make more money than any of us will ever see. Only I don't look that good or make as much money being a spiritualist."

Regina and Mr. Prophet both gave me odd looks.

"What? It's a fact. And the only reason I'm a spiritualist is that I pretended I could use the Ouija board when I was ten years old. My career is a fluke made up out of thin air."

"Not anymore," said Mr. Prophet.

"I guess that's true," I agreed.

"My goodness," said Regina.

A huge crash came from the far stacks. I bowed my head. "I'm almost sorry not to be a fake any longer. That sounded like fallen books."

"It probably was," Regina said with a big sigh.

We saw Mr. Smith and a couple of other library employees hurrying to see what had happened this time.

Just then Harold Kincaid walked through the library's front door and strolled up to us. "Good morning," he said. Then he peered more closely. "Or not."

"Not," Regina, Mr. Prophet, and I said in a discordant trio.

FOURTEEN

I walked between Harold and Mr. Prophet as we made our way out to his magnificent red Hispano-Suiza.

"Ah," said Mr. Prophet, sounding pleased. "This is much better fer me than that dinky little red car you used to have."

"I loved that car," said Harold.

"Yeah, but I damn near broke in half before you got us to that lion farm," said Mr. Prophet. "This is at least high enough for me to sit in."

"True," said Harold. "Daisy's the one who made you ride in my Stutz Bearcat."

"Tattletale," I said as Harold opened the front door for me. I slid in before his sister's revenant could do me any harm.

"You don't need to tell me that," said Mr. Prophet. "She's had it in for me ever since we met."

"I have not!" I said, trying to sound indignant. "But that was mean of me. I thought it would be funny, but it wasn't, was it?"

"No," said Mr. Prophet. "It hurt." He shoved himself into the front seat beside me. I'm glad the Hispano-Suiza had big seats, because we wouldn't be squished as we all three sat in the front.

"I'm sorry," I said. "I hadn't thought about it hurting you."

"That don't surprise me none."

"Very well, children, stop quarreling," said Harold, getting in on the driver's side. "Is Mrs. Rattle still at your house, Daisy?"

"Yes, but I left Spike at my parents' house. I don't trust your sister not to murder my dog."

"But you don't care about Mrs. Rattle?" asked Mr. Prophet.

"Of course, I care about Mrs. Rattle!" I said, miffed. "But why would Stacy hurt her?"

"Dunno. But I wouldn't trust her not to."

"I wouldn't trust her not to either," said Harold.

"Oh dear," I said, beginning to fret about Mrs. Rattle's fate.

"Stacy always was a nasty, vicious little bitch," said Harold. "Even when she was young, she was a spoiled monster of a child. Mother indulged her."

"I hope Mrs. Jackson can figure out how to get rid of her."

"I do too," said Harold. "And I can't believe I believe any of this."

"That's pretty much what Sam said earlier today," I told him.

"Yup," said Mr. Prophet. "Don't surprise me none. I've had dealings with spirits before coming to Pasadena. In fact, so far, the only interesting things I've found about Pasadena are the ghosts. Well, and little Billy."

"What about Miss Li?" I asked him.

"Yeah," he said with a satisfied grin. "Her too."

"I don't even want to know," said Harold.

"She's a lovely Chinese woman," I told him. "She and Mr. Prophet are special friends."

"I said I don't want to know," Harold grumbled.

"You don't expect Miss Daisy to keep her mouth shut, do you, son?"

"Well, no. You're right about that," said Harold.

I thought about whacking his arm because he was being hateful, recalled his beastly sister and how she might make Harold crash his car, and didn't. Mercy sakes. Life has always been complicated, if you're me, but before Stacy died, I'd never had to fear a ghost slaughtering me. She'd been trouble enough when she was alive.

Harold pulled the Hispano-Suiza into our driveway and parked beside the gate to the front porch railing. Mr. Prophet managed to squeeze himself out of the passenger door, which wasn't easy because of his peg leg. Then I slid across the seat, clutching my handbag and Sam's library book. I stood stock-still, glancing around in fear of an evil act by Stacy's ghost, but Harold hurried to my side before she could do anything malicious, if she'd intended to.

"Let me walk between you, please," I said to the two men.

"Sure," said Harold.

"I'll go first," said Mr. Prophet. He trod up the two steps, unlatched the porch gate, and walked onto the porch. I was right behind him, and Harold darned near walked on my heels in order to stay close to me.

We arrived at the front door without mishap and entered the house.

Where we found Mrs. Rattle weeping!

"Mrs. Rattle!" I cried running up and putting my arms around her. "Whatever is the matter?"

"I don't know!" she cried back. "But every time I make a bed or dust a piece of furniture or something, my work gets instantly undone. I don't know what's happening!"

"Aw, shi-oot," said Mr. Prophet.

I bowed my head. "It's all right. I think I know what's going on, and I intend to do my best to fix it. Why don't you go on home now. And...and...Oh, dear. I'll telephone you when everything's fixed. I'll pay you, of course, for your full work week. But something odd is going on in here, and I think I need to call a...a..." Aw, cripes. I couldn't tell the woman I aimed to call on a Voodoo mambo or an exorcist.

"She has to call a specialist," said Harold, bless him.

"Yeah. A specialist," echoed Mr. Prophet.

Glancing at me—she'd had her head bowed with her hands covering her face—Mrs. Rattle appeared confused. "But what's going on?" she asked, sounding pathetic.

"We're not sure, but it has to do with the...Um, it has to do with the pipes."

"The pipes?" she echoed.

"Yes, and the plumbing. I know a professional who will fix everything," said Harold.

"And the foundation needs work," said Mr. Prophet.

Just then a whoosh of dust engulfed us. It was as if Stacy had gathered all the dust in all the houses in Pasadena and blown it at us.

"Ack!" I cried, shoving myself away from poor Mrs. Rattle and flapping my hands to wave the dust away from my face and hers.

"That's what I mean!" she said. "That sort of thing has been going on all morning. Oh, Daisy, I can't believe the pipes are at fault for everything."

"It's the foundation," said Mr. Prophet, also flailing at the dust cloud. "It's unsteady. Best if you go on now. Miss Daisy will let you know when it's safe to come back here."

"Safe?" Mrs. Rattle brushed dust from her arms and the scarf she'd tied around her head. "Well, if you say so. But really, dear, you needn't pay me when I don't work."

"Yes, I do. I need to," I said firmly. "I'm sorry about this. I think it all started with a mistake I made yesterday, but we'll get it all repaired shortly."

Looking at me oddly, she said, "Well, if you're sure—"

"I'm sure," I told her before she could finish her sentence. "Be careful when you gather your things and walk cautiously. Things are kind of falling apart in here. Try not to trip over anything."

"Very well. Thank you, dear."

"Thank *you*," I said. "And I'm so sorry this happened."

Harold, Mr. Prophet, and I finally got rid of the poor woman, who still appeared confounded as she left the house. I watched her like a hawk, but evidently, Stacy decided not to make her stumble or shove her or anything of a like nature, because she made it to the street safely.

"Stacy Kincaid!" I said to the air around me. "Stop it!"

"*Nooooooo! This is fun*," an eerie, evil voice answered back. As if to prove how fun it was, she made a picture fall from the wall. Fortunately, although the frame broke, the picture itself—a pretty autumn scene in New England—remained intact. Sam could fix the frame, but I didn't say so out loud for fear Stacy would ruin the picture itself.

"All right," said Harold. "Stacy, go to hell."

We heard something that sounded like *pthhhht* come from the empty air around us. All right, so Stacy wasn't going to hell on Harold's say-so. He'd given me a darned good idea, but I'd have to wait to act upon it.

"Will you go upstairs with me, Harold? Mr. Prophet, I know stairs aren't easy for you—"

"Hell," he said, interrupting me. "I've dealt with worse than the Kincaid witch. I'll go upstairs with you. But lemme get a weapon first. You got a yardstick or something around here?"

"Sure. In my sewing room upstairs."

"*How dare you,*" screeched Stacy's ghost voice.

Mr. Prophet pulled something out of his trouser pocket and waved it in the air. I'm not sure what it was, but it looked like some kind of Indian artifact. Given what I knew of his past, I suspected it was a charm or token a Mescalero Apache had given him.

"*Aaaaaaahhhhh!*" squealed the Stacy voice, sounding alarmed and not at all amused this time.

And just like that, life was peaceful again.

"Good heavens, what did you do?" I asked Mr. Prophet.

"I got me some powerful medicine. Just used some of it on the witch-ghost. I'm the only one it works for, but if we stick together, she can't get at any of us fer a while anyhow."

"Thank God," muttered Harold.

"Thank old Mrs. Tsedikezin. She's the one made it for me."

"Apache?" I asked.

"Mescalero," he agreed.

So that made me right for once that day. Didn't feel appreciably better for having deduced the talisman's origin, but I was awfully glad we'd be rid of Stacy for a while.

Harold, Mr. Prophet, and I climbed the stairs and, after visiting the sewing room to retrieve a yardstick, went to the spare room where I kept my spiritualist paraphernalia in a closet. I opened the door slowly and with great care, in case Stacy had decided to rig the closet so a box would fall off a shelf and bash me.

It turned out I'd been wise to move slowly and cautiously. As soon as I fully opened the door, darned if a big kitchen knife didn't fall from wherever Stacy had stashed it. If I'd rushed right to my back of tricks, it would have stabbed me. It most likely wouldn't have done a whole lot of damage, but it would have hurt and bled.

"Damn," said Mr. Prophet. "She really is a witch from hell, ain't she?"

"Yes," said Harold before I could. "She is."

I nodded. Then I took great care in reaching for the lovely embroidered fabric carrier I'd fashioned for my Ouija board and my tarot cards and lifted it off the hook on the closet door. I'm glad I didn't keep my crystal ball hanging anywhere, or surely Stacy would have beaned me with it. As far as I could tell, however, it still sat in its fabric sack—one I'd also fashioned personally—on the closet floor.

"Be careful opening it," advised Harold. "Stacy might have induced a herd of tarantulas to take up residence in there."

"Tarantulas ain't dangerous," said Mr. Prophet, surprising both Harold and me.

"I thought they were venomous," I said.

"Some are. The ones we get here are just big and fuzzy. It takes a lot to rile 'em enough to bite, and even then it'll just hurt for a day or two. If you scare 'em, they'll get on their hind legs and wave their front legs in the air and look pretty silly. Still, she might have dumped scorpions in there. They hurt more than tarantulas."

"Crumb," I said. Very carefully, I set my bag of tricks on its side on the floor. Then I pulled the drawstring so that if anything had been secreted in there, it would crawl out away from the three of us watchers. I bethought me of rattlesnakes, but decided not even to mention them. Unless, of course, one or two of them slithered out of the bag.

Nothing, however, crawled therefrom. Still being careful, I tugged the bottom of the bag so that my card bag and the Ouija board and planchette gently slid from it.

Mr. Prophet believed in being careful, I guess, because he produced his yardstick and whacked the bag a few times. Then he used it to heft the bag's drawstring and lifted it. The three of us peered inside.

"I don't guess she messed with this," said Mr. Prophet.

"She might be afraid to," said Harold. "Now that she knows about the ways of the netherworld, she'll probably treat Daisy's communication devices to it with more respect than she treats the rest of us."

"Might could be," said Mr. Prophet. "Lemme open that card case, though. I want to make sure there's nothin' but cards in there."

"I can do that," I told him.

"Yeah, but don't," he commanded.

So I let him open the card bag. He warily lifted it via his yardstick and, even more cautiously, pulled the drawstring so that the bag opened. As we stood near a window under which a table sat, he emptied the cards onto the table.

"Huh," he said when an almost transparent scorpion, which couldn't have been more than two or three inches long, crept out from between a couple of cards. He maneuvered it to the edge of the table with his yardstick until it fell off onto the floor and then stamped on it with his peg.

"She's truly going to kill me if she can, isn't she?" I asked mournfully.

"Yeah, but we won't let her, so don't worry. That scorpion wouldn't've killed you anyhow. It'd just have stung and hurt. I'll stay in the house with you and Sam until we get rid of her."

"Do you have any ideas about how to get rid of her? Permanently, I mean?" I asked him.

"One or two. Let's go see the Voodoo woman first. I'll bet she can set up some magic in the house to at least keep her under control until the devil rips her soul off the earth and down to hell where it belongs."

Dramatic. I didn't say so. What I said, and humbly, was, "Thank you."

"Welcome," he said.

Harold, whose mouth still hung open after watching the scorpion incident, snapped it shut and said, "I want to see how you do that."

"Sure," said Mr. Prophet. Then he said, "You know where the Voodoo woman lives? I think we should visit her before we go to see your ma, Harold."

"Fine with me," said Harold.

"Yes, I know where her house is," I said. "I don't know if she has a telephone. She didn't a couple of years ago."

"We can just drop by," said Mr. Prophet. "If she's like the other mambos I've met, she won't mind."

"Really?" I peered doubtfully at him.

"Aw, what can it hurt?" said Harold. "Anything to put off visiting Mother."

Very well then. When we returned to Harold's Hispano-Suiza, I carrying my spiritualist supplies, we all smooshed into the front seat. I told Harold where to go. In the region of Pasadena, I mean.

FIFTEEN

A lthough I hadn't been to Mrs. Jackson's home on Mentone Avenue often, I knew where it was. I'd taken her a few items I'd sewn for her and her grandchildren for Christmas and taken her treats from Aunt Vi occasionally. In return, she'd been instrumental in saving Sam's life and had given both of us Voodoo jujus she claimed would bring us luck. She'd also gifted us several times with the lightest, most delicious beignets I'd ever tasted before. Which doesn't mean much, as I'd never even heard of a beignet before meeting Mrs. Jackson. Still and all....

As perhaps I've mentioned before, the jury was out on whether or not the jujus, in fact, brought either Sam or me luck, but they'd helped solve a case or two of Sam's in the past couple of years. So I guess that's some kind of luck.

When I'd first met Mr. Jackson, I'd been a kid, and I hadn't known about Pasadena's so-called "red lines". The red lines designated where a family could live based on the color of its members' skin. The Jacksons of Pasadena, along with the Lis, the Castillos, the DeLoeras, and, probably, the Tsedikezins and others who weren't lily-white, could only own property in certain areas. Therefore, one didn't see many white faces when one visited the Jacksons' home.

This fact didn't bother any of us. So Harold parked his car across the street from Mrs. Jackson's tidy home, and we all walked across. Sweet alyssum lined the paved walkway to the front door along with pansies and johnny-jump-ups. Narcissus bloomed behind them along with snapdragons, and the rosebushes planted behind them were full of little buds.

Orange trees, which had been planted closer to the house, were also blooming like crazy. The fragrance from citrus trees is probably *the* most heavenly one in the world. In short, the Jacksons had a gorgeous garden. I knew for a fact, because I'd seen it up close and personally, they had a big kitchen garden in back of the house.

"Smells good here," Mr. Prophet observed. "Kinda like home."

"It does indeed," I agreed.

Speaking of observations, I observed that he'd removed his Apache charm or totem or whatever it was called from his trouser pocket and held it in front of him as we walked the path. I heard no squeals from Stacy's ghost, so I approved this foresight on his part. On the other hand, as we were approaching the home of a powerful (I'm only assuming that part) Voodoo mambo, perhaps her ghost feared being anywhere near the Jacksons' abode.

Mrs. Jackson, a huge woman, had seen us as we approached her door. I knew that because she'd already opened it and smiled broadly at the three of us as we walked up her porch steps.

"Welcome to you all, Mr. Harold, Miss Daisy. And who is this young man?"

Young man? Oh. Mr. Prophet.

"Mrs. Jackson," I said, after deciphering of whom she spoke, "please allow me to introduce you to Mr. Lou Prophet. Mr. Prophet is helping Harold and me as we attempt to foil a ghost's attempts on my life."

"Aaaaah," said Mrs. Jackson, nodding wisely. Stepping aside, she said, "Come on in. I knew a wicked soul had been released from its mortal body, but I didn't know who it belonged to. That's the one hauntin' you, child?"

"The ghost of Stacy Kincaid, Harold's sister," I agreed as we all entered the Jackson home.

"Mmm, she's a bad one. I'm sorry she's taken to haunting you, child."

"Me too," I kind of whimpered.

"Is that some kind of Injun juju, Mr. Prophet?" asked Mrs. Jackson nodding at the charm he held in his callused old hand.

"Sure is," said Mr. Prophet. "An Apache wise woman give it to me nigh onto thirty-five, forty years ago." He handed it to Mrs. Jackson, who studied it carefully before shutting her eyes for a second or two, nodding, and then handing it back.

"Interesting. And powerful. But come in and sit. I'll make some tea, and I have some fresh beignets. Just made 'em this morning. I had a hunch I'd have visitors today. You can tell me your story over tea and beignets."

"Thank you so much," I said, feeling guilty for barging in on her. "I'm sorry we didn't warn you we were coming, but—"

"No apologies necessary, young lady. *You* had no warning. Haints don't ever give folks warnings. They just show up if they've got it in for you. I'll be more than happy to help. You still wearin' your juju, I see." Her gaze was fixed on my lumpy chest.

"Yes. Sam and I wear our jujus every day. I was also given a charm by a Mestizo fellow a few months back. And a Tongva ghost gave me another one."

"Ah. Your powers are growing," said Mrs. Jackson, smiling as she headed to the kitchen.

I didn't say what I thought about her words, which was, "I wish they weren't."

From her chuckle as she disappeared into the other room, I had a feeling she heard them even though I hadn't spoken them aloud.

"Interestin'," said Mr. Prophet.

He and Harold waited until I sat on the sofa before they also sat. Then, when Mrs. Jackson returned to the room a minute or two later, carrying a tray, we all rose to our feet again. Manners. I don't understand them sometimes, but I appreciated them then because Mrs. Jackson deserved all the respect we could give her.

"Let me help you with that," said Harold, stepping up to take the tray.

"Thank you kindly, Mr. Harold," said Mrs. Jackson giving Harold the tray and returning to the kitchen. He set the tray on the table sitting in front of the sofa. Two comfy-looking chairs had been placed on the other side of the table across from the sofa.

When Mrs. Jackson returned, bearing with her a pretty plate of her spectacular beignets, she set them beside the tray on the table. "I'll just pour everyone a cup of tea. You can fix it however you want with milk and sugar. Just use napkins for your beignets. There's no way to eat one of those things without getting sugar everywhere, so napkins work better than plates." She chuckled. She was also correct.

"Thank you so much for this. I hope we aren't eating your family's dessert," I said, pouring some milk in my teacup before pouring the tea in it. I don't know why I did it that way except that Aunt Vi said I should. She also believes that tea isn't ready to be drunk until it's strong enough to walk out of the pot on its own. I didn't bother telling my companions so.

After she made sure we all were provided with tea and powdery beignets, Mrs. Jackson sat back on her chair and said, "So tell me about this spirit. It's your evil sister's ghost, Mr. Harold?"

"Yes. I'm afraid it is."

With a small shrug, Mrs. Jackson said, "Don't surprise me none. She was wicked from the start, and I figured she'd come to a bad end. Somebody kill her, did they?"

"Yes," I said, a trifle startled. "How did you guess that?"

"Wasn't much of a guess, child. I felt it. Knew that girl was near her end when Joseph told me she'd escaped from the hospital. Stupid girl. I expect the other stupid girl who helped her escape is the one who did her in. Knifed, was she?"

Feeling a trifle eerie, I said, "Er...In a way. She was stabbed with a broken liquor bottle. You think a woman did it?"

"Must've been. Her gent friend died a couple of years ago, didn't he? I 'spect she met someone in jail, and it'd have to be a woman because they don't house men and women in the same buildings."

"That makes sense," I said. "Mr. Prophet and I found her body." I swallowed a sip of tea. "Unfortunately."

"Ah. There you go. Her spirit lingered, and she didn't like it that you found her. That's probably why she attached herself to you. She never liked you much, did she?"

"No. She also blamed me for her male friend's death. But that's only because she'd hit me with a chair and I'd fallen down. He tripped over me and fell down some concrete steps."

"Of course she'd blame you. When the Klan came after Joseph, she told her ma to fire him, but you told her not to. And then you saved me when the Klan came after Mrs. Armistead and me."

"I didn't save you," I demurred. "You saved yourself by showing me what to do." It was during the episode to which Mrs. Jackson referred when I became familiar with her backyard and, therefore, knew about her kitchen garden.

"Yeah, but you did it," she said. Nodding wisely, she went on, "The Kincaid girl never liked it when folks got in the way of her meanness. She always held a grudge against her ma and people who live straight lives." She turned to peer at Mr. Prophet. "You ain't lived a straight life, but you're a good man. I can tell."

"Don't spread it around," said Mr. Prophet in a gruff voice. "I like it better when folks are scared of me."

With a big white grin, Mrs. Jackson said, "You don't ever have to worry about that, Mr. Prophet. You scare people just by bein'." She nodded knowingly. "I've met others of your kind."

Oh Lord, I hoped she was joking.

"Yeah," said Mr. Prophet. "I've met me a couple of Voodoo mambos, too."

"New Orleans?" said Mrs. Jackson.

"Yup. New Orleans."

"Figured as much." She turned her attention to me. "Very well, so what has the Kincaid girl been doin' to put you in a lather, Miss Daisy?"

So I regaled her with all the stunts Stacy's ghost had pulled, including hurting the Buckinghams' baby and Spike, trying to smash our gorgeous lamp, her harassment of poor Mrs. Rattle, and her attempt to take over the steering wheel of the Chevrolet.

"And you don't want her to hurt you or the baby," said Mrs. Jackson musingly. "I see."

How'd she know about the baby? I was only three months along and didn't hardly show yet.

Oh, that's right. She was a Voodoo mambo. And to think I never even used to believe in this stuff.

I said, "Mr. Prophet suggested you might know of a way to keep her from…well, haunting our house and hurting us while we're inside it. I'm afraid she'll shove us downstairs, or kill my dog or Sam. She's hated me for years."

"About as long as you've hated her," suggested Mrs. Jackson with a soft smile.

"Well, yes. That's because her mother was forever calling me in a tizzy over something Stacy was doing."

"I've hated her for longer than Daisy has and she's not haunting me," Harold piped up.

"That's because you didn't find her. Miss Daisy did. She probably hates you too, but Miss Daisy stands as an example your mother wanted her to follow."

"I do?" I said.

"You do. You help Mrs. Pinkerton—and that's not a small task, according to my Joseph—while Stacy only ever hurts her."

"Huh, I guess that's true," I muttered.

"It is," said Harold.

"So kin you help keep her out of Sam and Daisy's house until we can figure out how to get rid of her altogether?" asked Mr. Prophet, who didn't much care for chitchat. "And how do you suggest we get rid of her? She needs to get off the earth and go to hell."

"True, true," said Mrs. Jackson. "I'll have to think on how to get rid of her permanently, but in the meantime, I can give you some tokens to take home, and some herbs and essences to sprinkle here and there. They should keep her away from your house for a while at least. We might have to talk again about getting her gone for good."

"Thank you," I said, appreciative, although I wasn't altogether sure if herbs and essences would do much good.

Truth to tell, I still didn't actually believe in magic. Yes, I believed in Stacy's ghost, because she'd presented her evil self to my loved ones and me several times already, and she'd nearly driven Mrs. Rattle nuts. I'd even watched a real live ghost appear at a séance. Twice. At two different séances. But Voodoo magic? I just wasn't sure.

"It don't matter if you believe in it or not, Miss Daisy," said Mrs. Jackson, startling me because it was as if she'd read my mind. "It'll work anyway." She laughed a big, hearty laugh and made the rest of us laugh too.

"Glad to hear it," I said when I hiccupped to a stop.

"What you'll need to do first is sprinkle salt all the way around your house. Get a lot of salt, because you probably have a big house."

"You mean on the outside?" I asked.

"On the outside," she confirmed. "I'm gonna give you some sage to burn in your fireplace." She squinted at me. "You got a fireplace?"

"Yes, we have a fireplace."

"Good. You should burn some sage in the fireplace, but don't do that until you pour at least two or three cups of salt in it first."

"Put salt in the fireplace and then burn sage on top of the salt?" I asked in a weak voice.

"Buck up, child," Mrs. Jackson ordered. "You got a killing haint after you, and you need to pay attention."

"I'll remember if she don't," said Mr. Prophet.

"And you," she said, pointing at him, "stay under the same roof as Miss Daisy and Mr. Sam until this whole sorry mess is dealt with. You got your own juju power." Peering at him sharply, she said, "I see some Chinese juju around you too. You got a Chinese lady friend?"

Although I couldn't be certain, I thought I saw Mr. Prophet's leathery cheeks take on a reddish hue.

"Yeah. I got me a Chinese lady friend."

"Good. Visit your lady friend and ask her if she can give you some Fu dogs or Fu lions. You can just borrow 'em until you don't need 'em any longer. Also, put a copper one-cent piece in the corner of every room in your house. Including the closets."

"Copper pennies?" I repeated.

"We don't got pennies in this country," said Mr. Prophet. "The Brits are the ones have pennies. We have one-cent coins. They're all copper. I got a collection of 'em. You kin borrow 'em for a couple of days."

"That's good," said Mrs. Jackson.

"Thank you," I said, bewildered. I didn't know the U.S.A. didn't use pennies. We *called* them pennies. Learn something every day, I reckon.

"Fill a bowl with water and put it under your bed before you go to sleep," said Mrs. Jackson. Keep as many lights on as you can. And burn sage in all the rooms in your house. You got any dried orange peels?"

"Um…not on hand, but we have a whole bunch of orange trees."

"Good. Stick some orange peels in the oven on low heat until they dry out. Then lay a bunch more of them around the house. Dried orange peels are good for keeping off ghosts. Stick some of those in your fireplace, too."

"Dried orange peels," I whispered. "Will do."

"Don't look so fuddled, child," said Mrs. Jackson, grinning. "We'll defeat that nasty haint. She got nothin' on Voodoo and Chinese magic. And whatever Mr. Prophet has in his pocket. You say that thing's Apache?"

"Yeah," said Mr. Prophet. "Mescalero Apache."

"Don't know what that kind of Apache is, but if you got more of them tokens, take 'em to Mr. Sam's house and lay 'em around here and there. Be sure all the windows are open during the day, too, but close them all at night. Haints don't like light. That's why you want as many lamps burnin' at night as you can get. You probably got on the electrics."

"Yes," I said. "We do."

"We're gettin' it here pretty soon. Along with telephones. Some folks around here got telephones, but the city fathers don't much care about us black and brown folk."

"I know. I hate it," I said, feeling guilty on behalf of my race.

"Oh, it ain't just you white folk," said Mrs. Jackson. "You let anybody get on somebody else's land, and you'll have trouble. It was mainly the Spanish did in the Injuns around here, and you got about as much Spanish in you as I have."

"And that's the depressing truth," said Harold. "You should talk to my houseboy, Roy Castillo, Mrs. Jackson."

"Where's he from?" she asked him.

"Tortuga."

"Ahhh. Yeah." She heaved a huge sigh. "All righty then, let me go gather up some sage and salt, and a few jujus to hang in different places. We'll fix you right up, Miss Daisy."

"Thank you," I said in a small voice. Then I thought about poor Regina. "Oh, there's also a ghost haunting the library. It seems to be the ghost of a mean old man who doesn't want the library to be replaced."

"He ain't tried to kill anyone yet?" asked Mrs. Jackson.

"He threw books at my librarian friend, but he hasn't gone as far as Stacy has. Yet."

Nodding, Mrs. Jackson said, "Pour salt around the library, put sage in the rooms, and place copper cent pieces in all the rooms there, too. It don't sound to me as if the library ghost is as evil as Stacy's."

"It would be difficult to be as evil as Stacy Kincaid, dead or alive," I said bitterly.

SIXTEEN

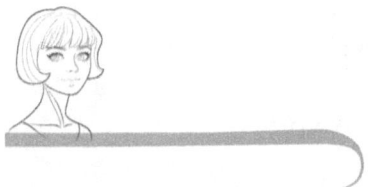

W hen Harold, Mr. Prophet, and I left Mrs. Jackson's home, both Harold and I carried cardboard boxes with us. Mine smelled rather like Thanksgiving. Harold's jangled. I got the sage; he got the jujus. Mr. Prophet carried a sack full of salt, so the only noise he made was the ka-thud of his peg and his boot as he walked.

"By God," muttered Mr. Prophet as we made our way to Harold's car, "she's the most powerful mambo I ever met, and she's here in Pasadena. By God."

"Technically, I think she's in Altadena," I muttered, walking carefully lest my carton fall and spill sage all over Mentone Avenue. It would probably keep the neighborhood free of ghosts, but sage on Mentone wouldn't assist us in protecting our house or the library.

"That's right," he said snidely. "You white folks don't want folks like the Jacksons living anywhere near you, huh?"

"The Jacksons could move in next door to me, and I wouldn't give a care," I snapped back. "I didn't make the stupid rules. And they *are* stupid. Look at this street! It's every bit as well-cared-for as Marengo. I think the city fathers are idiots. Anyhow, you're the one who fought for the Confederacy in the Civil War, trying to keep slaves slaves. My ancestors are Yankees, and we won."

"Stop fighting, children. I swear, you two are worse than siblings."

"We are not," I said.

"It's Miss Daisy," grumbled Mr. Prophet. "She brings out the worst in me."

"Likewise, I'm sure," I growled back.

"Stop it," said Harold, sounding more than a trifle forceful.

Both Mr. Prophet and I shut up.

Once we had stowed our boxes and Mr. Prophet's sack in the back seat of the Hispano-Suiza, and got into the car, Harold spoke again.

"What we're going to do from here is first, take Lou back to your place, Daisy." He bent over and looked across me at Mr. Prophet. "Does your Chinese lady friend live nearby? Oh, she's the one down the street in the big house, isn't she?"

"Yeah," said Mr. Prophet. "I kin go see her and ask if she can find any Fu dogs or Fu lions."

"What the heck are Fu dogs and Fu lions anyhow?" I asked.

"Chinese ghost repellants, evidently," said Harold. "It doesn't matter, Daisy. If Mrs. Jackson said we should get some if we can, we should get some if we can."

"Miss Li probably has other Chinese magic charms too," said Mr. Prophet in a meditative voice. "She's kinda like that Voodoo mambo, only she's a Cantonese wise woman."

"Like that Mescalero Apache wise woman?"

"Kinda. Only Miss Li's a lot better lookin' than Mrs. Tsedikezin."

"Only the best for you," I said sarcastically.

"You want my help or not?" he snarled.

"I'm sorry. Yes, I want your help. And Miss Li's. And anyone else's you can think of."

"Too bad Emilio's so far away," Mr. Prophet said musingly. "He's probably got some Tongva tokens to use against ghosts."

"He probably does," I said, thinking San Gabriel wasn't all *that* far away—Mr. Emilio DeLoera lived at the mission there—but it was too far for me to drive. Anywhere was too far for me to drive at the moment, thanks to Stacy Kincaid's ghost. Hmmm. Probably sage would work in the automobile. And maybe salt. And I could drop a couple of pennies —I beg your pardon. One-cent pieces—in the Chevrolet.

Might also be a mess to clean up. I'd wait to see about the Chevrolet.

"Let's just deal with what we have to deal with now. If you can get your lady friend to come to Daisy and Sam's place, Lou, maybe the two of you can start sprinkling salt and placing copper penn— um, I mean copper one-cent pieces in every corner of the house. I'll drive Daisy to my mother's house and take her home later. In the meantime, I'll talk to Roy. Maybe he has some Tortugan arcana we can use to fight my evil sister's evil ghost."

"Maybe you and Li can pick and peel some oranges, too," I suggested. "If I'm not there, I don't think Stacy can burn them in the oven. I guess it's only when I'm around— Oh, wait. That's not true. She bedeviled Mrs. Rattle, didn't she?"

"Yeah, she did. But I think Miss Li and I can keep her under control together," said Mr. Prophet.

"Thank you. I'm sorry I bring out the worst in you. I don't mean to. Not most of the time, anyway."

A rusty chuckle preceded Mr. Prophet's, "Yeah, I know it. Just like to give you a hard time, is all."

"Thanks heaps," I said.

"Do you have a key to Daisy's house?" asked Harold of Mr. Prophet.

"Yeah."

"Good. In case my sister's...What did Mrs. Jackson call her? A haint? In case my sister's haint has locked the doors, at least you have a key."

"I got other ways to get in too," said Mr. Prophet.

"You do? Even with your peg? I should think climbing through windows would be difficult for you."

"I wasn't talkin' about windows, fer gawd's sake," the old sinner said. "You just never mind how I do things. Miss Li and I will be able to get into your house." He squinted at me, saw me open my mouth and hurried to say, "Without breaking anything."

I heaved a sigh. "Thank you."

"Welcome."

So Harold dropped Mr. Prophet off at Mrs. Mainwaring's mansion down the street from my parents' house—because that's where Li Ahn lived—and then we went back up to Sam's and my house and dropped off our cartons and the sack of salt. We left them on the front porch, figuring that if they were meant to keep Stacy away, they'd keep Stacy away wherever we put them. I hoped we were right.

Then Harold drove us both to his mother's house. Again, he parked at the back of the house and we walked through the service porch and into the kitchen. Vi was there, cooking something that smelled wonderful. She smiled when she saw us.

"Oh, Daisy and Harold, I'm so glad you finally got here. Mrs. Pinkerton is in such a state about Stacy."

"I know she is," said Harold in a resigned voice.

"She should be thanking her lucky stars," I muttered.

"Daisy!" said my aunt in a reproving tone. "You don't have any idea what it's like to lose a child of your own."

She was right. "You're right. I'm sorry, Vi. I'm just so irked at Stacy's ghost for trying to kill my loved ones. Why isn't she haunting her mother? Why is she haunting *me*?"

"*What?*" Vi looked at me as if I'd lost my mind, and I only then recalled that she wasn't privy to Stacy's antics since her demise.

"Um…" I glanced at Harold.

"You go on and see my mother, Daisy. I'll tell Vi all about it."

"Thanks, Harold. I'm sorry, Vi," I said.

Then I stood up straight, tugged my lovely blue serge suit coat down, squared my shoulders, touched each of the good-luck charms I had on my gold chain, and gave a special squeeze to Billy's wedding ring. Then I hefted my bag of spiritualist nonsense and walked out of the kitchen and down the hall to the drawing room. I heard voices before I got there and thanked whoever might be in there for being in there so I wouldn't have to face Mrs. P alone.

Pausing outside the door, I listened to hear if I recognized any friendly voices.

And by golly, I did! Mrs. Bissel was in the drawing room! And so was Mrs. Hanratty! Two of my favorite people in the whole world. I was so glad, I darned near hyperventilated and fainted on the hall runner. I braced myself against the wall until I got my equilibrium back, then I walked into the drawing room.

As luck—bad in this case—would have it, Mrs. Pinkerton saw me first. The poor thing looked old and haggard and ill-used, but when she spied me, she squealed, "*Daisy!*" and leapt to her feet. In doing so, she upset a vase of flowers someone had given her. In fact, the place looked like a funeral parlor it was so full of flowers.

Reaching to set the vase upright and put the floral arrangement to right, Mrs. Bissel turned and smiled at me. "So good of you to come, Daisy."

"Ooooooh!" squealed Mrs. Pinkerton. And she collapsed back onto the sofa.

"Don't mind her," honked Mrs. Hanratty—her voice sounded like she was talking into a barrel and reminded me of a goose. "She's been fainting and crying all day long."

"Oh dear. I'm sorry," I said. "But I'm really glad you and Mrs. Bissel are here, Mrs. Hanratty."

"When I telephoned," said Mrs. Bissel, grabbing a doily and mopping up water, "Madeline told me you'd be visiting her today. I figured you might need reinforcements."

"Madeline said you found the body. That must have been awful," said Mrs. Hanratty, who'd picked up one of Mrs. Pinkerton's limp wrists and was chafing it.

"It was awful, all right," I told her honestly. "Mr. Prophet and I had walked to the gazebo in the library's park, and that's where we found her. It was just...horrid." I shuddered, remembering.

"I heard she'd been stabbed," Mrs. Bissel whispered. "Bother. I don't think this doily is going to get all this water up."

Peering at the puddle from the fallen vase, I agreed with her. "Let me find Featherstone or Edie Applewood. They'll know where the towels are," I said.

"Don't bother," said Harold from behind me. I turned to see him walking into the drawing room.

"How's Vi?" I whispered when he got close enough for him to hear a whisper.

"Shocked but recovering."

"Allow me." Featherstone, who had recovered a hundred percent —perhaps more—of his dignity, glided into the room, carrying a towel in one hand and a pitcher of water in another.

Mrs. Bissel rose from the sofa, dropping Mrs. Pinkerton's still-limp wrist onto a cushion. "I was trying to wipe it up with this"—she held out the dripping doily for Featherstone's inspection—"but it didn't work."

"I shall repair any damage, Mrs. Bissel," said Featherstone in his crisp English accent.

"Thanks, Featherstone," said Harold and Mrs. Bissel together. Harold added, "Why'd she faint?" He glanced at me and saw me still holding my embroidered bag.

"She just did," I said, feeling guilty and helpless. "I hadn't even got out the Ouija board yet."

"This is a terrible time for her," said Mrs. Hanratty. "She's over-wrought. I know she's been looking forward to Daisy's visit."

"Ah. I see," said Harold. He stepped aside as Featherstone carried the sopping towel, doily, and vase with its disarranged flowers toward the drawing-room door. Guess he thought more than water from the pitcher was required in this instance.

A knock came at the front door. Featherstone stopped in his tracks and looked from right to left and back again, I guess trying to think of where to put all the stuff he was carrying so he could answer the door.

Harold saved the day. "I'll get the door, Featherstone. Go ahead and fix the flowers."

"Thank you, Mr. Harold," said Featherstone, unruffled.

So Harold got the door. Mrs. Hanratty and Mrs. Bissel propped up Mrs. Pinkerton between them on the sofa, and Mrs. Bissel withdrew a vial from the pocket of her perfectly gorgeous, if large, two-piece cream-colored suit. She opened the vial and held it under Mrs. Pinkerton's nose.

And that did the trick. With a "Yeek!" of shock, Mrs. P sat upright on the sofa and attempted to swat Mrs. Bissel's hand away. Mrs. Bissel, who knew Mrs. P of old, had already removed her hand from swatting distance.

In a firm but soothing voice, Mrs. Bissel said, "Get your nerves under control, Madeline. Daisy is here, and if you'll let her she may be able to help you in this time of sorrow."

"Daisy?" Mrs. Pinkerton looked blank for a second or three, then sat to attention. "Daisy! Oh, *Daisy*, you've come!"

"Indeed, I have. I'm so sorry I couldn't be here earlier." I decided not to explain further.

"It's good of you to visit, dear," said Mrs. Bissel. "How are Spike and Rosebud getting along?"

"Beautifully," I told her truthfully. "Rosebud's a little on the wild side, but Pa wants to take her to the next class Mrs. Hanratty holds at Brookside Park." I smiled at Mrs. Hanratty.

"An excellent idea," said Mrs. Hanratty. "How old is the dog? Rosebud, did you say?"

"Yes. My parents call her Rosie. She's about three years old, isn't she, Mrs. Bissel?"

"Yes. She's just about three."

"Good. That should work. I doubt she'll be as cooperative as Spike because you got him to class when he was a couple of years younger, but you're good at working with dogs." Mrs. Hanratty gave me an approving smile.

Harold walked into the room carrying a gigantic floral display. "Where do you want me to put this, Mother?" he asked, trying not to sound grumpy.

"Flowers? More flowers?" Mrs. Pinkerton began dithering. I recognized the signs.

"Just put them on the table here," suggested Mrs. Bissel. "Featherstone can find another place for the ones he took out."

"Grand idea," said Harold, executing Mrs. B's suggestion with alacrity. "All right now, Mother. No more fainting. Daisy is here to help you. She can't stay here all day because she's been having car trouble, and I'll have to take her home. In the meantime, I need to get a few things done at my house. So I'll be back here in an hour. Don't keep Daisy any longer than that." He spoke with benign authority.

"Oh, dear. Oh, Daisy, is your auto all right?"

"It will be, Mrs. Pinkerton. Don't fuss about my car. I'm here to help you right now, so what would you like to do first? Would you like to consult Rolly with the Ouija board or would you prefer that I read the cards first?"

"Oh," said Mrs. Pinkerton in a confused tone of voice. "Oh." She pressed her hands to her ravaged cheeks. "Oh, I just don't know. What do you suggest, dear? You're the expert."

Right. "How about we use the Ouija board first?" I said then glanced hopelessly around the drawing room, trying to discern a flat surface upon which to put the board. Or the tarot cards, for that matter. Every single surface had been covered with floral arrangements. "Um, we'll have to clear a space, I guess."

"I'll do that before I go," said Harold, who never dithered, thank God. He marched to the table upon which he'd just set the latest sympathy bouquet, lifted it, and carried it out of the drawing room. "I'll put this somewhere else for a while. Maybe the kitchen. Mrs. Gumm can use some cheering up, too."

I'm sure that was true, especially after Harold explained to Vi about Stacy's ghost having taken up haunting me. "Thanks, Harold," I said.

"I'll come back in an hour," he said. "Be ready to leave when I get here."

"Yes, sir," I said. An hour would be too long to spend with a bereaved and hysterical Mrs. Pinkerton, but I'd spend it anyway. It was my duty.

Opening my embroidered velvet container and recalling having done so at my own home, I slid the Ouija board out onto the table without touching it with my own personal fingers. Nothing except the board slithered out, so I did the same thing with the planchette's embroidered velvet case. Again, only the desired item slid out of its container.

"Very well, Mrs. Pinkerton," I said, attempting to sound sweet but firm, which wasn't easy. "You need to recall that you can only ask questions pertaining to yourself." I'd been Ouija-boarding with Mrs. Pinkerton for more than half my life, and I *always* told her the same thing. Previously she'd ignored my injunction and insisted upon asking questions regarding Stacy. Now that Stacy was dead, maybe I was safe.

I should have known better.

"Who killed my daughter?" she asked instantly.

"It's probably too soon to ask that question," I told her, forgoing Rolly for the time being. "It often takes a spirit a while to adjust to the world on the Other Side."

"Oh, dear," she said. "I know. I know." She stopped, bowed her head, and sucked in a deep breath. Then she said, being pertinent for once, "Rolly, when will the pain go away?"

Good question and one Rolly could answer. I had him spell out, "It will ease, but it will never cease entirely."

Rolly wrote from my own experience.

"Oh, dear," she said again. "Is there any way to know precisely what happened to my daughter?" she asked forlornly.

Good old Rolly spelled out, "The police will find that out."

"But don't you know when?" she said piteously.

"No," wrote Rolly. It was the truth. I didn't know, so he didn't know.

SEVENTEEN

From the tail of my eye, I'd noticed Mrs. Bissel becoming fidgety. She was a commonsensical woman who knew how to deal with Rolly and the Ouija board—and Mrs. Pinkerton. She didn't ordinarily fidget, but suddenly she burst out, "Madeline, ask Rolly questions he can answer, for pity's sake! How can he know what happened in that park? He can only answer questions about *you*. Perhaps you should request advice on what you can do now in order to feel better. I can't even imagine losing Dennis"—Dennis was Mrs. Bissel's son—"but mothers all over the world have lost children, and most of them have survived with considerably fewer resources than you have available to you."

"Oh!" said Mrs. Pinkerton, shocked. "Griselda, you're being cruel." Griselda was Mrs. Bissel's first name.

"No I'm not. It's the truth. First we had that horrible war, and then we had that influenza epidemic, and mothers lost children to both of those catastrophes. You and I are fortunate to have money and the wherewithal to assist us. Can you imagine a poor French mother whose only child was killed during that horrible war? Or a woman who, to this day, doesn't know if her child is alive or dead?

You and I don't have those problems, although we all have our sorrows. I think you should ask Rolly what you can do to help yourself feel better during these painful days instead of screaming and fainting."

"Oh!" whispered Mrs. Pinkerton once more.

"Listen to Griselda, Madeline," hooted Pansy Hanratty. "She's right, you know."

A brilliant idea occurred to me. Maybe. Have I mentioned it sometimes takes a while to determine if any idea is actually brilliant or not? Well, it does.

After gulping and wiping her dripping eyes with a sodden handkerchief, Mrs. Pinkerton said, "Perhaps you're correct, Griselda."

"She's correct," honked Mrs. Hanratty.

"Well, then," said Mrs. Pinkerton in a hesitant voice, "perhaps I'll give the matter some thought."

That would be the day. The day Mrs. Pinkerton thought about anything, I mean. That's unkind of me. I'm sorry.

At any rate, Mrs. P sat still for several seconds, then said, "Rolly, is there anything I can do that might make me feel less pain about Stacy's horrible murder?"

Rolly instantly sent the planchette to the word "Yes" painted on the top left corner of the Ouija board.

"Oh?" Mrs. P sounded surprised. "What do you suggest?"

"The only people who never gave up on Stacy are those at the Salvation Army. Donations to the Salvation Army in Stacy's name might help ease your woe."

Good old Rolly! Exactly what I'd have written. Well, I did write it. But you know what I mean.

"Oh," said Mrs. Pinkerton, still surprised. "You're right, Rolly. In fact, Captain Buckingham came over here as soon as he heard the news of her p-p-passing." She sobbed into her hankie once more.

"There you go," said Mrs. Bissel. "I knew Rolly would be able to suggest something worthwhile."

"Absolutely," agreed Mrs. Hanratty. "Excellent suggestion."

Rolly wasn't through with Mrs. Pinkerton. He then wrote, "And join the library guild. The new library will open early next year."

"But that's where Stacy was k-killed!" howled Mrs. Pinkerton.

"She was killed in the library park. The park will be gone when the new library opens," wrote Rolly. "You can help erase the site of her foul murder."

Very well, so Rolly just suggested something to which I wasn't looking forward: the destruction of the beautiful old library and its grounds. Donating funds and time might assist Mrs. P in dealing with her grief. There wasn't anything I—or the ghost of that awful man haunting the place—could do to stop the library's demolition. Any distraction in a time of heartache might assist the poor woman, however.

"Oh. Oh. Yes, I see," said Mrs. Pinkerton. "Perhaps that's a good idea."

"It's a wonderful idea," said Mrs. Bissel. "And don't you belong to the board at the Women's Hospital? Perhaps you can donate some time and money there too."

"And don't forget the Pasadena Humane Society," said Mrs. Hanratty. Except for her son, the stunningly gorgeous Monty Mountjoy who was a brilliant star in the Hollywoodland firmament, Mrs. Hanratty preferred dogs to people. I understood perfectly.

"Excellent idea," Rolly spelled out.

"Oh, of course," said Mrs. Pinkerton, forgetting to cry for a moment. "I held a party in aid of the Pasadena Humane Society once. Do you remember that, Daisy?"

"I certainly do," I said, recalling with fondness the fortune teller's tent Harold had created for me. "That's an excellent idea."

"And the Pasanita Dog Obedience Club is another worthwhile charity," said Mrs. Hanratty who, as mentioned earlier, taught classes for the club.

"Indeed it is," I said. "Spike went to obedience school there. They worked wonders."

"There," said Mrs. Bissel. "You have some great ideas. There's no way you can *not* grieve for your lost child, although she caused you nothing but trouble through the years, but you can think beyond your pain and do some good in the world."

Boy, I wish I'd said that. Of course, as a spiritualist-medium paid to give aid and comfort to the bereaved woman, I couldn't have. But Mrs. Bissel was correct. Stacy had been a pain in the neck.

"Sh-she wasn't all bad," whimpered Mrs. Pinkerton. "When she was a little girl, she was a sweet little thing."

"Mmm," said Mrs. Bissel, whose son was Stacy's age. It sounded to me as if she remembered Stacy's childhood a bit differently from Mrs. Pinkerton.

"Mmm," said Mrs. Hanratty.

I glanced at the two women, both of whom had screwed up their faces into moues of distaste. Okay, so they both had memories of Stacy's little girlhood different from those of Mrs. Pinkerton. Mine were too, although I hadn't really come to know her until I began working for her mother. But Stacy had always been condescending to me when she wasn't outright rude. Icky person, overall, from the beginning to the end. And even after the end, curse it. Curse her, if it came to that.

"All right, Daisy, why isn't your spiritualist mumbo-jumbo put away yet?" asked Harold as he marched into the drawing room, making us all give starts of alarm. "You've had more than an hour here. If you haven't helped Mother in more than an hour, you'll never do it."

"Good Lord, has it been that long?" I said, surprised.

"Oh, Harold, she's been an absolute blessing!" said Mrs. Pinkerton, almost smiling.

"She has been helpful," said Mrs. Bissel.

"Indeed," said Mrs. Hanratty.

"Good. Then pack it up and let's go. I have things to do," said Harold.

I hurriedly packed up my Ouija board and planchette. "We'll do a tarot reading another time, Mrs. Pinkerton," I told the poor woman. Rich woman. Fiddlesticks. "But please consider putting everyone's suggestions into actions. They won't cure your pain, but perhaps they will ease your unhappiness as you help others."

Harold grabbed my arm as soon as I had everything packed away and hauled me toward the drawing-room door. "Do as she says, Mother," he called over his shoulder.

"I shall, Harold," hollered Mrs. Pinkerton. "Thank you, Daisy!"

"Thank you, Mrs. Pinkerton," I called back.

As soon as we got to the hall, I yanked my arm from Harold's grip. "What the heck is wrong with you, Harold Kincaid? Why'd you drag me out of there like that? I'd have come on my own, you know."

"Why the devil were you thanking *her*?" barked Harold, not answering my question.

"Because she pays me," I said.

"Guess that's a good reason. But listen. I stopped by the library on my way back to Mother's place, and one of those uniformed fellows—Doan? Is that his name?"

"Stephen Doan is a policeman, yes," I said.

"Well, he's going to drive your car home. Some other fellow will follow him in a police car and then drive him back to the station."

"It was nice of you to consider how to get the Chevrolet back to my parents' place, Harold. Thank you."

"I didn't do it. Sam did. I went to the library to sprinkle salt and sage and pennies here and there."

"I thought we didn't have pennies in the U.S.A."

"I don't care what we have," said a thoroughly peeved Harold. "Everyone calls them pennies, so they're pennies. Your friend Regina was in a state almost as bad as one of Mother's."

"No! You're kidding. What happened?"

"The nasty ghost dropped a book on her, and her specs fell off and broke. Well, they bent. They're all cockeyed now."

"Poor Regina!" I said as we shoved the pantry door open on our way to the kitchen.

"What's the matter with Regina?" asked Vi, turning from the oven, from which she'd just lifted a fragrant and perfect loaf of bread.

I heard Harold mutter, "Hell," under his breath.

150

"She broke her glasses at work," I told Vi, deciding to leave the malevolent library ghost out of my explanation.

"I don't suppose that's too much of a catastrophe," said Vi, taking off her own cheaters and looking at them. From where I stood, they looked a trifle floury.

"She told me she's blind as a bat without them," said Harold.

"I hope she has a spare pair at home," said Vi.

"She telephoned her husband. He's going to bring her the spare," Harold assured her.

"That's good. What were you doing at the library, Harold?" asked Vi. "Do you have to do anything there because of your sister?"

"I stopped by because I knew the good detective would be there, and I wanted to ask him a couple of questions about what happens now."

I peered at Harold. "What do you mean, 'what happens now'?"

Harold drew out a kitchen chair and waved for me to sit in it. So I did. He pulled out another one for Vi, so she sat too. Then he got one for himself, turned it around, straddled it and folded his arms over the back. "I need to find out precisely what rigmarole my mother and Algie will have to deal with now that Stacy's been violently removed from this life. I mean, they'll have to do an autopsy—"

"Ew," said Vi, wrinkling her nose.

"Standard practice, according to Sam, when there's been a murder. Or even an unattended death. Then, depending on what the results are, they may need to keep the body for a while before it can be released for burial. I was hoping Sam could give me an approximation of how long this will take, but of course he can't, because he doesn't know."

"Did they find anything that might point to her killer?" I asked. I'd have asked Sam, but he wouldn't tell me.

"Oddly enough, yes, although I'm not supposed to know," said Harold.

"What do you mean you're not supposed to know?" I asked.

"I overheard a conversation I wasn't supposed to hear," said

151

Harold with an impish—or, perhaps, evil—grin. "They're convinced a woman did it."

"A woman killed your sister?" Vi asked, sounding amazed.

"I figured it was a woman when we found two sets of ladies' footprints in the mud," I said. "Mr. Prophet and I had to sit on a bench, but we kind of looked around, and there were two sets of footprints, and they were both from high-heeled shoes. I suspect one of them was from Stacy's shoes, and the other was from another woman's shoes. Unless she knows any men who wear high-heeled shoes."

"I'm not saying a word," Harold muttered softly.

Deciding to ignore his comment because I didn't want to shock my aunt, I said, "They took impressions of the shoe prints this morning, I think. That's what they said they were going to do anyway."

"Yes, they did," said Harold.

"You don't know the names of any of Stacy's female friends, right?" I asked Harold.

"I already told you I didn't. I tried to stay as far away from Stacy as I could. Anyhow, in these past couple of years, she's either been on the run, in jail, or in the jail ward of the hospital. I didn't visit." His voice was as dry as a mummy's thumb.

"Maybe a jail wardress will know the names of any friends she made in jail," I said, thinking out loud.

"Maybe. I'm sure not going to the jail to ask," said Harold.

"Oh, Harold, you sound so coldhearted," said Aunt Vi pityingly. "Think of your poor mother."

"I am thinking of my poor mother," said Harold in a hard voice. "Stacy caused her nothing but misery from the time she was…oh, maybe four years old." He shook his head. "She caused everyone trouble. Face it, Mrs. Gumm, Stacy was a chip off the old paternal block. She got all of our father's ghastly traits and none of our mother's…not-so-ghastly ones."

"I'm so lucky to have my mother and father," I said, thinking Harold and Stacy had lost out on the parental sweepstakes. They'd grown up with money, but precious little else.

"Yes, you are," said Vi.

"Yes, you are," said Harold.

"And even my brother and sister," I went on, thinking about how my big brother Walter used to tease me and my big sister Daphne used to get mad at me for borrowing her clothes. Now we were good friends, although they lived in different cities and we didn't see each other very often.

"Lucky you," said Harold. "But listen, Daisy, let's get you home. I know you have a lot of stuff to do there. I didn't stop to see if Lou and his lady friend were working on the house."

"Do you really think your sister's ghost is haunting Daisy, Harold?" asked Vi, shaking her head.

"Yes," said Harold.

"It sounds incredible," said Vi. "And kind of insane, to tell the truth."

"It's both of those things," I told my aunt. "But she darned near made me crash the car, and she drove poor Mrs. Rattle to tears. And she hurt Spike!" That last one really irked me. Anybody who would hurt my dog deserved to rot in Hades.

"I still don't understand what's going on, but I guess you know best," said Vi. "Why don't you and Sam come to dinner tonight? Harold said it's not safe for you to use the stove at your house."

"Thanks, Vi. She might be able to follow me wherever I go— although she hasn't messed with me in her mother's house." It hadn't occurred to me before to wonder why she hadn't, actually. Stacy'd always treated her mother like dirt. I didn't know why she wasn't bedeviling me in her mother's house.

"I think she's afraid of Mrs. Jackson," said Harold.

"Mrs. Jackson?" said Vi, puzzled.

"We visited Mrs. Jackson this morning," I told her. "She gave us a lot of things to ward off evil. I guess some of the sage and salt stuck to my hands or something."

"Oh, is that what I've been smelling?" said Vi. "Interesting. Sage, eh?"

"And salt. And copper one-cent pieces," said Harold. "We've got to get Daisy home to see if Mr. Prophet's lady friend has found any Fu dogs or Fu lions. They're supposed to keep ghosts away, too."

Vi stared at us as if we were a couple of strangers in Harold and Daisy costumes. "Whatever you say, dears."

"Honestly, Vi, I'll tell you everything once we get it figured out," I promised. "I can hardly believe it myself—but I heard her cackle at me!"

"Good Lord," said Vi faintly.

Harold and I took our leave.

EIGHTEEN

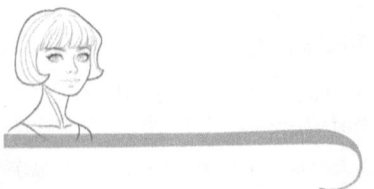

B y George, when Harold drove me home, it was clear that both
Mr. Prophet and Miss Li had been hard at work. As soon as I
stepped out of Harold's Hispano-Suiza, I saw a little path of salt
leading from the sidewalk, up the front walkway and to the porch.
When I opened the front porch gate, the drizzle continued on the
porch.

"We salted the driveway and all the way around the house, too,"
came Mr. Prophet's rusty voice from the front door.

"Thank you!" I said, looking at him with awe. "Did you have
any trouble getting behind the camellia bushes?"

"Miss Li said the salt wouldn't be good for the camellias, so we
sprinkled sage there and dumped some dried orange peels and
juniper berries." Mr. Prophet didn't even sound disgruntled.

"If *I'd* told you salt wasn't good for the camellias, you wouldn't
have paid me any attention," I said, feeling underappreciated.

"You ain't Miss Li," said he.

He was right about that. "And what did you say about juniper
berries?"

"Nothin'," said Mr. Prophet.

"Good afternoon, Daisy," came Li Ahn's lovely voice. She

walked up behind Mr. Prophet, put a hand on his shoulder, and nudged him over a pace.

"Good afternoon. Thanks so much for helping us with this project." Harold and I walked to the front door, the couple standing there stepped aside, and we entered the house. "Wow, it smells good in here!"

"Sage and orange," said Li. "Along with several bundles of dried juniper and some plum flowers."

"Oh. I didn't know juniper and plum flowers repelled ghosts."

"I don't know that they do, but they're used in Chinese preparations, and they can't be any worse for your home than salt, sage, and dried orange peels. Besides, except for the salt, they all smell good." She laughed her pretty tinkling laugh.

"Hmm," I said. "Maybe we should plant some juniper bushes. I think junipers grow well here."

"Yes. There are juniper bushes all over the place in Pasadena," said Li.

"I've never even noticed them," I admitted.

"No surprise there," grumped Mr. Prophet.

"Cut it out, you two," said Harold. "Need me to place copper pennies anywhere? And don't tell me we don't use pennies in the United States."

"Wouldn't dream of it," said Mr. Prophet with a creaky chuckle. "I think Miss Li and I managed to put copper pennies in all the corners of all the rooms."

"Including the closets?" I asked, feeling like an idiot as I did so.

"Including the closets," said Li. "And I brought over four Fu statues. I'm not sure where to put them."

"May I see them? I don't think I've ever seen a Fu dog or a Fu lion."

"You probably have if you've ever been to Chinatown in Los Angeles," said Li. "They're all over the place. They're supposed to keep evil spirits at bay. And, really, Fu dogs and Fu lions are the same thing. They're called lion dogs."

"Yet something else I didn't know," I said, feeling even more like an idiot than I did before. I braced myself for another snipe from Mr. Prophet, but Li spoke first.

"Well, why should you?" she asked, "You're not Chinese. They're part of our culture. I think you use horseshoes for luck." She squinted at Mr. Prophet. "Do I have that right, Lou?"

After huffing out a disparaging puff of air, Mr. Prophet said, "Some folks put horseshoes up for luck. I prefer Injun tokens myself."

"That makes sense," I said, thinking it made no sense at all. "After all, you scared Stacy's ghost away with that Apache thing you brandished."

"I'd like to see the lion dogs," said Harold. "Then I have to go."

"Sure," said Li. "Lou and I put them on the kitchen table. I think they'd be better guardians at the front and back doors, but you can decide that, Daisy."

"I think you're the one who knows what's best to do with them," I told Li.

"Front and back doors it is," said Mr. Prophet, making up everybody's minds for us. "Harold, you and I gotta carry 'em, because they're heavy."

"Oh!" I said, "How'd you get them in here?" A crippled old man and a delicate Chinese lady seemed an odd pair to be carrying heavy Chinese statuary around.

"Cyrus helped," said Li.

"Ah, of course." I nodded.

Cyrus Potts worked for Mrs. Mainwaring as...Well, I'm not sure what he did. I know he chauffeured her around here and there, but I think he had other duties as well. His wife, Hattie, worked as Mrs. Mainwaring's cook, and she was rumored to be as talented in the kitchen as Aunt Vi. She sure made a great apricot pound cake, but that's all I knew for certain about her culinary skills.

The house did in fact smell good as we walked from the front entry and past the living room to the hallway. I noticed Li had arranged a little bowl of juniper berries, dried sage, and dried orange peels in a tiny bowl on the telephone table. Maybe I'd keep little bowls of that sort of thing in the house even after we got rid of Stacy's ghost. If we ever did.

Out of curiosity, I asked, "What did you do with the fireplace?"

"Sprinkled a ton of salt in there, then dumped some sage and juniper and orange peels on the salt. You kin have a fire in there tonight, and it should smell great," said Mr. Prophet with a chuckle.

"Thank you. You two have thought of— Oh, my Lord!"

The last, loud, part of my sentence was yanked from my mouth when I walked into the kitchen and saw the four enormous Chinese figurines sitting and staring balefully at all of us from the kitchen table.

"You wanted Fu dogs. You got Fu dogs," said Mr. Prophet.

"Wow, I didn't know what they were," I said, awed.

"I've seen some of those things at friends' houses," said Harold. "They're quite...um..."

"Ugly?" suggested Li with a smile.

"No! Not ugly," said Harold. I could tell he meant his words. "Intimidating, I think is the word I was looking for. And interesting."

"You can see that one pair looks more like dogs and the other looks more like lions," said Li, gesturing at the quartet of...ornaments? Not sure what to call them. It appeared to me as if one pair was made of marble (maybe) and the other of some kind of metal. Bronze? I had no idea.

"Wow. If I came across one of those guys in the dark, I'd sure be intimidated," I said, confirming Harold's choice of adjectives.

"Li says you should put one on each side of the door. On the outside," said Mr. Prophet.

"Oh, they go outside?"

"Generally, yes," said Li. "If they're this big, they do. I can probably find some smaller ones if you want a pair on the fireplace mantel."

"That's okay," I said. "I think Mrs. Jackson gifted us with some Voodoo statuary to put on the mantel."

"You're going to scare away every evil spirit from all over the world," said Li, grinning. "You've got, what did you say? Apache?

Apache charms, Chinese guardians, Voodoo talismans, and about a dozen cultures' worth of herbs to protect you. I think your ghost will have a hard time getting through."

"I sure hope so," I said.

"So, let's carry these Fu characters to the doors," said Harold. "Where do you want which ones?"

I looked at Li, who put a hand to her chin, gazed at the two sets of guardian statues, and thought. Finally, she said, "Put the marble ones outside the front door. They'll be protected there."

"I thought they were supposed to protect Daisy," said Harold.

"Well, yes," said Li. "But they're marble, for Pete's sake! I don't want them to get ruined by weather, should we have any." She turned, looked apologetically at me and added, "If you could keep the dog from peeing on them, it would help too."

I didn't say anything, but my confidence in her Chinese talismans began to wane slightly. I mean, if a guardian lion could be pitted by dog pee, rain, or hail, what good was it? Guess I'd find out.

"Oomph," said Harold, as he lifted one of the heavy bronze lion dogs. "Crumb, these are heavy."

"Want me to call for Cyrus to help?" asked Li. "I'm sure he wouldn't mind."

"No, no," said Harold. "I'll sacrifice my back for the sake of Daisy's safety. I feel kind of responsible—oof!—because it's my sister who's haunting her."

"Daisy, I think you and I can carry the other one," said Li, gesturing to the second marble lion dog.

"I kin get it," said Mr. Prophet huffily.

"You be still," said Li.

"Yeah," I told him. "You've done enough today."

Boy, that marble statue was heavy! But Li and I hauled it out the front door and sat it on the porch. Harold had dumped—I mean carefully settled—the first one to the left of the door, so we sat ours to the door's right.

"Whew!" I said, shaking out my arms.

"You shouldn't have carried that!" Harold hollered at me.

"You're going to lose that baby if you don't stop carrying heavy stuff and running all over the place!"

Whirling and staring at me with horror, Li said, "You're *pregnant*? Why didn't you tell me? Lou and I could have carried that monstrous thing!"

"I'm all right," I assured them. "I'm not sick or crippled. I'm pregnant. I thought women in China had babies in rice paddies and then slung the newborns in sacks over their backs and went back to working in the rice paddies."

"I've read that too," said Li. "But I don't believe it. And you may *not* carry either of those bronze lions. Harold and I can carry them."

Mr. Prophet said, "I kin—"

"Hush up, Lou," said Li, sounding downright menacing. Maybe she'd be willing to stand guard at a window or something.

"Hellkatoot," muttered Mr. Prophet.

"Good for us," said Harold, not overjoyed but game.

So they did. Harold and Li set each bronze lion dog—in truth, the bronze ones seemed more like dogs than lions—on either side of the back door. They looked positively ferocious.

"I really like those lion dogs," I told Li. "Maybe if Sam will let me, I'll get some and put them beside the back door."

"Just don't carry them yourself," she told me. "I think that's a myth about women giving birth in rice paddies and instantly returning to work, by the way. Not unless somebody urged them on with a whip. The whip scenario wouldn't surprise me much, given the value of women in Chinese society."

"Oh, dear, is it even worse than it is here?" I asked, thinking women *never* received proper respect for their contributions to society. Have you ever heard of any of America's Founding Mothers? No? Neither have I. Dolley Madison springs to mind as a brave soul, but she's an exception, and nobody would ever talk about her if she'd rescued, say, her mother's portrait from the White House walls instead of George Washington's as the British burned our Capitol.

"Much worse than here," said Li. "Why, do you think Evangeline could own an orange grove in China? Ha!"

Mrs. Evangeline Mainwaring, as I might have mentioned, lived down the street from us on Marengo. What I didn't mention until now is that her home was the very first one built on Marengo, and it's a mansion. Whoever built the place began selling off lots upon which to build other homes before Mrs. Mainwaring bought it, but she could only manage to purchase it because she'd become wildly wealthy growing oranges. And doing other things, but those are best not spoken of.

"That's a shame," I said.

"Huh," said Mr. Prophet.

"Most of the females I've known in my life have been either like my mother or like my sister," said Harold. "I know most women aren't dimwitted or evil, but if the only ones a fellow is exposed to are like those two, I think he can be forgiven for believing women are of less worth than men."

"Harold Kincaid, you take that back!" I snapped at him.

He held up both hands in an I-give-up gesture. "I didn't say *I* believe it! I know better, but that's only because I've *learned* better."

"Huh. All right then," I said grudgingly.

After sharing a laugh, Li and I toured the house. She pointed out where each copper cent piece was placed in every room and closet, indicated several more pretty bowls with fragrant ghost-repelling herbs in them, and explained a few Chinese knickknacks she'd set out in various places. We ended our tour in the utility room.

"Thank you so much, Li," I told her.

"Not a problem," she told me. Then she gestured at the utility room. "There are more windows in this room than anywhere else in the house, so I opened them all. Be sure to shut them before it gets dark, and keep as many lights on in the house as you can stand."

"Mrs. Jackson—she's the Voodoo mambo—told us the same thing about lights," I murmured. "I guess some evil-spirit repellants are universal."

With a chuckle, Li said, "I guess they are. But I'd better get going now. Lou is going to stay overnight in this house with you and Sam until the Stacy problem is solved permanently."

"Yes, he offered to stay in the house."

"Good for him," Li said. "He's an old rogue, but he's dealt with ghosts before."

"I know," I said.

"Even before your Tongva ghost," said Li. "Maybe you can get him to tell you about the Mescalero witch."

"Is she the one who gave him the Mescalero amulet or whatever it is?"

"Oh, no. She's the one who tormented him into asking the Mescalero wise woman to make him an amulet."

"Interesting!" I said. "He probably won't tell me. I annoy him."

"He's just a grouchy old goat," said Li with a smile.

Couldn't argue with her there.

NINETEEN

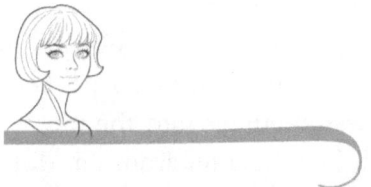

Shortly after I bade farewell to Li and she began walking down the street toward Mrs. Mainwaring's house, I saw her wave her arms in the air over her head. Squinting, it took me a few seconds to realize she was being pelted with dried peppercorns from the pepper trees creating a canopy over Marengo Avenue.

"*Stacy!*" I shrieked. "Stop it!"

Harold walked up behind me. "Huh? What are you yelling about?"

"Look! I'm sure Stacy's the one hurling those peppercorns at Li!" I pointed. Li had started running. Fortunately, Mrs. Mainwaring's house wasn't too far away, but I felt bad that Li should be rewarded for helping us by being bombarded with peppercorns.

"What's goin' on?" asked Mr. Prophet, looming over both Harold and me from behind. He was even taller than Sam, although he stooped a bit.

Again I pointed at Li, who was graceful as a gazelle as she dashed down the middle of Marengo Avenue. "Stacy's ghost is flinging peppercorns at her!"

"Shit," said Mr. Prophet. "I should'a give her one o' them Voodoo jujus."

"I should have thought of doing that too," I said, feeling guilty for not having anticipated this sort of thing. "Stacy isn't going to approve of anyone who tries to help us."

"Well," said Mr. Prophet philosophically. "If there's any woman in the world can save herself, it's Li. Look there. She's reachin' into her pocket."

By this time, it was difficult for me to see Li through the thick foliage of the pepper trees, but I could just make out what Mr. Prophet had seen. Li did reach into her pocket. When she removed her hand, she threw something into the air. It looked like sand or something, although I couldn't tell from this distance.

I did hear a loud, "*Eeeeeeee!*" issue from the air around Li, and the peppercorn storm stopped instantly.

"Ha," said Mr. Prophet in a satisfied voice. "Told ya so."

"I wonder what she threw at Stacy," I said.

"Could'a been salt," said Mr. P.

"Or juniper berries," said Harold.

"Li, she's got her own magic," said Mr. Prophet. "Stacy better not mess with her."

"I don't want Stacy to mess with her either," I told him. "I appreciate her help so much. And yours too."

"What about mine?" asked Harold, pretending to be offended.

"I appreciate your help, too, Harold. In fact, you help me all the time."

"Better believe it," he said. "But I'm going home, too. If Mother isn't still in a state tomorrow, we really should figure out what to do with Stacy's body. I mean, her physical body. We know where her non-physical body went."

"You mean her soul? Is her soul the ghost?" I asked, honestly curious.

"Did she have a soul?" asked Harold.

"If she did, it was a rotten one. Her dead body will be decomposing pretty soon too," I said. Mean of me, I know.

"Ew. Daisy!" said Harold reproachfully.

"They keep corpses in refrigerated rooms," I said. "At least I think they do. I'll ask Sam."

"I expect they do," said Mr. Prophet. "You either got to freeze 'em or plant 'em fast. The weather ain't been too hot, so she might keep for a few days. They begin to stink something fierce after a couple of days otherwise."

"Good God," whimpered Harold who looked as if he might faint, so I stuck an oar in.

"I think the medical examiner has to do an autopsy first. That might delay a burial, although I don't know it for a fact." And I still didn't know if Stacy had possessed a soul and if it was her soul haunting me.

"Oh, gawd, Mother's going to screech when she hears about the autopsy."

"So don't tell her," I suggested. "She most likely won't ask."

"I suppose you're right. Okay. I'm going now. Call if you need me."

"Thank you, Harold." I threw my arms around him and gave him a big hug. "I don't know what I'd do without you."

"Good Lord, there's no need for that," said Harold. But he hugged me back. "And I don't know what you'd do without me either."

The telephone began ringing, so I didn't wait to see Harold and Mr. Prophet shake hands.

"Rotondo residence. Mrs. Rotondo speaking," I said into the mouthpiece.

"Daisy, did you and Harold get home all right?"

"Vi! Yes, we did, and I think we, Mr. Prophet, and Miss Ahn from down the street ghost-proofed our house."

Vi didn't speak for a minute. Maybe two minutes.

Thinking perhaps we'd been cut off, I said, "Vi? Are you there?"

"Yes, I'm here." Another pause ensued. Then she said, "You know, Daisy, I don't really believe in ghosts and so forth.

After heaving a huge sigh, I said, "I didn't used to either. I mean, when I started being a spiritualist-medium, I thought it was all hooey. Unfortunately, I learned better a few years ago. Really and truly Vi, Stacy has started playing havoc in my life. I hope we've

Stacy-proofed the house, but we still have to figure out some way to get rid of her forever."

"She's dead, Daisy," Vi reminded me. "That's about as gone-forever as a person can get."

"Her spirit didn't go to heaven, Vi. It stuck around, and it's haunting me."

"That sounds crazy, Daisy," said Vi in a flattish voice.

"I know it does. Try not to think about it."

"I'll try," she said. "Do you and Sam and Mr. Prophet want to come to supper tonight? Since nobody's eating much at the Pinkerton place, I have a gigantic pot of fricasseed chicken and dumplings along with carrots and English peas. There's tapioca pudding for dessert."

"Sounds delicious. I'd like to, Vi. Let me ask Mr. Prophet. Sam isn't home yet."

"And I think Spike is getting tired of Rosie wanting to play with him all the time," she added.

"Spike!" I cried, having forgotten all about my beloved dachshund for the very first time since he came into my life. "Oh, my Lord, I forgot Spike! Stacy's ghost did something to hurt him last night, but I'll bring him home. I think the house is Stacy-proof now. I hope." Oh, dear. How in the world could I have forgotten Spike? I hated myself so much in that instant, I don't even like to remember it.

"Daisy," said Vi, sounding concerned, as if she feared I'd suddenly lost what was left of my mind, "please stop talking about ghosts as if they were real!"

My heart, already at my feet, sank down below the basement. It almost made its way to China. I can't remember feeling so awful since Billy died.

Meekly, I said, "I'm sorry, Vi. I'll come over and get Spike. I'll ask Mr. Prophet and Sam if they'd like to have dinner with you. What time? Oh, my goodness, I don't even know what time it is now!"

"Calm down, Daisy," said Vi. "It's about five now. I got home early, so I'm here now. Would you like me to bring Spike over?"

Recalling the peppercorns that had nearly battered Li Ahn to death, I said quickly, "No, no. I'll get him. I hope he hasn't been a bother."

"Spike is never a bother. Rosie, on the other hand, can become slightly rambunctious."

Great. Now the dog I got to keep my father company because Spike used to live at my parents' house was giving everyone grief. I clearly couldn't win. "I'll be there in a minute, Vi."

"There's no rush. Spike is being a good dog."

Then why'd she say Rosie was bothering him? I didn't ask. "I'll be there as soon as I can be."

"Very well. Just come on over for dinner at six-thirty if you want to," said Vi. She sounded as if she were talking to a mere acquaintance.

I hated Stacy Kincaid in that instant even more than I hated myself. And I loathed myself. Nevertheless, I said, "Thanks, Vi," and hung up.

When I placed the receiver on the hook, Mr. Prophet was leaning up against the archway leading to the living room from the hallway. "You look like you swallered a toad. What's the matter?" he said, sounding almost sympathetic.

I glanced up from the telephone, and I'm pretty sure there were tears in my eyes. "Vi doesn't believe in Stacy's ghost," I said miserably. "But she invited us to go there for dinner if we want to."

"Well, she's never had anything to do with ghosts, has she?" asked Mr. Prophet, sounding reasonable, curse him. "Unless you've been through it, you don't understand it. If we go there for supper, we better stuff our pockets with salt and copper cent pieces. And mebbe hang a copper on Spike's collar."

"What a good idea!" I said, forgetting to be unhappy for a second. "How do we do that?"

"Hammer a nail through a penny—or a one-cent piece, if you wanna get technical—and hang it on his collar with a piece of wire."

"Can you do that?" I asked him, my voice full of wonder.

"Fer gawd's sake, it's not a miracle. It's hammerin' a nail

167

through a copper coin. Ain't even magic, but it might help Spike. Wouldn't hurt to rub a little sage on him, either. Sage smells good anyway."

"True." I slumped on the chair at the telephone table, feeling despondent because my aunt didn't believe me and my dog might still be in peril.

"Buck up," commanded Mr. Prophet. "Bein' miserable won't fix a thing. What we gotta do is figger a way to get rid of Stacy's ghost—and the one in the library—permanently. They're both danger-ous, although I expect Stacy wants you dead so she's more danger-ous. The library ghost is just pissed off about the library closin'. He shouldn't be hard to send away."

"But how?" I asked.

"Well…Mebbe Mrs. Jackson can help. And that séance you did for the Tongva feller worked pretty well."

"It wasn't the séance that got rid of him. It was Mr. DeLoera, and he went through a long ceremony that included smoke and fire and chanting and clanking and a whole lot of other stuff."

"Yeah, but that Tongva'd been dead for more'n a hundred years. Stacy's been dead a day or two, and the library feller's been dead for…I dunno. How long?"

"Two or three weeks, I think," I said, trying to remember what Regina had said about the late old misery.

"There you go. I'll wager you or Mrs. Jackson together can kick both of 'em out o' this world in one séance." He stood there for several seconds, leaning against the wall with his arms folded across his chest and staring at me. He had an odd expression on his face.

"What?" I finally barked. "What have I done wrong this time?"

"Not a damn thing," he said at last, surprising me. "I was just thinkin' you got some powers of your own. If anybody kin get rid of those two spirits, you can. I don't want you to get swell-headed or nothin', but I was impressed by the way you handled gettin' that Tongva feller back to his family."

I'm pretty sure my mouth fell open in astonishment. After it clanked shut, I opened it again and asked in a quavery voice, "You were?"

"Yeah. Like I said, don't go gettin' swell-headed, but you got your own powers now. You thought you was a fraud, but I've seen fer myself that you ain't. Not anymore you ain't, anyhow."

"Thanks, I guess," I said. "I mean, I think life is easier when you stay on one side of it or the other. I don't like ghosts and spirits intruding into my everyday life. Do you know what I mean?"

"I know what you mean. But you know, if we go to your folks's house for supper, we better drop a few copper coins there. Just to make sure. We can protect ourselves and the dawg, but if Stacy can't get at you, she might try to get at other folks. Like she did to Elvira and Li."

My head drooped. "True."

The telephone rang. As I sat right next to it on the chair at the telephone table, I jumped and let out a short squeal. Patting my thundering heart with one hand, I lifted the receiver with the other and started my usual greeting, "Rotondo resi—"

"Daisy!"

"Vi! Whatever is the matter?"

"You mother nearly got battered to death with peppercorns as she walked home from work today! She just arrived, and she's got peppercorns in her hair and her handbag and I think she's going to have *bruises*!"

"Oh no!" I said, peering at Mr. Prophet with eyes probably pleading for help. "It's Stacy. We've Stacy-proofed our house and me, and how she's going after people I love!" Thinking about Mrs. Rattle, I added, "And people who work for me."

"Daisy!" said Vi. "Stop talking nonsense."

"If my mother almost got pelted to death by peppercorns, I'm not talking nonsense, Vi. The same thing happened to Miss Li when she went home. Luckily for her, she had some kind of Chinese talisman with her, so she managed to get Stacy to stop throwing the peppercorns." Something then occurred to me that might or might not have been pertinent. "Listen, Vi, I'm coming to get Spike right now. We won't be able to take dinner with you tonight, but I think if Spike is out of your home, you'll all be all right."

"What in the world are you talking about?" My aunt sounded seriously annoyed.

"Oh, Vi, never mind. I'll be there in a few minutes."

"All right. I'll pack up some dinner for you. It will all fit in a cooking pot. Well, and a bowl for the pudding."

"Thank you. You're very kind."

Vi huffed out something that might have been a sigh or a gust of indignation. "It's all right. I just wish all this nonsense would stop, Daisy."

"It will, Vi. Promise." Okay, so I'd just made a promise I didn't know I'd be able to keep. Why not?

We hung up our respective receivers and I lifted my gaze to Mr. Prophet's wrinkled old countenance. "Stacy nearly killed my mother by heaving peppercorns at her when she walked home from work. My mother, not Stacy. Stacy's never done a day's work in her life. Or her death."

"Yeah, I figgered as much," he said. "You want me to punch a hole in a penny and stick a wire through the hole? We can fix it to Spike's collar when we go get him. And be sure to stuff your pockets with sage and salt. And I'll take some more copper coins to your folks's house to scatter here and there."

"I'll make sure they don't see you do it," I said.

"Don't matter if they see me. They might believe you if they see I do."

I thought about his words for a second or two. "Hmm. Maybe you're right."

"And we've gotta get that Voodoo lady, Li, Harold, Sam, and your librarian friend to join in a séance. You should probably do it at the gazebo in the park there at the library. Kill two ghosts with one stone."

"You really think so?"

"Cain't think o' nothin' else that might work," he said.

After contemplating things for several moments, I couldn't either.

TWENTY

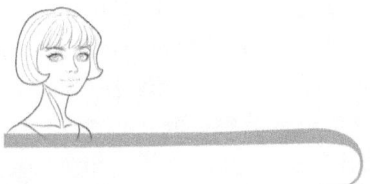

S am came home not long after Mr. Prophet had deftly pounded a nail through a copper one-cent piece and stuck a strip of thin wire through it. He made a nifty little S with the wire so I could hook it onto Spike's collar and twist the wire so it would dangle nicely and not fall off. His collar was at my parents' home because it was buckled around Spike's neck.

"What's going on?" we heard Sam call from the front door. "Daisy? Where are you?"

"Here I am!" I said, beginning to run from the utility porch until I remembered Sam's opinion about running, so I slowed to a fast walk. "We were getting ready to Stacy-proof Spike. What do you have there?" I asked, staring at the large file Sam held under his arm.

"Information about Stacy and her friends," he said. "I spent the afternoon with Johnny and Flossie Buckingham. They gave me names of people they think were friendly with Stacy."

"Wow," I said after giving my wonderful husband a kiss on the cheek and taking the folder from him. "I didn't know she had any friends."

"You just didn't like her," said Sam with a chuckle. "We still need to find out who killed her, and these names might give us a place to start."

"I suppose so," I admitted.

"Smells good in here," said Sam, sniffing the air kind of like Spike did sometimes. "What am I smelling? Turkey stuffing and oranges?"

"Pretty much," I said. "Mrs. Jackson told us to sprinkle salt all around the house and stick bunches of sage and juniper here and there. Oh, and you can't smell them, but we also put copper one-cent pieces in every room of the house. And we burned some sage. And Li Ahn prepared little bowls full of dried orange peel, sage, and juniper berries and put them all over the house. She and Mr. Prophet poured salt around the outside of the house and in the fireplace and put sage, orange peels, and juniper on top of the salt. In the fireplace, I mean."

"Good Lord, you don't think that's a little excessive?" Sam sounded skeptical. Guess he'd forgotten about last night. Also, he didn't know about today's goings-on.

"After we left the library, we came here to get my Ouija board and tarot cards, and Mrs. Rattle was crying because Stacy had been tormenting her all morning."

"What?" Sam's beautiful brown eyes opened wide.

So I explained about Mrs. Rattle and Li Ahn. Then I told him about my mother's bombardment with peppercorns.

After staring at me as if I was insane for far too many seconds, and just before I could batter poor Sam with my fists, Mr. Prophet said, "She's tellin' the truth, Sam. Miss Li, she had some Chinese magic with her, so she sent Stacy away. Poor Mrs. Gumm didn't know what the hell was goin' on, and Stacy nearly peppered her to death."

"Oh," said Sam. Then he said, "Are those two Chinese-looking statues beside the front door from Miss Li?"

"Yes," I told him. "We're borrowing them. Those are Fu dogs. Or maybe they're Fu lions. I guess they call them lion dogs. They're supposed to scare away evil spirits."

"Ah." He hung his coat on the rack and stuck his hat on the

shelf. "What about Spike? How do you plan to keep him safe from Stacy? When he's not inside the house, I mean. I guess you've ghost-proofed the house so well that no self-respecting ghost would dare enter it."

"That lets Stacy out," I muttered. "She has no respect for anything."

"Still, she can't get in, right?" asked Sam.

"Right," said Mr. Prophet.

"I hope not," I said.

"I punched a hole in a copper penny and put a wire through it. We kin attach it to Spike's collar." Mr. Prophet stopped speaking and tilted his head to one side. "Hmm. Mebbe I should do somethin' like that fer Yuyu to keep that ghost-bitch from gettin' to him."

"You think Stacy would try to hurt Yuyu?" I asked, thinking not even Stacy would be foolish enough to tangle with Mr. Prophet's cat.

"Dunno why not. She hurt Spike," said Mr. Prophet.

"Well, yes," I said, "But she knows how much I love Spike."

"Huh," said Mr. Prophet, looking daggers at me.

And then, as if he'd summoned a devil from hell, there came a sudden feline yowl from the backyard, and a responsive, "*Eeeeeeee!*" I recognized as coming from Stacy's ghost.

We all took off race-walking to the back door. Well, Sam ran. I didn't dare run, and Mr. Prophet couldn't run. Nevertheless, they both beat me to the door. As soon as Sam opened the door, we saw Yuyu, hackles on end, standing like a Halloween cat on one of the lion dogs guarding the door. He didn't move, even though he usually did when confronted with anyone other than Mr. Prophet. His one yellow eye all but glowed at us. I stepped back a pace, more frightened in that moment of Yuyu than of Stacy.

"Cripes," said Mr. Prophet, reaching out and grabbing his cat. Then he said, "Ow! Dammit cat, quit stickin' yer claws in me!"

Thinking quickly, I dashed to the utility room, where the remains of the sage, juniper, salt, and orange peels still lay. I scooped up a handful of salt, grabbed some orange peel pieces and some sage, and went back to the door. There I threw the salt at what looked like the empty air, eliciting another "*Eeeeeeee!*" from

173

Stacy's ghost. Then, taking my life in my hands, I rubbed some sage on Yuyu's back and stuck a piece of dried orange peel on his hackles.

"Quick thinkin'. Thanks, Miss Daisy," said Mr. Prophet.

"Ow! Dammit!" hollered Sam.

When I glanced at him, I saw his hair, which was thick and wavy and generally sitting smoothly on his head, being yanked this way and that. So I tossed some sage and orange peels on him, grabbed him by the arm, and yanked him into the house. Mr. Prophet and Yuyu followed on his heels. One last eerie "*Eeeeeeeee!*" got quiet when I slammed the door on it.

We stood in the back entrance, panting, and I looked at Sam. "So," I said. "What do you think now?"

"I think we have a couple of big problems on our hands," He said, attempting to smooth his hair back down. I don't think Stacy had managed to pull any of it out. "Damn, that hurt."

"This might not have happened if we hadn't been the first people to find her body," I said, peering up at Mr. Prophet.

"Mebbe," he said. Yuyu didn't like being indoors, but he finally sheathed his talons, and Mr. Prophet let out a relieved, "Whoo, boy. You got some claws on you, Yuyu."

"And Spike isn't here to calm him down," I said. "Oh, but wait! I have some catnip in a cupboard in the pantry!"

"You do?" asked Sam, astonished.

"Yeah. I saw some growing in a yard down the street, so I picked it and brought it home. Thought maybe Yuyu would like me better if I gave him some catnip."

"Cain't hurt," said Mr. Prophet. He appeared as astonished as Sam had.

I turned and strode to the pantry. "I'm going to plant some in the yard. What the heck. It's not poisonous. The Colonists used to brew it in their tea."

"They did?" asked Sam, now sounding befuddled.

"They did. I read a recipe in one of my father's great-grandmother's recipe books from Auburn, Massachusetts. In fact, there are lots of old recipes and things in that book that are interesting.

She spelled pumpkin p-u-m-y-o-n. I wonder if they called them pumyons."

As I disappeared into the pantry, I heard Sam's faint, "I have no idea" behind me. Sure enough, there sat a brown paper parcel neatly tied with string. I'd printed "Catnip" on it when I'd brought it home a couple of weeks before and had promptly forgotten all about it.

Sam, Mr. Prophet, and Yuyu had gone to the kitchen by the time I'd taken what I considered a reasonable amount of catnip from the parcel. Yuyu looked mad as an old wet hen, as my aunt sometimes said, but he was no longer attached to Mr. Prophet's chest. He stood, hunched, on Mr. P's lap, glaring balefully at Sam and then me when I entered the room.

"I don't want to spook him," I told the two men. "I'll just lay the catnip on the table, and you decide what to do with it."

"Sounds fair," said Sam.

So, with slow, gentle movements, I took the catnip out of the pocket of my day dress and laid it on the table, shoving it close to Mr. Prophet. It was still in stalk form, but withered, if you know what I mean. Boy, that was one pungent herb!

"Smells...strong," said Sam.

"Yeah," said Mr. Prophet. "I've smelled it before. Didn't know it was catnip."

Moving slowly, I pulled out a kitchen chair and sat on it. I didn't want to startle Yuyu into exposing those vicious murder-hooks.

He wasn't startled. Rather, as the aroma of the catnip wafted over to him, he twitched his nose. Then, after staring at the shriveled strands on the table, he reached out one furry front paw. Tentatively, he touched the small pile of catnip and drew some of it toward himself. He sniffed and sniffed. And then darned if the silly cat didn't stick his entire face in the pile of 'nip! He finally jumped on the table—which was always covered with a white oilcloth to keep it free from splashes, cooking catastrophes, and now, cats—and rolled in the stuff!

"Well, hell," said a dumbfounded Mr. Prophet. "I reckon we can go get Spike. Yuyu seems set to amuse himself for a while at least."

"Excellent," I said. "Sam? Want to come with us? Vi is giving us dinner in a pot and a bowl. And Mr. Prophet is going to stick some pennies in corners of my parents' house."

"Sure," said Sam in a what-the-heck kind of voice. "Why not? Let me get some more of that stuff to stick in my pockets." He bowed his head before me, not in reverence. "Do I still have enough of that salt and sage in my hair to prevent Stacy from pulling it out as we walk?"

"Yes. And I have plenty of salt, sage, and orange peel all over me still. And so does Mr. Prophet. He and Li have been Stacy-proofing the house all afternoon."

Sam just shook his head and rose from the table. Mr. Prophet and I also stood, and as Yuyu rolled in a small pile of catnip, we walked to the front door and exited our house. Stacy's ghost didn't attempt to interfere with us as we walked across the street, although she did screech at us and whoosh around some. I hoped our preventive measures would last until she figured out how to get around them.

My mother was still dealing with peppercorns when we made it across the street. We just knocked on the front door and walked on in. Spike and Rosebud greeted us with ecstasy. Rosebud added some high-pitched barks of greeting. Fortunately, they didn't last long. Her barks could shatter glass.

"Vi told me you said Stacy Kincaid's ghost is responsible for this mess," said my mother, sweeping peppercorns from the dining room floor. "Are you serious?" She didn't believe me any more than Vi had.

"Yes, I'm serious, but I don't expect anyone to believe me," I told her. "She almost made me crash the Chevrolet, and she hurt Spike, and she scared Yuyu—"

"She scared that *cat*?" Pa repeated as if he'd never heard of such a thing. "Shoot. I should think that cat would more likely be a ghost's familiar than a ghost's victim. Or am I thinking of witches?" He added, "Sorry, Lou."

"It's all right," said Mr. P. "Yuyu's just fine."

"So you believe this ghost nonsense too?" asked Ma, looking up from the dustpan into which she'd swept an enormous pile of peppercorns.

"Unfortunately, it isn't nonsense," said Sam. "Believe me, I thought it was nonsense too. Then Stacy tried to yank my hair out by the roots."

"She *what?*" Ma stood abruptly, jarring the dustpan and scattering peppercorns again. "Oh, bother."

"I'll sweep those up," I told her.

"I'll sweep 'em up," said Mr. Prophet. "You put this penny on Spike's collar. You can kneel, and I can't."

"Here, I'll do it," said Sam, taking the coin from Mr. Prophet.

My parents and Vi stared at us as we went about our tasks. Rosie just bounced around, happy to have company. Spike seemed pleased to have an ornament attached to his collar. Mr. Prophet began dropping copper coins here and there throughout the house and handed Vi several pennies.

"Here," he said. "Take these upstairs with you and set them in corners. Mrs. Jackson, the Voodoo lady, told us they keep ghosts away. And sprinkle some sage here and there too. And mebbe some salt."

"Good Lord," said Vi faintly as she took the coins from Mr. Prophet. "Very well. If you say so I'll do it, but this is all nonsense."

"Tell that to Ma," I said, lifting the dustpan full of peppercorns, carrying it to the kitchen, and dumping the peppercorns in the trash.

"I…" My mother stared at Sam and me, and then her glance followed Mr. Prophet as he dropped copper coins here and there in the dining room and living room. When he was finished in those rooms, he coppered the rest of the downstairs rooms.

"I put some on the staircase, too, in case Stacy manages to get past the stuff we already put out. Better sprinkle some sage—you got some sage?"

"Yes," said Vi. "I always have sage on my spice rack."

"Good. Got any oranges?"

"Oh, yes. We always have a bowl of them on the kitchen table," said Ma.

"Peel a couple and stick pieces of orange peel around the house, too."

"Orange peels?" said Pa in a sort of strangled voice.

"Mrs. Jackson said to do that," I told him. "And Miss Li and Mrs. Jackson both told us about the sage. Oh, and if you have any juniper berries or branches anywhere around, they're supposed to be good, too. And salt. Sprinkle salt outside."

"I can't believe this," said Ma faintly.

"I couldn't either," said Sam. "Until Stacy had at my hair." He patted his head. "Still hurts, curse her."

"And she might not bother you," I told my parents and my aunt bracingly. "I'm the one she's after. She wants me dead."

"Daisy!" my mother cried, only not in her *you're-being-rude* voice. Her tone, this time, sounded horrified.

"Can't help it, Ma. It's the truth." I made sure my voice was apologetic.

I swear, if Stacy Kincaid were still alive and if I had a gun and did such things, I'd have shot her dead.

TWENTY-ONE

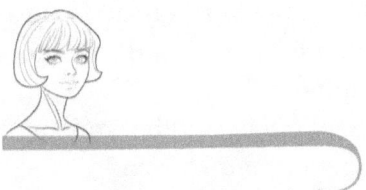

W e went home shortly after that, Spike with his nice copper cent piece dangling from his collar. I made sure to dust him with a little sage and salt before we set out. Mr. Prophet carried the bowl of tapioca pudding and Sam carried the rest of our dinner across the street.

As we walked, Stacy's ghost *Eeeeeeed* and whooshed, but she couldn't get at us, thanks to the precautions we'd taken.

Yuyu seemed to have gone into some kind of kitty coma on the kitchen table, but Mr. Prophet managed to move him to the utility room on a cushion I snabbled from a spare chair. The cat didn't seem to mind, and Mr. Prophet made sure the cushion and cat were both dusted with sage and salt, along with the now-crushed catnip before shutting the door and letting him sleep it off.

I got a whisk broom from under the sink and brushed the catnip tatters and several orange cat hairs into a bowl, which I set aside in the pantry. I don't know how long catnip's "nip" lasted, but maybe there was still some left in the shreds. Then I scrubbed the oilskin nearly to death.

Dinner was delicious, as are all of Vi's meals. After dinner, as I washed up the dishes, Sam and Mr. Prophet sat at the kitchen table.

Sam had retrieved his work folder and plunked it down in front of him.

"Do you think Harold would agree to visit and go over some of these names with us, Daisy?" asked Sam. "Or maybe I could just talk to him over the telephone."

"Shoot. I don't know," I said, rinsing soapy dishes and setting them on the counter in the wooden draining rack Sam had made for the purpose. "I can telephone and ask him. I don't know if he's at his house or his mother's."

"Hmm," said Sam. "His mother might know the names of Stacy's friends even better than Harold."

"Maybe," I said, "But she's in no condition to think about them now."

"She don't think a whole lot anyhow, does she?" asked Mr. Prophet.

With a sigh, I said, "Not much. At any rate, I don't think Stacy confided in either one of them, especially during these past couple of years. She's been in trouble or in jail for most of them."

"True." It was Sam's turn to sigh.

"But I'll telephone and see if I can find Harold somewhere," I said, thinking Sam already had better answers about Stacy's possible companions from the Buckinghams than either Harold or his mother could provide.

Harold wasn't at his own home, but Roy Castillo said I might be able to reach him at Mrs. Pinkerton's place. So, fearing what might befall me if Mrs. Pinkerton knew I was telephoning her home, I did it anyway. Brave soul, huh?

Luckily for me, Harold was there, and his mother was in bed after having been sedated. This was according to Featherstone, who fetched Harold to the telephone.

"What is it now?" he barked into the mouthpiece on his end.

"And a good evening to you, too, Harold," I said.

"It's *not* been a good evening," he snapped. "My mother is insane, poor Algie is at his wits' end and I'm afraid Featherstone is about to give notice. What do you want?"

"Um, to offer my sincere condolences. I'm sorry you have to

handle everything, Harold. I know your mother is unfit to deal with everyday matters, much less with death certificates, undertakers, policemen, and so forth."

"That's better," he said in a softer tone. "I just wanted a little understanding from somebody who *knows*."

"I do know," I said. "And I'm sorry. However," I added crisply, "if you could find it in your heart to visit us this evening and go over some names with Sam to let him know if any of them ring a bell, he'd appreciate it. And we have some of Vi's tapioca pudding left over too."

"I don't suppose you have anything of substance to eat there, do you?" he asked, still sounding edgy but no longer angry.

"There's leftover fricasseed chicken and dumplings, too. And some English peas and carrots."

"I'll be there in a few minutes," he said and hung up.

I relayed Harold's message to Sam and began heating leftovers for him. It was nice to know Stacy couldn't foil my efforts to heat food. By the time Harold rang the doorbell, I had a nice plate all ready for him.

As I opened the front door with Spike wagging at my ankles, I said, "Hope you don't mind if Sam continues to go through Stacy's file on the kitchen table while you dine."

After stooping to give Spike the greeting he was due, Harold said, "Don't mind at all. I didn't expect you to have anything for me to eat here. I just asked because I'm hungry and I didn't want to bother poor Roy, who's having enough trouble dealing with Del."

"What's the matter with Del?" I asked, surprised.

As he hung his coat on the rack and shoved his hat on the shelf, Harold said, "He's all in a flutter because Stacy was murdered. Fears her death and the manner of it will be bad for me. That's because he didn't know her well. His family still lives in Louisiana, too far away to be problematic if they object to Del living with someone whose sister was killed. He doesn't know how lucky he is."

"Oh. Well, it's nice that he's concerned," I told him.

"Don't play the innocent with me, Daisy Gumm Majesty

Rotondo. You know very well he's actually worried that news of Stacy's murder will somehow affect the bank."

Delray Farrington, Harold's life partner, had saved and now ran the bank Harold's father attempted to ruin a few years back. The bank, after teetering on the brink, now had a sparkly reputation.

"I can't imagine how Stacy's murder will be any worse for the bank than your father's dirty dealings were," I said.

"I can't either, but bankers are a touchy bunch." He paused to sniff the air. "Smells good in here. Maybe Stacy will prove to have been good for something after all."

"Are you telling me my house didn't smell good before we dumped the sage, juniper, and orange peels all over it, Harold Kincaid?"

"No! Not at all. But you have to admit that stuff smells good."

"Yes, it does," I acknowledged. "But come to the kitchen with me. I have a plate all ready for you in the warming oven. The peas and carrots kind of got mixed in with the chicken gravy, but that will only make them taste better."

"Did you fricassee the chicken?" he asked dubiously.

"How the heck would I have had time to cook after Stacy-proofing the house all afternoon?" I asked indignantly. "Vi fixed dinner."

"Ah," said Harold, sounding pleased. "Good." Then he said, "Ow!" because I whacked him on the shoulder.

"I can cook!" I declared. "Maybe not as well as Vi, but I'm getting better."

"It's true," said Mr. Prophet. "As much as I hate to admit it."

"She's becoming a good cook," Sam lied nobly.

"At least I don't burn everything any longer," I said.

Using a couple of hot mitts I'd made, I retrieved Harold's plate from the warming oven and set it on a placemat I'd also made so the heated plate wouldn't crinkle the oilskin.

"This looks good, Daisy," said Harold.

"And if you finish that and want more food, there's still some Chinese grub in the Frigidaire," I told him.

"I think this will be fine, thanks," he said, and started to dig in.

"Mind answering questions while you eat?" asked Sam.

"Not at all," said Harold after swallowing his first bite.

So Sam shuffled through a bunch of papers and withdrew one upon which he'd written several names. He read them to Harold slowly so Harold could think about them if he needed time. It was I who spoke first, though, after Sam read a name.

"Darlington," I said. "Isn't that the name of the fellow those women murdered at Regina and Robert's wedding?"

"Cecil Darlington?" asked Harold, lifting his head and peering at me. "I remember him. He was a miserable person. Glad he's dead."

"So am I," I said, "but some of those women—well, they were hardly more than girls, really—weren't prizes themselves."

"True," said Harold. "And I don't suppose it's nice to kill people, although I might pin a medal on Stacy's killer when you find him, Detective."

"We think it's a her, actually," said Sam.

This time when Harold lifted his head, he stared at Sam. "A *woman* killed her?"

"We think so. From the footprints and the evidence found in and around the library's gazebo, we think a woman was the culprit."

"Hmmm," said Harold. "Interesting."

"The late Mr. Darlington had two sisters," Sam said, "Geneva and Roma."

"I've never heard of either of them," I said.

"That's why we asked Harold over," Sam said a trifle testily. "I don't expect you to recognize any of these names."

"Oh. Well, then, I'll just be quiet," I said.

"Good idea," said Mr. Prophet.

"Nertz," I said. I put the last of the dishes away and sat on another chair at the kitchen table.

"I vaguely recall somebody named Geneva being a bosom pal of Stacy's," Harold said thoughtfully. "Not sure how long ago that was. When Stacy started hanging out at the Salvation Army, lots of her friends figured she'd lost her mind and sloped off."

"Unsurprising," said Sam. "These are names I got from the

Buckinghams, though. Maybe they came back into Stacy's orbit after she left the Salvation Army, took off with that Petrie character and began her life of crime."

"Do you have the names of females who visited her in the hospital?" I asked, thinking the question pertinent.

"Some of them, yes," said Sam. "I looked at the visitor register from the jail ward. The hospital is going to make me a copy of it. A couple of the women on the Buckinghams' list also appear on the jail register."

"Oh," I said. "Which ones?"

"Let me finish reading these names to Harold first. Is that all right with you, Daisy?"

"Sure," I said when I realized Sam was speaking through clenched teeth. Sheesh! I was only trying to be helpful.

"Go on, Detective," said Harold, grinning as he forked up more chicken and dumplings.

"Jervis," said Sam. Then he shot me a don't-you-dare-say-a-word glare.

I shut my mouth, which I'd only barely opened, with a clink of teeth.

"The Jervises are all a trifle loony," said Harold. "One of them helped kill Cecil Darlington, didn't she? And then she shot some other people after she was arrested?"

"Yes." Sam heaved a huge sigh.

Sam had long considered Alma Jervis's antics at the Pasadena Police Station after her arrest one of his major failures, although I didn't. Still don't. It wasn't his fault there were no female police matrons available to search the women brought in that night. And he certainly couldn't be faulted if Alma Jervis had decided to stick a pistol in her garter belt. She shot herself, too, but only damaged her vision and her hearing. Which, in my opinion, served her right. She and a couple of her pals decided it would be fun to pin Cecil Darlington's murder on *me*, of all people, and I'd never even met the man. After I learned about him and his evil ways, I was glad I hadn't. I was also glad he was dead, but that's not very nice of me.

"How about a Miss Louise Trunick?" asked Sam of Harold.

"My mother has some friends named Trunick, and I've met a couple of Trunick girls at parties," said Harold.

"I think a Trunick fainted at one of my séances once," I said musingly. Then I remembered I wasn't supposed to speak and slapped a hand over my mouth.

But Sam wasn't mad at me. Rather, he asked, "Do you recall the name of the woman who fainted?"

I contemplated Sam's question. "It was an unusual name, I think."

"Medora," said Harold.

"That's right. Miss Medora Louise Trunick. Oh." I peered at Sam. "Louise. Maybe she dropped the Medora part of her name."

"Guess I'll have to ask," said Sam in a resigned voice. Poor thing. He'd have to question a whole lot of people, some of them young women from wealthy Pasadena families who wouldn't be happy about it. But again, he'd chosen his profession, even if a policeman's lot wasn't always a happy one.

"Wait a minute," said Mr. Prophet. "Wasn't it some lady named Trunick who had that Darlington's sumbitch's baby?"

"By golly, I think you're right," I said. To Harold I asked, "Do you recall which Trunick girl it was?"

Harold munched thoughtfully on some carrots and peas, then shook his head. "Don't think it was Medora. Louise. Whatever she calls herself. What's the other one's name? Elizabeth? Betsy? Betty?"

"Betty," I said. "It was Betty Trunick who had that cad's baby. I think they sent the baby to live on a farm in some place called Fresno. I don't know how Betty can stand it. How horrible to be used by a louse believing he loved you, and then have him deny his part in creating the baby she was carrying. If I were Betty, I'd have happily murdered Cecil Darlington, but I don't know what that has to do with Stacy Kincaid."

"I don't either," said Sam, "but I'll have to ask. Perhaps Stacy was friends with Darlington. If she could fall in love with Percival Petrie, she clearly had no sense when it came to men."

"Or anything else," said Stacy's brother.

"I don't suppose you came across anymore Petries, did you?" I asked. "When you were talking to Johnny and Flossie?"

After staring at me far too long for my comfort, Sam said, "No, but that's a good thought."

It was? Glory be!

"When I'm questioning people, I'll ask about Petries. And Gauldings."

"Oh, my goodness, yes!" I cried. "Definitely ask about Petries and Gauldings."

A Petrie had done his level best to kill me on more than one occasion, and a Mrs. Gaulding, whose maiden name had been Petrie, had shot and almost killed Sam.

Sam went through the rest of the list of names with Harold, and I fed him the last of the tapioca pudding. Neither Harold nor I recognized any further names.

Which didn't mean a blessed thing, darn it.

TWENTY-TWO

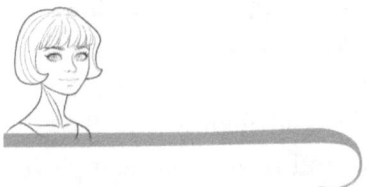

Before we went to bed Tuesday evening, I telephoned Mrs. Rattle to let her know she didn't need to come in the next morning.

"I suspect it will take another couple of days to fix the problems with the house," I told her, attempting to sound matter-of-fact.

"Have you called in a contractor?" she asked.

"Um…" Crumb. What had we told her was the matter with the house? I think I'd mentioned plumbing, which had been asinine. The foundation! That's right. "Yes. A fellow will be here to inspect the foundation tomorrow." I swear, even when I wasn't spiritualist-mediuming, all I seemed to do was lie.

"That's nice, dear. Which contractor are you using?"

Another frantic search through my cranial convolutions came up with the answer. "Bullis!" I said triumphantly and perhaps too loudly. "Ahem. The Bullis Construction Company built the house, so I called them." That almost wasn't a lie. I had called them several months prior about a different matter entirely.

"I see. Well, let me know when I should come back. I miss you and Spike. And Mr. Prophet is always amusing."

He was, was he? I'm glad she thought so. At present, he was in a spare room next to the utility room with his cat. I'd made up the bed for him. To be on the safe side, and because I didn't trust Stacy not to burn down Mr. Prophet's cottage if she could figure out a way, we'd ghost-proofed it too.

"Yes, Mr. Prophet is quite amusing," I said to Mrs. Rattle, hoping my words didn't sound as prickly as they felt on my tongue. "I hope this foundation work won't take long."

"Very well, dear. Hope to see you soon."

"Thanks, Mrs. Rattle."

Before turning in, and taking Mrs. Jackson's advice again, we shut all the windows and turned on nearly every light in the house, including those on the front and back porches. Mr. Prophet said he didn't want a light on in his and Yuyu's room, which I understood because I didn't want a light on in Sam's and my room either. And then, with Sam carrying Spike, we went upstairs. I don't know about Sam and Spike, but I was asleep almost before my head hit the pillow.

The next day, Wednesday, I decided to telephone Regina Browning at the library to see how things were getting along there. We were supposed to get together that afternoon for our weekly exercise class, but I figured it would be nice to ask her about the library ghost.

"It's not throwing books at people," Regina said, sounding slightly perkier than she had the day before. "It still shoves books off shelves and startles patrons, but it's not as vicious as it was before we threw all those copper coins around. Of course, people find them and pick them up, so we have to keep replacing them."

"Of course they do," I said, thinking we should have anticipated something of the sort.

"Mr. Graves, the custodian, tried to sweep up the salt, but I asked him not to. He thinks I'm crazy."

"My parents think I'm nuts, too," I told Regina. "They don't understand."

"To be fair," said Regina, "Mr. Whitehall's ghost didn't turn off the lights, lock the door, and heave books at them."

"True. But Stacy's ghost nearly battered my mother to death with dried peppercorns from all the pepper trees on our street."

"Stacy's ghost?" said Regina in a small voice.

Whoops. "I didn't tell you?"

"Uh...No. We talked about ghosts in the library yesterday, and I know Miss Stacy Kincaid was killed in the library's gazebo, but I didn't think she'd...um...become a ghost."

"She not only became a ghost, she's haunting *me!*" I said.

"Oh dear. Will you be able to go to our exercise class this afternoon?"

Would I? "Huh. I hadn't even thought about a possible haunting of the exercise class. I expect I'll be okay if I dose myself with sage and orange peels and so forth."

"Sage and orange peels?"

"Ghost repellents," I told her. "Along with copper coins and salt."

"Oh. Well, then, I guess I'll see you there."

"Right. I'll be there," I said, not looking forward to the class. Then again, I *never* looked forward to the class.

Mind you, the exercises weren't difficult, and we ladies generally had a good time gossiping and so forth, but I'd rather take my dog for several walks than go to the church's fellowship hall and do exercises to music from Miss Betsy Powell's radio. But I'd go.

Nothing of an alarming nature happened when Pa and I took Rosebud and Spike for our daily walk around the neighborhood. To be safe, I had Mr. Prophet create another copper ornament for Rosie's collar. He'd already made a collar and a copper token for Yuyu. Rosebud strutted as if she knew she was wearing a new and charming item of jewelry. She and Spike took turns watering the same bushes and spots of grass and sidewalk. They were so funny. It was as if they each wanted to have the last word. Or squirt, I guess.

At any rate, when Pa and I came home again, I took Spike across the street with me. After Mr. Prophet and I salted and saged both Spike and Yuyu, Mr. Prophet sat on the back porch and kept an eye on the two animals. He couldn't run and save them if Stacy managed to do anything wicked to either of them, but he had various Apache and Chinese totems on his person, and he wasn't afraid to use them.

As for me, I went to my sewing room and studied the various pieces of fabric I had stored away. What I wanted to do was visit Maxime's Fabrics on Colorado Street and look at patterns and fabrics for Easter dresses for my sister's two daughters, Polly and Peggy. But I didn't dare stray too far from home yet.

This was becoming absolutely *insane*. We had to think of a way to get rid of the ghosts in our lives, and soon, before we all went nuts.

Along about eleven-thirty, I went to the back porch and asked Mr. Prophet if he'd like some lunch. He squinted at me, which might have been a sign that he didn't trust me or might have been because the sun was in his eyes.

"Whatcha got to eat?" he asked doubtfully.

"Well, not a whole lot. There's some Chinese food left. I expect it's still edible. We got it on Monday, and it's only Wednesday."

After tilting his head to one side and then the other, he said, "Yeah, why not? You gonna heat it up?"

"Yes. Do you mind if I combine the two chicken dishes? And maybe dump in the rice and noodles? I can't imagine they'd taste bad all mixed together. They're all good separately."

He shrugged a shoulder. "Why not? They all end up in the same place anyway."

"True. Very well, I'll taste as I go along, just in case."

"Just in case," he repeated. Then he grinned. "You ain't so bad, Miss Daisy, you know that?"

"Gee, thanks," I said. "You're not so bad yourself. Pa said to thank you for Rosie's charm."

"I'll go tell him he's welcome after this is all taken care of." He swept an arm in a gesture meant to take in the whole of the yard, the dog, the cat, the arbor and, I'm sure, Stacy's ghost. Which I hadn't heard *eeeeeing* or whooshing. Lordy, I hoped she wasn't taking lessons from Satan on how to un-ghost-proof houses.

Shaking my head hard to clear it of nonsense, I turned and went back to the kitchen, where I prepared lunch. By golly, all that

Chinese grub mixed together was darned good. Mr. Prophet and I pretty much finished it all up. Which meant I didn't have anything to feed Sam for dinner, but I'd think of something during exercise class, I hoped.

Because the day was a fine one and because the church was not far from our house, I walked to the class that afternoon. I filled one of the little fabric bags I had lying around with as much ghost-repellent as it could hold and boldly strode up the street.

Our church sat on the corner of Marengo and Colorado. The door to the choir room and the one to the corridor leading to the fellowship hall were on the Marengo side. I had my key ready to stick into the lock when I realized someone had beaten me to it. Fearing subversion—would even so vicious and vile a person as Stacy Kincaid sabotage a church?—I carefully pushed the door open. I breathed a sigh of relief when I saw Miss Betsy Powell had arrived before me and been let into the church by our pastor, Rev. Merle Negley Smith.

This, by the way, was a first in the history of my life. Me being glad to see Miss Betsy Powell, I mean. She wasn't my favorite person mainly because she screamed at the drop of a hat, and her screams could shatter glass. For another thing, she had deplorable taste in men. Two of her swain had made attempts on my life in past years. We remained friendly, although I tried to keep my distance and never, ever startle her.

As I entered the fellowship hall I said, "Good afternoon, Miss Powell."

"Mrs. Rotondo," said she. "How good to see you. I'm just setting up the radio so we can begin our exercises. I'm not sure who'll be here, but I think Mrs. Dermott will come. We chatted about it at fellowship last Sunday."

"I'm glad to hear it," I said, not quite fibbing. I liked Mrs. Dermott, a fellow church member. "Mrs. Browning will be coming too. I hope Mrs. Buckingham can get away. She's so busy with her two children and her Salvation Army Church duties."

"A busy life indeed," said Miss Powell. I think she disapproved of Flossie because she belonged to the Salvation Army and wasn't a

Methodist-Episcopal, but Miss Betsy Powell was an idiot so I didn't pay much attention to her.

What a horrid thing to say. I'd say I'm sorry, but I'm not so I probably shouldn't do any more lying than I already did.

"Oh, and here's Lucy Zollinger!" Lucy and I sang in the choir together. She was a soprano and always got the melody. I sang alto and always had to learn a part. I tell you, life is unfair in so *very* many ways.

"Good afternoon, gals," said Lucy, kind of a string-bean of a woman, but a nice one with a gorgeous voice. "Should you be leading the class, Daisy? In your condition?"

Bother my condition!

I didn't mean that. I was looking forward to starting a family with Sam. But golly, you'd think I had tuberculosis or something. Women had been having babies since God invented them.

"Until I get too big to bend, I think I'll be fine," I told Lucy in a sprightly tone so she wouldn't think I was irked.

"Actually," said Lucy, "you can probably lead us even if you get too big to bend. All you have to do is count out the repetitions."

"True," I said. "Or you could."

"Oh, no!" she cried as if I'd suggested she lead the D'Oyly Carte Opera Company's next production of *The Mikado*.

"It's not that hard, Lucy," I said.

"But you're a natural leader and I'm not," she said back.

I squinted at her to judge if she were being sarcastic, which would have been most un-Lucy-like, but evidently, she meant it. "If you say so," I told her.

"I've got the radio plugged in," sang Miss Betsy Powell in her screechy voice. The radio of which she spoke was an expensive RCA Radiola. Sam, Harold and I believe it to have been stolen by the last of Miss Powell's felonious gentleman friends, but we didn't tell her that.

"Okay," I said, attempting to sound chipper. "Just let me get a few things out of my bag here, and we can begin our stretches."

So I reached into my flowered bag, withdrew a handful of salt and sage, which I'd cleverly mixed together and pretended to balance myself on the table where Miss Powell had set the radio. As I balanced, I sprinkled some of the mixture around the radio. I *really* didn't want Miss Powell's radio to fall over and smash. Not only would it be a terrible waste of a nice, if stolen, radio, but Miss Betsy Powell would certainly scream. When I was through, I shucked the skirt I'd put on over my gym bloomers and turned to face "my" class.

The exercises we used came from a book called *Eating Your Way to Health*, by Dr. J. Douglas Thompson. As mentioned before, they weren't strenuous. I turned on the radio and tried to find a station that played stretching music. I finally managed to find a station playing popular tunes.

When I turned back to the class, Regina had shown up. The class members were a well-scrubbed bunch, but a motley one for all that. Most of us wore either the gym slips or gym bloomers we'd worn in high school. Mrs. Dermott, who was older than the rest of us, had fashioned an outfit for herself that looked kind of like a gym slip she'd made out of a couple of her husband's old shirts. She didn't look any worse than anyone else in the class.

"She Knows Her Onions" played and sung by the Happiness Boys, whoever they were, began playing on the radio, so I started with toe-touches and counted out repetitions. Hmm. Toe-touches were easy as pie—well, easier than pie if you were me—but I discovered that my slightly increased bulk seemed to wear me out more easily than I used to wear out. And this was only one week after our last exercise class. Fiddlesticks!

But I persisted. After we touched our toes an appropriate number of times and the announcer on the radio told us more doctors recommended Camel Cigarettes over any other cigarette, Whispering Jack Smith sang "Baby Face", which seemed appropriate somehow, probably because I was going to have a baby and I'm sure he or she would be cute. We did lunges to that one.

We did a different set of toe-touches to Paul Whiteman's "Moonlight on the Ganges". Then we twisted our bodies to "When the Red, Red Robin Comes Bob-Bob-Bobbin' Along" as Al Jolson urged us to get out of bed. As we were already out of bed and bobbing, this seemed inappropriate, but I wasn't going to argue with Mr. Jolson.

We were about to wrap things up with some slow stretches along with "Tea for Two" sung by Marion Harris. I recalled a time a year or so back when I'd played "Tea for Two" on my parents' piano and both Sam and Mr. Prophet had begun singing it. It struck me as funny, so I started to chuckle.

My chuckle was cut short with a *bang* when one of the tables— the tables were shoved up against a wall under the windows during the week—fell over. Or was pushed. When I noticed an open window just above the fallen table, I suspected ghostly interference.

Naturally, as I grabbed my flowered bag full of ghost-repellent, Miss Betsy Powell screamed. I didn't pause to smack her face, but raced over to the open window, threw some salted sage on the sill of same, and closed the window. I locked it to be on the safe side.

Then I marched back to the group of women standing around Miss Betsy Powell, their hands covering their ears, and shouted, "*Hush up!*"

The last of Miss Powell's screams stopped right, smack in the middle of itself. She looked at me as if I'd slapped her.

"There's no need for that hideous racket," I told her. "A table fell over. We were all startled, but no one else felt the need to scream."

"I...I..." Miss Betsy Powell's gaze went from me and made a circuit of the women surrounding her, all of whom were nodding as if to agree with what I'd said. After one final gulp, she said, "I'm sorry."

"There's no need to scream whenever anything unusual happens," said Mrs. Dermott. "I don't mean to criticize, dear, but you do have a mighty loud scream, and you seem to use it more often than is strictly necessary."

Miss Betsy Powell bowed her head. "I'm sorry," she said again.

"Just take a minute after something startling happens and look around before you begin screaming," suggested Flossie. "If a child has been hurt or the house is on fire, scream. If you're only startled, screaming is unnecessary. It works for me."

"Really?" Miss Powell looked at Flossie as if for redemption.

"Indeed," said Flossie.

"What a good idea!" said Regina, stressing her enthusiasm a trifle, but probably Miss Powell was too dim to notice.

There I go again. I beg your pardon.

But at least Miss Betsy Powell drove home with her stolen radio a chastened and, with luck, a less noisy person.

TWENTY-THREE

I was so glad to get home again, I hauled Spike up onto the sofa with me and took a nap in the living room. And this, without giving a single thought to what I'd feed poor Sam for dinner that night. I was as bad as Miss Betsy Powell, only in a different way.

Then again, maybe she couldn't cook either.

I don't have a clue how long we napped, but it wasn't long enough. As Spike and I yawned in the living room and attempted to wake up, I heard the back door open. Because I was pretty sure ghosts didn't bother opening doors, I figured Mr. Prophet had arrived to fulfill his duties as guardian of the Rotondo homestead.

Spike leaped off the sofa and dashed off to greet him. I remained, exhausted, on the sofa, contemplating canned and preserved foodstuffs in kitchen cupboards and on basement shelves.

Nertz. It wouldn't be nice of me to feed Sam canned chicken, would it? What would I fix with it? How come I could be creative when it came to sewing, but my mind remained blank when it was supposed to think about preparing meals for my beloved spouse?

Mr. Prophet appeared in the doorway, squinting at me. "Lazy-bones," he said.

"You're right," I said, not even bothering to argue.

"You're still in your exercise outfit," he said.

I glanced down at my wrinkled skirt over my wrinkled gym bloomers. He was right again. "You're right."

"Go upstairs and change into somethin' decent. Sam'll be home soon, and I don't think he'll want to know you've been jumpin' around in them things."

"I wasn't jumping in them. I was merely doing some stretching exercises."

"Huh. Well, get dressed anyway. Mrs. Potts down the street fixed some supper for us."

"She did?" I asked, dumbfounded. Mrs. Cyrus "Hattie" Potts lived with Mrs. Mainwaring, Miss Li, and whatever waifs or strays Mrs. Mainwaring had taken in recently. "Why'd she do that?"

"Miss Li told her we was goin' through some rough times with ghosts, so Mrs. Potts said you shouldn't have to worry about anything else and made dinner for everyone. I put the pot on the stove." He tilted his head and squinted at me some more. "Unless, o'course, you've got somethin' I can't smell that you fixed for supper."

"You know I haven't. I went to the stupid exercise class, Stacy managed to knock over a table somehow, and Miss Betsy Powell nearly screamed the church down."

"Somebody ought to strangle that woman," opined Mr. Prophet, who had heard Miss Betsy Powell's powerful screams more than once.

"Not a bad idea, but I don't want to be anywhere around her if somebody does it. One ghost haunting me is more than enough."

"That woman's crazier than a loco shoat and dumb as a rock. She wouldn't know how to haunt anybody."

"You're probably right." I didn't ask what a loco shoat was because I didn't have the energy.

"Sam'll be home any minute now," said Mr. Prophet, who'd traded his squint for a frown. "He don't deserve a wife looks like you do now."

"I don't look *that* bad, do I?"

"You look like you've been given a Dutch ride over some sharp rocks," he said.

I knew what a Dutch ride was. It meant being dragged by a rope behind a horse. "I feel kind of like I have," I said bleakly. "I want Stacy's ghost to go away."

"Miss Li's been workin' on that," said Mr. Prophet. "Turns out Mrs. Potts and Mrs. Jackson are chums. They're fixin' their attention on the Stacy problem."

"Really?" By golly, his words made me feel better than I had all day.

"Yeah. So get changed, and show Sam he wasn't a fool to marry you."

"He probably was," I said. "But I'll try not to look like a Halloween ghost when he gets home." With a groan I couldn't suppress, I rose from the sofa.

"Aw hell, you don't look *that* bad," said Mr. Prophet.

"Thanks heaps," I said, heading for the staircase.

When I got to our bedroom and checked myself in the cheval glass mirror, I was unhappy to observe that Mr. Prophet had been correct about my overall appearance. For one thing, gym bloomers aren't the most flattering things a woman can wear even at the best of times. For another thing, I looked approximately as exhausted as I was.

Still, while Sam was partly responsible for my condition, he was a good man and an excellent breadwinner. Being a detective was also a difficult job, and he deserved a wife who looked a heck of a lot better than I did then. So I shucked off my gym bloomers and coordinating shirt, dumped them in the laundry basket, and went to the bathroom to see if I could repair myself. I took a quick bath, which was kind of reviving. Then I brushed my hair, peered in the mirror at my ashen face, and decided my cheeks needed help, so I rubbed a little Tangee Natural on my cheeks and lips.

Better. At least I didn't look dead any longer. But boy, those dark bags under my eyes didn't add much glamour to my overall self. So I got some white grease paint stuff I'd used a time or two when I conducted séances and wanted to look unearthly and ethereal and smoothed it over my eye bags.

Still better. I decided to powder my whole face then fluffed off the excess and used a tiny bit of Zona Eyebrow Pencil, which was a brand-new invention I'd found at Nelson's Five and Dime Store. I hadn't used it yet because it was black, and I've got dark red hair. But darned if a little of that pencil didn't make my eyebrows look rather nice. I didn't have any desire to attempt the skinny-brow Clara-Bow dramatic thing, but a little bit of color didn't hurt. Neither did a little bit of Maybelline's mascara, which came in a cardboard box with a tiny brush. I wet the brush, rubbed it on the caked mascara and then applied it lightly to my eyelashes.

By gum, I'd conquered the just-risen-from-the-dead look!

Happier, I went back to the bedroom and put on a pretty green day dress, some everyday lisle stockings, and my nice-looking but comfortable brown shoes. There. I think I was ready to see my husband.

That was a good thing because he came home just as I was buckling the strap on my low-heeled pumps. I took one last quick look at myself in the mirror and decided Sam would be glad he'd married me when I went downstairs to greet him.

I was right.

"Hey, sweetheart, Lou told me you'd had a rough day, but you sure look good to me," he said when I met him in the front hallway.

"Thanks, Sam." I got on my tiptoes and kissed him. "Spike and I had a good nap, so I'm feeling pretty good now."

"You look a helluva lot better than you did a half hour ago," said Mr. Prophet.

"Thanks," I said, wanting to smack him.

"Hellkatoot, at least you don't look like one o' them Voodoo zombies any longer," he said.

"High praise," said Sam, laughing as he hung his coat on the rack and stuck his hat on the shelf. "I'm glad you took it easy today. You did too much yesterday." Turning, he squinted at me narrowly. "Did you go to that exercise class today? You probably shouldn't be doing any jumping around, you know."

"We don't jump," I told him. "We stretch. It's good for us. Dr. Benjamin said stretching is good even for women who are in my condition."

"Well, all right," Sam said. "Just don't overdo it."

"I won't," I promised, wishing he'd stop being so fussy about my pregnancy. So far everything had been going fine. Doc Benjamin wasn't worried and said I was healthy as a horse. I'm sure he meant a healthy horse.

"I interviewed a plethora of ladies who were acquainted with Stacy Kincaid today," Sam went on, heaving his briefcase on the telephone table. "I have a lead or two and a pretty good idea of who might have helped her escape from the hospital ward. Not sure if the same woman killed her, but a bit more digging might solve the case."

"Really?" I said, surprised. "That was quick work on your part."

"Harold Kincaid helped," Sam admitted as we walked toward the kitchen. I picked up Sam's briefcase on the way because I figured we could go through his findings in the kitchen.

"Mrs. Potts made supper for us. Want to eat before we go through your papers?" asked Mr. Prophet. "My belly's rubbin' against my backbone."

"Sounds good to me," said Sam.

I glanced at the kitchen clock, which announced the time as being six-fifteen. "Good enough for me, too. What kind of dishes do you need for whatever Mrs. Potts fixed?"

"Probably bowls," said Mr. Prophet, his brow wrinkled in thought. "And little plates for the cornbread."

"Oh, I love cornbread," I said. "I'll get the honey out, too, because it's so good on cornbread."

"What did she make?" asked Sam.

"Red beans and rice," said Mr. Prophet.

Sam and I exchanged a glance. I personally had never heard of a dish called red beans and rice, although I'd eaten rice and beans in Mijares Mexican Restaurant in Pasadena.

"From New Orleans," explained Mr. Prophet. "They're good. Trust me."

"Excellent," I said. Anything I didn't have to cook was all right by me. "I'll just set the table."

"You got one o' them things that you put on the table to hold hot pots?" asked Mr. Prophet.

"A trivet or a coaster? Sure. I'll get a couple of those too."

So I set the table, using our everyday china—thanks to me having worked for so many wealthy Pasadena ladies, we had china for every conceivable occasion—and put a couple of ceramic tile coasters in the middle of the table. Flossie had given us those. I made sure the butter dish and the honey pot were on the table too.

Mr. Prophet carried a large black pot to the table, set it on a tile, and put a plate of cornbread he'd cut into squares on another one. When he lifted the lid off the pot, a delectable aroma filled the air.

"Smells kind of like ham," said Sam, sniffing.

"I think it's got ham in it. Get a big ladle, Miss Daisy, and we can just fill our bowls."

So I got a big ladle, and boy, that was one of the best meals I've ever had in my life. I'd have to ask Mrs. Potts for her recipe. Red beans and rice. What a concept. I'd never have thought of it in a million years. That's probably not a big surprise, is it?

"Where do you get red beans?" I asked nobody in particular as I savored my supper.

"Grocery store, I reckon," said Mr. Prophet.

"I've never noticed any dried red beans at Mr. and Mrs. Bennett's store. I'll ask her the next time I'm there. She carries dried lima beans, navy beans, and pinto beans there."

"Maybe Mrs. Potts orders them from New Orleans," suggested Mr. Prophet.

"Nertz. Well, I can ask her. This is delicious."

"It is," agreed Sam. "I wouldn't mind if you fixed this several times a month, in fact."

"If I can figure out the recipe and find the ingredients, I'll give it a whirl," I told him, thinking poor Sam deserved a better wife than I and also that I could probably ruin the simplest of recipes, of which this didn't look like one. Did that make sense? Oh, well. I'd worry about finding red beans and learning what to do with them after our current set of problems had been solved.

"When I was out on the desert, I ate beans and bacon," said Mr. Prophet. "You have to soak the beans to soften 'em up before you cook 'em, or they'll stay hard." He shrugged. "You kin eat 'em hard, but they're better if they soften up."

"How do you soak beans when you're on the trail of a criminal in the desert?" I asked, honestly curious.

He looked up from his bowl of beans and rice, spoon suspended in his hand, and squinted at me. "You serious?"

"Yes, I'm serious! I just thought about you eating all those beans with bacon and wondered how you didn't break all your teeth. I may be the worst cook in the world, but I know you have to soak dry beans. When Pa makes his Boston baked beans, he soaks his navy beans in water overnight and then cooks them the next day."

"Yeah, that's it," said Mr. Prophet. The spoon finished its way to his mouth.

Rather than throw my knife at him, which might have been overreacting under the circumstances, I said, "How did you soak them? In a container of some sort?"

"Coffee pot," he said after he swallowed. "Overnight."

"Oh! That's brilliant," I said before I could stop myself.

"We all did that. All of us who had to ride for days, I mean."

"How did you carry them the next day?" I asked, thinking he probably wouldn't dangle a coffee pot full of beans and water from his saddle, although I might be wrong.

"Dumped out the water and poured the beans in a heavy sack. They'd be soft by the time we stopped for the night."

"How interesting. Thank you very much."

"Gonna put that in your book?" he asked dryly.

Have I mentioned my book dedicated to Mr. Prophet's old-western sayings? Well, when we first met, his speech was so filled with what I considered odd turns of phrase, I began writing them down. I only realized he knew what I was doing several months after I'd begun doing it.

"Yes. I am. I think that's an outstanding solution to the bean problem, although I think eating beans and bacon for days on end must get kind of boring."

"Did," said he. "Sometimes we'd find stuff to put in with the beans and bacon. Or maybe a prairie chicken to cook and eat with 'em.'"

"Interesting. You ought to write a book," said Sam.

"I'm leavin' that up to Miss Daisy." Mr. Prophet actually winked at me.

"Maybe I will one of these days," I told him.

"So, do you like your father's beans or these beans better?" asked Sam, who had partaken of Pa's Boston baked beans along with the brown bread he cooked to eat with it.

I lifted my gaze from the butter I was smearing on a piece of cornbread and looked at my husband. "Um…Please don't tell Pa, but I like these better. In fact, these are absolutely delicious. Pa's baked beans are kind of sweet. These are more savory. And—again, *please* don't tell Pa this—I don't like brown bread. It's sweet, too, and I'd rather have a piece of cornbread."

"On which you spread butter and honey," Sam pointed out.

"Well, yes, but the cornbread itself isn't sweet and molasses-y. Not that I don't like molasses, but—"

"Never mind," said Sam, grinning. "I agree with you."

"Me too," said Mr. Prophet.

"Oh, good." For some reason, I felt relieved. For a second or two, I'd felt as though I'd betrayed not merely my father but my entire Massachusetts heritage for preferring beans from New Orleans over beans from Boston.

People can be so weird sometimes, myself included.

TWENTY-FOUR

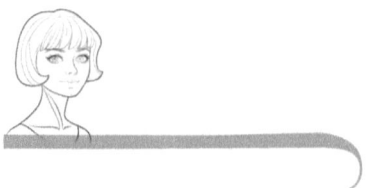

After dinner, I cleared everything away, wiped down the oilcloth, transferred the rest of the red beans and rice to another container, and put it in the refrigerator. There wasn't any cornbread left, but thanks to Mrs. Bennett at the local grocery store and the instructions on the back of the Quaker Cornmeal box, I could actually prepare cornbread myself. It tasted good, too, as long as I didn't cook it too long. Sam never chided me if I let something singe a bit. Neither did Mr. Prophet, but his snicker was just as bad.

As I began the washing up, Sam hefted his briefcase to the table and opened it. Mr. Prophet sat on a chair at the table and sipped from a cup of tea I'd made for him. He never drank my coffee. I hate to admit that preparing tasty coffee had thus far eluded me. Every now and then I could fix a pot of coffee that wasn't too weak or too strong—or percolated until it was dry and burning—but I could handle tea like a champ. Anyhow, Mr. Prophet put so much milk and sugar in his tea, he probably wouldn't have noticed if I'd served him sage and juniper berries steeped in boiling water. And then his innards would be free from ghosts!

Never mind.

"All right," said Sam in his serious policeman's voice, "I've interviewed several women today. All of them were known associates of Stacy Kincaid."

" 'Known associates' makes them sound like criminals," I said as I ran water into the sink into which I'd already shaken some Oxydol soap chips.

"One of them might be a criminal. I'm not sure how we can compare the women's shoes to the sample we took at the park."

"A warrant?" I asked, not quite sure what a warrant was or how to go about getting one.

"We can't get a warrant on a whim or a faint suspicion," said Sam. "We have to have solid evidence or a rational reason to ask a judge to sign a search warrant. I can't finger any of these women without more of a case than I have at present."

"I wish Stacy would stop pestering me and tell us who killed her. That might help," I said as I began scrubbing dishes with the sponge.

"Oh yeah," said Mr. Prophet. "Sam could just tell the judge Stacy's ghost told you who killed her, and he'd sign a warrant in a snap."

"Spoilsport," I muttered.

"Yeah," said Sam. "Still, I wonder if there's some way we could coax Stacy into telling you who killed her. Cripes." He shook his head hard. "I can't believe I just said that."

"I don't think Stacy would ever stop hating me enough to finger her killer."

"That's a shame," said Sam. "I want to get this case closed."

"Well then, who are your suspects?" I asked, continuing to scrub and rinse and place dishes in the wooden rack.

Sam huffed a big huff. "None of the people whom we thought about at first seem to know anything about Stacy. In fact, both of the Trunick sisters told me they tried to stay as far away from Stacy as they could, because Stacy was so wild."

"Smart, those Trunick girls," I said. "Well, except for the one who fell in love with Cecil Darlington."

"She's as quiet and tucked-away as a nun these days," said Sam. "She could hardly make herself talk to me, and I'm a policeman. I think Darlington gave her a fright—maybe a loathing—of men."

"I can understand that," I said.

"The other one, Medora Louise, seems like a straight arrow, too. She also lives at home with her parents, but she's engaged to a fellow named Kenneth Sanders. He's a professor at the California Institute of Technology."

"Doesn't sound like someone who'd hang out with Stacy," I said.

"No. I've pretty much eliminated both of the Trunick girls. I interviewed Geneva and Roma Darlington. They're part of the country-club set and wouldn't be seen dead with Stacy Kincaid. Or so they said. They both turned up their noses when I mentioned their late brother and didn't want to talk about that 'sordid scandal,' as they called it."

"Well, it was," I said.

"True," said Sam. "I had more luck with names I got from the Buckinghams and the hospital ward register."

"You got the register?"

"I said I would, didn't I?" Sam said, sounding peeved.

"Yes, but I didn't know you'd done it. So what names have you gleaned from Flossie and Johnny and the ward register?" I asked eagerly.

"Just to be clear," said Sam in his take-note-of-this-or-beware voice, "the only reason I'm talking to you about this case is that you're involved to a degree."

"More than a degree," I said. "The stupid woman's ghost is trying to kill me!"

"Exactly," said Sam. "So pay attention."

"Yes, sir," I said snappishly.

"Don't get huffy," said Mr. Prophet. "Just pay attention. Maybe we can figger out a way to get Sam's suspects and the wise women together."

Both Sam and I stopped what we were doing and turned to look at him.

He shrugged. "Mebbe not. Just a thought."

"Let's go over the names I've whittled out of the dozens of

names people have given me," Sam suggested. "Then maybe we can figure out how to convict the one who did it."

"Or pin a medal on her," I muttered.

"Convict her of a bloody murder," Sam corrected me.

"It was bloody, all right," I said and shuddered when I remembered all that blood in the formerly pristine and beautiful library gazebo.

"Very well, so have you ever heard of a woman named Claudia Wells?"

"Claudia Wells…" I thought for a second or two. "Yes! I have. She was one of the people who used to hang out with Stacy in speakeasies. She and…Oh, shoot, I forget her name…Somebody Steadman. I can't remember— Oh, yes I can! Valerie. Valerie Steadman. She was a couple of grades ahead of me in school. She was in Billy's class, and she was always in trouble of one sort or another. Good grief, do you mean she hung out with Stacy? From what I knew of her, I thought for sure she'd end up in Hollywood trying to be a star. Or get pregnant and have to spend some time in a home for unwed mothers. I don't know where the unwed fathers have to go. Probably nowhere, since men never have to take responsibility for their sins."

This anomaly in societal morality had plagued me for some time. It was always the *women* who paid for unwanted pregnancies. If men could get pregnant, a whole lot of things would change in this old world, and quickly too.

Sorry. It's hard for me to stop once I get started. Back to the kitchen.

"I don't know about that," said Sam mildly. "However, Valerie Steadman visited Stacy quite often, as did Claudia Wells and a woman named Grace Ellen Farmer."

"Grace Ellen Farmer visited *Stacy?*" I asked, astonished. "But she was a straight-arrow Christian girl when I knew her in school."

"She still is," said Sam. "Said she visited Stacy to try to get her to see the light and to pray with her. She said it was for the sake of Stacy's soul. Said Stacy didn't welcome her visits."

"No surprise there," I muttered.

"Cripes," said Mr. Prophet. "Keep her away from me."

"I doubt that will be difficult to do," I told him, laughing a little.

"Johnny visited her more than anyone else, but I ruled him and Flossie out even before I started investigating. Apparently, while Stacy no longer wanted to be a Salvation Army lady, she still liked and respected Johnny. When I talked to him and Flossie, they both just sighed and said they'd tried, but Stacy was one tough nut."

"Or she was just nuts," I said.

"Ain't someone gonna plan a funeral for the Kincaid gal?" asked Mr. Prophet out of the blue.

His question jogged my brain a little. "Hmm. I don't know. Sam? Do you know?"

"Mrs. Pinkerton is still in a dither," said Sam. "I don't think she's capable of organizing a funeral or a memorial service or anything at the moment."

"She couldn't organize her way out of a cardboard box," I said unkindly.

"I suspect you're correct," Sam said, sighing. "Still, she lost a child. That's a big blow, even to a rich woman."

"You're right. I should try to be more respectful of her loss."

Mr. Prophet grunted.

"I imagine Father Frederick and Harold will organize services," I said. "Harold will hate it, but he'll do it, because that's the way he is."

"Everybody who knew her would go to her funeral," said Mr. Prophet. "They'd all be together. Mebbe you could trap the killer at the funeral."

"Hmmm," Sam murmured. "There's a thought."

We all jumped about six or seven inches when the telephone rang. I quickly wiped my hands dry—I was still rinsing dishes—and hurried to the telephone.

When I lifted the receiver, I barely got out the, "Rotondo—" when I was interrupted.

"I know who you are," said a clearly crabby Harold. "What I want you to know is that you have to go to Stacy's funeral. It's this coming

Saturday at All Saints Episcopal Church. It will be a short service. Then there will be a graveside service at Mountain View. Mother is, of course, too distraught to do anything but weep and faint, so Father Frederick and Johnny Buckingham are conspiring to bring it off."

"I think it's called cooperating, Harold Kincaid," I said. "I also think it's nice that Father Frederick and Johnny are working together."

"For Stacy?"

"It's for your mother and the other people who will grieve Stacy's passing." It was evil of me, but I couldn't help adding, "If there are any."

"Except for Mother, I don't think there are," said Harold grouchily.

"What time is the church service? Lordy, I hope Stacy won't try to kill me there."

"She still haunting you?"

"Yes, and it's not pleasant."

"Maybe the church service will make her go away."

"I doubt it," I said, and told him about how the day's exercise class ended.

"Is that Harold Kincaid?" came Sam's voice from the kitchen.

I put my hand over the receiver and called back, "Yes."

"Ask him if he knows any of the women we identified as possibles," he said. He had stopped speaking loudly and appeared in the hallway with his list of names.

"Sure. Say, Harold, Sam found names of a few women who are possible suspects in Stacy's murder. Mind if I read you their names and maybe you can tell us something about them?"

"I tried to stay as far away as possible from my sister. I didn't know her friends."

"I know, but maybe you'll recognize a name or something," I said.

"Oh, all right," said Harold with an aggrieved sigh.

So Sam handed me the sheet of paper with the names on it, and I read them to Harold.

"I knew Claudia a little bit, but I tried to avoid her. Never heard of the other two," said Harold.

After I relayed Harold's message to Sam, I said, "You never told me the time of Stacy's service at All Saints."

"Ten-thirty. The graveside service will follow. Then there will be a light luncheon at Mother's house after the burial."

"Backing and forthing," I murmured.

"Something like that," said Harold.

"You're organizing the light luncheon, I presume, since your mother is too distraught to organize it."

"Boy, you're smart," said Harold. "Your aunt and Featherstone are helping. Fortunately for them, Mother has pretty much stuck to her bed since she learned about Stacy's demise. Makes it easier for everybody else."

"I feel sorry for your mother," I said. "I know she's...difficult, but still, as Sam reminded me a few minutes ago when I was saying mean things about her, she lost a child. I can't even imagine losing a child of mine. I'm sure her grief is real and painful."

"Yeah, I know," Harold said, still sounding grouchy, "but she's a real pain in the neck."

"Say, Harold," I said, suddenly having an excellent idea. Or maybe it wasn't. Only time would tell. "You don't mind if a couple of Voodoo mambos and a Chinese wise woman go to Stacy's service, do you? Maybe one of them will convince Stacy's ghost to vanish."

"Are both of the Voodoo mambos of African heritage?" asked Harold.

"Yes," I said.

"Have them and the Chinese woman come to the cemetery for the graveside service. Mother might faint if they show up at the church. But they can just stand around as if they're merely visiting the cemetery if they go to Mountain View."

"That's so unfair," I said, getting indignant about people's irrational biases. I did that a lot, and it didn't make a hill of beans' worth of difference.

"Yeah, I know. I'm me, remember?"

"Good point." Harold was actually illegal, I guess. People of his persuasion could be arrested and jailed. So senseless. "Well, okay. Thanks, Harold. Ten-thirty at All Saints on Saturday. I might be wearing some kind of protection at the graveside service. You won't mind if I smell of sage and orange peels, will you?"

"No. I understand. I might stick an orange peel in my own pocket. Stacy wasn't one of my more ardent admirers."

"She had no taste," I said.

"True," said Harold. "Very true."

TWENTY-FIVE

Lest you think I'd forgotten about the library's resident ghost, I hadn't. We'd managed to subdue it according to Regina, but she and everyone else who worked in or visited the library wanted the nasty old man to go away forever. I mean, they might run out of copper one-cent pieces. Besides, nobody wants to trample on salt and sage leaves in a library—or anywhere else, most likely.

In that regard, as soon as I hung up the telephone on Harold's call, darned if the stupid thing didn't ring *again*. Scowling at it, I lifted the receiver and said recited my speech: "Rotondo residence. Mrs. Rotondo speaking."

"Oh, Daisy!" cried Regina Browning, "Have you thought of a way to get Mr. Whitehall's ghost to leave the library?" I heard her suck in a breath. "I'm sorry. I didn't even say good evening."

"It's all right," I said soothingly. "I understand how unsettling it is to have a ghost haunting you. Believe me."

"I'm so glad I know you," said Regina, sniffling a little. "I don't know what we'd have done if you hadn't become involved. Thanks to the pennies, the salt, and the other stuff, there hasn't been as much mischief done as before, but patrons have started telling us we need to keep the library cleaner. And children have been pouring through the doors and picking up pennies. We try to get them all back again, but we're going to break the bank if we have to keep dumping copper coins on the floor."

"Can you put them in little tucked-away nooks or something?" I asked, feeling and sounding inadequate.

"We've been doing that today because the coins are such a temptation to people. Although I don't know why children are coming into the main library when there's a children's library right across the street."

"I imagine some kid came in with his parents, saw the pennies— I mean one-cent pieces—and told all his friends," I said.

Regina heaved an audible sigh. "You're probably right."

I bethought me of Pudge Wilson, the kid who lived in the house directly north of my parents' bungalow. Pudge was a Boy Scout, and he was always looking for good deeds to do. "I wish school was out for a holiday or something. I know a Boy Scout who'd *love* to stand guard at the library doors and make sure nobody left with any coins."

"Too bad I don't know any Boy Scouts," said Regina.

"I'll chat with a friend who's good at supernatural stuff. She might have an idea on how to eradicate Mr. Whitehall's revenant."

There was a slight pause on the wire. Then Regina said, "You know more interesting people than I do, Daisy."

"It's because of what I used to do for a living," I said. "It started out pure make-believe, but then weird things began happening."

"You mean you're giving up your...whatever you call it? Your job?"

"As a spiritualist-medium?" I thought about it for a second and three-quarters then said, "Yes. I'm going to be a plain old Pasadena matron, taking care of my husband, my house, my child, my dog, and my garden. No more séances for me."

"People will miss your services," said Regina.

"Perhaps, but I won't miss them," I said tartly. Relenting slightly, I added, "Maybe on special occasions I'll pretend to be a Gypsy fortune-teller if some rich woman throws a shindig for a good cause."

"Oh, my, do you do that?"

"I have done it," I said. "I had a fortune-telling tent at a party Mrs. Pinkerton held to benefit the Pasadena Humane Society. And I was a fortune-teller at a Christmas party once. That one wasn't much fun." It had served its purpose in unearthing a murderer, but I'd nearly battered the killer to death with Sam's cane because I'd mistakenly thought he'd shot and killed Harold Kincaid. I shuddered.

"Well, I imagine Detective Rotondo is a good provider," said Regina tentatively, as if she didn't think it was polite to ask about other people's finances. I agreed with her, but because she was Regina, I didn't get mad.

"Yes, he does. He also has investments, and I've saved quite a bit of money over the years."

"That's good. I love my job, or we'd live on Robert's salary, which is quite good as he's now a partner in the Underhill firm."

"Glad to hear it," I said. "But let me talk with my friend who might be able to rid the library of Mr. Whitehall's ghost. We'll figure out something." I hoped.

"Thank you so much, Daisy," said Regina.

"You're welcome," I said back at her, only hoping Mrs. Potts or Mrs. Jackson or Miss Li could actually perform an exorcism on the library's ghost. And on Stacy.

What a mess.

I walked back to the kitchen, only to discover Mr. Prophet had finished washing the dishes while I'd been on the telephone! I'd been feeling unsettled and weary and wondering why all of a sudden so many ghosts had shown up in my life, but seeing the pristine counter perked me right up.

"Thank you!" I said to Mr. Prophet, who had resumed his seat at the kitchen table opposite Sam's.

"You're welcome," he said. "I heard you talkin' about the library ghost. I'd dang near forgot about that one, Stacy bein' so damn pesky."

"Yes," I said, sighing heavily and sinking into another kitchen chair. "The library's ghost is, or used to be, Mr. Enoch Whitehall.

I'm hoping Mrs. Potts or Miss Li—or Mrs. Jackson—can perform an exorcism. Or at least tell me how to do one. Mrs. Bissel asked me to exorcise a ghost—or a spirit—from her basement once, but it turned out to be a runaway girl."

Mr. Prophet chuckled. "You do get in some tangles, don't you?"

"Not on purpose."

Sam said, "Huh." Then he said, "But listen here, Daisy, maybe you can talk to these females. You know, just chat with them about Stacy. Maybe you can get an idea about which one of them—if any of them—killed the woman."

"Me?" I pointed at my chest. "You always try to keep me out of your cases. How come you want me in this one?"

"Because you found the body and Stacy's haunting you."

"Well, yes, but I doubt those three women would believe me about the haunting."

"Hell," said Mr. Prophet. "Don't tell 'em about the haunting. Cain't you come up with some sob story about how awful it was to stumble across the hell-bitch's body at the library and how you just want to condole with her friends?"

"But do they even know each other? I can't imagine going to each one's home—remember I don't know any of them except Grace Ellen Farmer, and I don't want to know her—and talking about Stacy."

"Hmm," said Sam. "You've got a point." He sat and thought. I sat and didn't think, both my body and my mind being worn out.

The telephone rang. I sagged only a little bit before getting up and trudging back to the hall. I spoke my speech and got a surprise in return.

"Daisy dear," said Mrs. Bissel, probably my all-time favorite client. "I've been thinking about the murder of Stacy Kincaid, and thought I'd ask if the police are having any luck finding the killer. I know you probably can't talk about it, but has your detective given you a hint or anything?"

"I've been thinking about it too," I said with perfect truth. "Detective Rotondo and his team have come up with a few names of people who might have something to do with Stacy's death, but it's difficult to pinpoint any of them."

"It was another woman, wasn't it?" said Mrs. Bissel, surprising me.

"Um…" I didn't know what to answer without giving away police secrets.

"It must have been," she went on, "because the only people allowed to visit her in the hospital were females except for that Salvation Army fellow, and he wouldn't kill anyone. From what I've gathered during Madeline's calm moments between hysterics, all the men Stacy was enamored of are either dead or in prison."

"Oh," I said. Mrs. Pinkerton knew more about Stacy and her men than I'd thought she did.

"Anyhow the point of this call is that Pansy and I figure Stacy's murderer must have been a woman because there don't seem to be any men left in her life."

"Um…that's interesting."

"Of course, I wouldn't have blamed dear Harold if he'd done her in, but he'd never do such a thing.

"You're right there. Harold would never jeopardize his freedom even for so noble a cause as ridding the world of Stacy."

Mrs. Bissel chuckled.

"But my point here is this," she went on. "While I know the names of some of that girl's contemporaries, I don't know all of them. Madeline has been of little help in remembering names of her friends. Dennis, who went to school with her"—Dennis is Mrs. Bissel's son—"gave me another couple, but he didn't consort with the people who consorted with her."

"Fortunate for Dennis," I said, plopping a spiteful comment into an infinitesimal pause.

Another chuckle. "Yes. But I'm sure the police have come up with some names. That gentleman from the Salvation Army must know some names. I can't remember his name. Lovely fellow."

"Yes, he is a truly good man. His name is Johnny Buckingham. He and his wife Flossie were about the only two people I know who stuck with Stacy to the bitter end."

"That's what Harold told me," said Mrs. Bissel. "Poor Harold. He's running himself ragged, what with trying to console his mother and getting a funeral planned but he's done it, bless him."

"Yes. He just called me. Ten-thirty at All Saints, a graveside service at Mountain View, and then a light repast at Mrs. Pinkerton's house."

"That's been changed," said Mrs. Bissel.

"What has?" I asked, confused.

"The light repast. I told Harold that since the graveside service will be at Mountain View, why have attendees drive all the way back to Madeline's house? Why not have it at my house on Foothill? It's closer to the cemetery, and I'm sure Madeline will be in no fit state to have people wandering through her home after she just buried her only daughter."

"That's kind of you," I said thinking, perhaps not strangely, of my beloved Aunt Vi who would otherwise have been tasked with preparing the funeral baked meats. Aunt Vi, who never even got to see her own son buried. Life can be so unfair.

"Only being practical, Daisy. You know Madeline. And I'm hoping you, with your unique skills with people, might be able to figure out who, among the guests attending, is the one who did Stacy in."

"*What?*" I cleared my throat. "I beg your pardon. I didn't mean to squeal into the telephone."

Yet another chuckle. "It's all right, Daisy. I know you undervalue your ability to uncloak people's outer shells, but I've seen you do it time and again."

"You have? I have?"

"Oh, for goodness' sake, of course you do And I'm sure Rolly is with you always, even when you're not conducting a séance. Perhaps as you chat with the young women at my house, you'll be able to discern if one of them is the villain."

Precisely what Sam wanted me to do. Crumb, people had awfully high expectations of one pregnant twenty-five-year-old woman who was attempting to put her mediumistic past behind her.

"That's what my husband said," I told her, a morose note to my voice.

"See? He knows you have powers of compassion too."

Powers of compassion? What the heck were they? "You think compassion will make Stacy's killer confess? I can't quite see it myself." Besides, it seemed to me I was more cynical than compassionate.

"There you go again," said Mrs. Bissel. "Underestimating your understanding of human nature."

"You think I understand human nature?" I asked, bewildered.

"Of course you do!" she said, cheerfully confident. "Why, if the killer is among those present, I'm sure you'll discover who she is!"

Crumb. Crumb, crumb, crumb. Wasn't being haunted by Stacy Kincaid enough pressure for one youngish Pasadena matron to be under? Evidently not. Now I was supposed to be a compassionate psychic who uncovered murderers. I know. It was my own fault for fooling so many people for so many years.

"Well," I said feebly, "I'll do my best."

"Of course. That's all anyone can ask. Thank you so much, Daisy."

I didn't ask for what. I did, however, go back to the kitchen and tell Sam he didn't have to worry about getting all the suspects together so I could talk to them. Mrs. Bissel had already planned a party for them.

Lord, give me help. Richard III might have been better off hollering for assistance rather than a horse at the Battle of Bosworth Field, although I'm not sure. People's unfounded beliefs in me were weighing me down.

Speaking of Richard III, I wondered if anyone in Pasadena—or anywhere else—sold old roses. I don't mean wilted ones, but ones that have been cultivated for hundreds of years. I vaguely recalled reading about people who cultivated what they called heirloom roses. I wouldn't mind having historical roses in my garden. I'd plant the white rose of York and the red rose of the Lancasters right beside each other and *force* them to get along. I might just entangle their thorny branches. That'd teach them.

Sorry. I think the pressure of being haunted and of other people's expectations were driving me a little nuts.

TWENTY-SIX

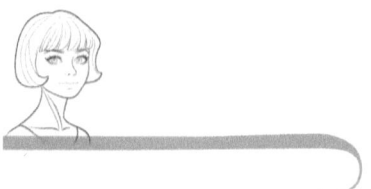

O n Thursday morning, after I took myself and Spike for a walk with my father and Rosebud, Spike and I returned home. Not finding Mr. Prophet lounging in the kitchen sipping his last cup of coffee, we moseyed out to his cottage hidden away behind a bunch of orange trees in our backyard.

As I'd anticipated, we found him sitting in his rocking chair reading a book, Yuyu on his lap. When I squinted at the book's title, I saw it was *Marching on Tanga*, by Francis Brett Young. I couldn't imagine why people wanted to read about that grisly war, but I didn't ask Mr. Prophet. He glanced up when he heard us approach. Yuyu looked kind of cute in his collar with the copper coin appended thereto. He didn't hiss at me for once, but only stared with his weird yellow eye—he only had the one. If ever a man and a cat were meant for each other, they were Mr. Prophet and Yuyu.

"Mornin' again," Mr. Prophet said, not sounding grouchy. I'd expected him to be unpleasant to me for interrupting his morning reading.

"Good morning," I said back. "Would you please go with me either to Miss Li's place or to Mrs. Jackson's? I told Regina I'd attempt to find someone who could exorcise the ghost of Enoch

Whitehall from the library, and she and Mrs. Jackson are the only people I can think of who might be able to do it."

He didn't answer for several seconds, during which I became antsy. Was he going to yell at me? Tell me he had better things to do? Tell me it didn't matter because the library was going to be torn down whether Mr. Whitehall's ghost was exorcised or not?

I startled Spike into a short yip when I jumped at Mr. Prophet's ultimate, "Sure. Why not?"

He closed the book. I noticed he was using a dried orange peel as a bookmark. He lifted Yuyu from his lap and placed the cat tenderly on the porch. There, Yuyu gave a big stretch, then bounded down the porch steps and pounced at Spike, who pounced back. And they were off, all orange (cat) and black (dog) playing for all they were worth. The sight of Spike playing with a cat still faintly surprised me. It also always made me smile and sometimes laugh out loud.

"They look like Halloween," I propounded.

"Wrong season," said Mr. Prophet.

"Maybe, but they still look like Halloween," I said.

"Lemme get my peg on, and I'll join you in the house," he said, not even bothering to bicker.

I squinted at him. "You feeling all right?" I asked, concerned.

"Yeah. Why?"

"You're not arguing with me."

"Hellkatoot. I want to get rid of the damn ghosts as much as you do. We'd best talk to Hattie Potts about an exorcism though. I don't think Miss Li can do 'em. But Hattie, especially if she gets together with Mrs. Jackson, should be able to roust any ghost and send it to where it belongs."

"Thank you," I said and turned to go back to the house.

I wanted to know where ghosts went when they were exorcised, but then I decided it probably depended on the person the ghost had been whilst alive. I figured Stacy should go straight to the nether reaches of heck, but I didn't know enough about Mr. White-hall to form an opinion. For all I knew, he'd been a fine man except for his fixation on the library and the park. As I was almost as sorry as he to know our beautiful library and its spacious green park would soon be no more, I figured that one idiosyncrasy wouldn't necessarily send him to dwell with Satan. If it did, I guess I was doomed too.

Spike and Yuyu had frolicked off to what Sam and I had begun calling the "back forty" because it was in the very back-back of our yard. The "back forty" was where a bunch of bones had been discovered earlier in the year. The bones were gone now thank heaven, but the dog and cat still liked to race around there and dig for things. I was about to open the back door when Spike caromed up to me, almost bumping into the door.

I looked down at him. "What's up, Spike? Did Stacy's ghost get to you again?"

But his tail was wagging a mile a minute and he was grinning like an imp—don't tell me dogs can't smile—so I guessed he'd just decided to trade Yuyu's company for mine. I was glad. I loved my dog.

That day I wore a plain but pretty day dress suitable for visiting neighbors, even Voodoo mambo neighbors. My gold chain, with its lumpy load of four charms, wasn't noticeable because this dress had a fabric bow at the neck. I'm not overly fond of bows or frills, so I only tied it once and allowed the ends to dangle, but they looked nice that way. They also covered the lumpy charms.

Spike and I didn't have a long wait. Mr. Prophet came in the back door about five minutes after we'd visited his cottage.

"Do you want me to drive us down the street, or are you able to walk that far?" I asked him. Then I wished I hadn't.

"Damnation, I been walkin' on this peg since I lost my leg. I walked you to the library and to the gazebo, don't forget. I kin walk to Miss Li's place. Hell, I do it all the time."

"All right," I said. "Please don't get huffy at me. I was trying to be considerate. And it's Mrs. Mainwaring's house, not Miss Li's."

"Mrs. Mainwaring." He chuffed derisively. "That's not the name I knew her by in Tucson. She's had more names than an actor in the flickers."

I sighed. A year or so earlier, I'd learned a whole lot about Mrs.

Mainwaring's earlier life in Tucson and other places, and Mr. Prophet was correct.

"Apparently she's settled on Mainwaring as the last of her last names," I said.

"Huh," he said back. Not an admirer of Mrs. Mainwaring, Mr. Prophet was a true fan of Miss Li Ahn, whom he'd also known in Tucson but of whom he harbored fonder memories.

We didn't chat as we walked down the street, Mr. Prophet carrying the cooking vessel in which Hattie Potts had prepared our last night's meal. Stacy couldn't get at us, because we'd armed ourselves with pockets full of sage and salt and orange peels. We heard her whooshing around us, and her shrieking and *Eeeeeing* were kind of eerie, but at least she couldn't harm us. She wasted a lot of dried peppercorns by throwing them at us, but they veered off to hit the street and the sidewalk. It was perhaps the most uncanny walk I'd ever walked, but we got to our destination eventually.

When we did so, the huge iron gate stood open, so we walked up to the big double doors and pressed the doorbell button. I heard chimes ringing inside the house.

When it came to Mrs. Mainwaring and her establishment, one never knew who'd answer the door when one came to visit. She had so many fingers in so many pies—many of them charitable—she often had what I thought of as waifs and strays being trained for legitimate work answering her bell. That day, one of her strays, a lovely young girl of Hispanic heritage, opened the door to us. She stood there looking and smiling and saying nothing. I let Mr. Prophet take the lead, which he did admirably.

"*Buenas días*, Maria," said he. He hung out at the Mainwaring place a lot more than I did, so he knew the inhabitants better than I. "Mind takin' this to Mrs. Potts?"

"Happy to," said Maria, taking the pot he held out to her.

"Are Mrs. Potts and Miss Li here, Maria?" asked Mr. Prophet

"Yes, they are," said the young woman—Maria, I presumed. "Will you please come in, and I'll get them." She had a thick accent, but I could understand her.

"Thank you," I said, stepping into the house. "Shall we wait in the living room?"

"*Sí.* I mean, yes, please. Dammit, I'm trying to remember to speak English." She slapped a hand over her mouth. "I'm not supposed to swear, either. I'm sorry."

"It's all right," I told her, trying not to laugh. Mrs. Mainwaring's strays generally came to her when they got tired of making their livings "on their backs," as Sam politely put it. Most of them were unlettered and had no families, money, or education to help them along the road to a better life. I applauded Mrs. Mainwaring's charitable leanings. In her own unconventional way, she was kind of like the Salvation Army and Johnny and Flossie.

Mr. Prophet and I walked into the living room where her grand piano sat. I'd played that piano and it was exceptional.

"Howdy there," came a deep masculine voice at our backs.

"Good morning," I said, turning to greet Mr. Judah Bowman, who had followed us into the living room.

"Mornin'," said Mr. Prophet. He held out his hand, and the two men shook hands. Mr. Prophet got along fine with Mr. Bowman. The only thing he didn't approve of when it came to Judah Bowman was what Mr. Prophet considered his inexplicable fondness for Mrs. Mainwaring. A handsome man, even though he certainly wasn't in his first youth, Mr. Bowman also lived in the Mainwaring home. At least, I think he did. A whole lot of Mrs. Mainwaring's life remained a mystery to me.

"We just came over to consult with Miss Li and Mrs. Potts," I told him.

"Ah, yes. Both of them tell me you've been having some trouble at your house. Something about ghosts? I never believed in ghosts until I met Hattie Potts, but I sure do now."

"Yes, we have a ghost. It's that of Stacy Kincaid, who is out to bedevil me and those close to me," I told him.

Mr. Bowman shook his head. "Too bad. But I expect Hattie can help you. I didn't know Li was in the ghost-removal line."

"Don't know if she is," said Mr. Prophet. "But she helped ghost-proof Miss Daisy's house."

"Good. I'll see if I can find Hattie."

"Maria's doin' that," said Mr. Prophet.

"I'll help," said Mr. Bowman, and he drifted off.

After he'd exited the room, I whispered to Mr. Prophet, "Did you ever know him in your bounty-hunting days?"

"Met him a couple of times in Tucson," Mr. Prophet said. "He was a kid then. I...wasn't, but I wasn't all *that* old." He sounded defensive, perhaps because he was about twenty years older than Mr. Bowman, at least by my estimation. Mind you, Mr. Bowman wasn't a spring chicken. I figured he was in his fifties, just as Mr. Prophet was in his seventies.

"Was he a bounty hunter too?" I asked.

"Naw. He was a good man with a gun and did jobs for people who needed jobs done."

"What kinds of jobs?" I asked.

Squinting down at me, Mr. Prophet said, "Jobs that needed help from folks that was good with guns."

"Oh," I said, only partially enlightened. Mr. Judah Bowman, along with Mr. Lou Prophet and others of their ilk, likely weren't people you'd want to meet at night in a dark alley.

"Mrs. Rotondo, Lou," came Hattie Potts's voice from the door to the living room.

I turned to see her beaming face and portly figure coming toward us. "Good morning, Mrs. Potts. Thank you so much for fixing us supper last night. It was delicious, and we brought back the pot this morning."

"You're more than welcome, child," said Mrs. Potts. "Li's been tellin' me about the problems you've got, and you don't need to worry about fixin' meals when you're tryin' to get rid of an evil emanation."

"Thank you," I said. "You're very kind."

"Yeah," said Mr. Prophet. "But what we want to know is if you or Mrs. Jackson can get rid of another ghost. There's one hauntin' the library. It's not evil like the one hauntin' Miss Daisy, but it's a pain in the ass and, the folks at the library want to get rid of it."

"Why are you standing?" asked Mrs. Potts. "Sit down."

ALICE DUNCAN

I'm not sure about Mr. Prophet, but I'd been standing because no one had invited me to sit yet. I sat in one of the gorgeous chairs in Mrs. Mainwaring's living room. However she'd spent her life before coming to Pasadena and becoming the wealthiest orange grove owner in town, she sure owned beautiful things.

"Anyhow," said Mr. Prophet, after we were all settled on comfy furniture, "do you think you can get rid of the library ghost? I expect it'll take more power to get rid of the ghost hauntin' Miss Daisy. But the library ghost is just an old fart who doesn't want the building to be torn down."

"Odd reason for haunting a place," said Mrs. Potts.

"His name was Mr. Enoch Whitehall," I told her. "He's been knocking books off shelves and throwing them at librarians. He turns off the lights sometimes and locks the doors so people can't get in or out of the building."

"Pesky feller," muttered Mr. Prophet.

"I should think a stern talking-to will get rid of him," said Mrs. Potts. She turned to me, her dark face registering concern. "But what about the ghost out to get you? Li told me she's vicious and pure evil."

"Yes," I said upon a sigh. "She was always trouble, even when she was alive. But now that she's dead, her ghost seems intent on seeing me dead too."

"That's not good," said Mrs. Potts, frowning.

"It sure isn't good for me," I told her. "She tried to crash the car when Mr. Prophet and I were going to the library on Tuesday."

"Who's Mr. Pro— Oh, you mean Lou here? Why d'you call him Mr. Prophet, girl? Don't you know him well enough by this time?"

I know I blushed because I could feel the heat creep up my neck and invade my cheeks. Curses! I decided to be honest. "I don't know. I've just always called him Mr. Prophet."

"You kin call me Lou if you want to, Miss Daisy," said the old reprobate, grinning like one of those weird kewpie dolls you see at fairs sometimes.

I looked at him, tilted my head a little, and decided something right there on the spot. "I'll keep calling you Mr. Prophet. My life is

226

already confused. If I have to call you by a different name, it'll only get more complicated."

Hattie Potts and Mr. Lou Prophet both laughed.

"Reckon you got a point there, Miss Daisy."

"Aha!" I pointed a finger at him, which I know to be impolite. "You call me 'Miss Daisy', when you could just call me Daisy. So I'll call you Mr. Prophet."

"Fair deal," he said.

Then both he and Hattie Potts laughed again.

TWENTY-SEVEN

I didn't mind their laughter, mainly because it ceased almost instantly and Mrs. Potts said, "But enough of this nonsense. Loretta and I can get rid of that ghost in the library for you."

"You can?" My heart leaped like a ballerina. Loretta is Mrs. Jackson's first name, by the way.

"Why do you sound so surprised?" said Mr. Prophet. "We come over here to ask her to get rid of the library ghost, remember?"

Mrs. Potts laughed again. "Don't tease the child, Lou! She was hopin', was all. She didn't know I could do it. But with Loretta Jackson's help, I'll bet we can get that snarly old man to leave the library alone."

"Oh, thank you!" I said. "The library staff is scared to death. They've scattered copper one-cent pieces all over the place, but people keep picking them up."

"Yeah, people will do that with money," said Mrs. Potts. "But let me get Cyrus. He'll drive us up to Loretta's place, and we can come up with a plan. Shouldn't be too hard to get a mean old ghost to leave a library. The ghost hauntin' *you* might take a little more doin', but not all that much."

"Oh, if you could send Stacy's ghost away, I'd be forever grateful!" I felt silly when tears filled my eyes. "She's trying to kill me, and I want to stay alive for my husband and my baby!" I kind of wailed the last couple of words and I also cradled my small lump. Pathetic, I know.

"Oh, honey, don't cry. We'll fix you up. Might require you to get your spirit-control fellow into the action."

I blinked away my tears and wiped the excess moisture with my fingers. "Rolly?" I said, surprised.

"That his name? Angie couldn't remember."

Angie was what people called Mrs. Mainwaring when they didn't call her Mrs. Mainwaring. "Oh. That's right. I performed a séance for her, didn't I?"

"Don't know, but she says you got a spirit control, and Loretta and me will probably need him."

"But I made him up when I was ten," I said. Then I wished I hadn't when I saw the knowing smile on Mrs. Potts's face.

"You were too young to know about spirits back then, child. But he's yours now, isn't he? You know he is."

I hesitated a second before admitting, "Yes. He is. And sometimes he gets out of control."

"That's only because he wants to protect you," said Mrs. Potts. She rose from her chair. Mr. Prophet, being polite, did likewise. So did I. "I'll go fetch Cyrus. You ready for a visit to Loretta Jackson?"

"Yes, indeed," I said. "We already visited her once and got some sage, salt, and other things to repel ghosts."

"That's good. And Li gave you some Chinese magic." She peered at Mr. Prophet. "I expect you still got some Apache magic from Arizona."

"Arizona and New Mexico," he said. "Not that they were states at the time." He sounded grumpy when he spoke the last sentence. Mr. Prophet didn't approve of modern inventions like statehood for his old stomping grounds.

"Nothing lasts forever," I said, trying to be sympathetic.

"Yeah. Like the library," he growled at me.

"Exactly. I'm going to be heartbroken when it and the gorgeous park are gone."

"Yeah, well…" He didn't go on, probably because he realized I actually *did* understand a little of what he missed from his younger days. Only a little, but still and all, I had a good imagination.

"Don't pick on Daisy, Lou," said Mrs. Potts as she exited the room, chuckling.

"Wasn't pickin' on you," grumbled Mr. Prophet. "Mebbe you'll understand someday when you're old and can't get around like you can now and your kids are grown and gone, and Pasadena's a big ugly city like Los Angeles."

"I hope Pasadena doesn't come to that," I said, thinking I hoped my kids—plural, for heaven's sake—didn't desert me when I got old. And that Pasadena didn't get to be a huge modern city I no longer recognized.

Mrs. Potts came back into the living room, Li on her heels and smiling at Mr. Prophet and me. "Good morning, you two. How's the house, Daisy?"

"Protected, thanks to you and Mrs. Jackson. I hope we can get rid of Stacy's ghost entirely, and you can have your lion dogs back."

"Good. I miss them," said Li.

Cyrus Potts drove Mrs. Mainwaring's gorgeous Marmon Touring Car to the front of the house and waited beside the front porch. The car was light blue and gleamed in the early spring sunshine. Cyrus must have been busy washing and polishing it. He opened the back door, and I got in first. Then Mr. Prophet hoisted himself into the car and sat next to me. The seats were roomy enough to give him plenty of room for his peg. Hattie took the front seat next to Cyrus.

We arrived at Mrs. Jackson's small but well-kept home on Mentone Avenue not more than ten minutes after we'd left Mrs. Mainwaring's house. Cyrus parked right in front of the house. Mrs. Jackson, who'd been watering her many flowers, smiled and waved when she saw us drive up, she had shut off the hose and was standing on the grass verge in front of her home by the time Cyrus parked the car.

"Good morning to you all," she said, beaming upon us. "I just made some doughnuts for Henry's children"—Henry Jackson was one of her sons—"but they won't be here until school lets out, so we can eat 'em, and they'll never know the difference." She laughed. She had a contagious laugh. By the time we'd all exited the car, we were laughing too.

"How'd the salt and sage do in keepin' that nasty ghost out of your house, Mrs. Rotondo?" she asked.

"Please call me Daisy, and they worked really well. Along with the bundles of juniper branches and dried orange peels. Miss Li gave us some Chinese charms too. We've got ghost-repellents all over the house. It'll take me a month to clean everything up once Stacy's ghost is vanquished."

"Might want to keep a few of 'em around, just in case," she said. "You never know what's going to happen." She led the way to the front porch.

"True," I said as I followed her along with Mr. Prophet and Hattie Potts. Cyrus opted to stay with the car.

Once we were settled in her cozy living room, a plate of donuts before us, Mrs. Jackson said, "All right, what's going on now? Hattie, you need me to help you get rid of a haint?"

"Yes. Daisy says there's one hauntin' the library that needs vanquishing. Not an evil one like the one haunting her, but a cranky old man who's peeved that the library's going to be replaced."

"Strange reason to haunt a place," Mrs. Jackson observed.

"I guess it is," I said, "but I kind of don't blame the guy. I'll hate to see that beautiful building demolished, and I'll miss the library park."

With a slow nod, Mrs. Jackson said, "Yeah. I'll miss that building too. And that green, green park." She shook her head. "But it's still no reason to haunt the place."

"I suppose not," I said. The library was doomed, with or without Mr. Whitehall's approval. Or mine.

"What time does the library close?" asked Mrs. Jackson.

"Six o'clock, I think," I told her. "My friend, Mrs. Browning, is a librarian there, and I think she said the library closes at six p.m."

"Six, eh? That should give us time. You think that'll be enough time for us to prepare, Hattie?"

"I think so," said Mrs. Potts. "You thinkin' about a Voodoo spell on the ghost?"

"Something like that," said Mrs. Jackson. "It'll need to be dark." She turned to me. "Do you think your friend will let us set up at around nine o'clock tonight?"

Set up what? I decided not to ask.

"Probably. I'll talk to her."

"Good. You do that. Hattie, you stay here while Cyrus drives Daisy and Mr. Prophet here to the library to see her friend. We can make arrangements. Can't be too much trouble to get rid of a grouchy old man's ghost."

"Sounds good to me," said Hattie.

So Mr. Prophet and I left Mrs. Jackson's home, full of the most delicious donuts I'd ever tasted, and returned to Mrs. Mainwaring's spectacular car. Cyrus Potts drove us to the library.

Regina was happy to greet us, and she didn't even flinch when she saw Mr. Prophet. "It's not been too bad here since we spread all that sage and salt around. As I told you, people keep picking up the pennies, but Mr. Whitehall has mostly just been making noise today."

"I'm glad he's not throwing books at you any longer."

"So am I," said Regina with fervor.

She and I made arrangements for Hattie Potts and Mrs. Jackson to visit the library at nine o'clock that evening.

"I'll have Robert come too," said Regina. "He'll be interested in how the two ladies vanquish the ghost."

"Sure," I said. "Why not? The more, the merrier."

When Mr. Prophet and I left the library, we noticed the police presence still in the park. The gazebo's entrance had been blocked by the nailing up of two boards. I felt sad seeing it. I'd miss that gazebo, even though I'd seldom been in it, and the last time had been horrible. But it was pretty, and so was the library pond. It was going to be gone soon, too.

"Why the heck did Stacy have to get killed in that gazebo?" I blurted out when Mr. Prophet and I walked back to Mrs. Mainwaring's car, where Cyrus waited for us behind the wheel.

"Dunno," said Mr. P. "Guess because she was there when somebody got mad at her."

"I guess so."

Still, I wondered. What had Stacy been doing in the park at that hour?

What hour? I didn't know, which gave me pause.

"How long had she been dead when we found her?" I asked.

"Hell, how should I know?"

"You've had more experience with dead bodies than I have. Couldn't you tell? At least approximately?"

"Aw, hellkatoot, lemme think. We found her when? Around ten? Ten-thirty? She was cool, getting cold, and she wasn't stiff yet. I think rigor mortis generally starts about four hours after death, and she wasn't in rigor yet. So...I dunno. Somebody done her in around seven or eight? That's awful early to be frolickin' around in a gazebo in the park."

"Hmm," I said, beginning to think instead of react for a change. "If she'd been out with one or two of her degenerate friends, they might have parked behind the library and decided to go for a walk in the park just for the heck of it. She'd been drinking, hadn't she?"

"The gazebo smelled like booze, and there was a broken bottle in there with her."

"That's right. The bottle had blood on it too, didn't it?"

"Yeah," said Mr. Prophet.

"So they'll have dusted it for fingerprints," I mused.

"I reckon they did," said Mr. Prophet.

"It wouldn't surprise me if Stacy and one of her awful friends decided to get drunk in the gazebo. Then maybe they got into a fight or something."

"Was she stupid or what? If she'd just escaped from jail, why didn't she run? Why'd she stick around Pasadena?"

"Yes, she was stupid, but she was more—or maybe less—than that. She always seemed to be looking for the easy way. When Mrs. Pinkerton's gate guard was being threatened by the Ku Klux Klan, she thought Mrs. Pinkerton should fire him so as not to draw the KKK's wrath to her."

"Not very nice," muttered Mr. Prophet.

"No. And she was madly in love with a vicious gangster until he got arrested. Then she fell in love with a man who belonged to a gang smuggling children into the country to be the playthings of perverted men."

"Shi—oot," said Mr. Prophet. "So she was stupid and didn't have any morals. That about it?"

"Just about," I said, contemplating the person who used to be Stacy Kincaid. "She was a terrible person."

"You don't know what you're talking about!" came a screechy wail above our heads.

"Oh, just go away, Stacy," I snarled, annoyed as all get-out about her continued abuse of my person and my friends.

"Noooo!" she howled as she swooshed and whirled around us. She couldn't do anything *to* us because we were practically reeking of sage and orange peel.

"Aw, hell," said Mr. Prophet, and he reached into his pocket and plucked out something that he waved above his head. Guess he still carried his Mescalero magic on his person. Good thing, under the circumstances.

A weird cry of *"Eeeeeeee!"* faded into the atmosphere as we finally got to the car and Cyrus Potts. Cyrus, I noted, hadn't been bothered by Stacy. I guess he was protected by his wife's strong Voodoo or something.

"I'm so sick of her," I said as I climbed into Mrs. Mainwaring's Marmon.

"Yeah," said Mr. Prophet. "Me too."

"That the ghost y'all's wantin' to get rid of?" asked Cyrus once we were in the car.

"Yes. Did she bother you?" I asked, surprised.

"Tried," said Cyrus. "Couldn't." He turned to grin at us, and I decided he had powers of his own to fend off ghosts.

Maybe I could learn how to bolster my own powers. If I had any. Oh well. One thing at a time.

Cyrus dropped Mr. Prophet and me off at our house and then drove the rest of the way to Mrs. Mainwaring's place. Stacy didn't even try to hurl peppercorns at us as we walked up the porch steps, unlocked the door, and stepped inside to be welcomed by an ecstatic Spike.

TWENTY-EIGHT

After we'd greeted Spike and I'd let him out the back door so he could relieve himself among the many plants and trees, I sat on a chair on the back porch and sighed. It was a little after noon by then.

"Want some lunch?" I asked Mr. Prophet, who'd also taken a chair on the porch. I loved our backyard and our porch and our flowers and trees and…well, just everything. Once we got rid of Stacy, life would be just about perfect.

"Any more of them beans and rice left from last night?" he asked.

"Yes, and that's exactly what I aimed to heat up for us."

"Good. I'll get the receipt from Hattie Potts next time I visit Miss Li," said Mr. Prophet with a smug smile. "Them New Orleans beans and Mexican beans must be easy to cook up. If you use beans and rice a lot, you'll probably get to cookin' good in no time."

I thought about his comment for a second or three. "By golly, I think you're right. And both Sam and I love Mexican food. Beans and rice. I'll bet I could fix lots of things with beans and rice and make tasty meals."

"Don't know why not. Most of the rest of the people in the world eat beans and rice. Why not you and Sam?"

"Why not indeed," I said.

We sat on the back porch for another few minutes until Spike had done his duty as a dog, decided the yard wasn't interesting any longer, and joined us there. Then I rose with a grunt and headed for the kitchen. My grunt had been unintentional.

Spike danced into the kitchen. He loved the kitchen. I reached into the Frigidaire to get the container of leftover red beans and rice. "Don't Mexicans eat something called *arros con pollo*?" I asked Mr. Prophet as he pulled out a chair at the table. "That's just rice and chicken, isn't it?"

"Yup. Good stuff, too."

"All right, the next time I go to the library I'm going to check out a bunch of cooking books that deal with foreign food. I don't think I can find the ingredients for most of the Turkish food I loved so much, but there are scads of Mexican and Negro people in Pasadena. I should be able to get ingredients for what they cook."

"Might have to go to different stores," said Mr. Prophet. "Trek over to the far west side of town to the corner stores there."

"You're probably right." Until quite recently, I hadn't even thought about my beautiful Pasadena having an ugly side. But it did. White people ruled here, and most white folks didn't want people with darker skins living next to them.

Oh, I forgot the U.S.A.'s eastern population. They didn't want Italians or Irish folks polluting their pristine places, and the Irish are as white as...well, as I am. I swear. People. Couldn't do anything with them.

But never mind that. I couldn't even solve my own problems, much less those of the rest of the world. I scooped out beans and rice into a small pot and set the pot over a burner I lit and turned to a low setting. I was sure glad Stacy couldn't get into the house and burn *this* meal!

It was just as tasty for lunch as it had been for dinner. Mr. Prophet and I actually ate two helpings each, and there was enough left over for dinner if Sam wanted it. I thought maybe I should have a sandwich for dinner because of the interesting conditions produced after eating beans. I told Mr. Prophet that and he laughed at me.

"That's one of the good things about livin' in the wild. You don't have to worry about other folks smellin' yer farts."

Very well then.

After I cleaned up the lunch dishes, Spike and I went upstairs to take a nap. I felt marginally better when we woke up.

I felt even better when Sam arrived home after work that day. Spike and I met him at the front door. I allowed him to enter the house, gave him a welcome-home kiss, and even let him hang up his hat and coat before I started in on him.

"That bottle in the gazebo with Stacy had fingerprints on it, right? Oh, Sam, they might point straight to her killer."

"Yes, I did have a good day, thank you, and hope you did as well," said Sam, trying to be funny. I could tell he wasn't best pleased by my greeting, which had been a bit abrupt.

"I'm sorry, Sam, but I want Stacy's ghost to go away, and I want her killer found. I want everything to get back to normal."

He hugged me. "I know you do, sweetheart. I do too, although 'normal' around you isn't necessarily anyone else's idea of normal."

I wrenched myself free from his embrace, which was a mistake because it hurt. "What do you mean by that?" I demanded, prepared to defend myself.

"Don't get mad, Daisy. It's only that I never used to have to worry about my wife tripping over dead bodies every time she walked out the door, and I've sure never been haunted before I married you."

My lip trembled, and the urge to fight vanished. What he said was true. I bowed my head. "I'm sorry, Sam. I had no idea that when I created Rolly and all that spiritualist-medium nonsense, I might actually be conjuring spirits."

"Don't fret, sweetheart. I love you. I knew all about you before I asked you to marry me, and I did it anyway."

I couldn't make myself lift my head and look him in the eye. "Billy used to say what I did for a living was evil, but I honestly thought I was helping people. They *told* me I helped them. They truly did! So many people had lost loved ones, and so many of them just needed someone to listen to them. I thought that's what I was doing."

"I know, Daisy. I'm only teasing. Sort of. I don't believe your spiritualist-medium profession is evil, but I do hope you'll slacken off now that you don't need the money so desperately."

"I've already decided to slacken off," I said. I sniffed, swallowed, and dared to lift my head and look at his face. It showed only concern. And love. He loved me. I could tell.

"Oh, Sam!" I said, throwing my arms around him again. "I'm so glad I have you!"

"Holy cripes," came a rusty voice at the door to the front hallway. "I don't even want to know what's brought on all this weepin' and huggin'."

I didn't loosen my hold on my husband, but I did get up on my toes and peer at Mr. Prophet over Sam's shoulder. "You've probably never cared for a person long enough to know what it feels like."

It didn't occur to me how cruel a thing it was to say to him. I realized my mistake a second after my words hit the air, and the expression on his face changed.

Another second or two ticked by before Mr. Prophet said, "You'd be wrong there, Miss Daisy, but it was a long, long time ago." He turned and started to walk away.

"I'm sorry!" I hollered after him, finally letting go of Sam. My tears still fell. "I'm so sorry! Come back. I didn't mean it. I know you've loved women in your time."

He stopped and peered at me over his shoulder. "One or two. One of 'em I'd've died for. Damn near did a couple'a times."

"Please forgive me," I pleaded. "I honestly didn't mean that to sound so...mean."

"Aw, hell, what's it matter now anyhow?" he said. "I'll just sit in the kitchen, if it's all right by you."

"Of course it is," said Sam, finally free of my clingy arms. He set his briefcase on the telephone table in the hall and loosened his tie as he too walked to the kitchen.

As for me, I felt about two inches tall. I peered down at my darling Spike, who never deserts me, even when I've been an unconscionable idiot. Well, except when one or two of his people goes to the kitchen, where the food lives. He trotted after Sam, leaving me in the hall wishing I could start my life over.

The telephone rang. I glared at it for several seconds until it rang again, then I stamped to the telephone table, lifted Sam's briefcase therefrom, set it gently on the hall floor, and lifted the received. "Rotondo residence—"

"Oh, for God's sake, why do you say all that garbage? Why can't you just say 'hello' like a normal person?"

"Harold. Do normal people really answer the telephone with a mere 'hello'? I didn't know that."

"That's because you don't have much to do with normal people on an everyday basis. If *you* telephone anyone, they belong to a church or a grand estate or something. Normal, every-day people just say 'hello' these days."

"I didn't know that. I appreciate you telling me," I said, now feeling maybe a quarter of an inch tall.

"You sound like you just lost your best friend, but I'm still around, so it's got to be something else making you blue. Has Stacy overcome all the repellants we put in place and entered your house?"

"No. I've only been cruel to Mr. Prophet and a bad wife to Sam."

"Oh. Is that all? Well, buck up. I'm going to bring you dinner tonight."

"You are?" I blinked at the telephone, uncertain if I'd heard what I thought I'd heard.

"Are you going deaf too? You really are having a bad day. I said I'm bringing you, Sam, and Lou dinner. Your aunt and my mother's friends have introduced so much food into Mother's house, I'm either going to have to send it to the starving people in China or throw it away. Your aunt told me she'd kill me if I threw it away, so she's taking some of it home to your parents' house, I'm taking some of it to your pals at the Salvation Army, and then I'll bring the rest to you. And don't worry about Mother's staff. They're all stuffed to the gills."

"Oh," I said. "That's nice. Thank you."

"For once," said Harold, "you might consider thanking Stacy. If she hadn't died, we wouldn't have this bountiful harvest of edibles."

After contemplating his suggestion for half a second or so, I said, "I think I'd rather thank her killer."

"Don't blame you. I hope you didn't just fix a feast for Sam."

"Lord, no. Mr. Prophet and I spent the morning and part of the afternoon preparing for a ghost-removal party at the library this evening. After that, I was so exhausted I had to take a nap. If you want to dine with us, you may also attend the...whatever it's going to be. A couple of Voodoo mambos and Rolly will be there."

"Good God."

"I guess," I said, still feeling miserable, "although I doubt God had much to do with the library ghost. Or Stacy."

"God avoided Stacy like the plague," said Harold.

"I think it was the other way around."

"If you say so. I can't imagine a good God wanting anything to do with my sister."

"Well...Maybe you're right. If God thinks you're bad because of something you can't avoid being, maybe you're right."

"Hell's bells, and don't forget about purgatory for the Catholics! I hear it from Del all the time. Do you know he's amassing money because if he dies before I do, he wants me to spend it all in the church to say Masses so he can get out of purgatory sooner?"

"I don't understand purgatory," I said. "Who invented it? I can't remember Jesus talking about purgatory in the Gospels. In fact, I don't think there's a mention of purgatory in the whole Bible, although I haven't read it for a long time."

"The leaders of the church invented purgatory in order to enrich themselves and their churches. If I get started on the Catholic Church, I'll never stop, so I'll just shut up about it," said Harold grimly. "I'll be there in a few minutes. And sure, I'd love to see tonight's...whatever it is. Are you performing a séance?"

"I don't think so, but one of the Voodoo ladies told me to bring Rolly with me."

"He's always with you, isn't he?" Harold's voice held a snippet of snidety (I'm sure that's not a word).

But his words gave me pause. After approximately two heartbeats, I said, "Actually, yes. He is. I had no idea when I invented him that he'd eventually turn into something almost real."

"Lucky you," said Harold. "See you in a few."

"Thanks, Harold. Bye."

"Bye."

We hung up our receivers. Then I took a deep breath, braced myself to do some groveling, and walked to the kitchen.

Where I saw Sam and Mr. Prophet having a big belly laugh over something.

Which taught me something. While my behavior might be good or bad, it doesn't necessarily affect other people as much as it does me. I'm not the center of everyone else's universe!

How about that?

TWENTY-NINE

When I entered the kitchen, I saw Sam and Mr. Prophet stop laughing and turn to look at me. Both of them appeared somewhat wary.

Very well, then. I might not be the center of everyone else's universe, but my behavior can affect those close to me. I didn't want Sam or Mr. Prophet to be afraid that I'd either have a tantrum or burst into tears when I approached them.

Spike, of course, didn't give a care. He trotted up to me, his tail waving like a flag, happy to have me join the party.

"I wish we humans were more like dogs," I said.

The two men exchanged a glance. "Yeah?" said Mr. Prophet.

"Yes," I said. "I'm sorry if I made you both uncomfortable. I guess I can blame it on being pregnant. My moods are all over the place, but I shouldn't take them out on either of you, and I apologize."

"Oh, fer gawd's sake," muttered Mr. Prophet.

Sam rose from the table and came over to give me a hug. "It's all right, sweetheart. It's been a rough few days."

"Thanks, Sam. I didn't mean to pester you the second you walked through the door."

"No?" he said, a doubtful note to his voice. "Well, it's all right. I'll tell you what I can about the case. Lou says Mrs. Jackson, Mrs. Potts, and you are going to get rid of the library ghost tonight."

"Yes. Mrs. Potts and Mrs. Jackson will do that. They told me to bring Rolly with me."

"Cripes," muttered Mr. Prophet.

I ignored him. "We're going to meet at the library at nine. I hope it works so we don't have to waste any more time on the ghost of Mr. Enoch Whitehall."

"That who's haunting the building?" asked Sam.

"Yes. I thought you were there when Regina told me about him."

"Guess not. I hope it works. Then, if we can get rid of Stacy, we can concentrate on who murdered her."

"Yes. It's just like a murdered Stacy not to reveal her killer's name but instead take out all her anger on me. She was always a waste of space." I sat in a chair at the table and slumped there. Then I remember Harold. "Oh!" I straightened. "Harold's bringing dinner."

"He is?" Sam sat up straighter too. "Why?"

"Too much food at his mother's house. He said it's either bring it here and to my parents or throw it out." I recalled his other option. "Or send it to the starving people in China."

"What about the Salvation Army?" asked Mr. Prophet. "They feed poor folks."

"He's going there before he comes here," I said.

"That's nice of him," said Sam.

"Yes, it is," I said. "He also wants to attend the exorcism or whatever it is."

"Why not?" said Mr. Prophet. "He's been to all of the rest of 'em, at least those I know about."

"True. Well, I'll feed Spike now so he won't bother us too much at the table when Harold gets here."

Spike, who understood human language and had even begun to spell—you couldn't say W-A-L-K in front of him because he knew what it meant—perked up and wagged some more.

So Spike and I walked to the service porch where I kept his dried dog food. The veterinarian said the dry stuff was good for him, but it didn't look awfully appetizing to me, so I always mixed it with something else. Usually, I mixed it with jarred chicken I'd chopped up.

I probably didn't need to feel guilty about it, but I know Vi preserved food for her human kin. I wasn't sure she'd appreciate knowing the dog got lots of it. A jar of chicken lasted Spike about a week and a half. I don't think that was wasteful.

Other people might think differently, but what they didn't know wouldn't hurt them. Or me.

By the time Spike had been fed, and I'd returned the jar of chopped chicken to the refrigerator, Sam had retrieved his briefcase and laid it on the kitchen table. Opening the briefcase, he looked up at me and smiled. "The broken liquor bottle did have fingerprints on it."

"Oh! Do you know who any of the prints belong to? Whom they belong to? To whom they belong? Whatever it's supposed to be?"

Mr. Prophet shook his head and said, "Huh?"

"Never mind," I said, deciding this wasn't the time for a grammar lesson, especially since I didn't know what I was talking about. About which I was talking. The English language drives me *insane* sometimes!

"Most of them are Stacy's," said Sam.

"Oh. Well," I opined, "that's not very helpful."

"There are prints from another person, but we don't have that person's prints on record. That's one drawback to fingerprinting. Unless the person belonging to the prints has committed a crime in Pasadena, we won't have them on file."

"But if you find the person belonging to the prints, he or she might be Stacy's killer?" I asked.

"We still think it was a she. She might be, but how do we get her prints to compare them to the ones on the bottle?"

"At the get-together after Stacy's funeral," I said, again feeling almost cheery because I'd just offered such a brilliant suggestion.

Have I mentioned how difficult it can be to determine if an idea is brilliant or not? Well, it is, as Sam's next comment proved.

"Are you going to collect glasses from everyone who drinks lemonade at the get-together?" he asked sweetly.

"Oh. I didn't think about that. We'd have to label the glasses, too."

"Yes," said Sam. "We would."

Mr. Prophet chuckled. "Good thought though, Miss Daisy."

"If totally impractical," I muttered, my teensy bit of cheerfulness flopping onto the floor like a dead trout.

"I still believe our best bet as far as finding the killer is to have you nose around at the funeral or at the get-together afterwards, Daisy," said Sam. "You should be safe there too. I can't imagine a lady at a funeral attacking another attendee."

"When it comes to Stacy and any of her associates, I wouldn't rule anything out," I muttered. Catching criminals was *so difficult* unless you caught the crook in the act. I didn't envy Sam his job.

Suddenly, Spike leaped up from where he'd been snoozing on the floor next to my chair. I feared for a second Stacy's ghost had managed to get into the house until I remembered Harold. Sure enough, about ten seconds after Spike's first warning, the doorbell rang.

Sam closed his briefcase. He and I rose to go to the door. We told Mr. Prophet to stay where he was, figuring the three able-bodied among us were better equipped to carry whatever foodstuffs Harold had with him.

I'd already turned on the porch light. As soon as I opened the door, the light spilled down upon Harold Kincaid, his fedora hat looking fashionable, holding a large cardboard box, which didn't appear fashionable but which sure smelled good.

"Here, Harold. Give me the box," said Sam. "Crumb, it's heavy," he added as Harold obliged him.

"Yes," said Harold, shaking out his arms. "It's very heavy. I swear I've never seen so much food in my life. First it was seven thousand floral bouquets, and now it's tons of food. I don't know how much food people think my mother and Algie can eat, but they overestimated by a good deal."

"Still," I said, stepping out of Sam's way as he carried the heavy box down the hallway and turned to go through the dining room to the kitchen, "it was kind of them to send it all."

"I guess," grumbled Harold. "I believe Mother would have preferred people donate to charities she supports rather than send flowers and food. She's already got a fabulous flower garden and the world's best cook."

"True," I said, glad Harold had acknowledged my Aunt Vi's contribution to Mrs. Pinkerton's...I was going to write happiness, but she wasn't happy at the moment. How could she be?

"You know, Harold, your mother might be the only person in Pasadena who's not glad to be rid of your sister."

"Believe me, I know it," snarled Harold. "I'm not even sure I want Sam to catch her killer."

"Don't say that," I said, helping him remove his well-cut overcoat and hang it on the rack. He plopped his rolled-brim fedora on the shelf, where it sat next to Sam's more sober derby. "Even if it was Stacy she killed, it might be someone nice the next time."

"What next time?"

"Well, I don't know, but I should think that if you get away with murder once, you might decide to do it again if someone annoys you. Heck, we all become annoyed with people every now and then. If we killed a person every time they irked us, there'd be nobody left in the world."

"You're always saying dogs are better than people. What would be so bad about getting rid of all the people?" Harold's mood was clearly as bad as mine, although he seemed more angry than gloomy.

"Who'd be around to feed all the dogs?" I said after thinking for a moment.

"Well, there is that. But I'm so sick of people right now I'd as soon they all just die. Maybe only for a day or two. They can come back when I feel better able to cope with them."

"You've had a lot of responsibilities heaped on your shoulders since Stacy's murder, haven't you?" I said sympathetically.

"You have *no* idea," he grumbled. "As if dealing with Mother wasn't bad enough, I had to deal with paperwork at the police department, the mortuary, the bank, the accountant, the church, and Mother's dressmaker, for the love of God. And I don't even believe in God."

"Harold!"

"Oh can it, Daisy. You wouldn't either if you were me."

Disquieting notion, but perhaps correct. And then, like a thunderbolt from God Himself, I remembered choir practice! "Oh, my Lord, tonight's choir practice! And I've got to go to an exorcism! Oh, shoot. This has been an awful week."

"Calm down, Daisy," Harold advised. "Can't you just telephone your choir director and tell him you're unable to attend practice tonight?"

"Telephone Mr. Floy Hostetter?" The mere idea nearly gave me hives. "I guess I'll have to," I admitted unhappily. Then, I thought of a possible way to work around talking to the choir director himself. "Go on into the kitchen, Harold. Set out food and stuff if you want to. I've got to make a telephone call."

"You're not calling the choir director, are you?" asked Harold slyly.

"No. I'm going behind his back," I confirmed. Then I sat myself down at the telephone table and dialed Lucy Zollinger's number.

Sure enough, she answered the telephone on her end with a simple, "Hello?" making it a question.

"Lucy, it's Daisy. I can't make it to choir practice tonight, and I'm afraid to call Mr. Hostetter because he'll berate me."

Lucy burst out laughing. "Oh, Daisy, he won't. He might be a little touchy, but he won't scold you," she said.

"I've had a terrible week, and I have to do something else I don't want to do tonight, so I can't go to choir practice. Please plead for me, Lucy."

"What's happened that your week has been so bad?" she asked.

"Didn't I tell you yesterday at exercise class?" I said.

"Tell us what?"

"On Monday morning, Mr. Prophet and I went to the library and found the murdered body of Stacy Kincaid!" I tried to make my announcement as dramatic as possible.

"Oh, Daisy, how horrible!" Lucy sounded suitably traumatized, so I guess I succeeded.

"It was. It still is. In fact, because of the murder, I have to go to the library tonight after it closes." There. I didn't even lie. "Please apologize for me. I was afraid that if I called Mr. Hostetter, I'd start crying, Lucy." That wasn't a lie either. I knew Mr. Hostetter of old. If one of his choir members missed practice, he got angry at the missing member. Heck, he'd pestered me to come back to choir practice even after I'd been hit by a car!

"I'll be happy...That is to say, I won't be *happy* to tell him you can't make it, but I'll do it. He's generally not as hard on me as he is on you for some reason."

That was true, too. "You're right, darn it. Why's he so darned fussy at me, of all people?"

"Probably because you're more confident than the rest of us."

"Me?" I said, fairly stunned. "Confident? Me?"

"Well, you seem confident," said Lucy.

"It's an act," I told her. "I generally feel about as confident as a two-year-old commanded to read Shakespeare."

"Hmm. Well, no one would ever know it. You always seem confident to me, too."

"Interesting. I'll have to rethink the way I conduct myself. I'm tired of everyone depending on me for everything." Instantly I thought of Harold and repented my words. "Well, that's not true, but—"

"Never mind, Daisy. I'll make your excuses. Will you be at church on Sunday? If so, Mr. Hostetter probably won't be too upset. You always practice the hymns and the anthem, so you're better prepared than the rest of us when Sunday rolls around."

I was? Hmmm. Interesting. I just thought practicing was something I should do. I never realized my fellow choir members didn't do likewise, although it explained some of the sour notes we produced occasionally.

"Thanks, Lucy. I owe you."

"You don't owe me anything," she said firmly. "I just hope your week gets better."

"Thank you. I do too."

And boy, that was another truth. We hung up our telephone receivers; I sucked in a deep breath, and uttered a short prayer that tonight's ceremony would help solve the library's problem at least. Then I got up and walked back to the kitchen.

THIRTY

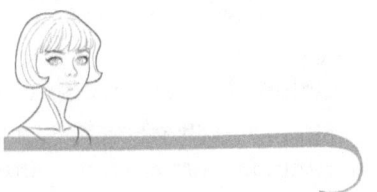

And there my mood got knocked up a couple of inches, by golly! Harold and Sam had set the kitchen table, and Harold had placed bowls filled with various foodstuffs on it. And here I'd thought I'd have to do everything. Just goes to show how little you can depend on in life, and that may be a good thing. Sometimes, anyway.

"Have a seat," said Harold as if he were hosting the feast, which he pretty much was. "I poured orange juice from the pitcher in the Frigidaire. Hope that's all right."

"It's perfect," I said.

We had a delicious meal composed of a slew of dishes that seemed incredibly fancy to me. I expect the wealthy Mrs. Pinkerton's wealthy friends had ordered special recipes prepared for the sorrowing mother of a slain child.

"This soup is delicious," I said as I politely scooped my spoon away from me. "Is it cream of asparagus?"

"Yes," said Harold. "And there's Steak Diane with mushrooms and Beef Wellington. The crust's a little soggy, but it's still tasty. Then there's salmon with hollandaise sauce, canvas-back duck, English peas, and *haricots vert*. Remember those?"

"Skinny green beans? Yes, I remember them." Harold and I had dined well in Turkey, which was where I learned the French words for skinny green beans.

"And," said Harold, spearing something on his plate and holding it up for inspection, "don't forget the lobster timbales."

"My goodness. I've never even heard of a lobster timbale. I know what a lobster is, but what's a timbale anyhow? Can you make it with something other than lobster?"

"Sure. It's just something cooked in a crust. Actually, I think the timbale refers to the kind of dish it's baked in. You can fix dessert timbales or salmon timbales or anything timbales." He looked across the table at me. We were dining on this exceptional fare at our kitchen table covered with an oilcloth. A rather casual venue for so exalted a meal. "I wouldn't recommend you attempting to fix a timbale until you've conquered a few easier dishes."

"Don't worry, I won't," I said, instantly feeling like a failure.

"Good grub," Mr. Prophet commented. "Helluva lot better'n beans and bacon. Probably get a belly ache if you ate this stuff every day though."

Sam chuckled. "You're probably right, but it's nice to indulge every now and then."

"Yes, it is," said Harold. "If I ate like this every day, I'd be even plumper than I am now. That would be tragic. I'd have to buy new clothes."

"Poor baby," I said.

"What time is this séance thing tonight?" asked Harold.

"Nine, and I don't think it's actually a séance. We'd probably better get to the library a little early. I'm not sure how Mrs. Potts and Mrs. Jackson are aiming to set up things. Maybe we'll just sit in a circle around a table or something."

"Huh," said Mr. Prophet. "If they're doin' Voodoo, I'd expect smoke and drums and music and so forth."

"Inside the library?" I asked.

With a shrug, Mr. Prophet said, "Dunno. Been to a couple of Voodoo rites in New Orleans. I expect folks could drum on tables, but you probably couldn't start a fire in the library."

"Not unless we want to burn it down along with all its books. Mr. Whitehall would really throw a fit if that happened."

"Mebbe," said the old sinner with a cynical grin. "Might be a good way to get rid of him."

"I'd hate to see all those books burn. Where would we procure reading material?"

"Why don't we wait and see what the ladies have in store for us?" Sam said reasonably. "No need to get carried away with speculation beforehand."

"You're no fun," I told him.

We finished our astonishingly fancy meal, and while I washed the dishes, Harold and Sam put the leftovers in the Frigidaire. We'd probably have breakfast, lunch, and dinner for tomorrow at least. Perhaps I *should* thank Stacy.

Naw.

We set out for the library in Sam's Hudson at about eight-thirty. Sam, Harold, Mr. Prophet, and I had taken the precaution of stuffing our pockets with sage, salt, juniper berries, and orange peels. We even sprinkled dried sage on our heads under our hats. I'd be *so* happy when Stacy's ghost was disposed of.

When we arrived at the library, it was to find Mrs. Potts and Mrs. Jackson already there, along with Cyrus Potts, Li Ahn, and several members of Mrs. Jackson's family. I recognized Jimmy, Joe Jackson's son. He played his horn in the Cocoanut Grove at the Ambassador Hotel in Los Angeles. Because he was a Negro fellow, he had to enter the grand hotel through the kitchen. I thought that was demeaning and stupid, but nobody had asked me.

Li came up to greet us. "The ladies are going to perform their ritual behind the library, where they won't attract too much attention. I'll be with them, although I won't do much. They're the experts at this sort of thing."

"Sounds reasonable, considering what they're aiming to do," I said. "Do you know what they have planned?"

Shaking her head, Li said, "Don't have an idea, but they seem pretty sure of themselves."

"Good. I'm glad." I was extra glad, truth to tell, since I didn't have the least idea how to get a ghost to depart this mortal plane and head elsewhere.

"I'm pleased too," said Li. "I sure don't know how to vanquish ghosts."

"Glad I'm not the only one," I told her.

She gave me an odd look. "I thought you did this sort of thing all the time."

"Me?" I pointed at my chest. "Good grief, no. I'm a fake. I thought Mr. Prophet would have told you that."

"Lou's told me your magic is pretty strong," Li said.

"He did?" I was shocked.

"I expect you don't believe you're powerful because you're white."

"Oh?" What did being white have to do with anything? Well, except for excluding everyone else from our white vicinity.

"It's not part of your culture," explained Li. "Lou's been around Apaches long enough to understand magic. And I'm Chinese. It comes with the territory."

"Oh. Interesting."

"Miss Daisy, please bring your spirit control to us," said Mrs. Jackson from behind the library building. "Hattie and I are setting up back here."

Regina, Robert, and the rest of the library staff showed up about then, so we all walked to the back of the library, I still puzzling about my supposedly strong magic. Crumb. It was true Rolly had occasionally become obstreperous during the past couple of years, but I figured that was my fault for not reining in my too-glib tongue. Well, except when a ghost had appeared during a séance. And the time when the Tongva ghost showed up at another one. Come to think of it, there were another couple of incidents I'd as soon forget.

Perhaps my spiritualist-mediuming *had* become genuine. Another reason to quit my job.

I attempted not to think about the oddities of my profession as we trekked to the back of the library. There I discovered Sam had exercised some powers of his own when I saw the police contingent barring access to the barren area serving as a parking lot for library patrons during the day. I also discovered a partial answer to Mr. Prophet's prediction of smoke and drums. To wit: a large round metal trash barrel had been commandeered by the organizers of the event, Mrs. Potts and Mrs. Jackson, and a fire built within it. Several more of Mrs. Jackson's grandchildren had been secured to tend the fire and keep it stoked and under control. They'd also filled buckets with water, probably from the library pond, just in case. Prudent.

A few folding chairs had been set in a semicircle on one side of the fire barrel. I assumed most of us would be standing and watching the spectacle until Mrs. Jackson beckoned to me.

Merciful heavens. In the few years since I'd first met Mrs. Jackson, I'd never seen her in full Voodoo mambo regalia. Tonight she wore *the* most colorful ensemble I'd ever beheld in my life, along with a big turban created from strips of different-colored cloth. In line with this startling raiment, she wore huge dangling earrings, about a thousand strands of different-colored beads around her neck, and bangles of bracelets on her wrists. Somewhat taken aback, I fingered the quartet of amulets making my chest lumpy.

"Come to me, Miss Daisy," intoned Mrs. Jackson. Her voice had already taken on a sepulchral tone.

So I went to her. Didn't dare not do so. However, when I approached, she gave me a huge smile and whispered, "Don't be afraid. This is mostly for show. Hattie and I have things under control, but you'll have to sit in this chair here between us."

"Oh, my goodness, I didn't even notice that chair," I whispered when she stepped aside to reveal it.

"How could you?" asked Hattie Potts reasonably. "With me and Loretta standing in front of it. You just sit right here and close your eyes. You're probably gonna have to call that spirit fellow of yours. We might need him."

Oh Lord, that was all I required to put me in a state of nerves the likes of which I hadn't seen since…Well, since I realized Stacy Kincaid's ghost was haunting me. And this was just a show.

"There you go, child. You'll be just fine," said Mrs. Jackson. "Mr. Sam?"

"Yes, ma'am," said Sam, promptly stepping up to do his part, whatever it turned out to be.

"Hattie and I'll need you and Mr. Lou there to keep an eye on things. Don't let anybody in, and don't let nobody leave. Cyrus and Mr. Wu will help."

As Cyrus was as big and powerful as a well-muscled draft horse and Mr. Wu was an expert in some Chinese martial art with which he felled large men with one kick of his soft-soled shoes—I wouldn't have believed it if I hadn't seen it for myself—I figured Sam and Mr. Prophet wouldn't have much trouble controlling a crowd should one gather. At this point, it consisted of several library staff members, Harold, Sam, Mr. Prophet, the organizers of the event and me.

"Now, Miss Daisy, you just close your eyes and think about your spirit— What's his name again? I can't recall." Mrs. Jackson peered down upon me with eyes that seemed to glitter in the increasing fire-light from the barrel

"Rolly," I whispered. Then, taking myself in hand, I said more boldly, "Rolly. His name is Rolly."

"Ah. Rolly. I see." Mrs. Jackson seemed to mull over this nonsensical name for a few seconds, then pursed her lips, nodded her head, and said, "Fine."

Suddenly, a single drum beat sounded, nearly shocking me out of my chair and onto the raked parking area. Mrs. Jackson's hand held me firmly in place. She'd expected this reaction from a rookie Voodoo session attendee, I presume. I heard gasps and a stifled shriek or two from the spectators, so I wasn't the only coward in the yard.

"And what's the name of the man whose ghost is haunting this library?" asked Mrs. Jackson.

"Mr. Enoch Whitehall."

I think she muttered something about it being no surprise the ghost was white, but I'm not sure. Wouldn't have astounded me, nor would I have blamed her.

A few minutes passed, composed primarily of people sitting in folding chairs and looking at the fire barrel, the three women standing in back of it—Li had joined Mrs. Potts and Mrs. Jackson—

and me sitting in my chair between Mrs. Jackson and Mrs. Potts. Then Mrs. Jackson, with quite a clanging of her several bracelets, pointed a finger at Cyrus Potts.

Without any other prompts, Cyrus boomed, "Silence!" in his deep bass voice.

After a short flutter of sound—I think several people jerked with alarm—silence pretty much ensued. Pasadena was a relatively civilized, well-behaved town, and not a whole lot happened in the city after dark, so there weren't many people out and about at that time of night.

Mrs. Jackson began a low chant. She might have been chanting in a language of which I was ignorant; there were thousands of them, after all. As she gained volume, the drum started again, and I saw the drummer was Jimmy Jackson. I couldn't see the attendees very well because the flaming barrel sat between them and me, but the few faces I could distinguish showed intense interest and more than a little trepidation.

After a while, some of Mrs. Jackson's chanted words became clear in English. I heard her call Mr. Enoch Whitehall's name. It sounded eerie in her Voodoo-song voice.

"Mr. Enoch Whitehall, come to me," she commanded. "Mr. Enoch Whitehall. Mr. Enoch Whitehall. Come. Come to me."

I don't know how long this chant lasted, but it was weird and echo-y and strange, and finally, a small, thin, grayish-white *whoosh* of vapor appeared before Mrs. Jackson. It wasn't much of a vapor, and it shivered in the light of the barrel.

"*What do you want?*" asked a querulous voice that seemed to issue from the flimsy puff of fog.

"Why are you haunting this library?" demanded Mrs. Jackson in a voice I'd have been in a hurry to answer had her question been aimed at me.

"*They're going to tear it down,*" sniveled the voice.

"Yes, and there's nothing you can do about it," said Mrs. Jacksons. "Your efforts are worthless. You're nothing but a petty annoyance."

"*They shouldn't tear down this library!*"

"What you want doesn't matter, Mr. Enoch Whitehall. You are worthless and useless and you can't stop progress."

"*I hate progress!*" whined the voice.

"Too bad, Mr. Enoch Whitehall." Mrs. Jackson flung some sort of powdery stuff into the burning barrel, making the flames turn blue. It was a most effective...effect. "Be gone! Go! The Other Side beckons. Your time here is over!"

"*Noooo!*" the whiny voice cried.

In spite of its wishes in the matter, both the voice and the flimsy cloud seemed to be drawn into the barrel. As we watched the little foggy wisp vanish, we heard one last pitiful cry of woe before the fire leapt up in a red flame, then settled into the barrel and happily burned on.

"There," said Mrs. Jackson in a satisfied voice. "That takes care of him."

The onlookers started making oohing and aahing whispers and various noises indicating amazement and pleasure. Regina took a step toward the barrel. "Is he really gone?" she sounded almost avidly agog.

"He's really gone," said Mrs. Jackson, smiling at Regina. "That wasn't too hard, was it?"

"No. I'm so...so...so astounded. And grateful." She took a few more steps toward the barrel, probably intending to shake Mrs. Jackson's hand and thank her, but her forward progress was halted when another, larger, darker cloud of fog appeared. Regina jumped back as if she'd run into a wall.

"*He might be gone, but I'm still here!*" came the ghostly voice of Stacy Kincaid. "*And you can't get rid of* me *so easily!*"

Suddenly, Mrs. Jackson's turban was jerked from her head, and it flew into the flaming barrel. Then Regina began flailing at nothing, as if she were being bedeviled by some invisible being. Which she was, darn it.

"*I hate you all!*" shrieked Stacy's ghost voice, messing up a few other people's hair and flinging hats here and there. "*Especially* you, *Daisy Gumm Majesty! And I'll get you yet!*"

Terror and fury seemed to stiffen my backbone. "My name is Rotondo now, Stacy. Sam and I are married."

"*Sam, Sam, Sam!*" she shrilled. "*Your Sam should have died when Eloise Gaulding shot him! If her aim had been better, you'd still be a Majesty with a dead husband and a miserable life catering to my crazy mother! Or you'd be dead instead of my darling Percy!*"

Her darling Percy had aided and abetted a man named Leo Banister to procure children for the perverted pleasure of ghastly men. Rage built up in me, even thinking about the horrors those poor children had endured.

"Your darling Percy was as evil as you are!" I hollered at her.

Mrs. Jackson threw some more of her powdery substance into the barrel, which burned blue and orange and rose out of the barrel as if it were Moses' burning bush.

Stacy shrieked, "*Eeeeeeee! I don't care about your Voodoo! You killed my precious Percy!*"

"Your precious Percy was a depraved coward who defiled and hurt innocent children!" I thought about my own unborn child as I yelled at Stacy's ghost. All of a sudden, I felt as if I were about to explode.

Then I kind of did.

"*Stacy Kincaid!*" roared Rolly from my own personal mouth. "*Go. To. HELL!*"

"*Noooooo!*" screamed Stacy's voice.

And darned if the huge, dark, ugly cloud of vapor from which Stacy had been wailing didn't get sucked into the fiery barrel along with Stacy's voice, which grew softer and softer until it gave one last angry keening wail and disappeared.

THIRTY-ONE

S tunned, I stared at the barrel from which now issued the
blackest plume of smoke I'd ever seen. It stank, too.

Then I think I fainted, because I don't remember anything else
until my eyes opened to find Sam kneeling beside my chair and
holding on to me. I heard Mrs. Jackson say, "She'll be all right, Mr.
Sam. She just needs to rest for a bit. Sending ghosts to the afterlife
takes a good deal of effort. She and her Rolly just sent one to hell. It
belonged there, but Miss Daisy will need to rest for a while."

"Dammit, I knew you shouldn't have done this," Sam growled
into my ear. "As if exercise class wasn't bad enough. You've got a
baby to think about now, you know."

Sam scolding me about our baby and this evening's unusual
proceedings put the icing on the cake as it were. And it wasn't gently
smoothed on, either. It was slapped onto the cake willy-nilly and
spread with a cleaver rather than an innocent butter knife. I turned
to my husband, whom I loved with all my heart and who had just
riled me beyond bearing.

"Don't you *dare* talk to me about our baby, Sam Rotondo! You
were as much a part of this as I was!" I jerked myself away from
him—once more nearly sending the chair and me tumbling to the

ground—and turned my head to find Mrs. Jackson. She was right there, patting her hair, which had been mussed when Stacy yanked off her turban. "Is Stacy's ghost gone for good now, Mrs. Jackson?"

"Yes. Stacy's ghost has gone to hell, where your spirit fellow —Rolly?"

"Yes," I said. "Rolly."

"Funny name for a spirit guide, but that's as may be," she said. "Yes, that gal's ghost is gone where your spirit fellow Rolly sent her."

"Forever?" I asked.

"Yes indeed. For good and forever." Looking at Sam, she said, "Don't scold the girl, Mr. Sam. She did a mighty lot of good tonight. All she needs now is rest and the support of her family and friends."

"I'll help," came the rather thin and quavering voice of Harold Kincaid. "I'll help you, Daisy. My God, I've never seen anything like what happened here." His voice became stronger as he used it. "Sam, stop berating your wife. She worked a miracle tonight."

"Yeah, Sam," said Mr. Lou Prophet, who had already stumped up to the group of us ghost-removers and put an arm around Li Ahn. "She done good."

I heard Sam suck in a huge breath and let it out slowly. "I beg your pardon. I didn't mean to yell at you, Daisy. But you nearly scared the life out of me."

"It's all right, Mr. Sam. Your wife has strong magic in her," said Hattie Potts. "She don't use it much, which is a good thing, but it sure came in handy tonight."

"Amen to that," said Mrs. Jackson. She then lifted her arms to the sky and intoned, "Thank you, God, for your many mercies, and hold this child and her child in your blessed arms. Keep her safe, and keep her family safe. Amen, amen."

The crowd of onlookers, which had remained silent for the most part during these past few fraught minutes, seemed to release a communal breath of relief. I heard many of them mutter, "Amen," after Mrs. Jackson stopped speaking.

And then I wondered if there were any Jews, Confucians, or Hindus in the group. Don't ask me why, because I don't have a single, solitary clue. Did Jews, Confucians, and Hindus say "Amen" or some version of it?

"Let's go home, Sam, if it's all right with everybody," I said faintly. "I think my brains are scrambled."

"Best idea I've heard all day," said Sam, helping me out of the chair. Holding me gently with his arms around me, he asked, "May we leave this to you and your helpers, Mrs. Jackson and Mrs. Potts? And Miss Li?" I was glad he remembered Li. "I want to get Daisy home."

"To an un-haunted house," said Mr. Prophet. "You did a mighty lot of good tonight, Miss Daisy."

I whispered, "Thank you."

"Thanks, Lou," said Sam rather grimly. "You coming with us, or you staying with Miss Li for a while?"

"Think I'll stay here and help get everything back to the way it usually is. I'll be home later, but I won't bother you two."

Sam nodded.

Harold said, "I need a ride to your house, Sam. My car's there."

"Right." With a still-gentle hold on my arm—which I needed because my knees felt rubbery—Sam said to the people still standing, confused, in back of the library, "Show's over, folks. With any luck, you won't have to worry about strange things happening in the library from now on."

"Thank God," murmured Regina. "Thank you, Daisy. And thank you, Mrs. Jackson, and...and your helpers."

"You're welcome, child," said Mrs. Jackson. "I ain't had so much fun since I moved to this boring place from Louisiana." And darned if she didn't let out with a huge cackling laugh.

I noticed her relatives had begun pouring buckets full of water into the fire barrel, which hissed and spat as if Stacy were making one last attempt at life after death. But the angry noises didn't go on for long. Soon the fire was out, and I saw everyone moving off in different directions, presumably to their automobiles.

"Thank you, Mrs. Jackson and Mrs. Potts," I said. "And Li and Mr. Cyrus Potts and Jimmy Jackson and...and just everyone who helped tonight."

"Go home, child," said Mrs. Jackson, clearly amused. "You can thank us all later if you want to, but there's no need. We're all put on this earth for a purpose, and this sort of thing is mine. You just go home and rest up for that baby you're carrying."

"Good idea," muttered Sam as he started steering me toward the Hudson.

Harold fell into step beside me and took my other arm. "I'll never forget tonight," he said solemnly. "I do believe you finally rid the world of the scourge that was Stacy."

"That big cloud of black fog sure seemed to get sucked into that barrel," said Sam, his voice no longer grumpy but holding a hint of awe. "And then there was that God-awful screaming and the fire leaping out of the can and that stench. I...I don't know what to say."

"Good. Don't say anything," I told him. "I feel weird, and I want to go home. I want some cookies and milk, but I don't think we have any cookies."

"They're probably a little mushy, but there's a bakery box full of chocolate éclairs in your Frigidaire," said Harold. "And I saw milk in there. Can we have chocolate éclairs and milk instead of cookies and milk?"

"Sounds perfect," I said, silently and fervently thanking what-ever powers that be—Christian, Jew, Confucian, Hindu, or what-ever other deities might be hanging about—for Harold Kincaid and his friendship. And for Sam, even though he nagged me.

The chocolate éclairs were a trifle soggy, but they tasted wonderful. Harold and I each had one and a half of them, and Sam had one and two-halves. They were delicious with glasses of milk. Then Harold went home, and Sam, Spike, and I went upstairs to bed.

In an un-haunted house.

I slept like a rock and didn't wake up until far later in the morning than I usually arose. When I peered with gummy eyes at the bedside clock, I almost fainted dead away when I saw its hands pointing to eight-thirty. Eight-thirty in the morning! Good Lord! Sam had to be at work at eight. I frantically turned in the bed to find his side of it empty and a note sitting there. I snatched it up and read it.

You looked so comfortable I didn't have the heart to wake you up. See you after work, Love. Take care of yourself and don't do anything strenuous today.

Love, Sam

Well.

I stared at the note. Then I looked for Spike. No Spike. He'd probably risen with Sam. I truly must have been dead to the world in order not to be awakened by those two male animals. Neither of them was noted for their sylph-like treads. Sam was apt to stomp around, and Spike's toenails skittered on bare floors like falling toothpicks.

I bunched up the pillows at my back and scooched to sit and take stock. If Spike were there, I'd have asked him to join me in the bed but I didn't know where he was. I suspected he was outside playing with Yuyu. It took me a few minutes to realize I felt relatively well. That was nice.

Then I wondered if Stacy were really and truly gone for good. Guess I'd find out. I slipped out of bed and stuffed my feet into my slippers. Because I wasn't sure where Spike was and might have to go outside in order to find him and be seen by passers-by, I put on my robe, tied it, and walked downstairs. If there was another chocolate éclair in that bakery box, I decided I'd eat it for breakfast. What the heck.

I smelled coffee before I got to the kitchen and was glad I'd donned my robe.

Sure enough, there sat Mr. Lou Prophet, sipping coffee and feeding bits of what looked like warmed-up chicken a la king to Spike in between bites for himself. He glanced up as I entered. As I hadn't even bothered to look into a mirror, I was neither surprised nor offended when he said, "Mornin', sleepy head. Don't you look beautiful this morning." It wasn't a question.

"Shut up," I said, bending to pet my hound.

Mr. Prophet laughed. "I made coffee, and there's about a ton of food in the ice box."

"Yes. Thank you, and I know."

"A little touchy this morning?"

"A little," I muttered.

"You got rid of two ghosts last night. Good job," said Mr. Prophet.

I squinted at him over the percolator as I poured myself a cup of coffee. I noticed there was a sugar bowl and a cream pitcher on the table. "There still milk in that pitcher?"

"Yeah," he said.

"Good." I took my cup to the table, stirred in a lump of sugar, and poured some milk into my cup. After stirring it sufficiently, I went to a cupboard and withdrew a plate, which I laid on the counter next to the Frigidaire. When I looked inside, I was pleased to see the bakery box. I pulled it out, opened it, and discovered two chocolate éclairs. Both had my name on them. Not literally. I put one on a plate, opened the drawer and got out a fork, and took my plate to the table. After setting my plate next to my coffee cup, I forked up a big bite of pastry with custard and chocolate sauce. Perhaps not the healthiest breakfast in the world, but I deserved it.

As I chewed blissfully, I squinted across the table at Mr. Prophet, who sat there grinning at me. Then I looked down at my darling dog, who was also grinning at me. "Just a minute, Spike," I said, and went to the Frigidaire and took out a bowl I vaguely remembered held some kind of beef.

When I lifted the lid and looked, sure enough, it was beef. Soggy beef Wellington, to be precise. I took the container to the table, grabbing a kitchen knife along the way, set the container and the knife on the table, and proceeded to cut slices of beef for Spike. Not too many, or he'd get fat and hurt his back, but this was a special morning and he deserved a treat too.

Mr. Prophet and I didn't speak again as I consumed my chocolate éclair, considered eating the other one, and decided I'd get sick if I did so I didn't. If I ate one of the oranges sitting in the bowl on the table, it would taste sour after the sweetness of the éclair, but I wanted something else. What the heck. I sliced off a piece of soggy beef Wellington and ate some of Spike's breakfast.

All things considered, it was a perfect breakfast to eat the morning after having dispatched a soul to hell. Good grief. Had I really done that? It seemed so...so...I don't know. Drastic or something.

On the other hand, we were talking about—well, I was thinking about—Stacy Kincaid and she'd honestly been worse than useless whilst alive. She'd done bad things and hurt people.

"Don't worry about it," said Mr. Prophet, startling me out of my convoluted thoughts.

I peered up from my empty breakfast plate. "Huh?" Inelegant, Daisy, but did I care? No.

"Don't worry about sendin' Stacy to hell. That's where she belonged. You did a good deed."

"You really think so?"

"Yup."

Very well, then.

"Poor Sam still has to find her killer," I said, thinking her killer deserved a reward.

"Yeah, and don't feel sorry for the gal who done it. She's just as bad as Stacy. People don't go around killin' people and then run off if they think the killin' was justified."

It took me a minute to sort out that sentence. When I did, I said, "You think so?"

"Yup."

"Maybe it was self-defense," I mooted.

"If it was self-defense, she'd'a stuck around and told the cops what happened."

"Not if she were Negro or Chinese or some other race. You know the police would lock up a person of another race even if the killing had been justified a hundred times over."

"Yeah, I know that, but do you think Stacy would hang around with Negro or Chinese folks?"

"Oh. No, I guess she wouldn't."

"Hell, she wouldn't even touch a Mexican, and you know it."

"True. Speaking of Mexicans, I'd like to go to Mijares again. Now that I can leave the house without Stacy attacking me, it might be fun to go out to dinner."

"Mexican food's easy to fix. You ought to try makin' some at home."

"Oh, bother learning to cook! Bother learning *anything*! I've had a hard week, I'm tired and pregnant and I want to go to Mijares, curse you!"

Mr. Prophet lifted his hands, palms out, as if warding off an encroaching swarm of yellow jackets. "Hellkatoot! Don't holler at me. I was just sayin', was all. Hell, even I can make Mescin beans."

"Well, then *you* cook for us," I snarled.

"Okay by me," he said. I think he was attempting to placate me, but it didn't work.

"I don't *want* you to cook for us! Not tonight anyway. I want to go out to dinner, and I want to go to Mijares!"

"That's fine by me, too," he said. After waiting to see if I would fling any more rancor his way, he asked mildly, "Mind if I ask Miss Li to join us?"

I heaved a gigantic sigh. "No, I don't mind. I think that would be nice." Then I sagged in my seat, pushed my plate and the container of beef Wellington aside, and laid my head on my folded arms on the table.

THIRTY-TWO

Fortunately for Sam, Mr. Prophet, and anyone else who had to deal with me on the Friday after the ghost-removal event, my lethargy and foul mood didn't last long. Perhaps ten minutes after I'd laid my head on my arms, Spike jumped up from where he'd been lying at my feet on the kitchen door and raced to the front of the house.

I groaned.

Mr. Prophet said, "It's probably your pa. Sam said he aimed to tell him you were sleepin' in this morning because you had a rough night. He's probably just comin' over to see how you're doing."

Lifting my head, I decided I'd wallowed enough. I picked up the beef Wellington, covered it again, and stuffed it into the Frigidaire. There was still a whole lot of food in there. Then I cleaned off the kitchen table, put all the dirty dishes—there weren't many of them—in the sink, wiped off the oilcloth, sucked in a deep breath, and went to the front door.

Mr. Prophet had been correct. Pa stood in the entryway with Rosebud in tow. Rosie and Spike were happily greeting each other, and Mr. Prophet was chuckling. I figured he'd found my morning mood to be humorous.

Although I didn't, I plastered on a smile and went to greet my father. "Pa! Sorry I was such a sluggard this morning." I kissed him on the cheek and stooped to pet Rosebud. She wasn't much interested in me but continued to greet Spike.

"Let me take the leash off Rosie. I think these two want to play," said Pa.

As soon as he'd done what he'd said he'd do, Spike and Rosie darted into the living room. I've heard it said that when dogs want to play, they'll make a bowing gesture to another dog. Not those two. Rosie and Spike squared off as if they were two boxers in a ring, looking as if they aimed to kill each other. But then Rosie jumped on Spike, Spike gave a pretend growl, and they were off, rolling around and playing like nobody's business. Or like Spike and Yuyu occasionally. Maybe dachshunds are too short to execute a proper bow. I'd have to ask Mrs. Bissel or Mrs. Hanratty.

"You feeling all right, sweetheart?" asked Pa as he, Mr. Prophet, and I followed the hounds into the living room and we all sat. "You look a little peaky."

"You mean I look like heck?" I asked sweetly. "That's because I had a late night and haven't even brushed my hair yet." I sucked in a big breath and told myself to get a grip on my nerves, my mood, and my day. Yes, I'd deserved a rest and maybe even a good sulk, but my father was here, he loved me, I loved him, and I didn't want to distress him. So I added, "But I'm just going upstairs to get ready for the day a little late. Want to take the dogs for a W-A-L-K?"

Instantly, the dogs stopped playing with each other, stood up on all fours, and wagged at Pa and me. I guess Rosie had learned to spell too.

"Sure," said Pa. "Take your time."

I didn't take much time but just brushed my hair, sniffed my armpits, and gave each of them two squirts of Guerlain's Eau de Fleurs de Cédrat. Harold had given me the perfume and an atomizer for Christmas, bless the lad. I didn't use it often, but I figured Pa would rather smell perfume than eau de fire barrel on our walk. Then I washed my face, brushed my teeth, threw on a blue-flowered day dress, and stuffed my feet (clad in sensible lisle stockings) in my sensible walking shoes and, with the addition of the baby-blue cardigan Aunt Vi had knitted for me an eon or so ago and my lumpy gold chain, I was ready.

We had a nice walk. Pa only commented on the faint odor of charring once or twice. He figured there must have been a fire somewhere during the night. I didn't say a word about the fire barrel, but only agreed with him.

After we'd walked around several blocks, Spike and I left Pa and Rosebud at my parents' house, and we walked across the street to our home. The whole time we'd been walking, I'd been mentally girding my loins to tackle cleaning my home of ghost repellents.

Darned if Mr. Lou Prophet hadn't beaten me to it! He was busy sweeping salt from the living room corners when Spike and I walked through the front door. Spike raced over to help him. After hanging my sweater on the rack beside the door, I stood and stared for a second.

"Thank you!" I said.

He glanced up from greeting Spike—he couldn't actually kneel, having only one leg and a peg, but he did a fair balancing act—and said, "I s'pect we can just leave the juniper bundles and sage in the fireplace. Might smell good next time you light the fire.

"Sounds good to me. I'll grab another broom and tackle the upstairs."

"Don't throw out the copper coins," he advised.

"I won't."

"Gotta take them lion dogs back to Li, I reckon."

"I suppose so," I said. "I'll be sorry to see them go. Kind of."

"Mebbe you can get some smaller ones somewhere."

"Good idea," I told him. "Maybe I can even find some Fu dog bookends or something of the sort."

"There's an Oriental shop on Raymond," he reminded me. "Some feller named Suey One owns it, accordin' to the sign."

"True. Guess we don't have to drive all the way to Los Angeles to look for Fu dogs."

"Well, you might have to. Don't know what that feller carries in his shop," said Mr. Prophet.

"I don't either. I've walked past his shop and was kind of afraid to go inside. It looked so dark and strange."

"Aw, hell, go with Li," he said.

"If she'll go with me, that's a good idea."

"She'll go with you," he assured me.

We worked until afternoon cleaning the house of Stacy repellents. I got a creepy feeling when I considered there being no more Stacy in any form whatsoever to plague the earth's inhabitants. The idea that I'd played a part in dispatching her to the nether reaches also gave me the willies, although in truth it had been Rolly who'd spoken the dire words. They'd come out of my mouth, however, and I'd invented Rolly, so I guess I was responsible.

Another chat with Mrs. Jackson seemed in order. And soon. Perhaps she could explain to me how a complete fiction I'd invented as a child could attain real power. As far as I was concerned, Rolly could stay tucked away with the Ouija board and the tarot cards until he'd lost some of his whatever-it-was. Juju? I patted the charms bouncing on their chain and wished I could consign Rolly to the chain.

But never mind. By the time we'd swept up all the anti-ghost paraphernalia, Mr. Prophet and I were both hungry. Therefore, we went to the kitchen along with Spike, who was always eager to visit the kitchen, and I hauled out dishes from the Frigidaire. We had a nice lunch of leftover gourmet snacks that had been prepared for Mr. and Mrs. Pinkerton. We split the last chocolate éclair. By that time, it was almost too squishy to eat, but not quite.

Then I went upstairs and took a hot, soaking bubble bath. I guess Mr. Prophet went to his cottage. He might even have bathed. He never smelled bad, so I guess his hygiene was adequate. I doubt Li would have visited him so often if he'd been stinky.

After I'd washed myself all over twice, including my hair, I rose from the tub, frowned at the smudgy ring I'd left, and cleaned the tub until it shown as whitely as an angel's wings. There. Every last spec of ghostliness was gone from my life forever. Well, except for the Fu lion dogs, and they'd be gone soon.

Then Spike and I flopped down onto the bed, I smelled the

smoke-infused sheets, rose again, and changed the linen. I stuffed the smoky sheets in the laundry basket, and Spike and I napped for a while. By the time we awoke, it was almost time for Sam to come home. I hoped he wouldn't mind dining at Mijares that evening. If he did, we could eat more soggy food from the Frigidaire.

Thank heaven he didn't!

"Sounds great to me," he said, hanging his coat on the rack. "Haven't had a good Mexican feast for a long time."

While I got dressed in an outfit appropriate for dining at a not-too-posh restaurant, Sam and Mr. Prophet put the lion dogs in the Hudson. We dropped them off at Mrs. Mainwaring's house before we went to Mijares. In effect, we traded the lion dogs for Li Ahn, who decided to come to dinner with us when asked.

"Are you any closer to finding the person who killed that young woman, Detective Rotondo?" Li asked at one point as we dined.

"A little," said Sam, who didn't like to talk about his cases while dining.

Li caught on quickly. "I wish you the best of luck," she said, and daintily shoveled some beans and rice into her perfect mouth.

"Thanks," said Sam.

"Li," I said, perhaps too loudly in an effort to divert the conversation, "would you be interested in visiting that Oriental shop on South Raymond with me? Mr. Prophet said you might be able to steer me to some Fu lion dogs of my own."

"Oh, you mean Suey's place?" Li asked. "Sure, although I'm not sure what he carries there. Your best bet might be in downtown Los Angeles. There's a big Chinese community there, and lots of shops that sell Chinese goods, including artworks in porcelain, jade, and bronze and pretty much everything else."

"I don't suppose you'd want to you go with me, would you?"

"Sure," she said. "Why not? Might be fun." She turned to Mr. Prophet. "You want to join us, Lou?"

"No thanks," he said. "I'm not much for shoppin'."

"Hmm," I said, mulling over possibilities. "I wonder if Flossie Buckingham would like to accompany us. She never gets to go anywhere because she's always stuck at the Salvation Army tending to her and Johnny's flock."

"Not to mention their children," said Sam.

"Them too," I agreed. "Maybe we could pick a day when there are people who can watch her kids. Then you, she, and I can go to Los Angeles and look for Fu dogs."

"Would she mind doing that?" asked Li, appearing concerned.

I blinked at her. "Why would she mind looking for Fu dogs?"

"Well, I mean...I mean, she and her husband run a Christian organization. Would she mind looking for sacred figures from another religion?"

"Oh," I said, flummoxed. "I never even thought about them that way."

"What a surprise," muttered Mr. Prophet. I'd have kicked him under the table, but with my luck, I'd have hit his peg and only hurt my toes.

"What religion are lion dogs from? Or do they represent? Whatever I mean?"

Li pursed her lips as she thought. Then she said, "Honestly? I have no idea. I think they're actually related to Buddhism, but most of the Chinese people I've known have been Confucians. They're basically just mythical creatures. At least, I think they are. I mean, they *are* mythical creatures, but they're placed in front of temples to guard them."

Very well, I was totally confused now. "Hmm, if they're not specific to any religion, I can't imagine why Flossie would object to taking a little vacation away from her kids to look for some. Besides, Flossie and Johnny are two of the least condemnatory people I've ever met in my life. Even if lion dogs were specific to any one religion, I doubt either of them would mind."

"And neither do you," said Sam, grinning at me.

"And neither do I, and I'm a firm Methodist," I said, grinning back at him.

"In that case, sure. I've met her, and she seems like a really nice person," said Li.

"She is. She's a great friend, in fact," I told her.

"And you don't even belong to the Salvation Army," Mr. Prophet said under his breath.

"That's right," I said. "I don't."

"Glad that's settled," said Sam.

So was I. We went home shortly after our conversation about Fu dogs. That night, I dreamed about Spike and a Fu dog challenging each other to a fight only to end up playing all over our backyard while Yuyu hissed at them and fluffed his tail like a feather duster. It was better than a nightmare.

And then came Saturday.

THIRTY-THREE

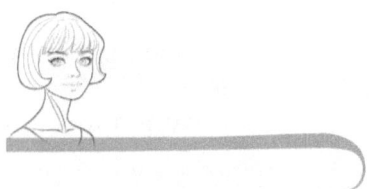

On Saturday morning, I was a little surprised when Mr. Prophet dressed himself in a somber black suit and told us he aimed to attend Stacy's funeral with us. Sam and I were just finishing a breakfast of goose-liver pâté on crackers, an orange each, and coffee. I'd be kind of sorry to see the end of all Mrs. Pinkerton's leftovers.

"Are you sure you want to go?" I asked him. "You don't have to if you don't want to."

"Would I dress up like an undertaker if I didn't want to go?" he snarled. "Don't ferget I was the one who found her. *And* I was in the car when she tried to kill us both."

"True," I said. "Then fine. We can all go. The graveside service will involve walking over some uneven ground at the cemetery, so be prepared for that."

"Not a problem," he grumbled. "What's that stuff?" He pointed to the jar of pâté on the table.

"Pâté de foie gras," Sam told him. "Goose-liver pâté. It's good on crackers. Want some? We had it for breakfast."

"Sure," said Mr. Prophet. "Don't mind if I do." So he got a plate and sat at the table and finished off the pâté. I was a little sorry to see it go, but I didn't begrudge him his share. "This stuff's good."

"Yes, it is," I said. "It's better for breakfast than soggy beef Wellington. I've got to throw that old wet crust away and chop up the rest of the beef for Spike."

"Don't give him too much," warned Sam. "He might get ideas above his station."

I peered down at my faithful hound. "Pretty much everything is above his station," I pointed out.

"True." Sam heaved a sigh. "Well, I'm going upstairs to dress in my own undertaker's suit. Today should be interesting."

"You think so?" I asked him. "I can't think of anything I'd less rather do."

"You're supposed to finger the murderer," Mr. Prophet reminded me.

"Crumb. I forgot that part." I finished clearing the table and washed the dishes. Then, as Mr. Prophet and Spike lingered in the kitchen, I too went upstairs to don my funeral attire.

I'd already set out an outfit to wear. During my years as a spiritualist-medium, I'd created many, many items of apparel suitable to wear at funerals or séances, so I had plenty to choose from. I'd selected what the pattern-maker called an "ensemble suit" of crepe-de-chine with a serge coat to go over it. The frock part was dark gray from the neckline to about mid-thigh, with black at the bottom and a thin black panel going from the neckline to the hem. The panel was adorned with metal bell buttons. The coat was black. The weather remained iffy this time of year, so if it got hot, I could remove the coat. If it remained chilly, I'd keep the coat on. As it was a waistless dress, nobody could tell my waistline was nearly gone.

Bother, everybody knew Sam and I were going to have a child, so who cared? I wore my black shoes with a strap across the arch, as they were most comfortable for standing and walking, and a black cloche hat. I carried my small black drawstring bag. It only held a hankie, my compact, and a tube of Tangee lip rouge.

Along about ten o'clock, we set out for All Saints Episcopal Church. The church itself was beautiful. It wasn't pointy all over as our Methodist-Episcopal Church was, but had a tall square stone tower attached to a pointy stone building that held the sanctuary. The inside was lovely too, with an arching ceiling held up by pillars. Chandeliers hung above the pews and glorious stained-glass windows lined the walls. A fellow named Ernest Batchelder had been commissioned to create the magnificent tiled floor in the sanctuary.

Floral arrangements nearly covered the chancel and spilled over to the steps leading up to it and even down the side aisles. It looked to me as though everyone who had sent condolence flower arrangements to Mrs. Pinkerton's home had also ordered them for the funeral. Zillions of roses, carnations, and stock had been used in the arrangements, and the church smelled heavenly, which was appropriate for the church if not for Stacy Kincaid.

Mr. Prophet, who didn't care for churches of any kind, gazed around as we entered and muttered, "Kind of a pretty place."

"I think so too," I said.

"Reminds me of a Catholic Church," said Sam.

"It almost is, I guess," I said. "Aren't the Episcopalians an offshoot of the Anglican Church? The Anglicans are pretty much Catholic without a Pope, aren't they?"

"Beats me," said Sam.

"I don't know what you're talkin' about," said Mr. Prophet.

"Never mind," I said.

Although we arrived at the church well before the service was scheduled, we weren't the first to get there. Mr. and Mrs. Pinkerton and Harold sat in a front pew reserved for family. Several other people I didn't know also sat in the same pew and the one behind it. It had never occurred to me that the Pinkerton family might have other people in it. Well, I'd met Mrs. Pinkerton's sister once, but it looked to me as if an entire Roman legion had gathered. Not sure why I was surprised. We sat in a pew more or less in the middle of the rows of pews mainly because Mr. Prophet refused to go any farther.

"Far enough fer me," he said and stopped walking.

"Sounds good to me," said Sam.

"Do you think I should offer Mrs. Pinkerton condolences?" I asked Sam in a whisper.

"No." He sounded firm and, because I didn't want to talk to Mrs. Pinkerton anyway, I let him have his way.

Just then, Harold stood up and glanced around the church, probably to see who'd come. I saw Del seated in a pew right behind the ones designated for family. As he and Harold might as well have been a married couple, I felt bad that he wasn't allowed to sit with Harold. As soon as Harold saw me, he gestured for me to go to him.

"Oh, he-heck," said Sam.

"I'll be right back," I told Sam and Mr. Prophet.

"Doubt it," said Mr. Prophet.

"So do I," said Sam grumpily.

"I'll try to be right back," I amended as I rose to go to Harold.

He met me halfway, grabbed my right arm, and whispered fiercely, "Daisy! Please sit with the family. I saved you a seat between Mother and me."

"But I'm not family," I protested.

"You are today," he said and fairly dragged me down the aisle with him. "Mother is absolutely *mad* with grief and drama, and she keeps saying she wants you."

"Oh dear. Let me tell Sam, all right?"

"I'm not letting go of you until you promise you'll sit next to Mother," he warned.

He appeared ravaged. The last week had been really hard on him. Having dealt with his mother for more than half my life, I understood. "I promise," I said.

"I'd better go with you, just to be sure Sam doesn't object."

"Harold Kincaid, I promise I'll sit between your mother and you," I whispered ferociously. "I keep my promises."

"I'm sure you usually do, but...Oh, God, Daisy, yesterday and this morning were pure hell."

"I'm sorry, Harold. Very well, you may come with me. I'm sure Sam won't mind."

Sam did mind, but he didn't kick up a fuss. So I returned with Harold to the front pew.

As soon as I appeared in her peripheral vision, Mrs. Pinkerton tried to rise to her feet only to collapse back onto the pew. *"Daisy!"* she shrieked.

"Shhhh, Mother," pleaded Harold. "We're in church, remember?"

"Oh yes, oh yes," whimpered Mrs. P. "I'm so sorry. Please sit with us, Daisy. I know you have a family of your own, but *please*. I *need* you!"

Whoo boy. "I'll join you, Mrs. Pinkerton. Just sit down and try to remain calm. For your daughter's sake," I added for the heck of it. "You don't want Stacy to look down"—clever devil that I was, I didn't mention the possibility of her looking up—"upon you and find you so..." Botheration! So what? Deranged? Insane? "...so unhappy."

"But I *am* unhappy," sobbed Mrs. Pinkerton.

"There, there, dear," said Mr. Pinkerton, trying to pat one of her black-gloved hands and failing because she was waving both them in the air along with her black-edged hankie. I hoped she had more hankies with her because that one already looked done for.

"Oh, Algie!" Mrs. P. cried and flung herself upon her cherub-faced husband. He didn't seem to mind, being a kindhearted and indulgent fellow.

"Gawd," whispered Harold in my ear. "Sit here. I'll sit next to you. If Mother gets out of hand, shove this under her nose." He handed me a corked bottle.

"What's in this?" I took the bottle and stared at it doubtfully.

"Chloroform," said Harold. "Don't worry. Doc Benjamin said to just give her a couple of sniffs to subdue her. But don't use it if she begins to flail around or—"

"Flail *around?*" I whispered furiously. "Is she *that* unhinged?"

After heaving a huge sigh, Harold said, "Probably not. She's feeling dramatic, so she'll probably just faint if given the opportunity."

"Fainting might be the best thing she can do," I said.

"Maybe," said Harold. "But here comes Father Frederick. He'll set her straight."

Sure enough, Father Frederick, whom I'd never before seen in his clerical garb, came up to Mrs. Pinkerton, holding out his hands for her to grab. She took full advantage of his offer and nearly yanked him off of his feet.

Nevertheless, he spoke quietly and soothingly to her, telling her everything would be all right and that Stacy was in a better place now and so forth and so on. It occurred to me as I listened to him consoling the afflicted Mrs. Pinkerton that he sounded a whole lot like me in spiritualist-medium mode. I attempted to suppress the thought as it might be considered profane.

Then Johnny and Flossie walked up to Mrs. Pinkerton, who let out a soft wail and grabbed a hand each and must have squeezed hard, because Flossie winced. Johnny also spoke soothing words to her, as did Flossie. They were both dressed in their Salvation Army uniforms, which, in years past, might have offended Mrs. Pinkerton. Not any longer. As the Buckinghams walked back to whatever pew they'd selected to sit in, Johnny tipped me a wink, and Flossie smiled as she flapped her gloved hand in order to get her circulation going again.

Shortly after the Buckingham incident, the organist began playing softly. As soon as she heard the first few chords of "Abide with Me", Mrs. P seemed to calm down some.

I heard Harold mutter, "Thank gawd," under his breath.

Things settled down after that. When I looked over my shoulder a few minutes later, I was surprised to see the church packed with people. I hadn't realized Stacy possessed so many friends. Then I realized the people weren't there for Stacy, but for Stacy's mother. I swear, I saw every wealthy woman I'd ever worked for in that congregation. How kind people were.

Once Father Frederick began the service, things trotted right along. Although he must have had to dig *really* deeply, he managed to say a few nice things about Stacy in his eulogy. The congregation stood to sing "Amazing Grace", which seemed appropriate as it was written by an Episcopal priest after he gave up his slave-trading business because he felt guilty about it. As well he should have.

The service concluded shortly after "Amazing Grace". Father

Frederick invited one and all to condole with the grieving family in the font pews, and then to assemble at Mountain View Cemetery for the graveside service and burial. I tried to scoot out of the way so nobody would think I was family, but couldn't because there were too many people in the way.

By the time the last of the attendees filed past and offered their condolences, etc., I needed to use a restroom badly. Have I already mentioned that so far in my pregnancy, I felt no sickness in the mornings, but I was tired and had to piddle a whole lot? Well, it was true, and I was almost squirming by the time I could stand up again.

I knew where the ladies' room was in All Saints, and I was about to dash for it when Mrs. Pinkerton took my hand and halted me in my quest. I hate to admit to swearing in my head, although I didn't swear aloud.

"Daisy, I need to use the powder room. Will you please go with me?"

Thank God! I rescinded my swear word and silently asked God to forgive me. "Certainly, Mrs. Pinkerton. I need to use the powder room, too." What a lovely euphemism.

Boy, I felt much better after having used the facilities.

We left the powder room together. Mrs. Pinkerton found her hubby and Harold waiting for her in the church lobby. I exited the church and found Sam and Mr. Prophet waiting for me next to Sam's Hudson. Mr. Prophet had rolled himself a quirley and was smoking contentedly. They made an odd pair. Sam in his formal duds looked like a member of Italian royalty, of which I guess there aren't any extant. Mr. Prophet looked rather like a disreputable funeral director in his dress-up clothes.

Anyhow, I joined them, and Sam drove us to the Mountain View Cemetery, where both of our first spouses were buried.

THIRTY-FOUR

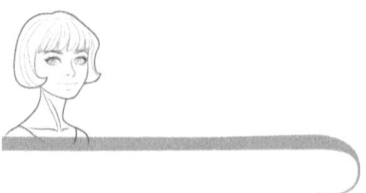

When we arrived at the cemetery, the parking area was nearly full, but Sam managed to find a spot next to Harold's beautiful red Hispano-Suiza. Sam's Hudson, while a nice, sturdy automobile that had recently been washed and waxed, looked kind of like a poor relation or, perhaps, a superior servant when compared to Harold's auto.

I fancied Harold's car telling Sam's car not to forget the spare cigarette case. Then I lectured myself to pay attention to our purpose. This was not merely to see Stacy's earthly remains safely bestowed in the dirt, but to attempt to discern who had killed her. I didn't want to.

"Find women Stacy's age," Sam muttered in my ear. "And try to draw them out. You might be able to extract some useful information."

"Here? In the cemetery?" I muttered back. "I thought I was supposed to do that when we were at Mrs. Bissel's place for light refreshments."

"No sense in waiting," whispered Sam. "Might as well start now."

"Yeah," said Mr. Prophet. "And look at the prints their shoes

282

make and see if you can find any that look like the prints we saw at the park."

"How delightful," I said sullenly. "I'll look at everyone's footprints. If I fall into the grave because I'm staring at the ground instead of the service, pull me out will you?"

"Naw," said Mr. Prophet. "You can stay there with Stacy." He gave a nasty chuckle.

"I'll pull you out," promised Sam, trying not to laugh.

"Thanks a whole lot."

But we had to cease our chatter because we'd arrived at the huge blue canopy the funeral home had erected to shade Stacy's family and friends. Rows of chairs were already filled with mourners —or at least people who'd come for the spectacle—so we had to stand. That turned out to be all right because many young ladies who were attending the rites had forfeited their chairs to their elders and stood in a group under a tree. Therefore, feeling not unlike the village idiot who was about to make a fool of herself, I made my way to the group of young women.

I recognized several of them, although I was a little surprised they'd come. I knew Medora Louise Trunick hadn't been close friends with Stacy. Nor had Gladys Pennywhistle Fellowes, who had been the class brain in high school—I mean, the woman actually liked and understood *algebra*. Her husband was a professor at the California Institute of Technology. I couldn't imagine why she'd have come to Stacy's funeral. Nor could I fathom why Lucille Spinks Zollinger had attended, but there she was.

There, too, were Valerie Steadman and Claudia Wells. They'd known Stacy and had visited her in the jail ward of the hospital. Oh, and Grace Ellen Farmer stood in the pack too. According to Sam, she'd attempted to convert Stacy from a life of sin and degradation to one of virtuous Christianity. I could have told her to save her breath, but I didn't know what she was doing when she was doing it.

I made my way to the cluster of women. Lucy, Gladys, and Medora smiled at me. When she realized I'd joined their clump, so did Grace Ellen Farmer who, I noticed, carried a Bible.

I whispered, "Good morning, ladies. A sad occasion."

"Yes," said Grace Ellen. "I tried so hard to help Stacy, but I fear I failed. It's difficult to help people who don't believe they need help."

"That's the truth," I said with perhaps too much fervor.

"Honestly, I didn't want to come today," said Medora Louise Trunick. "Stacy and I had very little in common."

I believed her. "Why did you come?" I asked.

"My fiancé, Kenneth Sanders, works with Dr. Homer Fellowes."

"Yes," said Gladys Pennywhistle Fellowes. "I'm only here because Mr. and Mrs. Pinkerton are generous donors to various projects at Caltech. I don't believe I ever met Miss Kincaid."

Consider yourself lucky, I didn't say.

"Stacy was fun," said Valerie. "She was a great pal, even though she went a little too far sometimes."

"I hardly knew her," confessed Lucy. "I'm only here because Albert is Mr. Pinkerton's accountant."

Claudia Wells appeared a trifle twitchy. She didn't seem able to stand still, but fidgeted with her skirt, her handbag, her hair, her earrings, and pretty much everything else on her person. "Stacy and I had great fun together," she said. "She sure didn't belong in that stupid jail."

I opened my mouth to set her straight but realized that to do so would dry up the conversation, so I didn't. "Did you frequent speakeasies with Stacy?" I asked Claudia in a mildly curious voice.

"I loved hanging out with Stacy," said Claudia, clasping and unclasping her handbag. "We had a great time together, even if we did...Well..." she giggled. "We drank a little. And, you know, a little sniff of cocaine every now and then never hurt anybody."

"Cocaine! Oh, Miss Wells, cocaine is from the pit!" said Grace Ellen Farmer. "And consuming liquor is illegal!"

"I don't know about any pit," said Claudia, visibly peeved. "Stacy was fun."

"Oh, my dear," said Grace Ellen, looking as if she'd just witnessed a terrible tragedy complete with blood and severed body parts. "May I lay my hand on you and pray for you? The Lord can help you overcome your weaknesses."

Yeesh, I'd known Grace Ellen as a fervent believer before, but I hadn't realized she'd turned into a radical proselytizer.

Now glaring, Claudia said, "No! No, you can't lay your hand on me. I don't give a hoot if you pray for me."

"I'm so sorry," said Grace Ellen, sounding melancholy.

"About what?" asked Claudia.

"About your wickedness. If you acknowledge your evil ways, you can overcome them with God's help. Your immortal soul is at stake."

"Oh, for Pete's sake, you sound like Billy Sunday. Quit preaching at me and leave me alone," said Claudia.

"Billy Sunday is a saint," claimed Grace Ellen. "He spoke the truth when he said, 'One reason sin flourishes is that it is treated like a cream puff instead of a rattlesnake.' Don't you understand that the so-called 'fun' you and Stacy had together was leading you straight to hell?"

"Shut up and go away," said Claudia.

Both women's voices had risen slightly, and I noticed people in the seats under the blue canopy looking our way.

"Um, perhaps you could speak to Claudia later, Grace Ellen. We're here to pay tribute to poor Stacy now." An inner, perhaps demonic, voice in my head screamed *like hell*! I probably needed saving too, but I'd never say so to Grace Ellen. She was quite annoying.

"That's right," said Valerie. "Preach at us at a more appropriate time, Miss Farmer. "This is Stacy's funeral."

"All times are the right times to spread the word of the Lord," said Grace Ellen piously.

Attempting to change the subject, I said, "Um, did any of you see Stacy after she"—I searched for a synonym for "broke out"— "left the hospital?"

The group of young women fell silent. This wasn't good. Any second now Father Frederick would start the service, and then I wouldn't be able to ask questions.

"She escaped from it, is what you mean," said Valerie with a grin. "She had guts, Stacy did."

"I guess so," I agreed weakly.

"Yeah," said Claudia, still opening and closing her handbag. The woman was a bundle of nerves. Unless that was cocaine. My goodness. "She had guts, and she was fun."

"Did she visit you after she…um, escaped from the hospital?"

Claudia fidgeted for several seconds and her handbag fell to her feet. She and I nearly clunked heads when we bent to pick it up at the same time. Because she'd dropped it during one of its unclasped states, when I grabbed one side and she grabbed the other, the bag tilted and everything fell out of it.

"Oh dear, I'm so sorry," I said. "I was trying to be helpful."

"Thanks," said Claudia through tightly gritted teeth. "I'll get it."

As I had already stooped to help her, I noticed a small corked vial, a compact, and another small tin container also held shut with a fastener. A few grains of white powder clung to its edges. When I handed it to her, I asked, "What's this for? Is it another compact?"

"Yes," she snarled.

"Oh, dear," said Grace Ellen. "Whatever is in that vial?" She clutched her Bible to her meager chest and appeared almost avidly sad, if that makes any sense. "Is that spirituous liquor?"

"It's medicine," said Claudia.

"I shall pray for you," declared Grace Ellen. And darned if she didn't put a hand on Claudia's head before Claudia could rise from her crouch. "Dear Lord, please help our friend Claudia mend her evil ways. She requires your many blessings and assistance to draw her away from evil and toward the light, dear Lord."

Claudia slapped Grace Ellen's hand away. "Oh, shut up!" she muttered. "And keep your hands to yourself. No wonder Stacy hated when you visited her at the hospital."

Face red and eyes gleaming weirdly, Grace Ellen said, "Poor dear Stacy hardened her heart to God, but I never gave up."

"I know you didn't," snapped Claudia. "You're a fanatic. Why on earth did you join us in the park that day? What the devil were you doing there at that hour?"

I perked up instantly. Not that I hadn't been perky before, but this sounded as if it might actually be pertinent. "When were you at the park?" I asked. "You mean the library park?"

"Yes," said Claudia. "Stacy and I had been having a good time until *she* showed up."

"When was this?" I asked.

"Oh, I don't know. Last Sunday or Monday. It was late. Stacy and I were having a good time. God, we loved to laugh together. I'm really sorry she's dead." Sincerity rang in Claudia's voice.

I turned to Grace Ellen, who stood with her chin in the air and her Bible still held in a death grip. "Were you at the library park with Stacy and Claudia early on Monday morning?"

After a short pause, she said, "Yes. I had been to a friend's house to pray with her. When I drove past the library, I saw Stacy and Claudia on a bench near the pond. They were passing a bottle back and forth. I knew it contained liquor and that they needed my help."

"We didn't need your help!" snapped Claudia. "What we needed was to be left alone. We were having a good time until *you* showed up."

Quivering, probably with righteous indignation, Grace Ellen said, "I shall not repay evil with evil. Remember the words of the Holy Bible: 'Ye have ploughed wickedness, ye shall reap iniquity.' But God can help you change your path onto one of righteousness. I can help you find God, Miss Wells, and save you from everlasting hell."

"Oh, just go away," said Claudia, sneering at Grace Ellen. "You made Stacy *so* mad with your holier-than-thou blather. She kept telling you to leave us alone, but you didn't. You just stuck like glue and harangued us. Preach, preach, preach. You just couldn't help yourself, could you?"

"I was and am doing the Lord's work," insisted Grace Ellen. "Recall Romans 5, verse 20. 'Where sin abounded, grace did much more abound.' Doing the work of God requires strength of purpose."

I hadn't realized this before, primarily because I didn't know the woman well, that Grace Ellen was something of a legalistic zealot. She cared more for the rules than she did the teachings of Jesus. Jesus didn't plague people with his vision of morality. He *did* the things he preached.

In an attempt to soothe tempers, I said, "I'm a Methodist and even sing in the choir. We Methodists preach love more than we preach damnation."

"You Methodists are *soft*," said Grace Ellen. "You have no idea how to conquer evil in the world."

"We don't?" I said, becoming a trifle alarmed. Grace Ellen's cheeks flamed red, and her eyes nearly glowed.

"No. Methodists distort the word of God. You're all going to hell," she intoned.

Good grief.

"To hell with *you*," said Claudia. "I got so sick of your preaching that morning I finally walked away. Your precious Lord is the only one who knows why *you* didn't leave. I shouldn't have left Stacy there with you blabbing on, but she said she didn't want to go with me. I don't know if she was listening to your garbage or laughing at you, but I couldn't take it any longer."

"You fled from the truth!" declared Grace Ellen. "Remember Proverbs 28:1: 'The wicked flee when no man pursueth; but the righteous are bold as a lion.' It is my duty to be bold as a lion and spread the true word!"

Things were becoming heated and, while this was an important conversation, I didn't want anyone to come over and tell us all to shut up. Therefore, I said, "Perhaps this isn't the right time for Bible lessons, Grace Ellen. And we Methodists are *not* going to hell!"

"Oh yes you are, and *all* times are right times to teach the word of God," she told me. She lowered her voice, though, for which I was glad.

"This is stupid," Claudia declared. "Stacy's dead, and I'm sorry, but I can't tolerate any more of this idiot preaching at me." She stuck her face close to Grace Ellen's. "Hasn't anybody ever taught you there's a time and a place for everything? This isn't the time or the place to tell me I'm going to hell. If heaven's full of people like *you*, I don't want any part of it!"

"That's the devil in you speaking," said Grace Ellen in a harsh, low voice. "You're rejecting the true path."

"Oh, this is just crazy," said Claudia.

She started walking away from our group. It looked to me as if she was heading to the parking area. I honestly couldn't fault her. I considered myself a good Christian girl, and I even sang in the choir, but being preached to by a fanatical zealot at a friend's funeral didn't appeal one tiny bit.

When Grace Ellen took off after Claudia, Bible forward, I followed her. Poor Claudia might be a sinner, but Grace Ellen seemed unhinged.

"Grace Ellen," I said, trying to keep my voice quiet. "Please don't chase Claudia. She just came here to say good bye to a friend. I don't think you're getting your point across very well at the moment."

"For heaven's sake, Grace Ellen, leave Claudia alone!" said Valerie. She caught up with me as we tried to catch up with Grace Ellen, who was by this time running after Claudia, who had also started running.

Claudia was right. This was stupid.

"What's the matter with that girl?" said Valerie.

It was probably a rhetorical question, but I asked, "Which one?" because I wanted to know.

"Miss Farmer," said Valerie. "She sounds crazy."

"She kind of does," I agreed.

A few minutes of Grace Ellen chasing Claudia and Valerie and me chasing both of them brought us to the parking area. There Claudia whirled around and confronted Grace Ellen. "Go away, you blasted idiot! Leave me alone!" She tried to open the door of a cute little Ford Roadster when darned if Grace Ellen Farmer didn't whack her over the head with her Bible! Poor Claudia hit the dirt as if the Bible had contained a brick.

"Grace Ellen!" I cried, trying to grab her biblical arm.

"She's gone insane!" shouted Valerie. She knelt to give aid and comfort to Claudia, leaving me to deal with Grace Ellen.

"You're all going to hell!" screeched Grace Ellen. "Why won't you listen to me? Why won't you accept the truth?"

"Stop it!" I hollered at her, trying and failing to capture her other arm. I'd managed to get the one holding the Bible under control. "Hitting people isn't what Jesus preached. He preached turning the other cheek!"

"What do *you* know?" Grace Ellen bellowed. "You're as big a sinner as *they* are! You all need to listen to *me!*"

"*Stop* it!" I bellowed again. Remembering a trick my brother had tried on me a time or two when we were kids, I hooked one of my feet behind one of Grace Ellen's knees. She lost her footing and plopped to the ground, more or less beside Claudia.

She glared at Claudia. Claudia didn't glare back.

"She knocked her out!" said Valerie, attempting to lift Claudia's head and cradle it in her arms. "She hit her with that book and knocked her out!"

THIRTY-FIVE

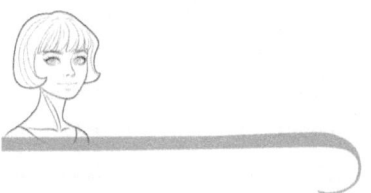

"What's going on here?" boomed a voice I recognized.

"Sam!" I cried, relieved. I scrambled to my feet, as I'd managed to lose my balance along with Grace Ellen.

"I'll *kill* you!" shrieked Grace Ellen. "You should all *die*! I killed Stacy with the tool of her damnation! She was sinning! She was drinking *alcohol*! She laughed when I told her she was damned!"

"Cripes, what's the matter with her?" muttered Sam as he knelt beside Claudia and Valerie. "What happened here?"

Then darned if Grace Ellen Farmer didn't race across the parking area and jump into the first automobile she reached. She slammed the door, pressed the starter button, and the engine roared to life. I heard a wicked grinding of gears, and the auto she'd appropriated gave a leap and backed up. Fast.

Sam, Valerie, and I dragged Claudia out of the way of the oncoming car. I cringed when Grace Ellen smashed it into what looked like a brand new Cadillac, crumpling its fender like so much paper. With another squeal of gears, Grace Ellen drove her car of choice out of the parking area.

"What's going on here?" a bewildered Harold hollered, running into the parking area. "What's that woman doing in my *car*?"

291

Sam had managed to get Claudia to her feet amongst the automobiles. She seemed a trifle woozy. Valerie held one of her arms and Sam held the other. I maneuvered my way out from between a couple of parked cars and hurried to Harold. I put a consoling hand on his arm.

"I'm so sorry, Harold. Grace Ellen Farmer just went crazy. First she decked Claudia with her Bible. Then she told us all that she killed Stacy, and we were going to hell and ran to your car. She backed it into that Cadillac there." I pointed.

But Harold wasn't interested in the crunched Cadillac. He had eyes only for his purloined Hispano-Suiza as it weaved wildly onto Fair Oaks Avenue. Grace Ellen didn't look either way or turn the steering wheel north or south on Fair Oaks but hurtled straight across the street. Several drivers going one way or the other on Fair Oaks squealed to a halt in order to avoid crashing into Harold's car.

"*Stop!*" bellowed Harold, running across the cemetery's parking area and stopping abruptly when he got to Fair Oaks. "Oh, my God, she's going to hit that—"

His last word, which was probably "tree", got buried under a hideous crunch of metal as his Hispano-Suiza jumped the western curb of Fair Oaks Avenue and rammed straight into a mighty Engelmann oak tree.

"My car!" whimpered Harold.

"Good heavens, what was she thinking?" I whispered.

By that time, a small crowd had gathered in the parking area of Mountain View Cemetery. Not everyone had left the blue canopy, but enough folks had come that Sam pulled out his badge, flashed it at the crowd, and said loudly, "Stay here, everyone. This is police business."

Naturally, traffic on Fair Oaks squealed to a halt as people gaped at the wreck of poor Harold's car. Several folks began to exit their own cars.

"Aw, hell," said Sam. "Harold, Daisy, and Lou, help me keep these people away from the wreck,"

"The wreck," said Harold in a shaking voice. "My car."

"What's going on here?" another voice said rather loudly.

292

When I turned to look, I saw it was one of the black-clad, somber fellows from the Mountain View office. I hurried up to him, took his arm, and said, "Please call the sheriff's station. There's been a terrible accident."

He seemed flustered, but when I repeated my request in a voice as firm as a slab of marble—which was almost appropriate—he gave a small start and said, "Of course. Of course. The sheriff's station. Of course," and hurried to the doors of the Mountain View office.

"Back up, everyone!" hollered Lou Prophet, standing in the parking area with his leg and his peg apart, glaring at the small bunch of fascinated funeral attendees. "Police business!" He held up his arms as if to warn people not to come any closer. I guess they believed him, because they stopped and stood and stared.

Only then did I realize he'd pulled out his trusty horn-gripped .45-caliber Colt Peacemaker. He always tucked it into the back of his trousers. If he were armed as usual, he also had a knife secured in a sheath strapped to his calf. The man hadn't given up his old ways. To his credit, he wasn't pointing the revolver at anyone. It was just there in his hand. Kind of as a warning.

"My car," whispered Harold as he walked, zombie-like, to where Sam stood in the middle of Fair Oaks. "My car."

I walked with him and took his arm. "I'm so sorry, Harold. Grace Ellen Farmer just seemed to go crazy. She said she wanted to kill us all like she killed Stacy."

Sam whirled around. "She admitted to killing Stacy?" He whirled the other way and gestured to people to stay in their automobiles. "Stand back! This is a crime scene. Police business! Get back!" He sounded and looked ferocious. Sam was like that. When he used his "Do as I say or I'll rip you into pieces and feed you to a bear in the San Gabriel Mountains", people generally did as he commanded.

"Yes," I said to Sam. "She said she killed Stacy."

"Cripes," muttered Sam. "Harold, can you stand here and direct traffic until the sheriff arrives?" Sam himself had managed to get traffic moving again at a snail's pace. The southbound traffic slowed considerably as it drove past the wreck, some of which had flown into the street. Drivers attempted to maneuver around large hunks of metal and piles of shattered glass.

I figured Grace Ellen Farmer was a goner. That poor Hispano-Suiza's front end was now shaped rather like two arms hugging the oak tree. It appeared the front seat had become one with the back seat. Grace Ellen must be in there somewhere. Perhaps she was now the glue binding the front seat to the back seat. I didn't want to look.

"My car," murmured Harold. He cleared his throat. "Yes, I can direct traffic. There isn't much of it. But my *car!*"

"Sorry," said Sam absently. "Daisy, come with me." He took my hand and guided me from the middle of Fair Oaks to the western curb where the mangled remains of Harold's automobile smoked. "Lord, she headed straight for the tree, didn't she?"

"That's what it looked like to me, although I don't know. She... she seemed to go crazy, Sam. I've never seen anything like it." I eyed the red car, which now sported splatters of red blood dripping into various hollows and cracks in its exterior. Its interior must contain a lot more blood. I turned away. "I don't want to see her, Sam."

"Don't blame you," he said. "But I have to, just in case she's still alive in there."

"Oh, no, she couldn't be. Could she?"

"Doubt it," said Sam. He walked to the smashed automobile and attempted to open the driver's side door. As it was crumpled rather like an accordion, he couldn't do it. "They'll have to cut her out." He turned abruptly after glancing into the shattered driver's window, and his face looked mighty pale. My Sam was as brave as one of Grace Ellen's lions, but evidently, the insides of Harold's late car made him sick.

Members of the Altadena Sheriff's Station showed up shortly after Sam had verified that Grace Ellen Farmer no longer breathed. After exchanging information with the sheriff's officers, Sam collected Harold and me, and we all walked back to the cemetery's parking area. When I glanced at the blue canopy, I saw people rising. Guess the service had ended.

Sam, Harold, Mr. Prophet, Del Farrington, Valerie Steadman,

Claudia Wells, and I all missed light refreshments at Mrs. Bissel's house. We had to go to the Altadena Sheriff's Station and give statements as to what we heard Grace Ellen Farmer say and do. It seemed to take forever, but eventually Sam, Mr. Prophet, and I made it back home.

As soon as we stepped foot inside the house, the telephone began ringing. I'd stooped to pet an ecstatic Spike and I lifted my head to stare at the instrument with hatred. I don't think I'd ever been so exhausted in my life.

"Let it ring," said Sam.

"Gladly," said I.

"I'm goin' home," said Mr. Prophet.

"Take some food from the Frigidaire on your way," I told him.

"Thanks," he said.

As soon as the telephone stopped ringing, Sam took the receiver off the hook. We scrounged some leftover rich people's food for dinner and went to bed.

I managed to sing the alto part of "Praise to the Lord, the Almighty" perfectly the following day at church, so Mr. Hostetter didn't scold me for missing choir practice. It's probably a good thing he restrained himself, because my mental state remained somewhat shaky.

Sam and I both felt considerably better after Aunt Vi insisted we go to my parents' house to dine with them after church. "Pot roast with onions, carrots, potatoes, and celery with floating island for dessert," she said as if we needed persuasion. "It's the oddest thing," she added. "I tried to call you last night, but I kept getting a busy signal."

"Yes," said Sam. "The receiver was off the cradle for some reason. We put it back this morning."

It wasn't even a fib.

The eventual end of the saga of Stacy Kincaid's murder was as follows. After the Altadena Sheriff's people or the Pasadena coroner's people (they cooperated) scraped Grace Ellen Farmer's corpse from the innards of Harold Kincaid's deceased Hispano-Suiza, they managed to take fingerprints. Some of those fingerprints matched the ones found on the broken bottle that had been used to stab Stacy to death.

Both young women had met gruesome ends, in fact, and I didn't like thinking about them.

And I still haven't figured out a way to wear all my good-luck charms so that they don't make my chest lumpy. Some mysteries are too tough for the best of us, I reckon.

The End

SPIRITS ADOPTED

A DAISY GUMM MAJESTY MYSTERY, BOOK 20

I sat at the kitchen table, pondering the merits of eating another orange versus eating another slice of buttered toast slathered with Aunt Vi's plum preserves, when the telephone's ring shattered my peace. Looking down upon my beloved dachshund, Spike, I said, "Crumb, Spike. I think the universe is telling me I shouldn't eat any more of anything at all."

Spike wagged his tail at me, but I knew he was on the side of buttered toast.

With a grunt, I shoved myself up from the kitchen table. The only reason I grunted was because I was seven months' pregnant and feeling slightly unwieldy. I kept repeating to myself, "Only two more months," but it didn't help a whole lot.

To be fair, my pregnancy thus far had been uneventful. I hadn't even been sick in the mornings. My husband Sam Rotondo, detective with the Pasadena Police Department, remained over-protective, but that's better than him not caring at all, I suppose.

According to people who claim to know these things, I was carrying the baby low instead of high—whatever that means—and that meant the child was a boy. As I already knew the sex of my baby because a Tongva shaman, Emilia DeLoera, had told me, I just thanked people and went on about my business.

As I lifted the receiver, I remembered to say a simple, "Hello?" Before my best friend, Harold Kincaid, had told me to stop doing it, I'd given the caller Sam's and my last name. Not sure why. It just seemed polite.

When a bellowed, "Daisy!" came through the receiver, I yanked it away from my ear. The only person who shrieked at me over the telephone wire was Mrs. Algernon Pinkerton, and I thought she'd gone to Santa Barbara for the summer. Surely she didn't need me in Santa Barbara. Did she?

Daring to put the speaker end of the receiver to my lips, I repeated my sedate, "Hello?" because I doubted the Mrs. Pinkerton theory.

"Daisy, it's Harold! You've got to help us!"

"Harold," I said, surprised. "Why are you in such a lather? I thought lathering was your mother's job." Harold Kincaid was the product of Mrs. Pinkerton's first and lousy marriage to a ring-tailed polecat named Eustace Kincaid.

Hmmm. I'll explain the "ring-tailed polecat" comment later. Along with Harold, who also needs some explaining.

"You'd be in a lather too if someone dumped a baby in a basket on your doorstep!"

"What?"

"Are you deaf as well as pregnant?" Harold demanded. "You heard me!"

"Somebody left a baby in a basket on your doorstep?"

"Isn't that what I just said?"

Harold was clearly in a foul mood. "Yes, you did say so. It's just...difficult to imagine."

The wail of an infant drifted to me through the receiver, and I revised my opinion.

"Do you hear that?" Harold bellowed.

"Yes. It sounds like a baby, all right. But who'd leave you a baby?"

"How the devil do I know? But what the heck am I supposed to do with it now?"

A poser, to be sure. "Um…I'm not sure. Would you like me to call Sam and ask him?"

Silence greeted my question.

I tried again. "Harold? Do you want me to ask Sam what to do with a baby left in a basket on your doorstep? I'm sure he knows."

"But…it's just a baby. I mean, I don't know much about babies, but I think this is about as newly born as a baby can get and still be out of the womb."

"Yes?" I wanted to ask, "So what?" but restrained myself.

"If you tell Sam, it'll get the authorities involved, and the poor kid will go to an orphanage or some other god-forsaken place like that."

"Do they send babies to orphanages?" I asked, never having considered this problem before.

"I don't know!" said Harold, who was back to shouting. "But I don't want this tiny pink thing going some place where nobody will care about it. It's only a baby! It deserves better than that."

"You keep calling it 'it'," I said. "Is it a boy or a girl?"

Again, silence filled the wire. Then Harold said, "Um…I don't know. Roy?" I deduced he'd turned his head away from the receiver because I only faintly heard the name of Harold's houseboy, Roy Castillo. Again, getting close to the speaker end of the receiver, Harold said, "Roy's looking. It barely looks human at this point."

"That's not very nice," I told him.

"Tell me that when someone drops a baby on your front doorstep," he growled. "Ew, good Lord, Roy, that's disgusting!"

"Harold," I said. "It's a baby. It can't help it."

"I know, I know, but it's still disgusting. Oh. Yes, I see. Thanks, Roy." To me he said, "It's a girl."

"Oh my goodness. Can you take care of her for a little while until we figure out the best thing to do for her?" I said. "I'll call Flossie Buckingham. If anybody aside from Sam knows, she will."

"That's better than Sam," said Harold. "At least Flossie won't send her to Siberia or an orphanage or anything."

299

"We don't know what will happen yet," I warned him. "There may be laws about this sort of thing."

"What sort of thing? Leaving babies in baskets on doorsteps? I imagine there are laws." Harold had taken to snarling. "But I still don't want to send the kid to an orphanage."

"Are you equipped to care for a baby?" I asked, thinking Harold, who lived with his companion, Delray Farrington, probably wasn't loaded down with the paraphernalia required to care for a newborn.

"No. No I'm not. I'm going to call Hazel Greenwood and hire her to be a nurse until we come up with a permanent solution to the problem."

"You sound as if you're planning to adopt her yourself," I said. I'd never before wondered what kind of parent Harold would be, but this was beginning to sound serious.

"I don't know what I'm going to do," said Harold. "But I know the kid's not going to end up in an orphanage if I have anything to say about it."

"What do you have against orphanages?" I asked.

"If you'd ever visited one, you wouldn't ask that question."

His answer surprised me. "Do you visit orphanages on a regular basis?"

"No, but I used to tag along when Mother was being Lady Bountiful and visited the Pasadena Orphanage for Children and the Los Angeles Orphan Asylum. Not sure why she made me go with her, but those visits gave me a horror of orphanages. I don't know who this kid originally came from, but she doesn't deserve a fate like that. Think about Oliver Twist and double it."

"Good Lord."

"The good Lord has nothing to do with places like that, even though half of them are run by religious organizations. But yes, please call Flossie. I'm going to get in touch with Fred and Hazel Greenlaw. I expect the kid should have a medical examination. And what am I supposed to feed her? Oh God, Daisy. Help me!"

"I'll drive down to your place as soon as I call Flossie. I'll stop at a store and get some infant formula, too."

300

"What the devil is infant formula?"

"Food, Harold. For the baby. I'm assuming you don't plan to nurse her yourself."

"We can't just feed her milk?" Harold sounded almost desperate.

"No, plain milk isn't good for babies. I'll bring you a book about babies, too. I have about a thousand of them thanks to your mother, Mrs. Bissel and Mrs. Hanratty and every other Pasadena matron I know."

"Hurry," said Harold. "Please hurry."

"I shall. Good luck."

"Thanks."

Harold hung up his telephone, and I gently replaced the receiver on mine. A baby. Somebody had left a baby on Harold's doorstep. Even thinking the words sounded insane.

Available in Paperback and eBook from Your Favorite Bookstore or Online Retailer

ABOUT THE AUTHOR

Award-winning author Alice Duncan lives with a herd of wild dachshunds (enriched from time to time with fosterees from New Mexico Dachshund Rescue) in Roswell, New Mexico. She's not a UFO enthusiast; she's in Roswell because her mother's family settled there fifty years before the aliens crashed (and living in Roswell, NM, is cheaper than living in Pasadena, CA, unfortunately). Alice would love to hear from you at alice@aliceduncan.net

www.aliceduncan.net

 facebook.com/alice.duncan.925